BOUND TO THE DARK ELF KING

JESSICA GRAYSON

Pur le Fall
Publishing

Published in the United States by Purple Fall Publishing. Purple Fall
Publishing and the Purple Fall Publishing Logos are trademarks and/or
registered trademarks of Purple Fall Publishing LLC.

Publisher's Cataloging-in-Publication data

Names: Grayson, Jessica, author.

Title: Bound to the dark elf king / Jessica Grayson.

Series: Of Fate and Kings

Description: Pleasanton, TX: Purple Fall Publishing, 2022.

Identifiers: ISBN: 978-1-64253-131-2 (paperback) | 978-1-64253-587-7
(ebook)

Subjects: LCSH Shapeshifting--Fiction. | Elves--Fiction. | Fantasy fiction. |
Romance--Fiction. | BISAC FICTION / Fairy Tales, Folk Tales, Legends &
Mythology | FICTION / Romance / Paranormal / General | FICTION /
Romance / Fantasy | FICTION / Fantasy / Paranormal | FICTION /
Romance / Paranormal / Shifters | FICTION / Romance / Paranormal /
Witches | FICTION / Romance / Royalty

Classification: LCC PS3607 .R3978 Cl 2022 | DDC 813.6--dc23

Cover Design by Kim Cunningham of Atlantis Book Design

PRINTED IN THE UNITED STATES OF AMERICA

DEDICATION

To my husband: You are not just my husband, you are my best friend and my rock. Thank you for all your love and support. I love you more than words can ever say.

-Jessica Grayson

CHAPTER 1

INARA

The full moon shines brightly overhead, bathing the landscape in an ethereal, silver light. Across the battlefield, the army of the Dark Elves lies in wait, their glowing eyes easily visible in the darkness as they stand in formation behind their king.

Everyone fears King Varys of Ithylian. Known as a fierce and lethal warrior, it is rumored that none can stand against his armies and expect to win.

He wears the dark green armor that is standard for his people. His vibrant blue eyes are trained on our army with a piercing gaze. Riding his dire wolf, he is terrifying to behold. The massive beast has the appearance of a common wolf but is twice as large as a horse. It rakes its sharp claws over the ground, snarling and gnashing its fangs as if impatient for war.

My chest tightens with worry as I think of my older brother—Raiden. The Dark Elves captured him less than a week ago, and I pray that he still lives.

Our eldest brother, Edmynd, moves to the front lines on his black stallion. With his short blond hair, striking green eyes, and only a hint of scruff along his jaw, he may be known as the young king of Florin, but Edmynd is no stranger to war. His armor is battle-worn. The dented metal lost its polish long ago in the many conflicts he has fought to protect our kingdom, and I know he wears this now to remind the Dark Elves of his resolve.

If they refuse to return our brother to us unharmed, Edmynd will declare war.

As my brother passes, his gaze sweeps over the men. I lower my hazel eyes to the ground, hoping he does not recognize me in this disguise.

My long, blond hair is tucked up under my helmet and the armor is rather large on me, but I sit on my horse and do my best to appear as if I am a man, and I belong here. I am a princess of Florin and women are not supposed to go to battle.

As the youngest, my siblings have always been overprotective of me ever since our parents died. If Edmynd knew I was here, he would be furious. But once I found out Raiden had been captured, I could not stay behind.

I'm terrified of the Dark Elves, and I hate that my brother is their prisoner. For the past two years, I've had a recurring nightmare. In my dream, a Dark Elf with raven black eyes stood over me and Raiden. He had a long, jagged scar that started just above his right brow and stretched down to his cheek. He offered me a green ribbon made of silk. But, like most of my dreams, I do not know what it means.

My mother used to dream things before they would happen. She said that the visions were not always clear and that it was a curse in our bloodline, passed down to the women in her family. A dangerous secret she taught me and my sister to hide by drinking *nylweed* tea, which suppresses magic and supernatural abilities. The Order of Mages has burned women at the stake for far less.

Not all of my dreams come to pass. I ignored one of these visions once, and I will carry that regret for the rest of my life. I refuse to make the same mistake again. I love my brother. Dearly. And if there is a chance, no matter how small, that my dream means I can save him, I have to try.

Prince Lukas of Valren rides up behind my brother, his golden eyes sweeping over the men. I lower my head even more, worried my betrothed will recognize me. He is a Wolf Shifter and their sense of smell is much more acute than a human's. He arrived this morning with several soldiers to support our cause.

"Edmynd, wait!" he calls out, riding his horse up alongside him.

My brother reins in. "What is it, Lukas?"

"You cannot reason with them. The Dark Elves are cold and ruthless." He runs a hand roughly through his short, dark-brown hair. "Raiden is probably already dead, and this meeting is a trap meant to lure you to your end."

Edmynd clenches his jaw, and the grim look on his face tells me he has already considered this. He moves closer to Lukas and rests a hand on his shoulder. "If I should fall, take care of my sisters."

His words settle like a heavy stone in my gut. We grew up with Lukas. He is like a brother to us, and has proved his loyalty and friendship several times. Most recently with our engagement, made only to shield me from Prince Aegryn of Kolstrad, who would have declared war over his wounded pride after I rejected his advances.

The Wolf Shifter kingdom of Valren has long been our ally, and today they prove themselves loyal once again.

"Of course, my friend." Lukas replies. "I will."

Edmynd dips his chin in a firm nod, then turns to head out across the field. It takes everything inside me to stay hidden when I want only to run to him. I love my brothers —both of them—and the thought I could lose them both this day, if Raiden hasn't already been killed, is almost more than I can bear.

Everyone is silent as the two kings approach each other in the center of the field.

My brother's black stallion snorts in distress and stops abruptly at the sight of Varys's dire wolf. Its thick gray and black fur bristles as it bares its sharp fangs in a snarl.

Edmynd manages to calm his mount, and they continue forward.

King Varys reaches the middle of the field first, his glowing, ice-blue eyes staring intently at my brother as he approaches. My heart thunders as Edmynd stops in front of the fearsome Elf king.

"I have come to negotiate the release of my brother —Raiden."

Varys straightens. "And what do you offer in return?"

"Our forces will withdraw, and we can negotiate a peace treaty between our two kingdoms."

"You have promised this before," King Varys says, his voice deep and cold as ice. "Why, now, should I think you might keep your vow?"

"You have my word, on my honor."

"The word of a human—even that of a king—means very little, in my experience."

Edmynd bristles. "I demand to see my brother. To know that he still lives before these negotiations go any further."

Varys turns back toward his men. The front line parts just enough for an Elf to drag Raiden forward, his arms bound behind his back, his nostrils flaring as his brown eyes burn with anger. I gasp as the Elf grips his short, blond hair and pulls his head back to place a knife at his throat.

"Edmynd!" Raiden cries out. "Do not—"

"Silence!" the Dark Elf shouts, pressing the knife closer to his flesh, and Raiden stills.

Even though they are far across the field, the moonlight provides enough illumination for me to see the trickle of blood running down Raiden's neck from the sharp blade.

"Release him," Edmynd grits through his teeth. "And then we may bargain for peace."

"You expect me to trust you?" Varys grinds out. "Given the history of your word to my people, I should end him right now, instead of allowing him to live to fight alongside you and wage war on my kingdom."

"If you release him, I vow that there will be peace between us," Edmynd counters.

"If you want trust, it must be offered in return," King Varys states firmly. "Have your Mages release the enchantment that binds our magic in these lands and I will release your brother and form an alliance with your kingdom."

My brother's head jerks back. "I'd be a fool to agree to such a thing. If your people had access to your powers on these lands, what is to stop you from attacking us?"

"If we had a treaty, as you suggest, why would it matter if we could use our magic here?" the Dark Elf King challenges. "We would be allies, would we not?"

"You know I cannot do this," Edmynd replies. "Ask me for something else."

"I have no need of anything else, King Edmynd." Varys tips up his chin. "I will give you until sunrise to consider my offer. We will meet here at dawn. If you do not agree to my terms, then I will execute your brother."

My heart hammers as worry twists deep in my gut.

Edmynd cannot agree to this demand. The Order of Mages cast this enchantment on our lands to bind the Dark Elves and the Fae from using their powers here. It is the only thing protecting us from invasion because it forces them to fight with swords and shields instead of their devastating magic.

There is no way Edmynd can ever do this. Bile rises in my throat at the thought of losing Raiden. Curling my hands into fists at my side, I vow to find a way to save my brother; I will not let them kill him.

CHAPTER 2

VARYS

As soon as I reach my tent, I close the flap behind me and begin pacing back and forth. My bedding has been laid out, and although it has been a long day and I should rest, I cannot.

I reach up and trace my fingers over the scar that runs from just above my right brow down to my cheek. The one that cost me everything, and the painful reminder of why I seek to negotiate true peace and avoid another bloody war.

No Dark Elf woman will have me now because of this disfigurement. The few that would consider me would only be after my title and the status our bonding would bring them. Although it is foolish, I hold out hope of someday finding my *Khio'ri*—my fated one. But such a blessing is rare, and I doubt this will ever happen for me.

I am fortunate I did not lose my eye to this injury when I fought Prince Aegryn of Kolstrad. His human army fought with iron because they know it is our weakness. Wounds made with this metal leave scars that Elven

JESSICA GRAYSON

healing cannot remove. We lost many in that battle, and I do not relish the thought of going to war again. The cost is always too high.

"The human king will never agree to this, Varys." Devyn says, stepping out of the shadows. As my personal guard and close friend, I know he is able to move with unnatural stealth, but sometimes it catches even me by surprise. "He cannot sacrifice the safety of his kingdom for one man."

"That *man* is his brother," I point out. "There is still a chance he will agree to my terms."

His amber eyes meet mine evenly. "And if you are wrong? Are you really going to execute the brother of the king of Florin?"

I cross my arms over my chest. "This is our only chance to achieve a true and lasting peace with Florin. If we can use our powers in their kingdom, they will think twice before ever threatening us again. Then we can concentrate our efforts on defending the Great Wall and keeping the Wraiths out of our territory."

"But the humans believe we would use our magic to invade."

"Our people were never the aggressors." I grit my teeth in frustration. "It was the humans who always sought to steal our lands and that of the Fae."

"That was over two hundred years ago, during the time of your grandfather."

"My grandfather was wise. He had the foresight to create a lasting treaty with the Fae by marrying the Fae princess, uniting us against the kingdom of Florin."

Devyn arches a brow. "King Edmynd has two sisters. Perhaps you could make a similar arrangement with Florin. That is why Prince Lukas of Valren is here. He is betrothed to one of them, creating a permanent alliance between the Wolf Shifters and the humans."

"Are you suggesting I offer my hand to a human?" I ask incredulously.

"Not *you*," Devyn replies. "Your brother Aryl is unmated. Or you could offer your sister, Nyrala, to the king himself."

I frown. I desire peace more than anything, but not at the expense of Aryl or Nyrala's happiness. "I will not force them to bind themselves to a human, Devyn. I cannot. Besides, King Edmynd is much like his father. He has a deep hatred and mistrust toward our people. I doubt he would agree to such a marriage. That's why it was a boon capturing his brother. We will not have another chance like this to make our demands."

"I'd thought the scandalous circumstances of Prince Raiden's birth would make him expendable to the royal family. But it seems I was wrong." Devyn shrugs. "I believe the king wants to save him, but I also believe that he cannot agree to your terms and still retain the loyalty of his subjects."

I have considered this. It is a gamble, but one that I had to take. "We will know one way or the other by morning."

"What will you do if the king refuses?" Devyn presses. "Will you truly execute his brother?"

"If I do, there will be war. But if I do not, I will appear weak." I sigh heavily. "If King Edmynd does not agree, I suppose Prince Raiden will have to escape our camp to return to his people."

Devyn frowns in confusion.

I meet his gaze evenly. "It is not outside the realm of possibility that you might make a slight mistake when securing the prince's bindings… leaving them a bit loose around his wrists." I arch a brow. "Humans are rather resourceful beings, and once he figures this out, he will naturally make his *miraculous* escape."

"Will that not still make you appear weak?"

"It might. But not as weak as if I simply return him after King Edmynd refuses my terms. Their father spared my life this way once, when their forces captured me. He had threatened that he would execute me if my father did not meet his demands.

"But the king of Florin did not realize how acute our hearing is, and I overheard him instruct one of his knights to loosen my bindings. And now, I will return the favor by sparing his son."

"There is a risk that King Edmynd might declare war before we are able to... enact this plan of yours to spare his brother."

He is right. It is a risk. "Let us hope it does not come to that."

CHAPTER 3

INARA

I t was not as difficult as I expected to slip around behind the Elven encampment. My father used to bring us hunting here when we were younger. I know these woods like the back of my hand.

Several Elven soldiers gather around various fire bowls spread out among the tents. At least six guards patrol the perimeter in a set pattern.

A chilly breeze cuts through the trees, and I shiver slightly as I crouch low on the damp earth. Spring is still several weeks away, and I wish, more than anything, that I was home in my nice warm bed, and that this entire ordeal was simply a nightmare that I'll wake up from at any moment.

The dark reality of the situation settles deep in my chest. I have to rescue my brother. If I do not, he will die tomorrow. As much as Edmynd loves him, I know he cannot make a choice that puts our brother before the safety of the kingdom. The thought of losing Raiden is unbearable, and I will do anything to save him.

Hiding behind the dense foliage, I take note of how many soldiers are nearby. The tents are closely grouped together, and they all look the same. I'm uncertain which one holds my brother. I cannot even tell which one houses the king because I can see no distinguishing marks.

This is smart. If anyone were to invade the camp, they would not be able to find the king easily to harm him. Whereas, in our camp, my brother's tent definitely stands out among all the others. It is much larger, and the banners of our house wave proudly on either side of the entrance.

Biting my bottom lip in frustration, I study the camp layout. I have to figure out how to locate my brother. I'll definitely be caught if I blindly search each tent I come across, hoping to find him inside.

A smile crests my lips as a solution forms in my mind. When we were little, we used to sneak out of the castle sometimes to play in the woods. Raiden would usually go first. He would call to us with a signal, making a sound like a *narwick* mouse, to let us know there were no guards nearby, so we could make our escape.

Drawing in a deep breath, I cup my hands around my mouth and make the soft trilling sound I remember so well. I remain completely still. My heart hammers as I listen for a reply, praying that Raiden hears me.

After what feels like an eternity, but I'm sure was probably less than a minute, I hear the sound in return, coming from a tent along the edge of the camp. Relief washes over me. Raiden is alone. This is his signal that all is clear. Now, I just need to free him and we can escape.

My muscles tighten in readiness as I gather my courage. I watch as the closest guard walks his route along the camp's perimeter, observing how long he takes.

When he turns and paces in the opposite direction, I creep toward the tent as quietly as I can. As soon as I reach it, I carefully lift the flap and slip inside.

Moonlight shines in through an opening in the ceiling, granting just enough illumination to see Raiden clearly.

His mouth forms a surprised O when I remove my helmet. "What are you doing here, Inara? When I heard the call, I thought you were Edmynd or Lukas," he hisses. "You shouldn't be here. It's too dangerous."

"I came to save you," I whisper as I move toward him.

He is sitting on a small bedding pallet, wrists bound with chains and tethered to a post in the center of the tent. There is a plate with crumbs and an empty goblet beside him. I'm surprised that his prison isn't as bleak as I'd imagined, considering the Dark Elves plan on executing him in the morning if Edmynd doesn't agree to their terms.

"You have to go," he whispers urgently. "If they find you, they'll—"

We both still as the soft trilling sound of a narwick mouse reaches our ears. Raiden's brown eyes widen. "Did you come alone?"

I nod.

"Gods above," he curses. "The Dark Elf King is going to have us all as prisoners before the night's end."

I purse my lips.

Raiden returns the trilling call. While we wait, I study his chains. "Where do they keep the key?"

"One of the guards carries it," he replies resignedly. "You must go, before you get caught."

The tent flap opens and Lukas slips inside. His mouth falls open. "Inara? What are you doing here?"

"You need to take her back to the camp, Lukas," Raiden says quickly.

"What about you?" I whisper. "We cannot just leave you

here. King Varys is going to kill you tomorrow if Edmynd does not agree to his terms."

All the color drains from Raiden's face. He turns to Lukas. "Please, Lukas," he pleads. "Take my sister from here. Get her safely back to camp."

Lukas turns to me, indecision written across his features. "No," I hiss, and then turn to Raiden. "We are *not* leaving you here."

Lukas clenches his jaw and walks over to my brother. Raiden opens his mouth to protest, but I glare at him. "If you keep talking, someone is going to hear us."

He clamps his mouth shut and Lukas starts to work on the lock with his blade.

I glance anxiously over his shoulder, watching him work. "Do you think you can open it?"

He shakes his head. "Not without making far more noise than I'd like."

I turn to Raiden. "You said a guard has the key?"

"Yes."

"Can you describe him?" I ask, grasping at any sliver of hope that we might be able to free my brother.

"All Dark Elves look the same," Lukas grumbles as he tries again to pick the lock. "All of them just as vile and as villainous as Orcs, except they hide their true nature behind stoic masks."

It is no secret that Wolf Shifters hate the Dark Elves as much as my people do. Both our kingdoms border their lands. Lukas and his men have fought just as many border skirmishes with the Dark Elf Kingdom of Ithylian as we have. That's why the announcement of my betrothal to Lukas has been so celebrated.

Little do they know our engagement is only a pretense.

"I will go search for this guard and retrieve the key," Lukas says, making his way to the tent flap. He stops and turns his sharp gaze to me. "If I howl, that is your signal to run, and do not look back. Do you understand?"

I nod.

When he leaves, Raiden turns his attention back to me. "Lukas is a good man. Are you sure you do not want to actually marry him?"

I huff out a frustrated sigh. We've talked about this many times over the past few months. "Must you bring this up now?"

"It's important to me," Raiden says.

"I've already told you. I care for him like family, not as a lover. And he feels the same."

"Are you sure it could never be anything else? Most good relationships start out as friendship first."

I purse my lips. "He is like a brother to me."

"I just—" Raiden's voice catches. "Wolf Shifters are an honorable people, Inara. Lukas is one of the best men I know. I just want you to have a husband who will be good to you after I am gone."

My chest tightens. "Do not speak like that. You are not going anywhere."

"If Lukas cannot find the key, you will have to leave me here."

"He'll find it, Raiden." Tears sting my eyes, but I blink them back. "I know he will."

"If he does not, and I—" He swallows hard. "If something happens to me, you must convince Edmynd not to go to war. Not for me. If there is any way to spare our kingdom from war with the Dark Elves, then that is the path he must take." He pauses. "Do you remember Grandfather's stories? The last Great War with their people nearly cost us everything." His dark eyes search mine. "Give me your vow on this, Inara."

I hate that he is talking as if his death is a foregone conclusion. A tear slips down my cheek. "I promise."

A sharp howl slices the air, stopping my breath, and Raiden jumps to his feet. Without thinking, I slam my helmet back on and rush to the entrance, determined to help Lukas. With my dagger in hand, I push open the tent flap and smack into something hard. Knocked off balance, I stumble back, dropping the blade.

Pulse racing, I scramble to my feet as a Dark Elf steps inside, followed by three more. Behind them, I notice at least a dozen others standing just outside the tent opening.

"What is this?" he snaps, voice low and menacing. His eyes are feral, obsidian black as he stares down at us.

My mouth drifts open as my fear gives way to shock. My gaze travels over the long scar on the right side of his face. He is the one from my vision... from my recurring dreams.

He stands tall and proud in his dark green armor. The silver moon casts just enough light to illuminate his short, black hair, the pointed tips of his ears and the sharp lines of his face. With a masculine, square jaw that could cut glass, and a sharp nose and brow, I would probably think him handsome, despite the severity of his expression, if I were not so afraid. I study again the long scar that trails down the right side of his face, the line a shade lighter than the rest of his gray-blue skin.

Two more Dark Elf guards appear, dragging Lukas behind them, his ankles and wrists bound with rope. They toss his motionless form at my feet. Only the rise and fall of his chest indicates that he is still alive. "We caught a Wolf Shifter in the camp, my King."

King? I blink up at the man looming over us.

"I'll kill you!" Raiden charges the king. Before he reaches the end of his chain, a guard jumps in his path.

Lightning fast, he hits Raiden's head with the pommel of his sword, and I watch in horror as my brother crumples to the ground, unconscious.

My heart hammers as I step in front of Lukas and Raiden, both lying helpless on the ground. I place myself between them and the king, spreading my feet in a defensive stance. "Let them go." I rip off my helmet, and my long, blonde hair falls around my shoulders.

Something cracks in King Varys's expression. He freezes, staring at me in shock.

"*Khio'ri.*" He whispers a strange word in Elvish, and the guards beside him gasp.

Varys examines me intently, eyes returning to his normal glowing, ice blue.

"Let them go, King Varys, and you can keep me instead."

He growls deep in his chest, speaking in Elvish to his men, and although I understand very little of their tongue, I recognize enough to know he is ordering them to stand down.

He turns to me and speaks in heavily accented Florinesh. "Who are you? What is your name?"

I raise my chin. "I am Princess Inara of Florin, and I demand that you release these men."

"I will free them, Princess, but I ask something of you in return."

"What is it?"

"Accept my hand in marriage so that we might form a permanent alliance between our people."

My heart seizes as I stare at him in shock.

CHAPTER 4

VARYS

Her luminous eyes stare up into mine—a vivid, unusual shade, somewhere between golden-brown and green. Long, silken hair cascades down her back and shoulders like spun gold. As I study her lovely, heart-shaped face, a pink bloom spreads across her cheeks, accentuating the light dusting of pigmented spots on her otherwise pale skin.

"*Khio'ri.*" The word ripples through me, suffusing body and soul, as awareness spreads like fire through my veins. My soul recognizes I am irrevocably hers; she is now as much a part of me as the heart that beats solidly within my chest. I am bound to her by celestial fate.

My heart stops when I realize she is not only human, but the sister of my foe. Our people have been enemies for centuries. The *khio'rinar*–the fated bond–is a blessing from the gods that many hope for but seldom find. I do not understand why the gods would bind my soul to a human, but I will not question their ways.

I meet her gaze evenly as I lay out my terms. "Will you marry me to forge a permanent alliance between our people?"

Her eyes widen, and she sways slightly before responding. "You promise to free them if I agree to this?"

"Do you want peace between our kingdoms?"

"Yes," she replies without hesitation.

I regard her unflinchingly. "Then this is how we accomplish that."

"Why not sign a treaty instead?" she counters. "Why ask for my hand?"

"My people have had many treaties with yours over the past several hundred years and none of them have lasted," I reply darkly. "We have learned that such agreements are too easily cast aside. An alliance through marriage is stronger than any piece of paper. I will return the three of you to your brother's camp as a gesture of goodwill." Astonishment flits briefly across her features. "Consider my offer."

My nostrils flare at the acrid scent of her fear, but she hides it well. Her people believe we are monsters, and she undoubtedly thinks this is some sort of trap. She digs her nails into her palms to still her trembling hands. Princess Inara is brave, which is not something I expected of a human princess. I'd always heard they were fragile.

Her luminous eyes meet mine steadily. "And what if I refuse to give you my hand?"

My throat closes, but I force my expression to remain impassive. I cannot reveal how important she is to me. She does not yet know the power of the fated bond.

I am the first to find my khio'ri—my fated one—outside of our race. If she senses the connection, she has said nothing… but, then again, neither have I.

If she were a Dark Elf, she would already feel its pull.

But because she is human, I do not know how it will affect her. All I know is that I do not want to lose her. I must find a way to make her mine.

"Then more blood will flow along our borders, and war will likely follow. Too much anger and hatred exist between your kind and mine. I grow weary of fighting with your kingdom when our resources could be better spent uniting to defend against the Wraiths."

"The Order of Mages uses its powers to reinforce the Great Wall," she says. "The Wraiths cannot break through it."

"They can and they do." I clench my jaw. "The magic of your Mages fails more often than you realize. My people guard the Great Wall to keep the Wraiths on the other side. And if we fall, they will not just invade Ithylian, they will come for Florin as well."

"I am already betrothed to Prince Lukas of Valren."

I still. I remember Devyn telling me one of King Edmynd's sisters was engaged to the Wolf Shifter prince. I had hoped it was not her. "It does not matter."

"You do not care if I am already promised to another man?" she asks incredulously.

Jealousy stabs at my chest. I know it must be an effect of the bond that makes me react so strongly, but I cannot ignore it. "No, I do not," I lie, knowing I will surely go mad if she refuses my hand and chooses to stay with him.

My gaze darts to the Wolf Shifter's unconscious form. Although I have never seen Prince Lukas, I suspect it is him. My fangs and claws extend as anger twists deep inside me. I cannot bear the thought of her being claimed by another.

She is mine.

"Allow us to leave, and I will consider your offer," she states firmly.

I dip my chin. "After the healers have treated your brother and your betrothed, I will have my men escort you back to your camp."

Her eyes widen slightly when I mention the Wolf Shifter. I was right. This is Prince Lukas—her betrothed. Jealousy flares brightly, but I force it back down.

"I will meet with you tomorrow for your answer."

Her eyes search mine, trying to gauge the truth of my words. She probably still believes I have some sort of nefarious plan. But I suppose her mistrust is to be expected. I captured her brother and threatened to execute him. She does not know I would have never actually gone through with it.

Trust is something earned, not freely given. And now I must find a way to earn hers.

CHAPTER 5

INARA

To protect his guards from a stray arrow, Varys sent word to Edmynd that he was releasing us. I'm not sure if he mentioned to my brother that "us" includes "me."

Edmynd still has no idea that I'm here, and I am already dreading that conversation. By the time my brother sends a dozen guards to the middle of the field to meet us, it is already dawn.

Varys stands beside me as his guards form up to escort us. Raiden and Lukas are still unconscious, and Varys has assigned eight of his men to carry them across the field.

As soon as we are ready to leave, I turn to the Dark Elf King. His ice-blue gaze meets mine, and I am reminded that the time to make my decision is fast approaching.

I cannot deny that he is handsome, but as I study him, I wonder if we would be a good match. I know so little of him and I've heard so many terrifying stories about his people, it gives me pause.

He steps forward, and I am struck once more by how tall he is. The top of my head is barely level with his chin. Strong, broad shoulders taper to a narrow waist. His armor accentuates his lean, muscular form. He moves with a preternatural grace, and as his blue eyes study me, I cannot help but think that he is fierce and beautiful all at once— ethereally handsome, with a lethal edge to his countenance.

He gestures to one of the guards beside him. A Dark Elf with short black hair and amber eyes. "This is my personal guard—Devyn. He will escort you across the field."

I dip my chin in acknowledgment to the guard, and he returns the gesture.

"There is something you must know before you leave," Varys says, drawing my attention back to him.

"What is it?"

"The last time I met your father in battle, his men captured me." I go still at the mention of my father, surprised by a sudden swell of grief in my chest. "When my father could not meet his demands, he chose to set me free rather than kill me as he had threatened." He pauses. "I have not forgotten this kindness, and I would have done the same for your brother."

Swallowing against the sudden lump in my throat, I'm not sure whether to believe him or if he is trying to manipulate me. "How do I know you speak the truth?" The question leaves my mouth before I even realize I have spoken it aloud. "How do I know you are not just saying this to try to gain my trust?"

"I *am* trying to gain your trust," he replies, startling me with his blunt honesty. "Ask Sir Geralt—your father's personal guard, who is now assigned to your brother. He is the one that was instructed to loosen my bindings so it would appear as if I escaped on my own. It spared my life without making your father look weak. And I had planned to do the same if your brother had been unable to meet my demands."

I consider him a moment before agreeing. "I will speak with him."

A slight chill hangs in the air, and the earth is soft and damp beneath our feet. I dart a glance toward my brother's camp, but I can barely make it out beyond the dense fog. The early morning rays of the sun scatter out across the battlefield landscape, painting the world in soft shades of orange and yellow. Yesterday, I'd feared this ground would be covered in blood, and that our kingdom would once again be at war with the Elves. A shiver moves down my spine. The fate of so many hangs on my decision.

Varys notices and removes his cloak, probably thinking I'm cold. He holds it out to me. "Will you allow me?"

I nod and he carefully drapes it around my shoulders, fastening it securely to keep me warm. Just that extra bit of care makes my heart clench, and gives me a small measure of peace. "Thank you."

The warm scent of cinnamon surrounds me, and I draw in a deep breath, pulling the pleasant smell into my lungs. I glance at the cloak and realize it is *him*. This is Varys's scent. A strange and heady mixture of cinnamon and earth.

Varys gives a subtle nod. "Of course."

Cautiously, he takes my hand. His skin is callused against my own, but this is natural, I would think, for a skilled swordsman. My traitorous heart flutters when he lifts it to his mouth and presses a soft kiss to the space between my thumb and forefinger. "I look forward to seeing you soon," he murmurs.

Heat rises in my cheeks. I definitely did not expect this sort of chivalrous gesture, especially from the Dark Elf King. "I—" I open my mouth, but no words escape me as my heart pounds in my chest. "I will see you soon," I finally manage.

When I turn and start across the field, I can still feel his gaze upon me. It is difficult, but I force myself not to look back.

Inhaling deeply, I remind myself that this man is technically my enemy, although he let us go free. Even if Sir Geralt supports his story, I cannot be certain that Varys would not have executed Raiden. He claims that he would have freed him, but I will never know if it is true. I want to trust him, but I'm not sure if I can.

My mother knew very little about my father before they were betrothed. It was not a love match, but a marriage to unite their two kingdoms. I always hoped to marry for love, but I also understand that women of my station seldom do. Our lives are spent in service to our people, making decisions that place their welfare above our own.

An alliance with the Dark Elves could avoid further bloodshed between us, potentially saving hundreds, if not thousands, of lives. Raiden will be against the idea of my marrying King Varys, no matter what. I am eager to speak with Edmynd and hear his thoughts on the matter. Of us all, he has the most level head, and I value his counsel.

Despite my poorly executed attempt to save Raiden, I always try to lead with my head instead of my heart. And yet I cannot deny that I find Varys intriguing. I am haunted by those ice-blue eyes that seem to pierce my very soul.

I have had many suitors, but none have ever made me feel like this. How is it possible that the Dark Elf King has such an effect upon me? I would think it was some sort of enchantment if not for the fact that his people are unable to use their powers in our kingdom.

Perhaps it is because I have dreamed of him before. I

wish my sister—Grayce—were here. She is like me. Both of us inherited our mother's curse. We often dream things before they happen, but more often than not, the visions are not clear. Just as in this case.

I dreamed Varys gave me a green silk ribbon, but I do not understand what it means. Was the ribbon a sign for marriage? Meaning that I should accept his hand? Or was the ribbon a symbol of choice, meaning I would have a decision to make?

Sighing heavily, I send a silent prayer to the old gods, asking for guidance. I just wish I knew what I was supposed to do.

One of the Florin guards notices us approaching. He shouts back at the others, and the camp bursts into a flurry of activity. Guards line up along the perimeter, dressed in full armor and ready to defend their king if this goes badly.

Edmynd stands at the front lines, waiting to receive us. The moment his eyes land on me, his jaw drops, but he quickly snaps it shut. "Inara, what are you doing here?" Raw panic rapidly replaces his surprise. "How did they capture you from the castle? Did they hurt you?" His eyes travel up and down my form, frantically searching for any sign of injury.

Varys's guards mutter under their breaths, obviously offended by Edmynd's questions.

"No," I reply promptly, desperate to stop this before it escalates. "They didn't take me from the castle, and they did not hurt me. I disguised myself to travel with the army." I gesture to my armor. "And then I snuck into the Dark Elf camp to free Raiden."

"And what about Lukas?" Edmynd's eyebrows climb and he gestures to the unmoving body, as a healer leans over him. "Did *he* know about this?"

"No, but apparently we had the same idea, because he

snuck into the Dark Elf camp shortly after I did."

Edmynd scrubs a hand over his face in frustration. "The battlefield is no place for a woman," he snaps. "You could have been killed."

"As soon as I told the king who I was, he let us go."

"Why would he do this?" Edmynd narrows his eyes. "I have not yet responded to his terms."

"He asked for my hand in marriage."

Edmynd's head snaps back. "He *what*?"

Devyn steps forward, holding out a folded piece of parchment to my brother. "This is the king's formal declaration of intent toward your sister."

Reluctantly, Edmynd takes it from him, his brow creasing as he unfolds it and begins to read.

I glance over the top of the page, surprised not only that Varys had time to write this, but that he did so in Florinesh, and with such elegant script.

When he finishes, his eyes lift to mine, full of concern. Clearing his throat, he turns to Devyn. "Tell your king we will meet him in the center of the field at dusk."

Devyn bows slightly. "I shall deliver your message."

With that, he turns, and the rest of the Dark Elves follow. We watch silently as they disappear into the fog, returning to their camp.

Once they are out of earshot, Edmynd turns to me. "I... Did you—" he starts, but stops, obviously at a loss for words. It is rare that my brother is so flustered, and it would be comical if my future did not hang in the balance. "How did *this*"—he holds up the parchment exaggeratedly —"happen?"

"I honestly do not know."

"Well, I'd like you to take a guess." He rakes a hand through his hair. "Because of all the things I thought might happen today, *this* was not it."

CHAPTER 6

VARYS

It was difficult watching her walk away from me. I have heard the pull of the bond is strong, but I never expected this. When I saw her shiver slightly from the cold, it called forth my protective instincts. It took every bit of my control to only offer her my cloak and not pull her into my arms to keep her warm.

Closing my eyes, I picture her face. I am completely and utterly captivated by her luminous eyes—a lovely mix of golden-brown with flecks of green. Princess Inara is beautiful in a way that I thought only our kind, or the Fae, could ever be.

"My King." Devyn's voice calls me back from my thoughts.

I turn to face him.

He glances around the tent, verifying we are alone before he speaks again. "Varys," he says, addressing me informally, as he often does when it is just us. He is not just my personal guard, he has been my best friend since we were children. He arches a brow. "It seems the king was completely unaware that the princess was even here."

"What?"

"Apparently, she was worried about her brother—Prince Raiden. So, she disguised herself in armor to travel with their army. And when she thought you were going to execute him, she snuck into our camp without anyone's knowledge to free him."

My mouth drifts open. She is even braver than I thought. So many things could have gone wrong. She could have been killed. If it had been the Orcs who held her brother instead of us, she would likely be dead now. They are not known for their mercy and would have executed her on sight.

"The king said they will meet you in the middle of the field at dusk," Devyn reports. "Shall I assemble a dozen guards to accompany us?"

Although it will send a message of mistrust, it would be foolish to meet King Edmynd unguarded. My father and I made that mistake once with Prince Aegryn of Kolstrad. I reach up and trace the scar again that Aegryn cut into my face. I will never make that mistake again.

CHAPTER 7

INARA

Edmynd's tent is rather sparse, with only a small cot in one corner, a desk, and a few chairs. Normally, he prefers to travel in luxury, but it seems my brother is more practical about such matters when faced with the possibility of war.

"Bloody Dark Elves," Raiden grits through his teeth as he takes a seat.

The healers released him and Lukas about an hour ago, saying they were well enough to leave the healing tent. They're bruised, and their pride is wounded, but at least they are alive.

"I wholeheartedly agree," Lukas seconds, as he sits down beside him. He glances at me. "Thank the gods they did not harm you, Inara. What were you thinking going over there by yourself? You could have been—"

"I know." I huff, cutting him off. "Believe me, Edmynd has already given me an earful."

Lukas gives me a commiserating grin. I overheard

Edmynd chastising him earlier, as well, for his rescue attempt.

"So, what exactly happened after they knocked us out?" Raiden leans forward in his chair. "Tell me everything."

I explain what happened while they were unconscious, including the story Varys told me about our father letting him go.

Edmynd sends for Sir Geralt to confirm this tale, and we all stand as he enters the tent.

He blinks at us in confusion as we stare at him expectantly. He bows low, his dark hair falling forward to cover his face. When he straightens, his gray eyes search Edmynd's. "You called for me, my King?"

"My sister has a question for you."

Sir Geralt turns to me. "What is it, Princess?" he asks earnestly.

"The Dark Elf King told me our father captured him when they last met in battle. Could you tell me how he escaped?"

"I—" Sir Geralt swallows thickly. "The king—your father—entrusted me to… keep this secret. He—"

"You were always loyal to him," Edmynd says, his expression softening. "And I know how much he trusted you, Sir Geralt. But right now, we need the truth. All of it."

He bows his head. "Yes, my King."

When Sir Geralt confirms Varys's story, Edmynd thanks him and the guard leaves.

"That proves nothing." Raiden slashes his hand through the air. "We cannot trust him. Especially with our sister. Besides, she is betrothed to Lukas, anyway."

Lukas exchanges a knowing glance with me. "Yes, but our betrothal is pretense, Raiden. I did it to keep that foul Prince Aegryn of Kolstrad from her. You know how volatile he is. If I had not asked for her hand first, he would have. And when she rejected him, he would have declared war on your kingdom out of wounded pride."

"The Dark Elf King does not know your engagement is false," Raiden counters. He turns to me. "You could refuse, saying you desire Lukas instead."

"He is right, Inara." Lukas flexes his very muscular biceps and flashes a teasing grin. "It is obvious that I'm the superior choice, is it not?"

A smile twitches my lips at his attempt to lighten the moment. "Of course you are, my dear heart. But there is just one problem." Lukas arches a brow. "We cannot keep up this charade forever."

His expression turns serious. "I would go through with it to keep you from him." He takes my hand. "You do not have to sacrifice yourself."

I squeeze his hand gently in return. "I know."

"He's right," Edmynd adds. "You do not have to do this."

I face Raiden. "Do you remember what you told me when I found you in the Dark Elf camp?"

He clenches his jaw. "Yes, but that does not pertain to this situation."

"Yes, it does," I counter. "You made me promise that if the Dark Elves executed you, that I would do everything in my power to convince Edmynd not to wage war." I pause. "You said one life was not worth the hundreds or thousands that could be lost in battle. That is what my marriage could do as well. If I wed King Varys, it could create a lasting peace between our kingdoms. Surely, it would be worth giving my life—my future—for this."

"I was referring to myself when I said that," he grumbles. "*My* life would not be worth going to war over. But *yours* would."

I shake my head softly. "Why do you say this?"

Without warning, Raiden stands and gathers me up in

one of his giant bear hugs. "Inara, why?" His voice is thick with emotion. "Why did you risk yourself for *me*? You could have died."

That he even asks, breaks my heart. He has never felt worthy of being loved, especially after how cold my mother was to him. It was not his fault he was born of Father's mistress. But I suppose he will always carry these scars. The best I can do is reassure him that he is my brother and that's all that is important. "Because you are my brother and I love you, Raiden."

"I was there too, you know," Lukas says, grinning cheekily. "It wasn't just Inara that came. Let's not forget that I came to save you as well."

We all laugh, and Raiden pulls Lukas and Edmynd into our hug, reminding me of when we were children. "I know," Raiden murmurs. "I know you did. You are like a brother to me, and I thank you, Lukas."

When we finally step back, Raiden looks at me. "I would not see you married to that monster. You do not know what he might be capable of. He could take you and—"

"I've had visions of him, Raiden." All eyes snap to me. "He is the one I have seen many times in my dreams. It has to mean something."

"Perhaps it is a warning," Lukas says. "That you should not accept him."

I lower my gaze as the images of my dream play through my mind. "In my dreams, Varys offers me a green silk ribbon, and I take it from him."

"A ribbon?" Edmynd frowns. "Why?"

"I do not know." I sigh. "Many of my visions have signs and symbols that I do not always understand until they come to pass. It is the same with Grayce."

"That is another thing," Raiden adds. "You and Grayce

have... abilities that you should not—inherited from your mother. No one knows about this, but us and High Mage Ylari."

High Mage Ylari has served in Florin since the time of our great-grandfather. He knows about me and Grayce, but he has kept it to himself. He has warned us, however, that if another Mage ever found out, he would be unable to protect us.

"But the nylweed tea suppresses them," I remind him.

"Not entirely," he says grimly. "And what if you cannot find any nylweed in Ithylian? What will your Dark Elf husband do if he discovers that you have visions?"

"The Dark Elves have magic, just like the Fae," Lukas points out. "They do not burn their people at the stake for it."

Raiden looks at me. "We have tried to hide your gift because of the Mages, but what if the Dark Elves try to exploit it?"

"It is a *curse*, not a gift," I state firmly.

"Only because the Order of Mages deems it a curse, Inara," Lukas counters.

"A curse punishable by death," I retort.

Edmynd leans forward in his chair. "Raiden is right. We do not know what the Dark Elves will do if they discover that you have visions. For all we know, instead of trying to exploit it, they might consider it a curse, just like the Order of Mages would. And that would put you in danger, Inara."

Raiden shakes his head slowly. "I cannot believe we are even discussing the possibility of marrying our sister to the Dark Elf King."

"I agree," Lukas adds. "The Dark Elves are dangerous, their king even more so. If you marry him, you will be at his mercy, and I cannot bear the thought of anything happening to you."

"King Varys will not hurt me; he wants a permanent peace between our kingdoms," I interject. "And he believes an alliance through marriage is the only way to achieve this."

"Even so," Edmynd says. "Lukas and Raiden are right. It is too great a risk. When we meet, I will offer Varys a treaty that does not include your hand as part of the bargain. If he truly wants peace, then he will accept this."

CHAPTER 8

INARA

I sit next to Edmynd while we wait for King Varys to arrive. My every muscle is tense as I try to project a calm demeanor, when I am anything but relaxed.

I allow my gaze to travel around the tent and the table before us. Raiden stands behind us, dressed in full armor, while half a dozen guards surround us. It makes sense to be cautious, and as I peer out the entrance, I see at least a dozen Dark Elves approaching. He is still rather far away, but I can make out Varys at the front.

His cloak is folded and lying across my lap, so I may return it to him. I trace my fingers across the collar. The material is soft as silk and carries his scent. I take in a deep breath, inhaling the smell of warm cinnamon and earth. Something about it calms me, although I do not understand why.

I close my eyes as I remember the feel of his lips upon my skin when he placed a gentle kiss between my thumb and forefinger. I have heard the Elves are very handsome and charming, and it seems the rumors are not entirely unfounded.

Tension is thick in the air as the Dark Elves approach. My heart pounds in my chest as King Varys steps inside the tent. His intense blue eyes find me immediately and heat scalds my cheeks as his gaze pierces mine.

Edmynd and I stand, and we each dip our chin in greeting, and Varys does the same. Varys's attention drops to his cloak in my hands and his brow furrows softly.

Flustered, I hold it out to him. "I wanted to return the cloak you so kindly lent me when I was cold." My hand trembles slightly, not because I am afraid, but because I have never been more nervous in all my life.

"Keep it," he says, his voice deep and smooth like velvet. "You are shaking. I do not wish you to be cold, Princess Inara."

"I'm not cold," I explain. "Just a bit… anxious." I offer him a nervous smile.

His brow furrows deeply. "I would never hurt you, Princess."

Raiden harrumphs behind me, seemingly unconvinced.

Varys's head snaps to him. "I apologize for having held you as my prisoner, Prince Raiden, and I hope that we can avoid any future… unpleasantries between us by forming an alliance."

"Unpleasantries?" Raiden says skeptically. "You threatened to execute me if my brother did not meet your demands."

"A negotiation tactic I learned when your father held me prisoner and threatened the same," Varys counters.

"Let us sit and discuss a treaty," Edmynd says, his glare pinning Raiden.

Raiden narrows his eyes at Varys, but finally nods. He

steps back behind us as we sit across from the Dark Elf King.

Awkwardly, I rest his folded cloak on the back of my chair, unsure what to do with it now that he has not taken it back.

Edmynd slides a parchment across the table to Varys. "I thought this might be a good start to discuss our treaty," he offers. "We can go through each point and make adjustments as necessary before finalizing the compact between us."

Varys studies the document, his eyes scanning quickly over the terms. Upon finishing, he taps the parchment and arches a brow. "There is nothing in here about my marrying the princess."

Edmynd straightens. "There is no need for a marriage when we could simply sign a treaty."

"Ithylian has had treaties with Florin before." Varys narrows his eyes. "None of them lasted beyond thirty years."

"Thirty years of peace is quite a long time," Edmynd says.

"For a human, perhaps, but not a Dark Elf."

"Why are you so determined to marry my sister?" Edmynd regards him. "I want peace just as much as you do, but we do not need a marriage for a treaty."

"You claim you want peace?" Varys asks darkly. "From what I understand of human customs, it is a common practice to forge permanent alliances through marriage, is it not?"

"It is," Edmynd reluctantly admits. "But she is already betrothed to Prince Lukas of Valren."

"Betrothed, but not yet wed." Varys gives him a condescending look. "Surely, a permanent alliance between your kingdom and mine would be the more advantageous match."

Raiden steps forward. "You have a sister, do you not?"

"I do."

"Then, take me instead."

"No," Varys states firmly. "I will not ask my sister to bind herself to a stranger."

My eyebrows fly up at his statement, for he and I are strangers, so his argument makes little sense.

I open my mouth to point that out, but stop when a commotion outside the tent puts everyone on alert. Florinesh guards surround us as the Elven ones do the same to Varys. I'm shocked when Varys moves directly in front of me, drawing his sword as if prepared to protect me from whatever approaches.

Lukas bursts in, his dark-brown hair completely disheveled, face red with anger, and sword drawn. "She is *my* betrothed," he thunders and points to Varys. "Not yours. You cannot have her."

My jaw drops.

"Lukas, stop," Edmynd commands, raising his arms out to my friend and apparently distraught betrothed.

Lukas growls low in his throat and Varys does the same, neither showing any sign of backing down.

"Lukas." I call out his name and he looks around Varys to me. "Stop." I shoot a pointed glance at the Elven guards. "I do not want you to get hurt."

Slowly, he lowers his sword, and everyone else relaxes slightly. I place a hand on Varys's arm, drawing his attention back to me. "I'd like a moment alone with him."

He hesitates before giving me a shallow nod.

I step around him to Lukas and grab his arm, pulling him to the opposite side of the large tent and behind a small divider, which affords us some privacy. We're as far from Varys and his guards as possible. I've heard Elves have very acute hearing, and I can only hope we are out of earshot.

Without warning, Lukas wraps his arms around me and pulls me close. "You cannot go through with this, Inara. Please. It is madness. You are mine."

I'm too stunned to even reply. My mind scrambles for something to say, but I cannot speak. I had no idea Lukas actually *wanted* to marry me. I thought…

"Do I sound convincing?" he whispers in my ear, and I go completely still. "Angry? Distraught?" He pulls back just enough that I can see the smirk that twists his lips. He waggles his eyebrows. "Violent, perhaps?" He flashes his fangs. "Like I'm about to go crazy and shift into wolf form at any moment?"

I swat at his chest. "What is *wrong* with you? Why are you—"

"Raiden and I talked about it," he says under his breath.

I roll my eyes. "Of course, you did," I say sarcastically. "Does Edmynd know?"

"We decided we couldn't let him in on this. We needed him to look just as shocked as you and the Dark Elf King did just now." He snickers. "You should have seen the look on your face."

"I should have known you and Raiden would try something like this," I practically hiss. "Did you see how jumpy those Dark Elves were? You could have been killed just now because of your antics."

"It's a good plan, Inara," he replies, shrugging off my concerns. "Trust me. Varys will think we're madly in love and that I cannot live without you. He'll back off on this idea of marrying you and—"

"No, he will not," Edmynd says, stepping around the

41

divider. He drops his voice to a low whisper as he looks at me. "Varys wants to talk to you. Alone."

"No," Lukas says.

I clamp my hand over his mouth. "Enough with the theatrics. This is serious."

"I know," he mumbles through my hand. "Why do you think I am doing this?"

A smile tugs at my lips. I cannot be annoyed at him when his intentions are good. "Thank you, Lukas. Truly. But it is not necessary. I can handle this myself; I will be fine."

Sighing heavily, he nods. "I know. I just worry for you, Inara. You are like a sister to me."

I hug him close. When I pull away, I straighten and smooth a hand down my dress as I draw in a deep and steadying breath. I look at Edmynd and Lukas.

Edmynd holds out his arm, and I take it. He guides me back to King Varys, still standing next to the table. Lukas follows close behind us. He turns to me and takes my hand, pressing a tender kiss to the back of my knuckles. "Whatever you decide, I will accept," he states firmly. His golden eyes snap to Varys and narrow slightly before he exits the tent.

Varys studies us warily a moment before sliding the parchment toward my brother. "I will agree to these terms, King Edmynd, but only on the condition of marriage to your sister, the Princess Inara."

Turning, he takes a step toward me. Then he reaches into his pocket and pulls out a green silk ribbon. My breath catches, as does my brother's beside me. It looks just as it did in my dreams.

I blink several times as he holds it out to me. "What is this?" I swallow hard, staring at it in disbelief.

"A symbol of my intent to bind you to me," he replies solemnly. "If you will accept my betrothal."

"And if I do?" I barely manage. "What then?"

"I will take you as mine and make you queen of the Dark Elves." He takes my hand and drops to one knee. His face is a perfect impassive mask, yet his eyes search mine with great anticipation. "I would know your answer. Tell me: Will you accept me as your mate, Princess Inara?"

As his sharp gaze holds mine, a peace settles over me that I cannot explain—a truth that resonates deep in my soul. "Yes." The word escapes my lips as a breathless whisper while I study the man who will be my husband. The face I will learn better than my own. "I accept your offer of marriage, King Varys."

He carefully wraps the silken, green ribbon around my left wrist, tying the end into a precise knot. It is not tight, but neither is it loose. Green light flashes around the ribbon, and then dims. "Magic," I whisper as a small shiver runs through me.

"No." Varys's luminous eyes hold mine. "A vow older than magic and far more sacred."

As I examine the ribbon, I'm only vaguely aware of Edmynd and Raiden staring at me, their mouths gaping.

Varys stands. He grabs his cloak from the back of my chair and carefully drapes it over my shoulders, surrounding me again with his masculine scent. "We will wed this night in a human ceremony, and leave for Ithylian in the morning, where we will have an Elven one when we arrive at the castle."

"Tonight?" Edmynd says incredulously. "That is much too soon. My sister needs time to prepare."

I turn to Varys. "I do not wish to be married without my sister present. It will take Grayce at least a half day to get here," I explain. "We can have our ceremony tomorrow evening."

He looks at my brothers. "Will tomorrow evening give you enough time to bring Princess Grayce here?"

"Yes," Edmynd replies. "I will send a raven to the castle immediately. As for the wedding, there is a temple nearby. It can be used to host the ceremony."

Varys frowns. "What sort of temple?"

"It is a temple of the old gods," my brother explains. "House Florin still keeps to the old ways."

My future husband cocks his head. "What is old for you is not so for my people," he says, referring to the longevity of the Elves. "Bonding ceremonies used to be held beneath the full moon and the stars, so that the old gods could observe from their celestial home."

"My sister is a princess of Florin, and she will have a proper wedding inside the temple as is the human custom," Edmynd states firmly. "You can honor *your* customs in a separate Elven ceremony when you return to Ithylian."

Varys looks to me. "Do you agree to this?"

"Yes."

"Tomorrow then," he says. His face is devoid of expression as his eyes hold mine. He bows low and then turns to leave. His guards follow him out of the tent and back to their camp.

As soon as they are far enough away, Edmynd turns to me. "Are you certain you wish to do this?"

"Yes, I am." I struggle to keep my voice even. Only now does the true weight of my decision settle in my chest. I will wed the Dark Elf King tomorrow. A man who was my enemy only hours ago is now my betrothed.

"What if he hurts you?" Raiden asks, his expression pained.

"It will be fine," I reassure him. "Varys wants peace

between Florin and Ithylian. Harming me would only damage our alliance."

Edmynd takes my hand, lifting it to study the green ribbon wrapped around my wrist. "It is just as you described from your vision." He pauses. "You are sure it was not a warning?"

"It did not feel like one," I reply softly. "When he presented it to me, it felt like a sign guiding my path."

Raiden gives me a pitying look. "I hope you are right, my dear sister."

I pray silently to the old gods that I am too.

CHAPTER 9

INARA

Today is the day of my wedding, and I am nervous, but not afraid. My sister, Grayce, arrived a few hours ago with tears in her eyes as she hugged me tight to her chest. "Inara, it should not be you making this sacrifice. You are the youngest. It should be me instead."

Unbeknownst to me, Grayce sent a raven to the Dark Elf King shortly after she received Edmynd's message explaining what happened and bidding her to come for my ceremony. She offered herself to him in my stead, telling him it was only proper since she is older than me.

I only found out about it when he sent a messenger to deliver his reply as soon as she arrived in camp. It was addressed to her and written in elegant Florinesh script, short and to the point: *I have pledged my troth to Princess Inara. And to that I will hold.*

Grayce is second in line for the throne and would have been a better political choice for him. She is also far more beautiful than I could ever be. That he chose to remain betrothed to me, when he could have had her instead, speaks to his character. He is not a man who gives his word carelessly.

In my tent, Grayce guides me toward the full-length mirror. Her long chestnut hair is tied back in an elegant braid and she wears her finest purple silk dress. Her hazel eyes, like mine, are brimming with unshed tears. She taps the green ribbon wrapped around my left wrist. "It is the same as your vision," she murmurs.

I nod. "A good sign, I believe."

She studies it a moment longer and then nods softly.

As I contemplate my reflection, a pained smile pulls at my mouth. This was our mother's gown. Grayce brought it from home.

"You are beautiful," Grayce whispers. "I wish Mother were here to see it." She pauses. "Are you sure you wish to go through with this? I can hardly bear the thought of you being gone."

I know what I'm doing is best for our kingdom, but it will be hard to say goodbye to my family. My sister is my best friend, and I will miss all of our late-night talks. Now, I'll never meet the mysterious man she insists is only a friend, but I suspect means far more to her than that.

"I'll miss you so much, Grayce." I bite my bottom lip to keep it from quivering. "But I do not believe King Varys is what we feared him to be. In the times we have spoken, he has been kind and chivalrous."

She hugs me close. "He'd better be kind to you, or our brothers and Lukas will hunt him down."

A soft laugh escapes me. A tear slides down my cheek, but I quickly brush it away. I've decided that I will not be mournful on my wedding day.

"Now that I am leaving, will you at least tell me who

your mysterious gentleman is, or is your secret too great for anyone to know?" I gently tease.

The smile falls from her lips. "He is gone."

"What do you mean?"

"I was such a fool, Inara." Tears fill her eyes, but she blinks them back. "We spent so much time together. I thought he loved me, but when I expressed my feelings, he pulled away." She sniffs. "He told me that he had something important to tell me. We planned to meet in our usual place, but... I waited until dawn, and he never came."

"I am so sorry, Grayce." I hug her even tighter. "Truly."

"It is all right. I will be fine. I am not the first woman to be left by someone they loved."

Before I can respond, she takes my hand and places a vial of nylweed in my palm. "I brought this from home. Keep this for emergencies; until you can find more, you will need it."

Grayce understands my curse better than anyone, for she suffers from it as well. It was passed to us from our mother.

Carefully, I tuck the vial into the pocket of the gown I will wear to travel to Ithylian, after the wedding. "Thank you. I still have some, but it is always good to have more on hand."

She gives me a faint smile and then adjusts my gold circlet crown to make sure it is perfect.

"There is my lovely sister." Raiden's voice rings out as he steps inside the tent. Edmynd and Lukas follow closely behind him.

Raiden gathers me in his arms in a great bear hug and spins me in a slow circle before placing my feet back on the ground. I've already requested that they not be somber this day, and it seems they are honoring my wish.

He pulls back, eyes twinkling. "You look absolutely stunning. I had no idea you cleaned up this nicely."

I laugh and playfully slap at his arm.

Edmynd places his hands on my shoulders. "You can still change your mind, you know."

I'm glad to know that if I had any second thoughts, he would support me without question. "Thank you, but I do believe this is for the best, Edmynd. It will mean peace between us and the Dark Elves, and hopefully, no more wars."

Lukas pulls a dagger from his belt and places it in my palm. His golden eyes meet mine evenly. "Keep this close and use it if you must."

I blink down at the knife. The handle is dark wood with an intricate carving of a wolf—the sigil of Lukas's kingdom. I curl my hands around the dagger. Lukas cares for me, and I appreciate the sentiment behind this gift, but I pray I never have to use it. "Thank you."

He embraces me and whispers in my ear. "You are like a sister to me, Inara. If you ever need me, send word and I will come for you."

I hug him even tighter because I know, in my heart, that he would come if I asked him to. He would do anything for me, just like my siblings. "Thank you, I'll miss you."

I tuck the dagger into the hidden pocket of my travel dress, next to the vial of nylweed. "Do not hesitate to use this if you are attacked," he adds. "Hesitation can mean the difference between life and death."

"I understand your reluctance to trust King Varys, but I doubt he will hurt me, especially since he could have when we were captured, but he did not."

"It is not him that worries me now," Lukas says gravely. "You will be the only human in Ithylian, surrounded by Dark Elves who were your enemies. There are bound to be some who will not want to accept their king's marriage to a human, nor this new alliance with Florin."

I swallow hard. He is right. Even my brother has enemies within the court. All rulers do.

High Mage Ylari enters the tent. The formal black robes he wears for my wedding envelope his gaunt frame. He leans heavily on his staff, his pale gray skin a stark contrast to the dark wood. Turning pitch-black eyes to me, he pushes his hood back, revealing the pointed tips of his ears peeking up through his silver hair. "Prince Lukas is right, Princess," he says, his voice low and deep.

I'm not sure how he overheard what they said since he was not even in the tent, but I learned long ago not to question such things.

"Will the Dark Elves be accepting of my visions?" I ask, hopeful.

He frowns. "You have not dreamed of this?"

"You know I cannot simply call upon my... curse at will," I gently remind him. "I never know what I might see in my dreams, and the things that I do are not always visions. Sometimes they are simply dreams, and nothing more."

"Then, I suggest you learn more of your new husband before deciding whether to entrust him with your secret." He rests a frail hand on my shoulder. "Until then, make sure you always have your nylweed."

"I will."

He offers me a faint smile, revealing two rows of sharp, white fangs. When I was a child, they used to scare me, but I am used to them now. Ylari would never hurt me. "I believe you have made a good choice in taking the Dark Elf King as your husband."

My ears perk up. "You do?"

He nods. "If your marriage is successful, you will bring many years of peace to both kingdoms, Princess."

"Hmph," Raiden grumbles. "We could have had peace with a simple piece of paper, but King Varys insisted upon this wedding."

Ylari arches a brow. "It is a wise decision. Marriage forged the permanent alliance between the Elves and Fae long ago."

"I still do not think it is a good idea," Raiden says. "King Varys threatened to execute me only a few days ago, and now he will become part of our family by marrying my sister."

"He would not have done it," Ylari says. "The Dark Elf King intended to let you go."

"How do you know this for certain?" I ask.

He exchanges a glance with Edmynd. "Your brother asked me to divine this. To see if the Dark Elf King spoke the truth when he claimed he had planned to let Raiden escape."

I am touched that Ylari did this. He has told us many times that divining is a very dangerous magic. Any time he uses his power to do this, he risks death by walking the line between this world and the next to find the answers that he seeks.

I reach out and rest my hand on his, squeezing it gently. "Thank you."

He inclines his head. "Of course, Princess."

When we reach the temple, Raiden, Grayce, and Lukas all head inside to take their seats in the front, while Edmynd and I stand outside the doors.

Several Dark Elf and human guards stand at the entrance, alert for any sign of trouble from either side. I hope that someday soon this tension between our people will be gone.

Edmynd offers me his arm. "Are you ready?"

I loop my arm through his. "Yes."

My heart hammers, knowing that my future husband awaits me inside. Drawing in a deep breath, I motion for the guards to open the doors.

As soon as we step into the temple, my gaze flies to King Varys standing at the end of the aisle with his personal guard, Devyn, at his side. His eyes snap to mine, and I inhale sharply.

He cuts an impressive figure, dressed in his dark green armor. Silver moonlight pours in from a nearby window, lending an ethereal yet fierce handsomeness to his features.

Beautiful ribbons and bouquets of lavender decorate the ends of each aisle. Scattered white rose petals line the carpeted walkway to the altar, filling the air with their sweet perfume.

I send a silent prayer to the gods to grant me strength and courage. Today, my former enemy becomes my husband and lover.

CHAPTER 10

VARYS

As I stand at the front of the temple waiting for my bride, I still can hardly believe my fated one is human. Our people have been enemies for hundreds of years, and while I have always desired peace, I never thought to achieve it in this manner.

Her brother insisted upon a human ceremony, but there must be an Elven one, as well, when we return to Ithylian, else my people will be hesitant to accept my bride, even though she is my Khio'ri.

The temple is rather small, but this is a remote area full of farmland and forests with a scattered population of smaller villages. It is a simple construct made of large, stacked gray stones with several wooden benches on either side of a central aisle.

There are a few statues near the front representing the old gods, but Gaila, goddess of fertility and the harvest, is prominently centered. Her ears are round, however, instead of pointed as they are in our temples.

I scan the crowd. Raiden sits on the front row of benches beside his sister Grayce. On the other side of her is Lukas—Inara's former betrothed. His golden eyes are practically burning as he stares at me. It is strange that he let her go so easily. I'd expected more resistance from a Wolf Shifter. Several of their guards and soldiers sit behind them, each eyeing me warily.

My own people sit on the opposite line of benches, emotions hidden behind impassive masks, but their eyes betray a mixture of fascination and disbelief. Since the moment the word "Khio'ri" passed my lips when I saw the princess, it has spread like wildfire among my warriors.

As far as I know, no one has ever had a fated bond to a *sanishon*—an outsider. We will be the first such pairing.

Devyn stands beside me. It is a human custom to have a relative or close friend stand next to the groom. He is as close to me as my own brother, so I thought it appropriate since my brother and sister are not here. Unable to use our magic in the human realm, I feel very exposed and appreciate his presence beside me. Devyn is one of our fiercest warriors.

My gaze pauses when I notice a man in black robes seated near the back. His gnarled hand is curled around a wooden staff beside him. His skin is pale gray and his eyes are fathomless pools of darkness, with no hint of white. The tips of his ears, while not as pointed as mine, are different enough from a human's to mark him as Other. He is from the Order of Mages—the High Mage likely assigned to Florin.

Humans fear magic because they do not have it. And yet, they made a deal with the Order of Mages, whose magic is far darker than anything we possess, to protect their lands.

Each human kingdom has a Mage advisor who maintains a binding over their lands, so otherworldly creatures —Elves, Fae, Orcs and such—cannot use their powers in the human territories. I wanted this lifted, but King Edmynd refused, and I suppose I do not blame him. Although I am marrying his sister to create an alliance, the peace between our kingdoms is still very new.

Devyn leans in just a bit to whisper in Elvish. "I researched more on the human bonding customs as you asked."

"What did you find?" I keep my voice low so no one can hear us.

"We do not need the dagger; there will be no exchange of blood."

I frown. "Then how do they seal their bonds to each other?"

"There is an exchange of rings."

"What?"

"Bonded humans wear a ring on the fourth finger of their left hand as a sign to others they are a mated pair."

Panic floods me in an instant. "I do not have a—" I stop short, remembering the ring on the chain around my neck. It belonged to my mother. It was the last thing she gave me before her death and she told me to give it to my mate someday.

I reach up and feel the small ring beneath my tunic. It is only proper, I suppose, to gift this to the princess. After all, she is my Khio'ri—a blessing from the gods I never expected to have.

Devyn continues. "The priest will tell you when the exchange should occur."

"Thank you, my friend," I tell him, and I mean it. I hate being caught unaware and am relieved to have this knowledge.

An elderly man dressed in long green and black robes

walks toward us. This must be the priest. He narrows his eyes disapprovingly at me before taking his place at the front of the altar.

Princess Inara is much beloved by her people, and they celebrated her betrothal to Prince Lukas only a few months ago. Now that she is to marry me, there are no celebrations, and I'm told the people have lowered their banners as if mourning the sacrifice they believe she is making on their behalf.

Prince Lukas sits with her family while Inara's sister fights back tears. She offered to marry me in her stead. I refused, but respect her willingness to fight for her sister's safety and happiness. Lukas and her brother, Raiden, keep giving me narrow-eyed looks, but I suppose I do not blame them. They care for Inara and worry for her.

The doors open, and my breath hitches when I see my bride. She is dressed in a long, white gown embedded with tiny, sparkling, clear gemstones on the bodice that trail down the skirt, reflecting the silver moonlight like glittering stars. A golden crown adorns her head. Her long blond hair is styled in a series of intricate braids, revealing the elegant column of her neck.

With her arm looped through her brother's, they begin walking down the aisle toward us. Everyone's eyes are fixed upon her as she moves toward me, for she truly is stunning to behold.

When they reach us, her brother levels a warning glare at me before he offers me her hand. I take great care to make sure my sharp claws are retracted, so I do not accidentally hurt her as I take both her hands in mine.

I acknowledge Edmynd's glare with a subtle nod, hoping he understands that I would never harm his sister.

Her dainty hands are warm, and her skin is petal-soft against my own. Despite her serene outward appearance, her fear is easily read in her eyes and the slight trembling of her hands.

She lifts her face to me, and her luminous gaze fixes upon mine. I note the softly curved shell of her ears where an Elf's would be pointed. A pink bloom spreads across her cheeks and the bridge of her nose, accentuating the tiny dots on her otherwise pale skin as she recites the vows of the human bonding ceremony.

When she promises to love, honor, and cherish me, I am completely taken aback. I had not expected such a promise of devotion. Especially since we are strangers and our people have been enemies for so long. When it is my turn to repeat these words, I have no problems promising her the same, knowing how freely she gave these vows to me first.

When the priest says it is time to exchange rings, Inara's eyes widen as I remove the chain from my neck and carefully place the ring on her finger. It fits perfectly. The delicate silver band is shaped like twining vines and in the center, a small heart-shaped stone shimmers like pale moonlight.

"This is beautiful." She lifts her gaze to me and I am once again fascinated by the lovely coloring of her eyes. Various shades of green fleck their golden-brown irises, reminding me of the spring fields of Ithylian. I could so easily lose myself in their depths.

"I am pleased you find it so," I murmur.

King Edmynd hands her a ring, and she slips it onto my finger. It is a bit tight, but not uncomfortable. As I study it, I pause, recognizing the Dark Elvish design: the thin silver band ringed with small moonstones. It is an ancient style, from the time of my great-grandparents—back when humans and Dark Elves had a tenuous treaty of peace which lasted nearly thirty years before it was broken. "Thank you."

Her lips curve up in a warm smile that grips my heart. She truly is lovely, my human bride.

At the conclusion of the ceremony, the priest instructs us to kiss. Inara stretches up on her toes, and I lean forward just enough to brush my lips against hers in a chaste kiss. Instinctively, I run my tongue over my bottom lip, tasting the delicate flavor of her kiss.

We then turn to face the crowd and walk arm in arm back down the aisle. King Edmynd leads us to a smaller wooden structure with a simple thatched roof beside the temple. Inside is a dining hall with several long rows of tables decorated with silk ribbon and flowers.

Great platters of meats, breads, fruits, and cheeses cover them, along with goblets overflowing with wine and mead. For having arranged everything on such short notice, I'm surprised by how much food and drink are on display.

Edmynd directs us to sit at the head table that looks out upon the rest of the room.

In the center is a cleared space for couples to dance. Lukas and Grayce spin and whirl across the floor, and I sneak a glance at my bride. They were betrothed, and I wonder if she was in love with the Wolf Shifter. He certainly seemed upset when he came into the tent yesterday during the negotiations.

Scent marking is very important in both my culture and his. As soon as she agreed to marry me, I quickly wrapped her again with my cloak, covering her with my scent. I wanted to make certain there was no doubt in his mind that she is mine. *Not his.*

I lean closer to Devyn. "How long is this supposed to go on? I am eager to leave for Ithylian."

"Most of the night," he replies. "It is a tradition to share at least one dance with your new bride. And then, after the reception, you are supposed to consummate the marriage."

"What?" I sputter. "But we barely know each other."

"I verified this with several sources." He arches a brow. "It is expected."

My mouth drifts open, but I quickly snap it shut. "We will leave at dawn, then."

He dips his chin in acknowledgement as I take a sip of my wine. While I find my new bride attractive, I had not thought to claim her so soon. I planned to wait until after our Elvish ceremony. If she were a Dark Elf, we would have had months of courtship before our bonding. If this is a human tradition, I will honor it, but *she* must be the one to choose.

I fidget, wondering how best to ask her feelings on this matter, but one of my men interrupts as he pours her a goblet of Elvish wine. We only had a few bottles with us, and I instructed it to be served only to Inara, myself, and her family.

Her eyes widen slightly as she takes the first drink.

"Is the wine not to your liking?" I ask.

"It tastes wonderful, but it is much stronger than what I'm used to, I believe. I think it might be safer not to drink too much of it." She laughs quietly. "If I have anymore, you'll probably end up having to carry me out of here at the end of the night."

I glance over at Raiden, watching as he downs one glass, then another. His cheeks are flushed bright red and, judging by his boisterous behavior, I wonder if it may be too strong for him as well. I purse my lips. "I believe someone may end up having to carry your brother."

She laughs again, and it is a lovely sound—airy and light, reminding me of chimes. It is the first time I have truly heard her do this, and I am glad she appears to be a bit more at ease around me. Hopefully, that will make things less awkward for us after the reception is over.

"It's a tradition for the newlywed couple to dance," she says, confirming what Devyn has told me. "Unless... your people do not dance."

"We do." I stand and offer her my hand. "Would you like to dance with me then, my Queen?"

Her cheeks flare red, and she smiles warmly. "Yes, I would." She slips her palm into mine, and I pull her up to standing. When we walk to the center of the room, the guests fall silent, watching us closely.

Many human traditions may be a mystery, but I *do* know how to dance.

Gently, I pull her toward me. I curl my arm around her waist, carefully resting my palm against the small of her back while my other hand takes hers. We're so close the warmth of her body radiates to mine. My nostrils flare as I draw her delicate scent deep into my lungs, memorizing the scent of my mate.

The music begins and we glide across the floor, spinning and whirling in a dance of give and take. The tempo changes and we part. She places her palm against mine as we circle one another. Her shining eyes stare deep into mine as we fall into rhythm.

My heart races as I study her. She is captivating in a way that I never thought to find among the humans. The entire room falls away until we are the only ones here. Our movements are smooth and fluid as we weave around each other in a series of intricate steps. I cannot help but hope this is a sign of what our union may be.

We change direction, and when she places her palm against mine, I dare to cautiously thread my fingers through hers, observing as a rose-pink blush spreads across her cheeks. My people conceal our emotions behind expressionless masks. I stare in wonder as a dozen emotions flicker across her face, completely and utterly enthralled with my lovely human mate.

As the dancing and feasting finally ends, I instruct Devyn to make sure we are ready to leave for home at dawn.

Raiden moves up beside me, his eyes practically burning into mine. "I want you to understand something about my sister," he says, the smell of Elvish wine strong on his breath, his countenance flushed from the drink. "She is everything good and light in this world. It never mattered to her that I was not born of the same mother as the rest of them were. She has a pure heart, and when she loves, she loves fiercely." He claps a firm hand on my shoulder and tightens his grip as he gives me a warning glare. "Be gentle when you consummate your marriage this night."

I struggle to hide my shock at his words. Devyn was right. They *do* expect us to consummate our vows this evening, after the reception.

"If you hurt her, I do not care that you are the Dark Elf King of Ithylian," Raiden continues. "I will hunt you down and I will end you."

I could remind him that I had him in my custody only a day ago, but I do not. I understand the sentiment of his words; I would probably feel the same, were our roles reversed.

Instead, I meet his gaze steadily. "I vow to you that your sister is safe with me. Contrary to what you believe, my people are not monsters."

He narrows his eyes. "That remains to be seen."

CHAPTER 11

INARA

With my arm looped through his, the Dark Elf King leads me into his tent. I know what is supposed to happen now that we are wed, but I cannot help but be nervous. I've never been intimate with anyone before, and while I have an idea of what to expect, I certainly do not know what I'm doing.

My gaze travels over the space, and I swallow hard when I notice the bed in the corner. It looks like two cots have been pushed together and piled high with blankets, pillows, and a few white furs.

There is a desk against the opposite side with a chair. At least a dozen scrolls lie on the desktop in a neat row, suggesting they are waiting to be read. Despite having come here prepared for a possible war, it seems King Varys did not intend to neglect whatever other matters he has to attend to for his kingdom.

Drawing in a steadying breath, I steel myself and glance up at my new husband. Although I know very little about the intimate act between a man and a woman, I *do* know that I'm supposed to undress.

I am thankful for the small amount of Elvish wine I had this evening, giving me a slight measure of courage I doubt I would have had otherwise. While my thoughts are not in any way muddled, the edge of my worry is not as sharp as it had been earlier, during our wedding.

Varys's expression is unreadable, and I swallow hard as I turn my back to him and pull my hair over my shoulder.

"Could you please help me unfasten my dress, my lord?" I try to keep my voice even despite my nerves.

A soft intake of air is his only response, at first. "Varys," he murmurs. "You may call me Varys."

"Varys," I repeat softly. "You may call me Inara."

"Are you sure you wish me to do this, Inara?" he asks gently.

My heart is beating so loudly I am sure he can hear it, but I understand this is expected to seal our marriage. It is tradition. "Yes."

He hesitates for so long I start to glance over my shoulder, but stop when I feel him beginning to unfasten the line of buttons along the back of my dress.

I draw in a shaking breath as my gown falls loose with each unfastened button. When he reaches the small of my back, I tense as my dress slips down and pools around my feet, leaving me in only my silken shift. The cool night air raises goosebumps along my flesh as I slowly turn toward my new husband.

Careful to retract his sharp claws, he cups my chin and tips my face up to his. His blue eyes swirl with black as they stare deep into mine as he leans down and ever so gently touches his lips to my own.

His mouth is soft and warm, and his kiss is tender and

exploring. I had not expected him to be so gentle, and I am glad that he is.

Despite my nerves, each light brush of his lips to mine warms something deep inside me, and tingling pleasure slowly replaces my worry. Heat permeates my entire body as he slips an arm around my waist and drags me closer.

I've never been touched like this before.

I place my palms on his solid, muscular chest, feeling his heart pound beneath. His masculine scent of cinnamon surrounds me, filling my lungs with each breath. He flicks his tongue along the edge of my mouth and I gasp, granting him entrance to gently coax my lips to move against his as we explore each other. Warmth pools deep within.

I did not know kissing could feel like this. A shiver runs through me when my tongue brushes lightly across the tip of one fang, reminding me that my new husband is not human.

He lifts me into his arms and gently lays me on the bed. His eyes search mine as he slowly moves over me. He brushes his lips again to my own in a reverent kiss.

Cautiously, I reach up to touch him. I run my hands over his broad shoulders and down his muscular arms, my fingers tracing over the thick cords of muscle easily felt beneath his robes.

He settles between my thighs and something long and hard presses firmly against my core. I gasp as I realize it is his manhood. Only the thin barrier of our clothing is separating him from my entrance.

My heart taps a frantic beat in my chest, and I go still beneath him as anxiety spikes through me. My previous courage and all of my pleasure disappears entirely.

He pulls back immediately and his nostrils flare. He cups my chin, forcing my gaze to his. "I can scent your fear," he says, his voice husky. "You do not want this."

"I am nervous." I swallow thickly. "I've never done this before."

He lifts away from me and then stands from the bed.

Quickly, I sit up, pulling the furs up to cover me, since I am only wearing my silken shift.

Still dressed in his robes, he folds his arms tight across his chest.

His eyes return to their normal glowing, ice-blue color. "You do not need to fear me, Inara. I will not take you like this. I vow I will not touch you until you ask."

"What if I never ask?" The question pops out before I even realize I have said it aloud. I cannot take it back, nor would I wish to. His response will tell me what I can expect from his character.

His gaze searches mine. "I hold to my vow. Now, rest," he says, turning his back to me as he strides over to his table. "We have a long journey ahead of us tomorrow."

At first, I hesitate, but then I sink back down into the bed beneath the blankets and furs, pulling them tightly around me.

I turn onto my side and bring my hands to my lips, remembering the feel of his mouth against mine.

My heart still beats erratically. I glance over my shoulder and find Varys sitting at his desk, studying one of the parchments. A deep frown mars his brow as he reads.

Although I'm still nervous, I am no longer afraid. Not of him—not anymore. He is not what I feared he would be. If he were a cruel man, he would not have cared how I felt. I've heard enough terrible stories of arranged marriages to know that many new husbands are impatient with their wives if they are nervous on their wedding night.

I am glad Varys's kisses were soft and gentle. All of this is so new. We are still relative strangers to one another, and

I am glad he respected that I was not ready to consummate our vows.

Exhaustion fills me. It has been a long, nerve-wracking day preparing for my wedding, and now that I know my new husband will not touch me without my consent, I allow myself to drift away into sleep.

~

When I wake in the middle of the night, he is still at the desk, head resting on his folded arms as he sleeps. It is a bit cold in here and I notice he has nothing but his robe covering him.

Quietly, I slip from the bed, gathering one of the larger furs, and walk to his side. His dark hair covers his eyes and I gently brush it back, tucking it behind the elegant, pointed tip of his ear. With his face relaxed in sleep, he appears so peaceful.

Looking at all the parchments laid out on his desk, I wonder how often he has any time to relax. The mantle of rule is a heavy one. I know because I have seen the toll it has taken on Edmynd ever since he inherited the crown.

Varys's own father died only a few years ago, from what I remember. A short life for an Elf, or so I am told. Varys is a young king, just like my brother.

My grandparents were strangers when they wed to unite their kingdoms. They ended up having a loving marriage that was the envy of many. I've always wanted something that beautiful, for I did not see it with my own parents.

As I study Varys, I wonder if we might someday be happy like my grandparents were.

Carefully, I drape the fur over his shoulders, tucking it

around him to make sure he is fully covered and warm before tiptoeing back to the bed.

This night did not end how I'd expected. I glance once more at my new husband before closing my eyes. As I fall away into sleep, I find myself wondering if this marriage can be more than I thought it would be.

CHAPTER 12

VARYS

When I wake, Inara is still asleep in the bed. I sit up and notice a large fur draped over my shoulders. I turn my gaze back to my bride. She must have covered me while I slept. It is a thoughtful gesture, and perhaps bodes well for our marriage that she shows this much care toward me, given the circumstances.

I'm surprised I did not awaken, as I rarely sleep so deeply that I am unaware of my surroundings. Then again, I have barely slept at all these past few days. When she agreed to our bonding, I thought it might be an elaborate trap, and have been on edge ever since.

Only after we spoke our vows before the old gods in the temple, did I realize both her and Edmynd's intentions were honorable. They truly want this alliance as much as I do.

As I admire her beauty, my thoughts return to last night. My desire for her is great and my fangs extend with the urge to claim her, but I force them to retract. I will not push my ardor upon her. I vowed that I will not touch her until she asks, and to that I will hold.

As if sensing my gaze upon her, she stretches her lithe body out on the bed and then sits up. She blinks several times before turning toward me.

"Did you give me this?" I gesture to the fur.

She nods. "I was worried you might be cold last night."

I cannot remember the last time someone was concerned for me like this. "Thank you."

Her lips curve up into a lovely smile. "Of course."

"My King," Devyn's voice calls from just outside the tent. "The queen has a visitor."

"It's me, Inara." I recognize her sister's voice. "May I come in to help ready you for your trip?"

"Come in," Inara calls out.

Her sister enters. Her eyes widen slightly when she sees Inara in her shift. "Forgive me, I did not realize you were still in bed." Her entire face turns bright red. "I should—"

"It's all right," Inara reassures her. "I just woke up. You do not need to leave."

I stand from my chair and bow slightly. "I will give you some privacy while you prepare."

She flashes a warm smile. "Thank you, Varys."

Her sister's gaze is hard upon me as she watches me leave, probably believing that I claimed Inara last night, even though I did not.

As soon as I step outside, Devyn turns to me. "Did everything... go well last night?" he asks a bit hesitantly. His cheeks and ears darken slightly.

I understand exactly what he is asking. "We did not follow tradition."

"The Wolf Shifter prince will be glad not to scent her upon you," he replies. "He paced back and forth all night along the camp, in his wolf form, probably worried for her."

I dislike the implications of this. Prince Lukas accepted her decision to marry me and she is no longer his concern. Perhaps he regrets letting her go so easily. "Make sure someone is watching him at all times," I command. "There may still be a trap in all of this."

"Yes, my King."

CHAPTER 13

INARA

Grayce helps me change into my travel clothes. I smile as I put on my favorite dress and touch the small rose embroidered along the collar. Mother sewed this. It was part of one of my dresses when I was a child. Grayce had it sewn into this one for me as a gift last year.

I pat the hidden pocket of my skirt, feeling the nylweed vial and the dagger still safely contained within. She packs up mother's wedding gown with the rest of my things.

"What about you?" I ask. "Do you not want to wear this for your wedding someday?"

Sadness reflects behind her eyes. "I will not be marrying anytime soon, my dear sister."

"I'm so sorry." I hug her close. "I wish I could take away your heartache." I remove the dress from my trunk and hold it out to her. "Keep it. It will be safer back home."

She nods and takes it from me. "I will miss you. You must write to me often, all right?"

"I will."

My family gathers around me as we ready to leave. I hug Grayce again, promising to visit, though I truly don't know when that might happen.

Raiden hugs me and whispers in my ear. "If you need me, I will come for you. I swear, I will find a way."

Edmynd wraps his arms around me. When he pulls back, the guilt in his eyes is almost more than I can bear. "This is my choice, Edmynd," I reassure him. "I'm going to be all right."

He gives me a reluctant nod.

Lukas embraces me warmly. He stills and then pulls back, his nostrils flaring. Although we did very little last night, I'm sure he can smell Varys's scent on me. His expression hardens. "Did he hurt you?"

"No, he did not."

He glances at Varys, then scowls before turning back to me. "If you need me, I will do anything for you. Do you understand?"

"I know. Thank you." A smile crests my lips. "When we were younger and played that game of looking at the stars to see if their patterns would tell us who we would wed, do you remember what I saw?"

"A bloody Elf," he grumbles. "How could I forget?"

"And then you made fun of me." I chuckle. "You teased me for at least two weeks, claiming I had an obsession with pointed ears."

Lukas laughs a moment before his expression sobers again. He wraps me up in a bear hug as he whispers. "I hope your stars were right, Inara. That they picked the right person for you."

"Me too."

When I walk over to Varys, he turns to me. His nostrils flare slightly, and he removes his cloak, draping it around my shoulders. It's a thoughtful gesture, and I thank him. So far, he seems very kind and caring. This is a good start to our marriage.

I lift my left wrist to him, gesturing to the green ribbon. "What do we do with this?"

His cheeks and the edges of his ears darken. Carefully, he unwinds it from my wrist and folds it into his pocket. "We save it for our Elven ceremony."

Before I can ask why, he turns to his warriors, shouting something in Elvish. I may not know the words, but I understand their intent when his guards line up in formation on their mounts.

I swallow thickly as I stare at the dire wolves. I wanted to bring my mare, but she is too skittish when surrounded by these predatory creatures. They may look like wolves, but they are at least twice the size of any horse, with sharp fangs almost as long as my forearm and lethal, black claws.

King Varys moves toward me and extends his hand. Cautiously, I take it, and he leads me to his mount. The dire wolf's sharp, yellow eyes meet mine, and the intelligence behind them is evident as it studies me. Varys places a hand on the dire wolf's shoulder while he gestures to me with the other. "She is my mate."

Mate. It's strange hearing this word instead of *wife*.

The wolf bobs his head almost imperceptibly, and my mouth drifts open in shock. I've heard Elves could speak to animals, but I always thought it was nothing more than rumor.

"This is Rhygar," he gestures to the wolf. "He will not harm you."

I study the wolf, unsure how to respond. Tentatively, I rest my hand on his thick, dark gray and black fur. "Hello, Rhygar." *Please don't eat me*, I want to say, but I do not.

Varys stares at me expectantly, then gestures to the

stirrup of the saddle. I look at my travel dress ruefully, wishing more than anything that I had my riding pants instead of this silken frock. When Grayce came, she brought only this dress and a few others. While it is one of my favorites, it is certainly not practical for riding.

I clench my jaw. "My dress... I'll have to ride sidesaddle."

"That is not safe." Varys frowns. "You could fall." An involuntary shiver moves through me as his gaze travels over my body. He arches a brow. "May I make an adjustment for your safety?"

Thinking he means to the saddle, I nod. Without warning, he extends his black claws and slices a line down first the front of my dress, starting mid-thigh, and then the back.

I stare at him, gaping. I *cannot* believe he just did that.

He steps back and dips his chin. "Now, you can ride safely."

I'm caught somewhere between thanking him and being scandalized that he just tore my fine dress. But as I gaze up at his stoic face, I decide it may be best not to say anything in front of my family. My brothers are still close enough that, if they thought something was amiss, they'd probably inadvertently start a war by trying to murder my new husband before we've even left camp.

My new husband seems to have no notion of propriety. But perhaps that is not a bad thing. I love that he is more concerned for my welfare than for appearances.

I put my foot in the stirrup and pull myself up into the saddle, swinging my leg over so I may ride properly, without falling.

Even my own parents used to insist that I ride like a proper lady, no matter the risk of potentially breaking my neck if I were to tumble over the side. Mother always used to admonish me for wearing riding pants when we were younger, claiming that my future husband would not approve of it in the slightest. Little did she know, I would someday marry a Dark Elf. And I wonder, not for the first time, what she would think if she was here.

I inhale sharply as Varys jumps up, settling behind me. I perch as far forward in the saddle as possible to avoid touching him. We may be married, but we are not quite that familiar with each other yet.

Straightening, I glance over my shoulder. The Dark Elves are known for their strength. I need to appear strong, not weak and helpless. "I am an experienced rider. I can ride by myself."

"Have you ridden a dire wolf before?"

"Not a dire wolf, of course, but I've ridden horses my entire life."

"A dire wolf is a very different creature from a horse." He arches a brow. "They are willful and headstrong, to a fault. You must properly bond to one for them to respect your commands."

"Bond? What do you mean?"

"You must share your mind with a dire wolf when you ride them. Each wolf is paired with their rider. And it is the wolf that chooses who his partner shall be." He pauses. "We will find one for you when we return home, but until then, you must ride with me."

I draw in a ragged breath, stealing myself for a long journey. Although I do not fear Varys, I'm not entirely comfortable with him yet, either.

My cheeks flare as I think of what happened between us last night. It has made everything that much more awkward between us this morning. I brace myself, waiting for Varys to wrap his arm around my waist and tug me back against him, but thankfully he does not.

He calls out to his warriors and we start forward, heading toward Ithylian.

I'm acutely aware of Varys's warriors watching me. It is a strange feeling being the only human amongst so many Dark Elves. Varys may not want to hurt me, but his guards might feel differently. After all, we were on the brink of war only a few days ago, before Varys released my brother.

Discreetly, I check the hidden pocket of my dress for my dagger. Then I straighten my spine and tip my chin up high. This is my life now, and I refuse to let fear rule me.

Even as I think this, however, my thoughts turn to my dreams. As long as I can find nylweed, I can keep my secret hidden. Part of me believes Varys would understand, if he knew. After all, his people are not afraid of magic, so why would they fear someone with visions?

But another part of me is afraid. I have hidden my visions my entire life for fear of being burned at the stake by the Mages for witchcraft. I always worried I might be discovered one day, and High Mage Ylari could no longer protect me.

I have never understood why the Mages consider such things heresy when they themselves have powers and magic. And while it is barbaric to burn people at the stake, the human kingdoms of the seven realms follow the laws of the Order for fear of losing the protection they provide us from the Fae and the Elves.

Closing my eyes, I force myself to push down my dark thoughts. When I open them again, I survey the landscape around us. Lush, green fields give way to rolling hills until we reach the dark forest between our two kingdoms.

The sun sinks low on the horizon, stretching shadows from the trees. Dark clouds gather overhead as lightning forks across the sky. The wind picks up, whipping around us with an icy chill as night begins to fall.

A loud crack of thunder booms above us, and I jump. I twist back just enough to glance at Varys. "How far away is your home?"

"Less than two day's ride from here. We will make camp once we are safely inside the Veil."

The Veil...

I've only ever seen the magic barrier that separates Ithylian from Florin once before, when I was still a child. A shudder runs through me. I remember my father telling me never to venture near for fear I'd be taken by the Dark Elves and trapped on the other side.

And now... I go to it willingly with a Dark Elf husband.

I peer up at the sky. Moisture hangs thick in the air. "We're not going to make it to the Veil before the storm hits."

His brow furrows. "It is only rain."

"Yes, but the temperature has dropped and it will only get colder as the night wears on. We'll catch our death out here if we have to ride through a storm."

He straightens and cocks his head to the side. "Humans can die from exposure to cold rain?"

It sounds ridiculous when he says it like that, but it's the truth. "Yes. We can develop pneumonia. Do Elves not get sick like this?"

Devyn rides up beside us. His amber eyes dart briefly to me, full of concern, before he addresses Varys. The few Elvish words I pick up are something to the effect of suggesting we find a place to make camp before I die from exposure to the elements because I am human and frail.

I hate that they believe I am weak. That is not the impression I wish to give to my husband's people.

Varys agrees we should make camp and refers to me as "his Khio'ri."

That word: *Khio'ri.* He said it the first time we met, but I do not know what it means. I turn around, about to ask, when movement catches the corner of my eye in the forest beside the road. "What was that?" I point off in the distance.

It's so dark now, I can barely see anything thanks to the dense cloud cover overhead.

Varys whips his head in that direction, his glowing blue eyes narrowing as he scans the woods. "What did you see?"

"A strange flash of light of some sort. I-I'm not sure what it was."

He raises his fist, and everyone stops, all eyes searching the forest for any sign of movement.

"I do not see anything. Are you sure you saw something?"

"I'm positive."

Another of Varys's men moves up beside us. "I've heard human eyesight is not as acute as ours," he says in Elvish, and I'm surprised by how much I'm able to pick up with my limited knowledge of their language. "Perhaps she is simply scared and seeing things as a result," he switches to Florinesh.

Indignation flares in my chest. "I am not imagining things. I saw something out there."

Varys's eyes widen and his brows shoot up.

"What is it? Why are you looking at me like that? Do you really not believe me?"

"I *do* believe you," he says. "I just... am surprised that you are speaking perfect Elvish."

"What?" I ask incredulously. "I am speaking Florinesh, as are you."

He shakes his head.

"Yes, you—" I stop abruptly, blinking several times as I realize he is right, recognizing the soft, lilting words as they leave my mouth. "How is this possible?"

"It is part of our bond," he explains. "It—" He stops, snapping his attention to the forest. He turns to me, dropping his voice to a low whisper. "I will explain as soon as I can. Right now, we must be very quiet. I believe we are being hunted."

I freeze. "By what?"

"Wraiths," he says under his breath.

Ice floods my veins. Wraiths are vicious and deadly creatures that are difficult to kill. Even one can take out an entire regiment of men. They feed off energy—usually the life force of any living thing around them—but they particularly target Mages for their innate powers. I imagine Dark Elves must be attractive to them, as well, since they possess their own sort of magic.

Varys tightens his arm around my waist and whispers in my ear. "Take my sword." Quietly, he unsheathes the long blade and hands it to me. "Do not hesitate to use it if they attack."

Raiden's archery lessons have made me deadly with a bow and arrow, but that does me little good right now. I know nothing about handling a sword. I grip the pommel firmly, while Varys pulls out another for himself.

The roiling black clouds block most of the moonlight overhead, plunging the landscape into darkness. I can barely make out the path in front of us or the forest off to the side.

I glance back at Varys and his men and hope the rumors of their excellent night vision are accurate. Their glowing eyes scan the woods as we move down the road in tight formation.

Rhygar's muscular form is tense beneath us, his fur bristling. Varys lays a hand on his neck. "Calm," he whispers. "Steady, my friend."

In the distance, the glowing barrier of the Veil stretches

83

out before us—the magical wall surrounding Ithylian. "We must get through the Veil," he whispers. "The Wraiths should not be able to follow us there. If they attack, run and do not look back. I will find you later. They should leave you alone since you do not possess the magic that draws them."

I swallow hard, wondering if my abilities might somehow attract their attention. I've never truly considered my visions to be a form of magic, and I hope that I'm not wrong. The truth sits on the tip of my tongue, but I cannot bring myself to tell Varys.

Edmynd's warnings echo in my mind. I have to make sure I trust my husband first, before I reveal this about myself.

"Take my hand," Varys says, reaching for me. "Your skin must be touching mine when we cross, or the Veil could kill you."

Without hesitation, I place my hand in his. He threads his fingers through my own and heat flares in my chest, startling me, but I bite my lip and remain silent. The air is still and the woods far quieter than only a few minutes ago. As if the very forest itself is holding its breath on our approach to the Veil while something terrible stalks us.

A bead of sweat trickles down my spine. We're less than ten paces from the glowing barrier. My heart hammers as we draw near, and I pray to the gods to grant us safe passage.

Without warning, something rushes from the woods. Varys raises his sword, but too late. It slams against us, knocking me from his grip and sending us tumbling off Rhygar's back.

The world spins, and then I hit the ground, the impact forcing the air from my lungs. Gasping, I struggle to right myself as chaos explodes all around me. I watch in horror as more Wraiths fly out of the forest, charging toward Varys's men.

They are even more terrifying than I imagined. Their ghastly skeletal forms are draped in raven-black shrouds; their blood-red eyes bulging above the razor-sharp teeth in their skulls.

Swords clang and shouts ring out as the Dark Elves fight off their savage attacks.

A Wraith rushes up behind Varys and panic claws through me as he spins to the side, but not fast enough as it slashes out with its talons. I swing my sword, cutting off its arm before it can touch him.

A shrill cry rips from its throat and crimson eyes lock onto mine. It charges me, but I swing my sword in a wide arc, catching its side. It releases an ear-piercing shriek before gripping my blade and setting it on fire.

I scream as the metal burns my skin, and drop my weapon. The Wraith strikes with dark claws, and I throw up my forearm to shield myself. White hot pain rips through my left arm as deadly talons rake across my skin, tearing through my flesh.

"Inara!" Varys cries out, rushing toward me.

His normally blue eyes are a feral, obsidian black and his fangs extend fully as he brandishes his sword, charging the Wraith like a demon possessed, before cutting it in half.

He pulls me to my feet, careful of his sharp claws. "We must go!"

Two more Wraiths attack, but he sweeps his sword through one's neck, severing its head. Dark blood splatters his face and armor as he stabs at the other with his lethal claws, ripping a hole in its chest.

"To the King!" I hear his men cry out.

Three more Wraiths rush toward us, and Varys jumps in front of me, shielding me from their attack. An inhuman growl rises from his chest as he moves with a fluid and lethal grace, wielding his sword with deadly precision.

Rhygar wraps his massive jaws around another Wraith, snapping it in half with a sickening crunch, painting his fur with dark blood.

Varys gathers me in his arms, lifting me to his chest as though I weigh nothing.

"To the Veil!" he bellows.

He swings us up onto Rhygar's back and takes my hand, clasping it firmly as we race for the wall.

My skin prickles with a jolt of power when we cross through the Veil. As soon as we're on the other side, Rhygar turns to face the barrier. Varys clutches me to his chest, and we drop to the ground. His men do the same.

Carefully, he sets me down against a tree beside him. "Reinforce the wall!" he shouts.

Crackling orbs of sparkling, blue and green light gather between their palms. Now that we're in Ithylian, they have access to their magic. My eyes go wide as they swing their arms sending their power arcing toward the barrier, where it slams into the side, making it glow even brighter.

Ear-splitting shrieks ring out from the other side as several Wraiths test the Veil, bursting into flames as they make contact.

Magic sparks like a firebolt across Varys's body. The ground rumbles and quakes as he grits his teeth, drawing energy from the earth as a massive blue flame gathers between his palms. The men stare awestruck at their king. His arms tremble as he fights to contain the power before hurling the flame toward the Veil.

It slams into the barrier, exploding in a brilliant display of light, and I squeeze my eyes shut against the assault. When I open them, the Veil is much brighter, energy crackling along the wall like lightning. It fingers out from the wall, catching the last of the Wraiths, incinerating them to ash in an instant.

Varys's chest heaves with exertion as he watches them burn. When they are gone, he spins to face me. His eyes widen as they rake over my form. He drops to his knees, running his hands over my body and my shredded clothing, stained with blood. "Where are you hurt?"

I'm still in shock, unable to speak. I glance down at my left forearm. The three jagged rents from the Wraith's talons pool with blood and drip down my arm. Angry red veins finger out from the wound as the Wraith's poison begins to spread. I pull my arm to my chest, doubling over as searing pain replaces my shock.

"Let me see." Varys reaches for my arm, but I jerk it away.

It's too painful to even touch. Clenching my jaw, I shake my head. "It burns," I grit through my teeth, struggling to hold back my tears.

He cups my chin, tipping my face up to his. His glowing blue eyes search mine with concern. "I can heal you, but you have to let me help you. Do you understand?"

I force myself to nod. Gently, he takes my hand as pain arcs through me like fire. I bite back a whimper as he pulls my trembling arm away from my chest.

"My King," I recognize Devyn's voice standing over us. "What are you doing? We need to get her to a healer."

"We will not reach one in time," Varys rasps. "Step back. I do not want to hurt you."

"You could die," Devyn counters.

"She is my Khio'ri," he says. "It will not kill me."

Khio'ri. The word echoes through my mind as I fight against the pain.

"But she is human, my King. You do not know that it will work."

"It will work," he growls.

Warmth radiates from his palm to mine, traveling up my injured arm, covering the agony like a soothing balm. My muscles relax as the fire in my flesh dissipates. I watch in awe as my skin begins to reknit before my eyes. Even the burn on my palm disappears.

I'm vaguely aware of his men gathered around us observing, their eyes wide.

The tension leaves my body, as Varys takes away the pain. When he is finished, not even a hint of a scar remains from the talon marks. I stare at my arm in wonder before lifting my gaze to his as exhaustion steals through me. My eyelids are so heavy I can barely keep them open.

He cups my face, brushing the soft pad of his thumb across my cheek. "You are safe now, Inara. My vow."

He pulls me to his chest, running a hand down my back in a soothing gesture as he whispers in my ear. "We are going to travel a bit farther, then we can rest. I'm going to pick you up. All right?"

This is not who I am; I'm not weak. Mustering my strength, I force my gaze to his. "I can stand," I protest.

His lips quirk up in a faint smile. "All right. Use my arm for balance."

I grip his forearm, and he helps me up. The world spins for a moment before settling again.

"You fought well."

"Did I?" I huff out a laugh as a smile curves my mouth. "In case you didn't notice, I dropped my sword."

His ice-blue eyes meet mine, glowing brighter now. "You saved me."

"And then *you* saved me. So, I think we're even."

He slips his arms around me and pulls me close. "My brave human wife," he murmurs, and something about the way he says it fills my heart with warmth.

CHAPTER 14

VARYS

I lift Inara onto Rhygar's back, positioning her with space for me to settle behind her. Dried blood covers our skin and clothing, and although it would probably be wiser to conserve my magic, I use it to cleanse us.

With a wave of my hand, I conjure a cleansing spell. She inhales sharply as it travels over her body. "What was that?" She blinks down at herself, then twists back to me, a faint smile curving her mouth. "Did you just use magic to clean us up?"

"Yes."

"Why am I so tired?"

I loop my arm around her waist and tug her back a bit so she can lean against me. "It is an effect of the healing spell."

That I could heal her proves that she is my Khio'ri. Only those with the fated bond are able to heal their mates in this way. Anyone else would have died in the attempt.

I was not sure it would work because Inara is human,

but I had to try, even if it meant risking my life. I know I must explain the fated bond to her, but not now. Not while she is still recovering. It can wait.

An icy wind blows through the trees and she shivers slightly. Dark clouds hover overhead as thunder rolls across the sky. The storm seems to have followed us across the Veil. I pull a blanket from one of the packs on Rhygar's saddle and drape it over her shoulders to keep her warm, praying the rain will not come until after we find a place to make camp.

"Thank you," she whispers, securing the fabric tightly around her.

"Of course."

Inara is very brave. My human wife fought well, even though she believes she did not, and I am impressed by her strength. She saved my life. I had my back to the Wraith when it would have attacked. If not for her, it could have dealt me a mortal blow before I'd even realized what was happening.

"Where did they come from, Varys?" she asks. "I thought Wraiths were only beyond the Great Wall."

They are supposed to be. That is the purpose of the Great Wall. It is reinforced with magic and heavily guarded to keep them from crossing into our lands. "I do not know." It bothers me that I do not have an answer. There should not be Wraiths anywhere near the Veil. "Our patrols have encountered them along the borders over the past few months. So have the Fae."

"Your people are friends with the Fae, right?"

"Yes. My grandfather sealed an alliance with them by marrying a princess of the royal family."

"I heard about this," she replies. "Does it mean you are part Fae? Because of your grandmother?"

"No. They did not have any children together."

"Then, how did—"

"My King," Devyn interrupts. "I would suggest seeking shelter in the old ruins of Elysarin castle this night." He lifts his head to observe the sky. "I believe the weather will hold until we get there."

I nod in agreement.

"Is that close?" Inara asks, turning her head back toward me.

"A few more hours, at least."

"We should warn my brother about the Wraiths roaming the forest near the border."

"I agree. I will send a raven as soon as we reach the castle."

A thought occurs to me as I glance down at my Khio'ri. "Why did you not wear your armor for our journey?"

"My armor?"

"Yes. The set you wore when I first saw you."

"Oh, that," she says, and it is easy to read the surprise in her tone. "I stole that from the armory."

"You are a princess. Do you not have a set of your own armor?"

"Women are not supposed to wear armor, much less march to battle," she explains. "When I heard you had captured Raiden, I disguised myself as one of Edmynd's guards so I could travel with his army to save my brother."

"I have heard this of your people... That human men are very protective of women and discourage them from going to war. But I thought it was rumor, not truth."

"They don't just discourage it. It is considered unlady-like to even learn how to wield a weapon. But that did not stop Raiden from teaching me to draw a bow." A soft laugh escapes her. "He did not care what others thought. He knew I wanted to learn, so he taught me. My mother hated him for it, but... she already hated him to begin with, so I suppose he no longer cared by that point."

My mouth falls open, shocked by her unfiltered words. I had heard Raiden was their father's illegitimate child, but until he mentioned how Inara loved him despite this, I never gave it much thought. After all, my own grandfather sired children with a mistress because his bride was Fae.

It is strange that human men do not want the women to learn how to wield weapons. Defensive training is something all Dark Elves receive from the time we are children.

I wonder if Inara might like a set of armor and weapons training. From what I have seen, she already possesses the heart of a warrior. Her brother was wise to train her, and I wonder if she would wish to continue that training when we reach the castle. I am about to ask, but pause when I notice her eyes are closed. Her head is resting against my collar as she leans back against me, asleep.

Devyn rides up beside us and arches a brow when he notices her sleeping. "She trusts you," he murmurs in a voice so low I almost miss it.

"And I trust her." I meet his gaze evenly. "She risked her own safety to save me during the attack."

He rubs his chin thoughtfully. "Did you notice how they all went for her? It was as though the Wraiths were more attracted to her energy than ours... But this makes no sense; they prefer feeding from beings with magic to those who do not possess it."

These same thoughts have been troubling me ever since the attack.

"What if she is the one spoken of in the prophecy?"

I shake my head, instantly dismissing Devyn's question. "She is human. They do not have magic. And the one prophesied is supposed to be extremely powerful."

"Are you certain she sleeps?" he asks softly.

Although our connection is new, I can already sense many things about her, and right now, I am sure she is slumbering. I nod.

"Those Wraiths sensed something about her, Varys. Something that drew them to her instead of us."

"If she were powerful like the one prophesied, I doubt her brother would have let her go... especially to one he has considered his enemy for so many years."

"Unless it was part of their plan," Devyn counters. "What better way to infiltrate your enemy than to send someone powerful to get close enough to kill a king."

"She *saved* my life, Devyn. If she wanted to assassinate me, she could have let the Wraith do it for her. She could have even ended me last night while I slept."

"Unless she is waiting to get close to the entire royal family."

I glance down at my bride as she so trustingly rests against me. "No," I state firmly. "I do not believe she would do that."

He frowns. "You have to consider that—"

"I do not believe she is a spy or an assassin, Devyn. I understand your concern, but it is unfounded."

"You are certain?"

My heart clenches as I stare down at her sleeping form. Perhaps it is the bond making me feel this way, but as I study her, fierce protectiveness fills me. "Yes."

"Melina will think differently," he says, a faint smile quirking his lips. "You know how distrusting she is of new people."

I sigh heavily and nod. I have anticipated this and am already dreading our arrival at the castle. Melina is another of my personal guards. She is critical of anyone new, always suspecting new guards of plotting either my assassination or that of the rest of my family.

Because Inara is human, she will be even more suspicious of her.

"I will deal with Melina," I tell him grimly. "If she wants to remain one of my personal guards, she must pledge to defend my queen without question."

Devyn straightens in the saddle, recognizing the thinly veiled meaning of my statement. He darts a glance at Inara. "I vow I will protect her with my life, as I do you."

I am pleased to hear this. He is one of the few people I can trust without reservation. "I appreciate your loyalty, Devyn, and I'm thankful for your friendship."

He dips his chin in a subtle bow. "You shall always have it, Varys."

An image of Rhygar protecting her fills my mind. I lean forward and rest a hand on his soft, thick fur. "Thank you for protecting her, my friend."

He projects another image of his own mate and I realize it is his way of telling me he understands how important Inara is to me. I am glad he already accepts her. Dire wolves are very loyal, and I have no doubt he will do all he can to keep her safe.

When we reach the ruins of Elysarin, it is very late. We make our way along the road leading up to the castle. The white stone towers stretch proudly toward the sky, their silver-capped rooftops reflecting the moonlight like sparkling gems. Thick, green vines full of glowing, white flowers climb up the stone walls and across the arched gateway that spans the entrance into the courtyard.

Much of the surrounding garden wall is either crumbling or missing entirely. The grounds are wild and untamed after so many years of neglect, and the forest has already begun to move in, overtaking much of it. But they are beautiful, nonetheless.

The large fountain in the center still flows, feeding into

several small streams that wind along the overgrown pathways lined with trees and bushes full of incandescent, vibrant flowers of purple, red, and blue.

The main doors guarding the palace entrance have a pattern of stars and the full moon etched into the silver metal. They are still lovely despite being rusted in place after so many years of disuse.

It is strange visiting the castle of my ancestors, as if their ghosts somehow still inhabit this place. These ruins are as much a part of my family's history as it is for all of our people. For some inexplicable reason, I wish for Inara to see it before we go inside. Gently, I call her name. "Inara."

Her eyelids flutter open. She blinks several times at the crumbling structure. "Where are we?"

"The once-great castle of Elysarin. Home of my ancestors."

CHAPTER 15

INARA

Silver moonlight spears through the clouds, illuminating the castle and the courtyard before me. Lightning fingers out across the sky, reflecting brightly off the castle's silver rooftops. I stare at the towering trees lining the path through the gardens and am completely mesmerized as flits of light dance between them in various shades of white and gold. "What are those?"

"They are Night Pixies."

As far as I knew, there was only one type of Pixie. "Night Pixies?"

"Yes. They are a bit more aggressive than Day Pixies and they have sharper teeth."

I whip my head back to him. "They bite?"

"Only if provoked."

That's rather disturbing, but good to know...

I scan the magical landscape through an entirely

JESSICA GRAYSON

different lens now, wondering what other possibly dangerous creatures may lurk here.

Varys shows me the courtyard containing a statue of a man and a woman with pointed ears and dressed in long, flowing robes. They stand before each other, palms pressed together and bound by some sort of ribbon or cord.

"The first king and queen of Ithylian," Varys says. "It is a depiction of their bonding ceremony. Elysarin castle was built during their reign."

I study the surrounding area, noting that several parts of what once must have been the palace have been reduced to crumbled stones jutting up from the ground. A glowing, green moss covers it all. It is common knowledge that the Dark Elves reside beneath the earth, but I never knew they once lived on the surface.

"We did not always make our home in the mountain," Varys says, as if having read my thoughts. "Our people used to live above ground, before the Great War. After the Great War, my ancestors moved everyone to Cyridil—our stronghold in the mountains," he explains. "It was supposed to be temporary, but we had lost so much they were afraid to rebuild the castle and the capital city. They believed the mountains offered greater protection, and they were right... but even that came with its own cost."

"What do you mean?"

"In withdrawing from the surface, we have isolated ourselves from our neighbors, neglecting to foster the relationships we once had." His expression turns grim. "Our choice to protect our people has led to much tension and subsequent fostering of mistrust between us and several of the other races, including yours."

He's right. We have a better relationship with the Fae and the High Elves than we do with Varys's kingdom. Probably because the others at least try to negotiate trade agreements and such instead of keeping to themselves. I place a hand on his forearm. "Hopefully our marriage can change this for the better."

"That is my hope as well," he replies solemnly.

Sadness weighs on me as I stare up at the ruined castle. Tears fill my eyes, but I blink them back, surprised by my reaction to this place.

Although the Dark Elves have been enemies of my people since before I was born, Varys's words tug at my heart as I think of all those who must have died here. It had to have been a devastating loss for them to retreat to the mountains and never rebuild above the surface again.

He pulls on the reins and we stop. I twist back to him, confused. "What are we doing? Is this where we're going to stay?"

He lifts his gaze to the sky. "The storms will overtake us shortly. Better to shelter here than be caught in the open."

He raises his arm, fist closed, and the rest of his warriors stop, listening to his uttered commands. I am acutely aware that he is speaking in Elvish again, yet somehow I understand every word of his instructions to the men to make camp here.

He says it's part of our 'bond' that helps me understand and speak his language, but I'm still not quite sure how that works. I make a note to ask him about it once we're settled.

When he dismounts, he turns to me, extending his arms to help me down. I do not want to appear weak or incapable. "Thank you, but I can dismount just fine on my own."

He retracts his arms, and I swing my leg over to dismount, but my dress snags on one of the saddle straps. It tugs against the fabric, causing me to lose my balance. With a pitiful shriek, I fall off the side, throwing out my hands to break my fall.

Strong arms wrap around my waist, catching me before I hit the ground. Varys pulls me back to him, steadying me on my feet.

Heat flushes my cheeks and I lift my gaze, acutely aware of his body pressed against mine. "Thank you."

He gives a tiny nod. His face and the points of his ears turn a shade darker. I cannot tell if he is angry, dismayed, or something else entirely. Or, perhaps, he is irritated because he thinks I'm clumsy. I do not know him well enough to read his expressions, or lack thereof.

Slowly, he unwinds his arms from around my waist. He pulls the saddle off Rhygar, then motions for me to follow him as he carries it toward the castle.

Instead of entering through the front doors, he guides me around to the side where the wall was destroyed, leaving a gaping hole.

I stop short, peering into the darkness. "Can you see anything in there?" I ask, worried that there might be some sort of terrifying creature making its home in the ruins. I certainly don't want to stumble upon something dangerous unknowingly.

He frowns. "I forget humans cannot see in the dark."

"We can see, just not very well," I say, hating how weak this probably makes me appear.

He raises his hand. With a sharp flick of his wrist, he conjures a blue orb. It hovers above us, providing enough illumination to light our path into the palace. The blue light casts eerie shadows around what appears to have been a great entry hall. Our footsteps echo along the stone walls as we walk through.

Broken furniture is scattered throughout and torn tapestries and paintings droop from the walls. A crumbling bust of, most likely, one of the great Elven kings who lived here sits on a pedestal at the top of a grand staircase leading above.

I trail my hand along the banister as we ascend, noting the intricate carvings of vines and flowers along the wood.

This palace must have been beautiful in its day.

A spear of moonlight cuts through the dark, and I lift my eyes to find a glass dome, somehow still intact. The rolling, black clouds quickly cover the moon, casting everything into darkness again. A loud clap of thunder crashes overhead, shaking the very floor beneath my feet, and I wonder how stable this structure is.

Surely Varys would not shelter here if he thought it might collapse on us.

As if reading my thoughts, he turns to me. "There is still lingering magic in these walls. They will not fail while we are here."

A soft scraping of stone in the distance draws my attention and I instinctively move closer to Varys. He places a hand on my shoulder and I feel foolish when he murmurs, "It is only a mouse."

So much for me trying to appear brave.

He leads me down a long hallway toward a set of double doors. He pushes them open, revealing a massive bedroom with a large hole in the ceiling in the far corner. Dark gray clouds still hang overhead and the smell of impending rain drifts in on the cool night breeze.

He sets down the saddle and pulls two bedrolls and a few glowing stones from the pack. I'm about to ask what they are when he taps them together and stacks them on the floor.

"These should help keep us warm," he explains.

I walk toward them, surprised when I feel the same level of warmth one might from a campfire. I take one of the bedrolls and set it across from his, on the opposite side of the warming stones.

His eyes snap to me. "We will sleep together this night."

I lick my lips nervously. I know we are wed, but we are still complete strangers. Surely, he does not intend to consummate our marriage now. I know it is expected, eventually, but he told me he would not touch me until I asked.

And I do not plan to ask this night.

I stop moving and he regards me with a deeply furrowed brow. "Is there another room I can sleep in?" I ask, hoping he'll understand my meaning.

"It is safer for you to remain here with me."

Now an entirely different worry fills me. "What do you mean? What are you worried about? We're inside the Veil. I thought—"

"The Veil is not perfect," he interjects. "My people are not the only ones with magic. There are many other-worldly beings that possess the power and strength to cross our wall, if they are determined. And as my mate, you are now a target for my enemies."

This, I understand. All kings have enemies, and the fact that he just married someone whose people have been opponents of the Dark Elves for so long makes me an even more tempting assassination target.

Silence settles between us while I ponder my potential demise. When I decided to marry Varys, I thought my sacrifice was worth it to create peace between our king-doms. It never occurred to me it could actually end in my death.

"Let us ready for bed," Varys says, interrupting my depressing thoughts.

I lower my attention to the stones and swallow thickly. I assumed we made everything clear last night, but perhaps we did not. While I want to ask what exactly he expects, I cannot push the words past my lips. I trust that he will not hurt me, but I am not quite ready to consummate our marriage yet.

I gesture to the bedrolls, grasping at the first excuse I pluck from my racing thoughts. "I know we are wed, according to my culture, but... technically we are not married according to yours. Yet." I clear my throat. "So perhaps sharing a... bed this night is not entirely proper."

His expression remains neutral, but his cheeks and the pointed tips of his ears flush a darker shade of blue. He opens his mouth to speak, but I continue.

"And while what happened between us last night was... pleasurable," I admit as my cheeks heat in embarrassment. "I believe it might be a much more satisfactory experience, for us both, if we knew each other a bit more before we do anything that intimate and—"

A discreet knock at the door interrupts my stumbling words. "Enter!" Varys calls out.

Devyn steps inside. Two guards carrying a sizable metal tub follow him.

"We retrieved this from one of the other rooms," he says.

They set it along the opposite wall and place a divider in front of it. With a wave of his hand, I watch, awed, as Devyn fills it with water, a light mist of steam rising from the top.

Dark Elf magic is certainly very useful, from what I've witnessed so far.

Two more guards enter and set up a cot that has just enough room for both of our bedrolls.

"Thank you," Varys says before dismissing them. He turns back to me and gestures to the tub. "You may bathe, if you would like."

Grateful, I nod and quickly make my way toward the divider. Although Varys used a spell to clean us up earlier, bathing will give me time to think of a plan to dissuade him in case he has changed his mind and wants to... do anything intimate this evening.

I remove my dress and throw it over the divider to keep it off the ground, but not before sliding my blade from the secret pocket. After his comment about Night Pixies, I think it may be wise to be prepared for anything.

Carefully, I step into the tub and sink beneath the warm water. My mind reels as I think up an array of excuses to avoid what might come next. The cot is of ample size to sleep side by side, with space between us. Perhaps I can simply line some pillows down the center as a divider of sorts.

When I'm finished bathing, I step out of the tub and discover a tunic hanging where my dress had been. Apprehension floods me at once. "Where is my dress?"

"It is still here," he replies. "I thought you might wish to wear something that is not torn until we can retrieve more clothing from your trunk in the morning. I have given you my tunic in the meantime."

"Why can I not have my trunk with my belongings now?"

"Some of the guards are still recovering from the attack. They brought the tub and the cot, but I do not wish to ask them to do much more this night. They need to rest and regain their strength for the journey ahead."

Now, I feel selfish for even asking.

"Oh," I tell him. "That's... understandable."

I pluck the tunic off the divider and slip into it, tucking the blade in one of the large pockets. The material is soft against my skin and lighter than anything I've ever worn—finer than silk. Because it belongs to Varys, it carries his masculine scent—warm cinnamon and earth. I cannot deny that I love the way my new husband smells.

When I step out from behind the divider, Varys is standing by the cot with our two bedrolls, dressed in only soft-knit pants. The moonlight filtering in from the window carves his lean, muscular form in light and shadow. His gaze wanders over my body before his eyes settle on mine. My heart is beating wildly and my mouth dries as he moves closer.

Last night, he never removed his robes, so I did not see any of his body. Despite my nerves, I cannot help but notice his toned abdomen and chest, and the thick cords of muscle that wrap around his arms. He is masculine perfection made manifest before me.

As he draws near, I notice the fine, silver lines covering his body—scars, I realize. They speak of a man who has fought many battles and survived many things that would have killed most others.

While studying his scars, heat flushes my cheeks as I observe the play of his muscles beneath his gray-blue skin. It occurs to me that I am blatantly staring at him, but I'm completely mesmerized and I cannot look away.

CHAPTER 16

VARYS

When Inara steps out from behind the divider, something dark and primal unfurls from deep within. Fierce possessiveness fills me when I see her in my tunic. I have heard the fated bond is strong, but I never imagined it would feel anything like this.

My nostrils flare as I inhale deeply of her delicate scent mixed with mine. No longer twisted up in an intricate braid, her lovely blonde hair cascades down her back in long, silken waves.

My tunic is so large on her it goes down to mid-thigh. She has rolled the long sleeves back to her forearm, and the neckline hangs off one shoulder, revealing a smooth expanse of bare skin.

I think of our kiss last night—the taste of her mouth and the feel of her lips against my own. Desire fills me, and I long to hold her close once more.

Her hazel eyes regard me warily, suggesting she is uncomfortable beneath the weight of my stare, but I cannot force myself to turn away. She is captivating, and I am completely in her thrall. When I first saw her, I thought she was the most beautiful woman I had ever beheld. Now that she is mine, I cannot take my eyes off her.

She tucks a stray tendril of hair behind the rounded shell of her left ear, and through the fated bond of the *Khio'rinar*, I can sense that my attentions make her nervous.

I wonder if she can sense me as I can sense her?

Her gaze snags on my chest, and her forehead creases slightly. She is studying my scars.

Fortunately, it is dark in here and humans have poor night vision because I can only imagine her disgust if she were to see them in the light. I decide to speak before she inquires about them. "Get in the bed while I bathe."

Her eyes widen at my rather curt statement. Inwardly, I curse myself as I move past her. I meant to say she could have the bed while I bathe, but it came out wrong.

Why does she make me so nervous I cannot think straight, or speak the correct words, much less make sense of the ones I manage?

I make quick use of the tub, then change back into my pants. The entire time, her anxiety pulses through the bond. She thinks I mean to take her this night, but I do not. And I'm not sure whether to be depressed or offended that she finds the idea of joining with me so terrifying. I am scarred, but I was once handsome, before all my injuries.

From her expression when she noticed my scars, apparently humans must be like Dark Elves—obsessed with perfection and beauty. Anything else is less in their eyes.

I draw in a deep breath, square my shoulders, and step

out from behind the divider. I cannot remove my scars, so she will have to learn to get used to them.

At least, I hope she will.

When I emerge, she is lying on the ground with a pillow and a blanket covering her shivering form. I purse my lips. "You will freeze down there. Get in the bed."

"No. I will be fine down here," she says through chattering teeth.

"Please, get in the bed, Inara,"—I press, stepping toward her—"before you freeze to death. I am not going to force myself upon you," I reassure her. "I would never do that. I'm simply trying to take care of you. I would see you warm this night, my stubborn human wife, instead of frozen on the floor."

"*Stubborn?*" She jerks up to sitting. "Only a few hours ago, I was your *brave* human wife." Crossing her arms over her chest, she gives me an indignant look. "I much prefer *that* term of endearment, my Dark Elf husband."

A smile tugs at my mouth. "I will keep that in mind." I blow out a breath. "Now, please, get in the bed."

Her eyes travel over me again, lingering a moment on my chest and my scars before moving up to the one that mars my face. As soon as she is aware of my noticing this, she quickly lowers her gaze. She picks up her blanket and pillow and places them on the bed.

I sigh inwardly. It seems my scars will be a much bigger issue for her than I originally believed. And right now, I am too exhausted to use any magic to hide them beneath a glamour.

She places a line of pillows in the middle of the bed, and I realize she will probably not sleep well if I share it with her. Even though I vowed to not touch her until she asked, I realize those are just words.

Now, I must show her with my actions that I meant

what I said. I want her trust, more than anything. And I will do whatever it takes to earn it.

I grab a pillow and blanket and arrange them on the floor next to the cot. Relief flits briefly across her features before she reluctantly gestures to the other half of the bed. "You can sleep up here if you wish."

While I would like to rest in the bed, instead of on the cold stone floor, I prefer that she be well rested for our journey tomorrow. "I will sleep here."

I roll onto my side and stare at the blank wall across the way. My thoughts turn again to the Wraiths. As tired as I am, my mind will not rest. Inara is human. She does not possess any magic; I do not understand why they were so interested in her.

I have heard that fated bondmates can sometimes inherit some of their mate's magical abilities. Although we have not yet sealed our bond, I wonder if this has happened with Inara... if she has gained some of my powers. Surely if it had, she would have said something.

Then again, we are still new to one another, and she may not trust me enough to confide this to me.

"Do you have many enemies in your court?" she asks, interrupting my dark thoughts.

I turn back to face her, curious why she would ask this. "A fair amount," I reply honestly. "But I suspect that is true in any royal court. Now that we are mated, I worry that some will seek to use this against me."

"Because I am human?"

"Not that," I reply. "Any who wish to harm me could do so through you. You are my weakness now."

Her eyes flash with anger. "Just because I am human does not mean I am weak."

I run a hand roughly through my short, black hair, frustrated by my inability to stop offending her with my choice of words. First, I called her stubborn, and now I have insulted her by referring to her as a weakness. I have to tell her the truth that I should have offered her from the start. "I do not say this because you are human. I say it because you are my fated one, Inara."

"Fated one?" She frowns. "What are you talking about?"

CHAPTER 17

INARA

I meet Varys's gaze evenly as he explains. "It is called the khio'rinar—the Fated Bond. It is a union of two souls and is sacred among my people: a blessing from the gods. You are my Khio'ri. My fated one."

I inhale sharply. "That word… you said it when you first saw me."

"I recognized what you were to me the moment our eyes first met."

"What does it mean?" I ask. "And why would it make me your weakness?"

"It means that we are bound to each other; my life is now tied to yours."

I blink several times. "Are you saying that… if I die, you do as well?"

"Those who have the Khio'rinar… when one dies, the other usually follows shortly after." He lowers his gaze. "It does not always happen, but it is common enough that anyone wishing to harm me might use you to do it."

"Do all Dark Elves have this connection with their mates?"

His ice-blue eyes snap up to mine, their soft glow illuminating the sharp, yet handsome, contours of his face. "No. And you are the first sanishon—outsider—this has happened with. So, I am uncertain how the Khio'rinar might affect either of us, if the other were to... die." His words settle like a heavy stone deep in my gut. "There are some who would take no issue harming you to find out."

That's why he saved me from the Wraith. Not because he cared, but because he worried that if I died, he might as well.

I'm not sure why this thought bothers me so much, but it does. I know this is a marriage of politics, but I'd hoped it might eventually become more than that, even if he *is* a Dark Elf.

My mother said that my grandmother's people were enemies of my grandfather's kingdom before they wed. Hers was a marriage of politics that turned into so much more. They fell in love after only a handful of days. I always dreamed of finding the same for myself, especially after seeing how miserable my mother was in her marriage to my father.

I doubt Raiden was the first child that Father had with another. If Raiden's mother had not died in childbirth, we might never have even known of his existence. When I grew old enough to understand, I felt so much sadness for my mother and what she had to endure. I hate the idea of sharing children with a man who does not truly love me.

I sigh heavily, weighing my probable unfulfilling future.

At least my new husband has a vested interest in keeping me safe, so I suppose there is that.

"My answer troubles you."

"How do you know?"

He places his hand over his chest. "One of the bond's

manifestations is an empathic connection to one's fated mate." He cocks his head to the side. "Can you not feel it as well?"

I think back on the deep sadness I felt when I looked at the castle. It was stronger than I thought it should be, especially since I have no connection to this place or these people except through a newly formed marriage. My lips part on a breath at my sudden realization. "When we first arrived, I felt this intense ache in my chest. I only remember feeling like that when my parents died," I admit. "But I did not understand why I felt it here."

"Because it was coming from me. This place reminds me of my mother. There is a *trianon*—summer home—in the woods near the castle. She used to take me and my siblings there quite often when we were young. We would explore the ruins here on our walks."

I recognize the pain in his voice that he tries to hide. I forgot until now that he is like me. He has lost both of his parents, too. Even though I hated how my father was unfaithful to my mother, I still loved him, and I know he loved me. There is not a single day that I do not think of them, wishing they were both still here. "You must miss her very much," I offer.

"Yes. I do." His voice is thick with emotion.

Grief is universal. It seems neither of us are strangers to the pain of loss. I wait a moment for him to speak. When he does not, I continue. "We had a summer home, as well. My mother used to go riding with us each day." A wistful smile crosses my face. "There was a lake we would race around to see who was the fastest rider."

"Is that where you learned to ride?"

Swallowing against the lump in my throat, I nod. "Those were some of the happiest days of my childhood.

Before—" My voice catches, and I cannot speak for fear I'll dissolve into tears.

"I am sorry about your parents," he speaks softly. "My soul grieves with yours."

Dark memories flood my mind of the day my mother was killed. Her dying screams still echo in my mind. I dreamed of it before it happened. But I was so young, I did not understand that some of my dreams were visions.

I thought it was a nightmare and ignored it, instead of warning her. It also led to my father's death. My father was so convinced the Fae had something to do with it. So certain he went to war and... never came back. I look at Varys. "Your father... I heard he died fighting the Orcs."

"He did." Sadness reflects behind his eyes. "And my mother followed shortly after."

My mouth drifts open. "The Khio'rinar..."

"Yes." His forehead creases. "Your father went to war against the Fae to avenge your mother's death. He died because of it. Why did he believe they were responsible?"

"The Fae king's brother died during a border skirmish with my father's guards, and the king vowed to seek revenge. When my mother was assassinated, my father believed he'd kept his promise."

"King Obyren died recently," Varys says. "His son is now king."

"I know. I have not met him, but Edmynd has. He claims he is just as bad as the Dark—" I clap my hand over my mouth as my cheeks flare with heat.

"Dark Elves?" Varys asks, arching a teasing brow.

A soft laugh escapes me. "Yes," I admit.

"And yet, he allowed his sister to marry a Dark Elf." Varys smirks.

"True. And not just *any* Dark Elf,"—I tease—"but the Dark Elf King himself."

A smile quirks his lips before his expression sobers. "We Elves have excellent hearing. I overheard your brother vow to get you out of our... arrangement, if you changed your mind." His ice-blue eyes regard me intently. "What made you go through with it—why did you marry me, even knowing your brother would have negotiated a way out for you?"

CHAPTER 18

VARYS

M y eyes lock on to hers as I wait for the answer
I have wanted the most.

"I love my family. More than anything," she begins, her conviction strong. "With the way relations have been with your people... I worried things would escalate into another war, especially with Raiden being your prisoner. I already lost both of my parents, and I don't want to lose anyone else."

Tentatively, she reaches out and rests her hand atop mine. "I know there may never be love between us, Varys, but I hope we can be partners in fostering peace and friendship between our kingdoms."

This is my hope as well.

"I've always wanted to do something important with my life." Her gaze breaks with mine and travels over the room and the damaged ceiling. "What happened here, in this place, must have been devastating. I look at these walls and imagine what this castle must have been before... and the people who used to live here." Her eyes return to mine. "If we can prevent something like this from happening to either of our people... that will be a life worth living, will it not?"

It seems the gods have chosen well for me. Through our connection, I can sense the sincerity of her words.

My mate is very wise.

"I believe it will, my Queen."

We talk a while longer before her eyelids grow heavy in the struggle to stay awake.

"Rest," I tell her. "We leave early in the morning."

I'm surprised once more at how easily she lets down her guard around me, especially after her earlier concerns. My chest swells with pride to know that she trusts me enough to fall asleep so readily in my presence.

She shivers slightly, and I remember what she said about humans dying from pneumonia after exposure to cold rain. I hate that this is the only shelter I can offer her tonight. We could have continued on to the village of Cael-rynd, to a proper inn or even to the trianon, if not for the impending rain.

However, I am not truly certain I could have brought myself to go to the summer home. It is too full of memories. I've not been back since my parents died. Devyn knows this, and I believe it is why he did not suggest it.

Carefully, I place my bedroll over Inara's shivering form, watching in satisfaction when she relaxes into the warmth. I take a moment to study her while she sleeps, allowing my gaze to drift over the delicate features and contours of her face.

Her softly arched brows are relaxed in sleep. Long lashes fan over petal-pink cheeks, covered with a smattering of tiny, pigmented spots. Idly, I wonder if she has these on the rest of her body. My fingers ache with the desire to count each one to see how many there are. Inara is the most beautiful woman I have ever seen.

My people believe perfection is the ultimate form of beauty, but studying my human wife, I do not believe this is true. I am fascinated by her eyes that can either appear brown or green, based upon the lighting, and the tiny spots dotting her skin that do not seem to follow any sort of pattern.

These things would be considered imperfections among my kind. But I find that the sum of these *supposed* imperfections is what makes her stunning to behold.

After speaking with her, it seems we have more in common than I first realized. It is encouraging to know she senses something of the Khio'rinar, even if she does not fully understand it yet.

She is human, and I have heard their love can be fickle. It would be wiser to keep her at a distance, not allow myself to love her. But I realize that, despite my better judgment, I am already beginning to fall.

My brother and sister will probably advise me against it. I'm almost certain my sister, Nyrala, will push me to treat Inara as my grandfather treated his Fae bride. She was his queen in name only, and nothing else. He never made her his *true mate*.

I find the idea of a marriage like his distasteful, and I do not want to take a mistress. He was unwilling to seal their bond and take the Fae princess as his true mate because he feared they could not have children. And even if they could, he worried that our people would not accept a child with Fae blood as their next ruler.

My people will expect me to follow in his steps, because Inara is human. But at the thought, a fierce possessiveness moves through me. Perhaps, it is the bond evoking this feeling within me, but I do not care. I only know that, as I look at my human bride, I would never do that to her.

I wonder if Inara has any feelings for me in return.

Sighing heavily, I realize I'll not get any answers this night. I roll onto my side away from her, and pull up the thin blanket. I train my ears toward her, satisfied when I no longer hear her teeth chattering as she sleeps beneath the bedroll I draped over her. Content that she is no longer cold, I close my eyes and allow myself to fall into a light sleep.

The wind howls outside as lightning arcs across the sky. Rain patters on the floor as the storm rages all around us, pulling me back into full consciousness. I turn back to her, searching for any sign she is cold, but notice nothing.

However, I still worry that, even beneath both bedrolls, she may not be warm enough. Quietly, I remove my own blanket and carefully drape it over her, tucking it around her shoulders.

Her hair spreads out beneath her like a golden halo, framing the dainty structure of her face and gently curved ears, and her lips are open in a small O.

I never expected to be so taken with her. I could blame it on the bond, but that would not be the entire truth. After our conversation this evening, I realize it is much more than that.

And I understand something else with sparkling clarity: The Wolf Shifter is a fool. Prince Lukas did not deserve her. If our positions had been reversed, I would never have let her go.

CHAPTER 19

INARA

*V*arys *stands over me, his eyes obsidian black. Gently, I reach up to cup his cheek, watching as they return to their normal ice-blue coloring. "Khio'ri," he whispers the words with sacred reverence as his gaze pierces mine, deep and intense.*

I trace my thumb across his bottom lip, remembering the taste of his kiss. I twine my arms around his neck as his hands slide to my hips, dragging me close. So close that there is no space between us.

His eyes drop to my lips and he leans in, sealing his mouth over mine in a passionate kiss. My heart pounds wildly as his hands trace over my form. Desire pools deep inside me as he kisses me like a man possessed.

My mind snaps back into awareness as I awaken from my dream. My pulse thunders in my ears, and my entire body is flushed with warmth at the memory of his lips upon my own. It felt so real.

I turn in the bed, taking a deep breath and slowly

exhaling as I try to calm my thudding heart. The soft, orange glow of morning light filters in. I blink several times and jerk up in bed when I remember where I am.

I'm in Ithylian and married to the Dark Elf King.

Peeking over the edge of the bed, I see him lying on the ground with only a pillow. I look back at my coverings, realizing he must have given me his blanket sometime during the night.

I'm surprised at this kind gesture, especially after I rejected him last night. From what I've heard, most men do not respond well when their wives refuse them.

He has proven, yet again, that he respects my feelings. The more I learn of him, it seems the Dark Elf King is not the cold-hearted monster I always heard he was.

It must be early, because I do not hear any movement outside the doors. I need to find more nylweed to keep on hand. And fast. I cannot afford for anyone to discover I have visions; I have to keep it hidden. While we were riding, I observed a few scattered nylweed plants along our path. The long, spindly, purple leaves with pink tips are hard to miss.

Gingerly, I rise from the bed, noting that someone left a fresh change of clothing for both of us on a chair near the door while we slept. I shiver slightly in the cool morning air. My chest constricts as I look at Varys, for I imagine he must have been cold sleeping on the floor. I pull the blanket from the bed and carefully drape it over him.

His short, dark hair is slightly disheveled. Dark lashes stand in stark contrast to his gray-blue skin. My eyes travel over the scar that starts at the top of his right brow and goes down to his cheek. Some might think this mark is ugly, but I find it only adds a lethal edge to his handsome features.

I brush my fingers lightly across my lips as images of

my dream replay in my mind. Looking at his ears, I'm struck with the irrational want to touch their elegant, pointed tips.

"Why are you staring at me?" he murmurs with his eyes still closed, his voice deep and rough from sleep.

I inhale sharply, startled. "I was just looking at your ears." I wince inwardly as my thoughts escape my lips unfiltered.

"My ears?" His eyes snap open and his brow furrows in confusion. "Why?"

"I—"

He sits up, and the blanket falls away from his body. My mouth drifts open. He is still only wearing his pants, leaving his torso completely bare. His broad shoulders and the thick planes of muscle lining his abdomen and chest are on full display.

Clearing my throat, I force myself to look away.

"My scars bother you," he says, and despite his impassive face, there is a hint of sadness behind his eyes.

"Why would you think that?" I ask, completely taken aback by his statement. "You're beautiful. Handsome," I mean, quickly correcting myself. My cheeks burn with embarrassment. "Not that I'm looking at you like that." I avert my eyes as I flap my hand at him. "I just… it's… you…" I gesture excessively. "You're not wearing a shirt and you have all those muscles and…"

His brow crinkles as he tilts his head, and I can't decide if he's confused or angry.

"I'm just—" I break off, mentally trying to salvage some dignity at this point. "Anyway"—I quickly grab the fresh tunic from the chair and hold it out to him—"put this on. It will be much easier to have a conversation if you are fully dressed."

His frown deepens.

"It's only proper that you be fully clothed when we talk," I add. "Even though we're husband and wife now, we still need to maintain appropriate boundaries and—"

"You find me handsome?" He blinks several times. "Despite my scars?"

"Why would your scars bother me?"

He inspects his chest. "Because they mark my skin."

"Well, I assume you got them in some sort of battle, right?"

He gives me a reluctant nod.

"Most warriors have scars. My brothers and their guards are always bragging over who has the biggest ones."

His head jerks back. "Humans are strange," he murmurs, more to himself than to me.

Annoyance at his insult vibrates through me.

CHAPTER 20

VARYS

My scars do not bother her.

I study her intently, searching for any sign of falsehood, but find none. They truly do not disturb her as they would a Dark Elf woman. Moreover, from her obviously flustered appearance and words, it seems she finds me attractive. Hope flutters in my chest. I thought she would have to learn to tolerate my scars, but it seems humans are not like my people. Imperfections are not hideous to them.

When she mentions humans bragging about their scars, I can hardly believe it. It's strange how different our two cultures truly are in this regard.

"*We're* strange? What about Dark Elves?" She gestures to my body. "Am I supposed to find your scars monstrous? And because I do not, I'm wrong somehow?"

I start to speak, but she cuts me off. "Well, I'm sorry I'm not what you expected." Her eyes flash with anger. "If you wanted a Dark Elf wife, you should have picked one instead of me. And I thought Elves had manners... Or is that just the High Elves and you Dark Elves are more akin to Orcs?"

Instantly insulted, I draw myself up and raise my chin. "I assure you we are *nothing* like Orcs."

"Well, you *certainly* fooled me," she snaps.

I narrow my eyes. "Have you ever *seen* an Orc up close before?"

"No." She sniffs. "Of course not."

"Pray that you never do," I reply darkly.

She huffs out a frustrated breath and rolls her eyes.

Inwardly, I curse myself. I always seem to say the wrong thing, offending her when I do not mean to. I'm about to say something else, but Devyn enters. His eyes lock onto my bare chest and the scars that cross my ruined flesh before his gaze snaps to mine, full of pity. "My King, we should be ready to leave in less than an hour."

"Good." I turn to Inara. "Are you ready?"

"Of course I am." She tips up her chin to stare down at me imperiously. "I may not be a Dark Elf, but I assure you, I am not some pampered princess who takes hours to ready herself for the day. I am much more practical than that."

She crosses her arms over her chest and stands ramrod straight.

Clenching my jaw, I mentally chastise myself. It is obvious I have deeply insulted her yet again.

My shoulders sag forward in defeat, and I regard her for a moment, wondering how best to explain myself without offending her further. "When I said that your people were strange," I begin, grasping for the right words, "I was simply... surprised that my scars did not... disgust you."

"Is that how a Dark Elf woman would react to them?"

"Yes."

"Well, fortunately for you, I'm not a Dark Elf, and I find all of this,"—she gestures up and down my body —"attractive."

She claps a hand over her mouth and her face is bright red, as if shocked that she said this aloud.

A smile quirks my lips.

"Is that a smile?" She cocks her head to the side. "Because sometimes, I cannot tell."

"Yes, it is."

She flashes a lovely grin in return. "Good." Her expression sobers. "How did you get your scars?"

I close my eyes as the dismal memories return. "Prince Aegryn of Kolstrad gave them to me. He captured me and tortured me with weapons of iron."

She brings her hand to her mouth. "That's awful. I'm so sorry." She curls her hands into fists at her side. "I knew he was a bad person."

"What happened?"

"He wanted to marry me, but I just... I knew there was something about him I did not like, but I was not sure what it was." She pauses. "I trusted my gut and thank goodness Lukas proposed first or I'm almost certain he would have declared war on Florin, once I rejected him, over his wounded pride."

"He probably would have," I agree.

As much as I dislike the idea of her with Lukas, I would have hated the idea of her having been betrothed to Aegryn even more.

"He is a power-hungry worm." She forces her words through a clenched jaw. "I believe he would even align himself with the Orcs if it meant he could gain more power and wealth."

"I wholeheartedly agree."

Squeezing my eyes shut, I force the painful memories of my torture from my thoughts. After a moment I clear my throat. "I must ready Rhygar for our journey."

"Can I help?" she asks.

"You wish to?"

"I love to ride. Horses, that is," she corrects. "But I assume from all the dire wolves I see here, you probably don't have them. You just have the wolves, am I right?"

"Yes. I do not think horses would last long in the stables with the dire wolves."

Her mouth drops open, but she quickly snaps it shut. "Well, I'd like to learn how to properly saddle a dire wolf and whatever there is to learn about riding one."

This is good. Yesterday, she seemed afraid of Rhygar, but today she faces and embraces her fear. "All right. I'll wait outside the door for you to dress."

The smile she gives me is brighter than the very sun itself, and for the first time in a long time, my spirits lift.

CHAPTER 21

INARA

I change into one of the few dresses Grayce packed for me. I choose the one that is blue because it reminds me of Varys. It has a row of buttons down either side, so I undo several to make it easier to ride today, and slip on a pair of leggings to hide my bare legs. But try as I might, I cannot reach to fasten the buttons down the back of my dress.

As I gaze at the lovely fabric, my thoughts turn to Varys's ice-blue eyes. He is handsome, my Dark Elf husband, but I wonder what he thinks of me. Surely, I am far different from a Dark Elf woman. I've heard they are fierce warriors, not to mention ethereally beautiful in a way humans can never hope to be.

I glance down at my body. I'm quite certain I am not who or what Varys thought he would marry someday, but then again, neither is he the one I imagined when I'd daydream about my future husband.

It is strange that I rode out from home in disguise,

hoping to help free my brother, unaware I'd end up not only negotiating his release, but marrying our enemy as well.

I open the door and find Varys waiting on the other side. My face heats as I force the words past my lips. "Can you please help me with my dress?"

He blinks several times and then steps back inside the room.

I turn my back to him, and he wraps his hand around my hair. He gently pulls it over my shoulder to keep it out of the way before he starts on the line of buttons.

Varys begins with the one at the small of my back. His fingers brush my bare skin and I inhale sharply. The mere touch sparks something deep within as the memories of our passion-filled kiss on our wedding night flood my thoughts.

As he continues up my back, the soft peaks of my breasts begin to harden against the fabric. And when he pulls back on the bodice of my dress, I bite back a low moan as the silken material caresses my already sensitive skin.

He leans in as he reaches the space between my shoulders. His masculine scent seems to grow stronger, surrounding me with a heady mix. His breath is warm across the back of my neck, raising goosebumps along my sensitive flesh.

When he finishes, he gently sweeps my hair over my shoulder, running his fingers through the long strands before pulling away.

I turn to face him, and find his pupils blown wide and swirling with black. The pointed tips of his canines peek out from beneath his upper lip.

My heart hammers as I stand before him. My tongue

instinctively darts out to trace over my lips as I drop my gaze to his mouth.

He clenches his jaw and takes a small step back, lowering his eyes and ending the moment between us all too soon.

Varys extends his arm out to me, and I take it. Despite his clothing, I can feel the lean muscle of his arm beneath my hand. He moves with a grace that belies his larger form as we make our way outside.

The early morning air is crisp and refreshing. A light fog blankets the ground, swirling mist around our ankles and feet. A chill breeze winds through the gardens and I wrap my arms around my torso.

Varys removes his cloak and carefully places it over my shoulders. He raises his eyebrows. "Is that better?"

I give him a faint smile, my heart melting at the extra care he takes to ensure I am warm. "Yes."

While Varys goes to speak to his men, I stroll through the unkempt garden. Despite its overgrown state, I cannot believe how lovely this is in the daylight. It was beautiful last night, but this morning I can appreciate all the things I missed in the dark.

I walk over to one of the long, hanging vines that has delicate red blooms along its length. When I trace my fingers over a bud, a crackle of energy flows from my fingertips into the plant. Jerking my hand back, I stare at my palm in shock.

I inhale sharply as all the buds unfurl and open into vibrant, crimson blooms. Glancing around to see if anyone noticed, I do not find anyone nearby, thank the gods. I've never had this happen before, and I do not understand why it is happening now.

Perhaps it is an effect of this realm. Or perhaps my

curse has gotten worse and now, instead of just visions, I have magic as well.

My mother always worried this could happen. She claimed some of our ancestors had powerful magic instead of visions, and she feared my sister and I would manifest it.

A sudden feeling of dread cuts through me, terrified I'll be discovered. I saw a woman burned at the stake for witchcraft when I was younger. We were traveling through a neighboring kingdom and my father covered my eyes, but I could still hear her screaming.

My hands shake with the memory of that trauma. It's been far too long since I took my nylweed to suppress my visions. High Mage Ylari says it can also hide magic.

Quickly, I remove the vial from the hidden pocket of my dress and take a few sips of my nylweed potion, rationing it until I can replenish it later. I hate taking the nylweed; it always makes me tired, but it cannot be helped. Until I am sure I can trust my new husband, I must make certain my abilities remain undetected.

I stride back to Varys, trying to still the trembling of my limbs and the rapid beating of my heart.

His head snaps to me as I approach. "What is wrong?"

Anxiety fills me as I wonder if he can sense my secret through our bond. "Nothing," I lie, doing my best to give him a convincing smile. "I was just… thinking of the Wraiths. That is all."

CHAPTER 22

VARYS

A sudden awareness ripples through me and panic stabs at my chest. It takes me a moment to realize it is not coming from me. It is from Inara. *Something is wrong.*

Her cheeks are slightly paler than their usual rosy hue. In response to further query she denies any problems, but through the khio'rinar, I can sense she hides something. I just do not know what.

I glance at my men. Each of them readies their dire wolves for travel with no sign of alarm. Her pale coloring causes me to worry she may be sick now because of the cold last night. "Do you feel ill?"

"No. Really, I am fine."

Through the bond, I can sense her fears dissipating. She is hiding something from me, but I will not push her to discover what it is. We may be wed, but we are still relative strangers. It is only natural that she does not trust me completely. Not yet, anyway.

I must earn her trust. To do that, I will not confront her to ask what she hides now. Whatever it is, I can wait until she feels comfortable enough to tell me.

"Are you ready to leave?"

She nods and walks past me to Rhygar. Resting a hand on his shoulder, she gently strokes his long black and gray fur as he turns to observe her. "Good morning, Rhygar," she murmurs. "Did you sleep well?"

His yellow eyes shift to me, and I walk up beside them, resting a hand on his fur next to hers. "Would you like to know his answer? If he agrees, I can link you to him, so you can communicate with him as I do."

She frowns. "How?"

I extend my hand, and she cautiously takes it. Entwining our fingers, I place my free hand on Rhygar's jaw as I reach to him through the mind link. *"She is my mate. Will you allow me to connect her to you?"*

What I ask is no small thing. Dire wolves are bound only to the rider they choose. It is rare for them to allow themselves to be linked to another. His sharp eyes meet mine and he dips his muzzle subtly.

Rhygar's mind reaches across the connection. Images of him running through the forest flash in my mind, and I know Inara also sees them when a beaming smile lights her face. "That's incredible," she murmurs. "Is that how you communicate with each other? Through images?"

"Yes."

An image of Rhygar's mate flashes through his mind and he looks at Inara.

"Who is that?"

"His mate," I tell her. "It is his way of saying he understands our relationship."

A rosy blush spreads across her cheeks, accentuating the spots across the bridge of her nose. "Oh."

"I believe he likes you."

She smiles radiantly when she looks at Rhygar. "Thank you. I like you, too."

He straightens, puffing out his chest and tipping his muzzle up with pride as the connection gives him a sense of her words and their meaning.

She laughs. "You are a magnificently, beautiful dire wolf."

He tips his chin up even higher.

"Enough of your preening, Rhygar," I gently chastise as I try, but fail, to suppress a laugh. "We must go."

She rests a hand on his cheek. "I would offer you an apple, but I somehow do not think you would appreciate that."

"Here." I pull a dried strip of meat from the saddle and hand it to her. "Give him this."

I watch as she places it on her palm, careful to hold her fingers and thumb back as she offers it to him, ensuring her delicate fingers are nowhere near his sharp teeth when he takes the meat from her hand.

Gently, he nuzzles her, and she turns to me. "Can I have another for him?"

I offer her another piece, and he takes it eagerly, then nuzzles her even more. A low rumble sounds deep in his chest as she buries her hands in his thick, soft fur to pet him.

My lips quirk up, and I arch a brow. "I believe you are his favorite person now."

She smiles. "Good."

I'd thought it would take him longer to accept her, since she is human, but it appears I am pleasantly wrong.

I offer her the saddle and show her how to adjust the straps for his comfort.

Once fitted, she climbs up in the saddle and I settle

behind her. She relaxes easily back against me, compared to the stiffness of her posture from the day before.

I observe the practical buttons down either side of this new dress she wears. When I was helping her with the buttons along her back, I could not help but notice how lovely this shade of blue is on her. "A good choice," I murmur.

"What is?" She leans back, tipping her head up to me, and she is so lovely I forget momentarily how to speak.

"Your dress," I finally manage.

"I thought it would make riding easier and save you having to shred another one of my perfectly good dresses."

I open my mouth to apologize, but stop when I notice her smirk.

She is teasing me.

She leans back against me, her head resting on my collarbone, and I inhale deeply of her delicate scent, drawing it into my lungs.

All Dark Elves have either black or white hair, but when Inara's catches the light, it appears like spun gold. I lean in, about to nuzzle the top of her head, but stop myself, thinking better of it. I do not know if she would welcome this sort of intimate contact yet.

She is beginning to trust me. I only hope that we can continue to build upon this.

As we wind through the forest, I am eager to return home but also dreading it, in the same measure. My family has no idea I've wed a human. It will be a shock to them, even more so when they learn she is the sister of our former enemy.

My thoughts turn to Melina—my childhood friend and personal guard. She hates humans more than most Dark Elves because they killed her mother. She will not be thrilled to know I am bound to Inara.

Her father—Lord Dralyn—feels the same about humans. I've always been able to rely upon his support on the Council. Now, I am uncertain I will still be able to count on it.

CHAPTER 23

INARA

As the nylweed takes effect, it becomes difficult to stay awake. I blink several times, struggling to keep my eyes open before giving up and resting back against Varys. Maybe it's this bond he says we have between us, but I'm not afraid of him like I was when we first met.

Part of me thinks I should just tell him about my visions and what happened in the courtyard. But then, dark memories bubble up and the fear grips me again. Even though I want to trust Varys, I cannot simply erase my concerns overnight. I have to be sure before I tell him. After all, it's not just my secret that I keep... it is my sister's as well.

"We will reach the village of Caelrynd soon," he whispers. "We will stop for a bit to rest."

"How much farther to the capital after that?"

"Cyridil is less than a half-day's ride."

"All right." I nod. "It will be good to stretch my legs."

When we reach the outskirts of the village, I straighten in the saddle, craning my neck to get a better look as we approach.

We continue along the road, the thick forest giving way to rolling hills and fields.

Farmland stretches out as far as the eye can see with a small village at the heart, directly in our path. A river runs straight through the center. The sparkling blue water cascades down several small rock waterfalls as it travels through the city.

Several buildings and houses made of white stone with black and silver rooftops line the streets. As we move down the main thoroughfare, I notice the cobbled stones seem very well kept. There is not even a hint of trash along the walkways. The people are all elegantly dressed in fine tunics and dresses, telling me they are not lacking in basic necessities.

Several villagers pass, stopping and openly gawking when they see me, their glowing eyes full of a strange mixture of disbelief and fascination. Only a few stare at me with unmistakable hatred in their expressions, but it is still concerning. A small twinge of panic ripples through my body, but I push it down and refuse to show any fear.

A large fountain graces the center of the town square. It cascades and overflows down three levels before pooling at the base and traveling on to rejoin the river. The statues at the top are the same as the ones we saw at the castle: the first Dark Elf king and his queen.

A woman with long, flowing, silver-white hair and dressed in green robes approaches us.

Varys dismounts first, then helps me down. I accept his aid without question, not wanting to risk my dress catching on the saddle again and falling.

He extends his arm to me, and I loop mine through his

as we walk toward the woman. She bows low. "My King," she says solemnly.

"Leilana, this is my bride." He gestures to me. "Inara, this is Leilana—the town's leader."

Her glowing, green eyes widen slightly in shock.

"This is Princess Inara of Florin, and my Khio'ri. Our marriage has secured a treaty of peace between our kingdoms."

"This is indeed good news." She bows again. "Will you visit the temple for your blessing?"

He turns to me with a questioning look. I love that he checks with me first, instead of assuming. I'm not sure what this blessing entails, but it sounds important, so I'm willing to find out. "Yes."

On one side of the town square is a gorgeous building made of dark wood. Intricately carved patterns line the structural columns and doorway, all of them various images of nature and Elves. When we step inside, I note the prominent placement of a statue of the Goddess of the Harvest at the altar. This is the Dark Elf equivalent of the temple we were married in.

"The Goddess of the Harvest," I murmur as we approach the carving.

"And of Life and Fertility," someone says off to the side.

I turn to find a Dark Elf woman dressed in flowing silver robes with long, silver-white hair braided down her back. Her sharp, glowing, lavender eyes study me with a piercing gaze. It is as if she can see straight through me into my very soul.

"My King," she says warmly. "It has been far too long since you have visited us."

"Forgive me," Varys says. "It is difficult to get away from the capital." He gestures to me. "This is—"

"Your Khio'ri," she whispers in solemn reverence. She bows low before us both.

I dart a glance at Varys, wondering how she knows this when we've only just met, but I say nothing. Perhaps this priestess is a seer. If she is, then there is hope the Dark Elves will not view my visions as a curse.

"My name is Priestess Syrila. I have known Varys since he was a boy." She gives him a warm smile. "I have prayed many times for him to find someone. I am glad you are here."

"Thank you," I murmur.

"Come," she says, "we will ask the gods for their blessing."

We follow her to an area behind the altar with a small reflective pool in the floor. She takes a wooden bowl and dips it into the water, and I am fascinated as it begins to glow with a lovely blue color.

A scraping sound along the stone floor draws my attention toward the entrance. Several of the villagers have followed us, gathering inside the temple. Thanks to Varys's guards and Devyn, they all stand a respectable distance away as they observe us.

It seems we'll have an audience as we receive our blessing.

I turn my attention back toward Priestess Syrila, feeling extremely self-conscious as the only human in the temple.

At least when we were married, Varys had his men. Here, I am alone.

She hands the bowl first to Varys. He turns to me, and she instructs me to place my hands under it, as well. We hold it between us while she recites a blessing in hushed and lilting tones. She dips her first three fingers into the water, then touches my forehead, tracing a symbol before doing the same to Varys.

When she finishes her blessing, the Elven symbol on Varys glimmers a soft blue, and in his eyes, I notice the reflection as mine does the same. Long tendrils of worry begin to unfurl inside me as warmth spreads throughout my body. I inhale sharply as the heat expands deep within.

"I am here," Varys's voice whispers in my mind. *"You are safe,"* he says, having sensed my concern.

His ice-blue gaze holds mine, and my confusion grows. "I can hear you in my mind," I whisper aloud.

"The prophecy," someone says in the crowd.

"Sanishon," another speaks softly.

"The sanishon of the Khio'rinar," another voice murmurs. "It is the prophecy."

The priestess raises her hands. Her sharp gaze meets mine and she turns to Varys, a hint of a smile playing on her lips before she turns to address the crowd.

"Let us all bear witness this day," her voice rings out with solemn clarity. "The gods have blessed this bonding between Inara, the sanishon princess of Florin, and King Varys of Ithylian."

The entire crowd bows low before us, and I turn to Varys. His expression is hard as he looks at Syrila, but I do not understand why.

She tips her chin up and looks down at him haughtily as she follows us through the crowd.

Varys leads me through the throng of people as they whisper words of blessing.

A woman touches my arm, her eyes brimming with tears. "Sanishon," she whispers.

Devyn's face is a mask of concern, and Varys appears worried, as well, as we make our way outside and back to Rhygar.

As soon as we are away from the temple, he turns to

Priestess Syrila. "Why did you do this?" he practically hisses, and I'm surprised by his anger.

"What's wrong?" I ask.

Syrila gives Varys a disapproving look. "You have not told her of the prophecy."

"It is superstition," Varys replies darkly. "Nothing more."

The priestess arches a brow. "You forget how long I've known you. I can see it in your eyes. You suspected before you came here, did you not?"

Instead of answering, he clenches his jaw. "And *you* forget there are many who would do anything to keep this prophecy from coming to pass."

She narrows her eyes. "Only those who seek to control the darkness are the ones that you must fear. In the prophecy, the sanishons are the catalyst that leads to their end."

"Do you know what the darkness in the prophecy is? Or who seeks to control it?" he asks heatedly. "If you know something, tell me, Syrila. Stop speaking in riddles."

"I do not speak in riddles, my King. I only speak the truth as I understand it from the Tomes."

"What are you talking about?" I whisper urgently. "Tell me. Now."

His eyes meet mine, anger brimming behind them, but I know it is not directed at me. "Not here."

He loops his arm around my waist and hoists me up with him into the saddle as if I weigh nothing. Each of his guards stares as if seeing me through fresh eyes before they mount up.

I don't understand what just happened, but it has put my new husband on edge. A knot of worry twists deep in my gut as we ride through the village. Varys sets a brisk pace, as if he cannot wait to leave this place far behind us.

With his arm around my waist, I can feel the tense set of his body against mine, but I do not dare ask anything until we are well outside of the city walls.

Once we are beyond the outer gates and almost to the thick forest beyond it, I twist back to him. Despite his impassive expression, it is easy to read the worry in his eyes. "What did all of that mean?" I whisper. "Please, tell me what happened back there."

Without speaking, he raises his arm in a bid for his men to stop.

Everyone halts and Devyn rides up beside us. "Tell the men to rest here," Varys commands. "I will speak with my mate, alone."

Devyn nods, then rushes back to relay the order.

Varys dismounts and then reaches for me, helping me down. He offers me his hand. "Come," he says. "There is much I must tell you."

His expression is full of concern. Whatever this is, it has him on edge, and it cannot be good. Drawing in a deep breath, I steel myself for the worst.

CHAPTER 24

VARYS

I guide us into the forest and away from the men. What I have to say is for Inara's ears alone. Through our bond, I can sense the anxiety building inside her. She is afraid, and I wish more than anything I could take away her worry, but I know now I cannot.

When we are far enough away, I stop and turn to face her.

"I heard you in my mind, Varys. I-I don't understand. Why were the people reacting that way?"

"Our scholars have studied the Ancient Tomes of the Lythyrian for many generations."

"What are they?"

"The Lythyrians were an ancient race of seers, long before Elves and men even existed," I begin, gathering myself for all I must tell her. "They passed from this world many ages ago, but they left behind much of their knowledge in a series of tomes discovered in the ancient ruins of their kingdom."

"I do not understand." She bites her lip. "What does this have to do with us?"

"There is a prophecy of the Great Uniters. They are outsiders—sanishon—that will unite the various races and bring an end to those who wish to control the darkness."

"That's why the Priestess made it a point to refer to me as the sanishon princess of Florin, isn't it? She was marking me as an outsider, because of this prophecy."

"Yes," I reply solemnly. "And while many will embrace this, there are others who will not. They will see it as a threat to their power. Many of them hate humans. I already knew they would be averse to the idea of me taking you as my mate, but if the people believe you are the sanishon spoken of in the ancient prophecies, it could make you an even bigger target."

Worry constricts my chest, and I realize it is not only my own.

"There is risk and danger in any political marriage," Inara says, taking my hand in hers. "There will always be those in support and others in opposition. Even among two human kingdoms, a treaty with a former enemy can be difficult to navigate. I'm sure a marriage to Lukas would have had its challenges as well."

Sharp jealousy stabs through me at the reminder that she was betrothed to the Wolf Shifter before me. A low growl rumbles deep in my chest.

"Fortunately for you, I grew up around politics," she says, pulling me back from my dark thoughts. "And what I do not know of this place, you can teach me, Varys. We will navigate these dangers together."

I blink several times, caught off guard by the poise with which she received the prophecy.

How is it my human bride always seems to surprise me?

I admire her strength. She is a stranger to my kingdom

and my people, yet… she hides the worry I sense through our bond so completely I would never know of it, were it not for this connection. "We will," I agree. A hint of a smile tugs at my lips as my admiration for her grows even more.

"About this prophecy—what do you believe?"

I consider my answer carefully before replying. "I am uncertain. Those with the fated bond can sense each other's emotions and heal one another, through shared life force, as I healed you after the Wraith attack. Another part of the prophecy is the ability for us to hear each other's words in our minds. There is more to it, but I admit that I am not well-versed. I have always considered it a myth.

"You are human. No Dark Elf has ever taken a human as their mate before. And all of this could simply be how the Khio'rinar has manifested because of our differences."

"What is the darkness she spoke of? Do you have any idea what it might be?"

"I do not know." I run a hand through my hair. "The prophecy speaks of a darkness being unleashed upon the land, controlled by those who would use it to assert their power and conquer the seven realms."

"What about your grandfather's Fae wife? Did they have the Khio'rinar? I mean… your people have an alliance with the Fae because of their marriage. How do you know *she* was not the Great Uniter from the prophecy?"

"They did not have the fated bond between them, so it could not have been her."

"You said they didn't have children," she says. "But they were married. So how—"

"He sired children with his mistress."

"Oh." She releases my hand and lowers her gaze. "I did not know Dark Elves took mistresses. I thought it was only done among humans."

My thoughts turn to her brother, Raiden. He is the

product of her father's affair with another. Apparently, it was a great scandal in their kingdom when her father took him to raise.

"Fae and Elves cannot have children together," I tell her. "My grandfather… he took a mistress because he needed an heir to secure his kingdom. His Fae wife gave him her blessing to take a Dark Elf woman—my grandmother—as his *true mate*, because of this."

"I suppose it was born of necessity then." She smooths her hands down her dress and tips up her chin. Through the bond, I can sense something akin to sadness and disappointment, but I do not understand why. Before I can ask, she changes the subject. "Do you think we'll make it to the capital—to Cyridil—before sunset?"

"If we leave now, yes."

"Then, let us go." She flashes a smile, but it does not touch her eyes. "I must admit, I'm curious to see my new home."

I extend my arm and this time, she is slow to take it. Reluctant almost. "Are you all right?"

She nods firmly. "I suppose I'm just nervous and… still trying to figure out my place here."

I can sense that it is more than just this, but I cannot tell what.

"I will help you, Inara," I offer, wanting to reassure her.

She opens her mouth to respond, but Devyn interrupts. "My King. We should leave, else we will not reach the mountain before dark."

Inara walks beside me as we make our way back to the group. I understand Devyn's concern. We have a treacherous path ahead, one I'd prefer to navigate in the daylight instead of darkness.

~

As we continue our journey, my mate is quiet for most of the trip. I know she is uneasy, but when I ask, she simply brushes off my concern, attempting to hide it from me.

She must not realize how well I can read her. Which makes me believe she either cannot read me or that it is so faint, she is unable to detect my emotions through the bond.

I have heard the Khio'rinar strengthens after the first mating, but I do not mention this to her. She has offered me her friendship. Despite vowing her love, I understand there are many forms of this emotion, and I am unsure which type she promised the day of our human wedding.

She is attracted to me. I could sense it even this morning when I helped her to dress. It took everything within me to maintain control when all I wanted was to pull her into my arms and crush my lips to hers.

Even now, as she leans back against me, desire pulses through my veins. Her delicate scent fills my nostrils and I long to brush my lips over her petal-soft skin and rain kisses along the elegant column of her neck.

But she does not wish to act upon our mutual attraction yet, and she might never wish to.

However, I feel protective of her, and fiercely possessive at the mere mention of Lukas—her former betrothed. She must have loved him. After all, they were engaged, and she'd known him since they were children. Yet, if she *did* love him, I can sense no heartbreak through the bond.

My thoughts return to the sudden spike of panic I sensed from Inara in the gardens of the ruined castle. She was hiding something then. If Inara can conceal such an intense emotion as heartache from me, I wonder what else she may be hiding and why.

CHAPTER 25

INARA

Riding toward Cyridil, I am both anxious and wary. If Ithylian is anything like Florin, word travels fast, and I wonder about my reception. The thought of living inside a mountain gives me pause, but I suppose I will get used to it. It will be strange to live in such a dark place when I've always loved the sun.

Varys's story about his grandfather's mistress replays in my mind. If Dark Elves and Fae cannot have children together, it's possible humans and Dark Elves cannot either. If not, I wonder how soon Varys will take a mistress to start a family.

And I wonder when he will cast me aside entirely. That is not the sort of life I ever envisioned for myself: to be a forgotten queen in a lonely tower somewhere. I cannot imagine a fate worse than that.

While I understand his culture is different from mine, I cannot stop thinking of my mother and how hurt she was by my father's affair. Edmynd told me he remembered a time when our parents were deeply in love. By the time Grayce and I came along, their relationship had transformed into something more akin to a partnership—a tense friendship, of sorts. It was easy to see Father still loved her dearly, but Mother's love was reserved... cold, almost. I never knew why until Grayce explained it one day, along with how Raiden came to be.

Straightening my shoulders, I push down my depressing thoughts.

If my mother could survive such a marriage, so can I.

Besides, Varys and I are only friends at this point. Nothing has happened between us that we cannot take back.

Even as I think this, disappointment washes over me. It's only been a few days, but I was already imagining a future with my new husband. Varys is intelligent, kind, and undeniably attractive. The way he always takes such extra care with me... I am already halfway to losing my heart.

I suppose it's best I temper my expectations now.

When we reach a clearing, my stomach drops as I realize we are on the edge of a cliff. I have always had a problem with heights. A steep, rugged valley spreads out before us and Varys points in the distance.

"Cyridil is in those mountains."

I've heard stories of the capital city of Ithylian, but I do not know anyone who has actually visited. The mountain is much larger than I imagined it would be. The obsidian stone is a stark contrast to the dense forest and vegetation that covers it.

I think of Varys's ancestors and their decision to remain in this stronghold to ensure the safety of their people after their devastating losses in the last Great War. There is a harsh beauty to this landscape that speaks of strength and resilience. Different from anything I've ever seen, it perfectly captures the essence of the Dark Elves.

They are survivors who chose to build a new way of life so far removed from all they had known. And they did this so that future generations would not have to endure the same terror and sadness as the ones who came before.

"We should reach they city by midday," Varys adds, pulling me back from my thoughts.

We begin the long trek down the mountain. Inhaling and exhaling deeply, I attempt to calm my racing heart as we wind down a narrow path.

Small rocks crunch beneath Rhygar's paws, skittering off the trail and clacking together as they fall over the side, tumbling to the ground far below. When we round a sharp corner, I grip his fur tightly, squeezing my eyes shut so I don't look down and panic even more.

Varys's strong arm circles my waist, holding me securely against him. He leans forward and his breath is warm in my ear. "I will not let you fall, Inara. My vow."

Unable to speak, I only manage a nod.

CHAPTER 26

VARYS

My nostrils flare as the acrid scent of Inara's fear fills the air. I glance down at the white-knuckled grip she has on Rhygar's fur, and it rouses my protective instincts. I lock my arm firmly around her waist and lean forward to reassure her.

"I suppose you take this route often," she says shakily.

"Yes. It is the fastest route to the capital."

"I wouldn't have minded the longer way, you know." She huffs out a nervous laugh. "Maybe next time be a good husband and ask your wife what she thinks first, all right?"

I stiffen, realizing that she is right. I did not even consider this particular trail might scare her.

"I'm just teasing you, Varys." Her eyes are squeezed shut again. "Sometimes, when I get nervous, I talk. Or… so I've been told. It calms me a bit."

Before I can reply, she continues. "My parents tried to break me of this when I was younger, you know."

"Why would they do that?"

"They worried my future husband would not want a chatterbox for a wife."

If she did not speak, I would not know what she is thinking beyond the fear that pulses through our bond. I am glad she talks freely to me. "You need not remain quiet around me."

"That's good to hear." A faint grin touches her mouth. "I was worried my talking annoyed you."

"Why would you think this?"

"You're not very expressive, for one," she says. "For another, I have not known you long enough to understand all the slight expressions you *do* make. Not yet, anyway." She pauses. "I suppose we have time to work on all that, however."

"Indeed."

"See?" She laughs nervously again. "Like that. I cannot tell if—"

"I am not annoyed," I quickly reassure her. "Just upset at myself for causing you so much distress with this route."

"Well, now you know for next time," she teases. "So... any other mixed marriages like ours in Cyridil?" she asks, changing the subject.

"No. We are the first since the time of my grandfather."

"So, I'll be the only person in the entire city who is not a Dark Elf?"

"No. The only one in the entire kingdom."

"Even better," she says, with a hint of apprehensive sarcasm in her tone.

"You need not worry," I assure her. "You are my Khio'ri. The bond is sacred among my kind. Most of my people will respect you for it, even though you are different."

As we approach the entrance to the mountain and the

city, a rider comes out to greet us. A smile quirks my lips as soon as I recognize Melina. She is one of our best guards. I should have known she would see us coming from far away.

CHAPTER 27

INARA

As we approach the base of the mountain, a rider gallops toward us, skidding to a halt only a few steps away. The dire wolf's green eyes lock onto mine, ears flattening against its massive head and baring its fangs in a feral snarl.

Rhygar answers with one of his own, and I smile at the realization he is defending me to one of his kin.

The rider removes her helmet, revealing a long, dark braid. Her features are exquisite, right down to her pointed ears. I heard Elvish women were beautiful, but this is the first time I've seen one up close, and the rumors do not do them justice.

She is absolutely stunning. Her skin is a shade lighter than Varys's and her glowing, golden eyes scrutinize me contemptuously.

"You brought back a prisoner? You should have just killed her. Humans are more trouble than they are worth, you know."

My jaw drops and I lean back into Varys at the venomous look in her eyes.

"She is not my prisoner." Varys growls. "She is my Khio'ri."

The gray-blue color of her cheeks pales. "A human?" She shakes her head in disbelief. "That cannot be."

"It is truth," Varys states firmly.

Her eyes snap to his, pain and sadness reflecting in them.

"Inara, this is Melina. Melina, Queen Inara."

With a tightened jaw, she dips her chin in acknowledgement even as she gives him an undeniably wounded look.

She turns to me, disgust breaking through on her features, and offers me a reluctant bow. "My Queen."

Dressed in the same green armor as the rest of his men, I recognize she is one of his guards, but I wonder if she may also be his lover. There is a longing in her expression that suggests their relationship is more than just guard and king.

Irrational jealousy stabs at my chest, but I force it back down. I have no reason to feel this way. It's not as if I'm in love with my new husband. Our marriage is based solely on politics, not emotions. Some part of me hoped, however, that he would be faithful, unlike my father. But, perhaps, Dark Elves are not immune to the same vices as human men.

"Your brother will be glad you have returned so soon," she says. "We heard rumors from Caelrynd, but were not sure of their veracity."

By rumors, I assume she means the ones regarding our marriage, even the prophecy Syrila and her followers believe.

"Take me to my brother," Varys says. "We have much to discuss."

She bows, and we follow her toward the base of the mountain. Two large, stone doors bar the entrance. They are so well concealed I would have difficulty finding them if I were alone. I suppose that is their purpose. This was the stronghold of the Dark Elves in times of war before they moved here permanently after the Great War that destroyed the former capital of Elysarin.

Varys raises his hand when we reach the doors. A swirling glow of magic travels out from his palm and pushes them open. They slide back with a heavy groan and a grating of rock upon gravel. Beyond them, a large tunnel awaits. Although dimmer than outside, I'm surprised by how light it is in here. Thousands of glowing gemstones embedded in the walls provide enough illumination that I can see clearly in this vast corridor.

I heave a deep sigh of relief. I feared spending the rest of my life in darkness, completely lost in cramped tunnels and buried deep in the mountain so far from light I might go mad. At least I can see where we are going. Still, I wonder how often I'll get to see any natural light. I'm not sure how much I'll relish the idea of living underground.

As we continue, the tunnel narrows a bit, but not much. Even though we're inside a mountain, this path is more like a road lined with a variety of glowing vegetation. Luminescent green moss and blue and green mushrooms the size of trees grow wild throughout the space, along with several plants studded with vibrant, glowing, white flowers that resemble enormous roses.

It's more beautiful than I ever would have expected.

The tunnel opens into a massive cavern with buildings carved into the dark granite, creating a city. Rows of houses and buildings line cobbled stone streets. Soft light filters onto the walkways from the various shops and houses, but it's the castle in the distance, towering over this astonishing city, that draws my attention.

Taller than any other structure, it overlooks everything. Carved into the sheer cliff wall, the obsidian stone castle is impressive and intimidating. With several formidable towers and built-out terraces, it appears to have been constructed more for defense than aesthetics.

A waterfall drops from the rock face above, straight into a large overhang at the top of the palace. It cascades into a series of waterfalls down the front of the structure before flowing into a pool at the base and feeding into a river winding through the city below.

Dark Elves walk back and forth as we make our way toward it, some traveling on dire wolves and others on foot. I'm glad when I see most of the women wear tunic dresses with pants and boots, a much more preferable fashion than the long dresses normally found in Florin. It was the same in Caelrynd as well.

All the Elves move aside, bowing low to their king as we pass, eyes locked on to me, with expressions ranging from curiosity to outright hatred and disgust.

Varys's arm tightens slightly around my waist, as if trying to shield me from the weight of their stares. His breath warms my ear as he whispers. "Many of them have never seen a human up close, and even more have lost someone they love in battle against your people."

I notice a woman with a small child, staring at me with anger flashing in her eyes. "I think I recognize the ones who hate humans," I murmur. "They do not appear pleased to see us together."

"They will once they know what you are."

"And what exactly is that?"

"A symbol of hope," he replies solemnly. "Regardless of

whether the prophecy is true, our marriage has been blessed with the Khio'rinar, and it has created a peace between our two kingdoms that would have been hard won otherwise."

The confidence in his voice is reassuring, but I cannot still my anxiety. So many of these people look as if they'd rather murder me than ever accept me as their queen.

When we reach the castle gates, I'm surprised they're open. Only one guard on each side stands at the entrance. It seems Varys and his family trust their people. I would think this a good thing, if not for the many hateful stares I received as we passed through the city.

When we step through the gates and into the gardens, I marvel at how wild everything appears, as if growing in a glowing forest instead of carefully manicured castle grounds.

Large, luminescent, turquoise and green mushrooms as big as trees line the winding paths carved from the same obsidian stone as the castle, punctuated every so often by various iridescent blue pools of water.

The gardens are so big it would be easy to get lost in here if one was not careful. I always loved the castle gardens back home, and I look forward to exploring this place more later.

When we finally reach the main entrance, Varys dismounts, then helps me down. I'm definitely going to talk to him about finding someone to fashion some Elvish clothing for me, so I no longer have to worry about dresses.

Two more guards stand on either side, bowing in respect as we pass. Their eyes widen slightly, the only indication in their impassive expressions that my appearance surprises them.

Varys offers me his arm and I loop mine through as we

walk toward the entrance. The massive, dark metal doors appear rather foreboding, but I remember this entire city was only used in times of war before they made this their permanent capital.

The main entry room is large and sparsely decorated. Our footsteps echo loudly on the stone tiles. Directly across from the entrance is a wide staircase and at the top of the landing is a portrait of Varys and Elves I assume are his brother and sister. They have the same ice-blue eyes, but his sister has long, flowing, black hair, and his brother's is shoulder length.

Varys guides me up the stairs to the second level. Knowing this place was built as a safe haven, I had expected a mostly utilitarian space, and I'm surprised by its elegance. It has just enough soft touches to make it feel like an actual home instead of a fortified castle. Thick rugs cover the stone floor, and there are several sofas and chairs scattered about with plush gray cushions that appear rather inviting.

Tapestries of nature scenes and beautiful carvings cover the walls on one side and rows of bookshelves on the other. I've always loved to read, but I wonder if any of these are in Florinesh. I know I can now speak and understand Elvish because of our bond, but I do not know if that extends to reading as well.

An enormous fireplace along the far wall emits a warm glow, but I notice the hearth has the same incandescent crystals that Varys used when we stayed at the abandoned castle ruins. I suppose it makes sense to not use actual flames that would cause smoke that might have difficulty escaping the mountain.

Melina guides us down a long hallway lined with several doors. "This is the family wing," Varys explains.

When we reach the second door on the left, Melina

gestures to it. "These rooms are always ready for guests. I thought the princess might find them comfortable, and—"

"There is no need." Varys turns to her. "She will stay in my chambers."

Melina's mouth drifts open slightly before she clamps it shut again. Her gaze slides to mine, disbelief and anger burning in her eyes.

Their relationship must be something more than just guard and king...

Without another word, Varys guides me farther down the hallway. Several rock carvings and tapestries depicting fierce battles decorate the walls. At the end is a set of double doors that he opens with a wave of his hand.

When we step inside, I'm surprised by how large the space is. Glowing, blue stalactites cover the ceiling, making the room both bright and intimate. A large bed stands along the left wall, covered in thick gray and black furs. The four posts are made of the same stone as the rest of the mountain, and I realize it is carved directly into the wall.

A desk and chair on the other side are piled high with books and papers, suggesting that Varys uses this space as more than just a bedroom. A sofa sits in front of what can best be described as a fireplace, but instead of wood in the hearth, several more of the stacked, glowing stones emit both light and warmth.

He guides me to another door and leads me inside. "This is the cleansing room."

A small waterfall cascades down from the ceiling and into a pool below. A light mist of steam rises from the surface, suggesting the water is heated. He gestures to a stone bench near the pool with towels and soap. There is a sink on the other side and the toilet area beyond another smaller door.

When we step back into the bedroom, I lament the

absence of windows. Despite how lovely it is in here, I will miss natural light.

Varys turns to me. "You should rest. I must go attend to a few things. Someone will be here with food for you shortly. If there is anything you require, you need only ask and it will be provided."

I follow him back out into the bedroom. As he opens the door to the hallway, I start to ask about finding some Elvish clothing for me but stop when I notice Melina is at the door, a visible scowl on her face.

Her gaze flicks to me and her expression darkens as she turns her attention to Varys again.

His shoulders tense, and he sighs heavily as he steps out and shuts the door behind him.

CHAPTER 28

VARYS

Melina is already waiting at the door when I open it. It is difficult, but I force myself to hold my tongue until we are far enough down the hallway that Inara cannot hear us.

I spin to face Melina. "What is it?" I struggle to hide the irritation in my tone.

"A *human*, Varys?" she snaps. "You *cannot* be serious."

"She is my Khio'ri, Melina."

"The Council will not care," she replies. "They will call you a traitor for taking her as your bondmate."

"Let them try," I grind out through clenched teeth.

"Humans are weak. They are pitiful and—"

"We may be friends, Melina, but that does not give you leave to disparage my bride."

Her head jerks back. "You are already bound to her?"

"We were married in a human ceremony before we left her people. Now that we have returned to Cyridil, we will have an Elvish bonding ceremony. There will be no question that she is mine and I am hers."

Melina stares at me in shock. "You truly mean to do this?"

"She is my Khio'ri." I meet her gaze evenly. "In the past you've made it very clear how you feel about humans. But I need to know now: can I trust you to protect her?"

She clenches her jaw. After a moment, she gives me a reluctant nod. "You know above all else, I am loyal to you, Varys. That loyalty extends to your bondmate." She pauses. "Are you certain she is not a spy or an assassin?"

Perhaps it is the bond that makes me so fiercely protective of my human bride, but I have difficulty biting back a growl at Melina's questioning of her integrity. "I have sensed nothing through the Khio'rinar to suggest she is either of those things."

She gapes at me. "You can already *sense her*?"

I nod, impatient to see my siblings. "Where is Aryl?"

"He is probably in the throne room."

I arch a brow. "How did he manage in my absence?"

She rolls her eyes. "Like he always does when you leave him to watch over things. He moped and prayed several times for your safe return so he would not have to rule a moment longer than he has to."

I grin. Aryl has always been rather dramatic.

As soon as we enter the throne room, Aryl's blue eyes light up. He runs a hand through his shoulder-length black hair and starts toward me. "Varys!" he calls out. "Thank the gods you are back."

I purse my lips. "You only had to watch over things for a few days."

He walks up and claps a hand on my shoulder. "A few days too long." He shakes his head. "I do not envy you,

Brother. The Council complained several times about the treaty being negotiated with the Fae for grain."

"Of course, they complained. They are always reluctant to accept change."

"There are reports of Wraiths along the northern edge of the kingdom," Aryl adds. "The Fae sent word that they have attacked some of their guards along their border as well. I sent scouts to verify."

"You can recall them." I give him a sober look. "We encountered Wraiths when we were crossing the Veil."

Aryl's face pales. "How did they make it past the Great Wall and to our borders?"

"I do not know," I reply grimly.

"Is it true, Varys?" My sister's voice rings out from the doorway. The clipped sound of Nyrala's boots echoes loudly as she crosses the smooth stone floor with a purpose. Her expression is thunderous, blue eyes narrowed. Her long, black hair is tied in a loose braid down her back. "Have you taken a human as your mate?"

"What?" Aryl's eyes widen and his head jerks back. "I thought those were rumors."

"They are truth."

Aryl's jaw drops. "Where is she?"

"In my chambers."

"Who is she?" Nyrala asks. "And why would you do this? Why bring shame upon our family in this way?"

"She is Princess Inara of Florin. She is my Khio'ri."

Aryl gasps. "Your Khio'ri?"

"That cannot be right," Nyrala counters. "No one has ever found their fated one outside of our race."

I curl my hands into fists at my side, angered that my own family would doubt me. "It is truth. I felt the pull of the Khio'rinar the moment her eyes met mine. We were bound in a human ceremony before we left Florin.

"We will have an Elven ceremony tomorrow. I will send for a priestess to perform the ceremony and invite the High Council and nobility. But I wanted to speak with you both first." I meet my sister's gaze evenly. "Inara has no family here. She will need someone to help her prepare."

Nyrala gives me a pitying look. "You know I will do anything for you, Varys." Concern laces her words. "But are you sure this is what you want?

It does not escape my notice how her gaze darts to Melina. Many times, my sister has tried to push me toward bonding with her. Even if I were not with Inara, I could never have been with Melina. She is like a sibling to me.

Melina's father, Lord Dralyn, holds the seat of power on the Council. He will not be pleased to learn of my bonding, especially since it is not to his daughter, as he has hoped for many years.

"Yes, I am," I state firmly. "The Khio'rinar is a blessing from the gods themselves. Why would I reject this?"

Yet, even as I hide behind this reasoning, it goes far beyond this. I did not expect to be attracted to my human bride, but I am. And in the short time I've known her, I already consider her mine and am very possessive of her. Even if these feelings are a product of the Khio'rinar, it does not make them any less real.

Nyrala looks to me. "When will we get to meet her?"

"I will bring her to last meal."

Nyrala nods. Her gaze darts briefly to Melina behind me. "I must speak with Varys. In private."

Melina excuses herself and leaves the room.

Aryl heads toward the door, but Nyrala grabs his arm, yanking him to a stop. "That includes *you*, as well."

"You said 'Varys.' I thought—"

"You *are* part of this family, Aryl, and despite how much

I'm sure you want to get back to your friends, you have a duty to your family first."

He heaves an exaggerated sigh. "Do you think I do not know that? I simply thought—"

I raise my hands in a bid for silence as I look between the two of them. "Please, can we not argue today? I need your support. Both of you."

They each give me a solemn nod.

Nyrala turns to me. "What exactly do you plan to do?"

I frown. "What do you mean?"

"Is she going to be your true mate? Or will she simply be queen in name alone?"

I understand what she is asking. She wants to know if I will be like our grandfather and take a mistress to produce heirs.

Closing my eyes briefly, the memory of the dowager Fae queen fills my mind. She died when I was very young, but I will never forget her kindness to me and my siblings, nor the sadness that I saw all too often in her eyes when she looked at my grandfather.

I understand his reasoning, but that does not mean I agree with it. The moment I took Inara as my bride, I decided I would never do that to her.

I lower my voice and speak clearly. "If she will have me as hers, I will be her true mate and she will be mine."

"Before you arrived, we heard rumors," my sister begins. "People are speaking of the prophecy of the Great Uniters."

I press my lips into a firm line. "The Priestess of Cael-rynd encouraged this when she performed the blessing of our union."

"We'll know tomorrow if it is true or not," Aryl says. "The bonding ceremony will tell if—"

"Enough," I cut him off. "She cannot be one of the Great Uniters foretold in the prophecy. She has no magic."

My sister lifts her brows. "Are you certain?"

"Surely, if she had the type of power spoken of in the prophecy, her brother would never have given up his greatest advantage against their enemies."

"You are right," Nyrala agrees. "No king would give that up. Especially to an enemy."

"Does her brother know what she is to you?" Aryl asks. "That she is your fated one?"

I shake my head. "Her older sister tried to offer herself to me in Inara's stead. She pleaded with me, since Inara was already betrothed to Prince Lukas of Valren, but I refused; I did not tell them why."

As I explain the events to them, their eyes widen.

"You took her from Prince Lukas—the Wolf Shifter?" Nyrala asks in astonishment. "He will wage war on us to get her back."

"He let her go without protest. He accepted her choice to marry me."

"Was it truly a choice?" Nyrala persists. "You had her brother captive and threatened to kill him. If she had not agreed to marry you, there was the threat of further war between us and their kingdom, in which her brothers and her husband-to-be would have had to fight." She shakes her head. "Do you not see, Varys? She sacrificed herself for the man she loves. She married you to spare her family and her betrothed."

My head jerks back. I had not considered this. I know they were engaged, but surely, if there was love between them, he would have fought for her instead of allowing her to sacrifice herself.

As if reading my thoughts, Aryl interjects. "Lukas is a Wolf Shifter. They are extremely territorial and possessive.

If he truly loved her, why did he just let her go without a fight?"

"Perhaps they had a plan." Nyrala narrows her eyes. "A plan to get close enough to assassinate you."

"No," I counter. "If she wanted to kill me, I would sense it."

Nyrala blinks several times. "You can already feel her through the Khio'rinar?"

"It is faint, but it is there," I explain. "Wraiths attacked along the border, and I was able to heal her by sharing my life force." My sister covers her mouth with a hand. "And when we received the blessing in Caelrynd, she could hear me speak in her mind."

Aryl's jaw drops. "No wonder the priestess believes she is one of the Great Uniters."

"We do not need to encourage this narrative," I state firmly. "As my Khio'ri, she is already a target for my enemies."

Nyrala wrings her hands. "How could you do this, Varys? She is a human; you know how weak they are. Now, you are vulnerable to any who seek to take the throne from you. And if you do not have any heirs—"

"Enough!" I rake my hand through my hair as frustration burns through me. "You act as though I had a choice. You know as well as I that the fated bond cannot be ignored."

Nyrala falls silent. She knows I'm right. As a healer, she has seen the effects of the bond on many others before.

Aryl tilts his head toward the door and raises his eyebrows. "What will you do about Melina?"

"What do you mean?"

"You know she has always desired you. Her father supports you on the Council because he hoped someday she would be your bondmate."

"I gave neither Melina nor her father any reason to expect this. She has always been my friend. Nothing more."

"Perhaps, for *you*," Nyrala says. "I have seen how she looks at you, Varys. How she has *always* looked at you. She has turned down several suitors waiting for you to choose her."

Sighing heavily, I shake my head. "I gave her no reason to ever believe that—"

"I know this." Nyrala places a hand on my shoulder. "I'll admit, I hoped you might grow to care for her beyond simple friendship. I'm sure the entire Council felt this way." She gives me a pitying look. "It would have been a good match. Certainly, one that would have been much easier for them to accept."

I look between the two of them. "I know the Council and many of our subjects will oppose this marriage. That is why I must bind her to me, in the ways of our people, as soon as possible. The sooner they accept what is done, we can move forward. And it will strengthen the bond between us, so I can sense her more than I do now. I will know if she is in danger and—"

"*She* is your greatest weakness now," Nyrala says sadly.

My sister would know. My parents had the Khio'rinar between them. Nyrala remembers how our mother succumbed shortly after our father's death.

"I know," I reply solemnly. "That is why I must keep her close to me at all times. Not only are the enemies outside our kingdom a threat, but the ones who hide within as well."

"And if the prophecy is true... you are both in danger," Aryl adds.

Nyrala blinks back tears, pushing down her emotions as she tips up her chin. "The fated bond cannot be ignored.

What's done is done." She glances at Aryl. "We will always support you. You know this."

My shoulders relax at her words. "I do. Thank you."

"Is she intelligent, at least?" Aryl asks. "I've heard humans can be very slow, like Orcs."

Pride fills me as I think of my bride. "She is intelligent, clever, and very brave."

"Good." He grins. "She will need to be brave to be married to you... She'll have to deal with your grumpy demeanor every morning before your first cup of tea. It often makes me wonder if you might somehow be part Troll, my dear brother."

I narrow my eyes, and he claps a hand on my shoulder. "You know I am only joking with you, Varys."

"Please try to restrain yourself when you meet her, Aryl. At least let her get comfortable around you before you start in with your relentless teasing."

"Relentless?" he asks, feigning shock. "I do not know what you are talking about."

Even Nyrala gives him a pointed look. "Varys is right. She is probably scared. After all, Dark Elves and humans have been enemies for a very long time. I suggest you be on your best behavior tonight."

"Of course." He rolls his eyes. "Why would you doubt me?"

Even as he asks this, I note the slight upward tilt of his lips. I hope Inara likes my family. I want her to feel accepted here.

CHAPTER 29

INARA

I take a seat on the sofa as my mind replays the events of the past few days. I still can't believe I am wed to the Dark Elf king but I wonder about Melina. Blowing out a resigned sigh, I accept I'll have to find a way to broach the delicate subject with him and ask if she is a mistress.

It is not the ideal way to begin a marriage, but this is not an ideal situation either, certainly not one I ever expected to find myself in. Then, there is the matter of my family and Lukas. I need to send word to them because I'm sure they are worried about me.

A soft knock at the door pulls me from my thoughts. I hesitate, wondering who it could be. Perhaps it's someone bringing food, as Varys promised.

"Enter," I call out, standing from the sofa to face whoever it is.

An Elven woman with long, dark hair streaked through

with silver enters. She bows low and then straightens. "King Varys asked me to attend you, my Queen."

Despite her neutral expression, her eyes shine with warmth and kindness. Only the fine lines across her brow and the silver in her hair suggest her advanced age. "I am Talyn and I will attend to you. I have brought you some fresh clothing."

I take the material that she holds out to me. As it unfolds, I study it appraisingly. It's a green dress tunic and light gray leggings with a matching set of boots. I noticed when we entered the city that most of the Elven women wore pants, and I am glad to see that it is acceptable here in the palace, as well. I do like to wear dresses now and then, but I've always preferred the practical comfort of leggings.

"Would you like to get washed up first?" she asks, a gentleness in her tone. "The king will be here shortly to take you to last meal."

"Oh," I reply uncertainly. I thought he was going to have dinner sent to my room. "All right."

I enter the cleansing room and Talyn follows me. She helps me out of my dress but, when she starts to remove my silken shift, I stop her. "I can do this."

She inclines her head politely. "I will wait in the bedroom if you need me, my Queen."

I allow my shift to fall on the floor and step into the water. The warmth seeps into my bones like a balm for my soul as I dip my head beneath the surface. When I use some of the soap, it is absolutely heavenly. It leaves my skin feeling soft and smooth, and I detect the delightful scent of jasmine.

When I'm finished bathing, I grab a towel from the bench and dry off before changing into my new clothes. They are a bit large, but I suppose that's to be expected, since I am smaller than a typical Elven woman. I'll need a seamstress to tailor garments that fit me better, but for now, this will do.

The material is soft as silk against my skin, just like Varys's tunic was last night. I suppose there is something to be said for Elven attire. I study myself in the mirror, admiring how lovely the tunic dress appears on me. It perfectly complements my hair and eyes.

Talyn helps me with my hair, making two small braids on either side of my head before tying them back and leaving the rest of my hair down. I much prefer this to the intricate and often painfully tight braids that are the current fashion in my brother's kingdom.

The door opens and Varys steps inside. He arches a questioning brow. "I was wondering if you might join me for last meal."

I'd thought I would dine alone this evening, and I cannot deny being glad he wishes to have dinner with me. There is so much we still need to discuss. I offer him a warm smile. "That would be wonderful."

He extends an arm to me.

Talyn steps out of the cleansing room. She must have gone through my trunk while I was bathing, because she holds out my ruined dress. "Would you like me to throw this away, my Queen?"

A pang of sadness moves through me as I study the dress. I run my hands over the fabric and the delicate embroidered flower along the collar. "Can you please clean it instead?"

"Of course, my Queen."

"It is ruined." Varys frowns. "Are you certain you wish to keep it?"

"My mother sewed this flower in here for me." I point at the embroidered edge along the collar. "I'd like to keep it. That part of it, at least."

His expression softens as guilt flickers across his features. "I am sorry, Inara. I did not know."

"It is fine." I rest a hand on his chest. "I'll simply remove the collar and save it for something else."

He nods and leads me into the hallway, down the stairs to the main floor of the castle, and to a large dining room.

A long, rectangular table that could seat at least twenty people sits in the middle of the spacious room. Tapestries and carvings of what I assume are former nobility decorate the space while a massive fireplace with warming crystals sits at the far end. Varys guides me to a place at the table near the hearth and takes the seat next to mine. I'm surprised when he does not sit at the head of the table, like my brother would have done.

An Elven woman appears, followed by a man. I recognize them immediately from the painting and know they are Varys's siblings.

His face lights with a smile. "Inara, this is my brother, Aryl, and my sister, Nyrala."

They both bow slightly. I dip my chin in polite greeting as they take seats across from us.

Aryl's lips twitch and his eyes dance with barely restrained amusement as he leans forward. "Tell me all the details about your scandalous affair." He grins. "How did my dashing brother sweep you off your feet? Was it his grumpy and brooding demeanor? Or was it—"

Varys growls low and Aryl stops.

I laugh and so does Nyrala.

"I am merely teasing," Aryl says quickly. He flashes an easy smile. "Welcome to our family."

"Thank you." I lean in and whisper conspiratorially. "If you want to know the truth, he captured me first."

Aryl's jaw drops.

"I was his prisoner for all of two minutes before he proposed to me."

"Truly?" Aryl asks, shocked.

"Truly."

A wide grin spread across Aryl's face as he turns to Varys. "I like her already. No wonder you look so happy, Varys."

My heart skips a little at his statement. I like the idea that I make my new husband happy because, if I am honest with myself, he makes me feel the same.

Servants come and set out food and wine before us. It is nothing I have not seen before, and I wonder if this is typical Elvish food or if they purposefully made human dishes for me.

Aryl clears his throat and raises his wine glass as his eyes meet mine. "To my new sister."

Varys and Nyrala join in the toast.

Awkward silence settles among us again before Aryl looks down at my hands, frowning. "What happened to your claws?"

"Humans do not have claws." I laugh softly as his mouth falls open again in shock, revealing the pointed tips of his two upper canines. "Or fangs," I add.

His brows shoot up toward his hairline. "No claws *or* fangs? How do you defend yourself?"

"You *have* seen a human before, Aryl," Varys chastises.

"Yes, but I never paid close attention," he counters. "When one is fighting on the battlefield, one does not pause to inspect their enemy's claws and fangs, now do they?"

"Enough," Varys warns gently, and Aryl rolls his eyes.

Watching them interact, it reminds me so much of my own family. I love that Varys is so close to his siblings. As Aryl lists off all of Varys's supposed faults to me with a teasing grin, I find myself laughing so hard my face begins to hurt, but in a good way.

"So, what do you think?" Aryl leans in, and arches a brow. "Are you sure you still wish to be bound to Varys... especially now that you know all of his shortcomings?"

A grin tugs at my lips as I decide to tease him in reply. "Better him, than his brother."

Aryl barks out a surprised laugh, and then raises his glass to me. "I believe we will get along well, Inara."

Varys takes my hand as his eyes sparkle with mirth. "Finally, there is someone in this family who can beat Aryl at his teasing."

"You act as though my joking is some sort of hardship upon you," Aryl replies in mock indignation. "I make every day interesting." He tips up his chin. "Without me around, your life would be boring, and you know it."

Varys sighs, and stops just short of rolling his eyes. "Of course, you do." He turns his attention back to me, his expression serious again. "Tomorrow we will have our Elven bonding ceremony. Nyrala will help you prepare."

I smile at his sister. "Thank you."

She nods. "Of course."

Aryl leans forward. "Since you are bound to my brother now, I would like to offer you one last bit of advice. Varys needs a good, strong cup of tea every morning." A teasing smirk plays on his lips. "Without it, you would think him a Troll, with his grumpy attitude, instead of a Dark Elf."

I blow out a soft laugh. Aryl reminds me so much of my own brother, Raiden.

"*Aryl.*" Varys narrows his eyes, but I can see the smile he tries so hard to suppress. His gaze shifts to me. "Allow me to apologize in advance. As you can see, Aryl loves to joke and tease everyone, *especially* family."

"It is all right; I am used to it." I wave a hand in dismissal. "I *did* grow up with two brothers, you know."

"Oh, that's right," Aryl says. "I have heard much about them. Especially Raiden. I've heard he is a fierce warrior. It is good that your father took responsibility and raised him in the castle. I've heard most human men do not even acknowledge their illegitimate offspring."

Varys makes a choked sound in the back of his throat, his eyes wide as he looks at his brother.

CHAPTER 30

VARYS

I look askance at Aryl. It is highly improper to mention Inara's father's infidelities. He should know better than this.

Aryl flinches and gives me an apologetic smile.

"He *is* a fierce warrior," Inara agrees, seemingly unfazed. "Raiden is the one who introduced me to the bow and arrow."

Nyrala frowns. "I heard humans do not train their women to fight."

"You are correct, but my brother began training me in secret after I begged. When my parents found out, they agreed to let me continue until I married."

"Why until then?" she asks.

"Because it is considered improper for a woman of nobility to do such things."

"All Dark Elves—men and women—learn to fight from a young age, so they can defend themselves," Nyrala says.

"A wise decision," Inara replies.

I previously wondered if Inara would like to continue her training, and this decides it. I will definitely start training my mate as soon as possible.

When we finish our meal, Nyrala excuses herself to return to her room.

Aryl swirls his goblet and downs the last of his wine. "Thanks to the two of you, I'm now the only remaining eligible bachelor in the royal family." He shakes his head and sighs dramatically. "Before you try to barter me off to one of the noble families, just remember that I would appreciate at least a few more years of freedom, dear brother."

I roll my eyes. "As if anyone would have you."

Inara coughs and spits out her drink.

Aryl purses his lips in mock irritation. "Great. Now there are two of you to laugh at me instead of just one." He points a stern finger at Inara, but the teasing glint in his eye remains. "I'll remember this, my dear sister."

She laughs, and I am struck again by how beautiful the sound is. I decide that I will try to coax laughter from her lips more often.

I turn to ask if she wishes to retire, but the words die in my throat. Her cheeks are flushed a lovely shade of pink from the wine, and her eyes are still bright with the echoes of her mirth. She is truly lovely, my human wife. Instead of asking if she wishes to leave, I find myself asking if she would like to walk in the gardens.

"I would love to," she replies. "They look so fascinating; I am eager to explore them."

When we reach the gardens, I guide her along the path near the back wall to afford us some privacy. She studies everything with a look akin to wonder. The softly glowing plants cast her in an ethereal glow, and I cannot take my eyes off her.

"This place is beautiful, Varys. I never imagined it would be like this."

"Beautiful enough that you will not miss living on the surface?" I ask.

She takes my hand. "I'm sure I will get used to it."

I am surprised by the intimacy of this gesture as I look down at our joined hands and entwine our fingers. Unable to stop myself, I reach out and brush my fingers across the delicate skin of her cheek, observing as a pink flush follows in their wake. "You are so different from a Dark Elf," I whisper.

She lowers her gaze and through the bond, I can tell I have made her uncomfortable.

Why am I always saying the wrong thing? "Forgive me, I did not mean to—"

"It is all right." She sighs heavily. "I know I am probably not"—she stops short as if searching for the right words, before finally settling on—"what you expected when you imagined your future wife. Dark Elf women are... stunningly gorgeous. Ethereal, even in their appearance, and humans... we're rather plain in comparison."

I blink several times.

She believes she is plain?

"I do not understand how you could consider yourself plain when you are anything but."

Her mouth drifts open and a rosy hue spreads over her cheeks and nose, emphasizing the several small spots that dot her skin. Again, I find myself wondering if they are present on the rest of her body. Before I can stop myself, I reach out and gently touch her cheek again. "What are these spots that you have?"

Her skin flares a deeper red. "Oh, um... they're called freckles. I inherited them from my mother."

"Freckles," I repeat the word for these markings,

committing it to memory. "They are lovely." Her head jerks back, and I cock my head to the side to regard her. "This surprises you. Why?"

"I used to get teased for them when I was a child. Some humans consider them ugly... imperfections on the skin."

I think of my scars and how she said humans often brag about them. I frown. "How is it that humans look down upon freckles but not scars?"

She shrugs. "I don't know."

Thinking back on her acceptance of my scars and what it meant to me, I move to reassure her of the same concerning her "imperfections" as she calls them. "Your freckles do not bother me, Inara. I do not find them ugly in any way."

She gives me a nervous smile. "Thank you." Her expression wavers. "There is something we need to talk about."

I wait patiently for her to continue, wondering what she wishes to speak of.

"Melina," she starts. "I..." She pauses, clearing her throat. "Is there something between you two? Because if there is, I will not hold a previous relationship against you, but I'd like to know, at least, how it stands."

I'm so shocked by her blunt question that it takes me a moment to respond. Aside from my brother, a Dark Elf would never have asked something this intimate so directly. Before I can explain it is not what she thinks, she keeps talking.

"Because, as you're aware, my father had mistresses... I mean, that's how my brother Raiden came along. And while I hoped to marry someone who would be faithful only to me, I *do know* how rare that is, and I understand this bond caught you by surprise. I'm not even sure I entirely understand it yet... Especially when I keep getting these strange impressions of what I think you may be feeling, but I'm not sure."

My ears perk up.

Impressions? Is she beginning to sense more of the bond as I do?

I try to ask, but she continues talking.

"Suffice it to say, I hope we can at least become good friends, if nothing else."

She wants more?

This is something I want as well. Desperately.

Inara continues. "I am human and you are Dark Elf, and we may be unable to have children. I mean… I know you said your grandfather had a Fae wife, but he had children with a mistress, because the two of them could not produce an heir. I just want you to know that if you are with Melina and anything ever comes of it… like a child… I just want you to know I would never shun it or be unkind."

I take a step back, shocked at her statement. I'm not only stunned she has even considered trying to have children with me, but that she would accept a child from a mistress.

My people mate for life, but it seems she does not know this.

She continues. "My mother treated Raiden very coldly when we were growing up, and I love my brother. I hated that he suffered, and I would never inflict that upon a child. I—"

I take her hand in mine, silencing her abruptly. "Melina is a friend. Nothing more. I swear."

"Oh," she replies, obviously surprised by my statement, before releasing a sigh that I can only construe as relief. "Thank goodness. I'll admit I was not looking forward to being cast aside while you—" She flashes a nervous smile. "I know I have a tendency to ramble, but—"

"It is all right, Inara."

"It truly does not bother you?"

A faint smile quirks my lips. "You speak enough for both of us, so it works out well, I believe."

She laughs again, and I find myself completely transfixed.

"My people—Dark Elves—we mate for life." Her lovely eyes stare up into mine. Feeling bold, I cup her cheek as I study them. "What is this color?" I ask softly. "Your eyes... they sometimes appear green and sometimes brown."

"Hazel," she replies.

"They are lovely."

Her gaze holds mine, and I find myself leaning closer. Her lips part slightly, and I can smell soft mint on each exhalation. My eyes drift down to the curve of her mouth, remembering the taste of her kiss. "We have not known each other long, but I would like to know if you might return my feelings. If you have considered the possibility of becoming my true mate."

"True mate?" she whispers. "What does that mean?"

"It means I would take you and no other for the rest of my life. You would be mine and I would be yours."

CHAPTER 31

INARA

His shining eyes bore into mine as he moves closer. The warm mint of his breath whispers across my lips, reminding me of when we kissed. I do not know why I am fighting my attraction to him. He is my husband. We are already bound to each other, and yet my mind urges caution even as my heart pulls me toward him.

And while we have not known each other long, it feels as if I have known him forever. My grandparents found love almost immediately. Would it be so strange if I did as well?

I stretch up on my toes and twine my arms around his neck. His hands go to my waist, and my heart pounds as he pulls me against him. Everything about him feels so right. As if his soul resonates with mine, recognizing its other half.

He leans in and brushes his lips to my own in a tender kiss. They are soft and warm, just as I remembered. My breath quickens as he tightens his arms around me, molding my form to his.

"You are perfect," he breathes.

His tongue curls around mine, and I melt into his touch. A low growl vibrates in his chest as he cups the back of my head, angling my mouth to his as he devours me with his lips and his tongue.

I have never been kissed before him, and I had no idea it could be this intense. My entire body hums in awareness of his as he pulls me even closer.

My hands slide to his chest, tracing over every dip and curve of the hard muscle beneath his tunic.

He cups my breast through the fabric of my dress, and I arch into him, completely lost in sensation. A low moan escapes my lips as he brushes his thumb over the peak until it stiffens into a hard bead, as if begging for his attention.

"My King," someone's voice calls out and we jump apart.

Varys immediately pulls me behind him, as if shielding me, as he turns. "Yes, Devyn?"

"Forgive me, my King. I-I simply was looking for you. I did not mean to—"

"It is fine," Varys says. "Leave us."

"Of course."

I listen as his footsteps retreat.

Varys turns back to me. I wonder if he regrets the interruption as much as I do. Awkward silence settles between us a moment before he takes my hand, threading his fingers through mine. "Let us go back to our chambers. We have much to do tomorrow."

Still a bit breathless from our kiss, I somehow manage to reply. "All right."

CHAPTER 32

VARYS

When we arrive at our rooms, she reaches into her tunic and pulls out a dagger. Her gaze holds mine a moment before she turns and places it on the table by the sofa. "I… do not think I need this. In fact, I am sorry I did not tell you I had it sooner."

I stare at her, staggered by the trust she is offering me. I did not even know she had this concealed on her person. She could have kept it hidden and used it while I slept if she wished.

I bow slightly. "You honor me with your trust."

Through the Khio'rinar, I sense her slight hesitance to my words, but I do not understand why. Then again, it must take a great deal of strength and bravery to trust someone who, only a few days ago, was her enemy.

I take both her hands in mine. "I desire for there only to be truth between us, Inara."

"I feel the same, Varys," she whispers softly.

It is a good start, and I feel hopeful in a way I have not in such a long time.

After I go into the cleansing room and bathe, I dress in my soft knit pants. When I come back out, I cannot help but notice how she eyes my form appreciatively before quickly looking away.

Happiness fills me. My scars truly do not bother her. I thought she was trying not to offend me the other night when she said they did not trouble her. It seems I was wrong, and she was telling the truth. They really do not upset her, just as her freckles do not repulse me in any way.

She goes into the cleansing room, and my thoughts scatter when she returns wearing my undertunic. "I hope you do not mind." She gestures to herself. "I did not see anything else to change into for sleep."

I would curse Talyn's inept caring of my mate by not providing any sleepwear, but she is clever, and I'm sure something like this did not simply slip her mind.

She knows the importance of scent marking upon mates. All Dark Elves do. She knew that even if I bathed after Inara, I would have offered her my tunic when nothing else was available.

Primal possessiveness floods my veins, and my nostrils flare as I draw our combined scent deep into my lungs. I love that she smells so strongly of me. "I do not mind." I can barely suppress a low growl of arousal.

Not in the least.

CHAPTER 33

INARA

Varys lies down beside me in the bed. Shadow and light carve his muscular shoulders, chest, and abdomen. When he catches me staring, I quickly look away. I cannot believe how attracted I am to my Dark Elf husband.

My mind replays our kiss. I long to kiss him again, but I do not even know where to begin. My lips tingle as I remember the feel of his tongue against mine and his hands on my body.

I know we are married in the human tradition, but we are not in the Elven, and I am not entirely sure I am ready to consummate our marriage. Besides, it would be wrong to do so when he does not yet know my secrets.

Staring up at the ceiling with its glimmering blue stalactites, my thoughts drift to the small amount of nylweed I have left to suppress my visions and newly acquired magic. Before it runs out, I'll need to either find more or tell Varys the truth, so he can help me locate some.

I cannot wait much longer. I want so desperately to tell him but I have to be certain of his response.

I want to believe he will accept me no matter what, but I cannot be sure.

Unpleasant memories flood my mind. If not for High Mage Ylari keeping my secret, I would probably be dead. Closing my eyes, I count silently to myself as he taught me, trying to calm the emotions churning deep within. I'm terrified of what might happen when Varys finds out.

I recall the Wraith attack. If I didn't suppress my visions, perhaps I would have foreseen it, but my visions are a double-edged sword. High Mage Ylari claims seeing the future is powerful... that this type of magic is stronger than others. But visions can be misinterpreted so easily.

Swallowing hard, I try to force the dark thoughts from my mind. Tomorrow will be our Elven bonding ceremony. Willing my tense muscles to relax, I drift into sleep.

CHAPTER 34

INARA

When I wake, I'm completely snuggled beneath two layers of blankets and furs. I roll onto my side and peek over, but Varys is not next to me. I smile to myself when I realize the extra blanket and fur are his. He must have placed them on me before he left. My husband is a thoughtful and caring man.

I sit up and swing my legs over the edge of the bed to stand. I'm about to make my way to the cleansing room when a soft knock at the door startles me. Thinking it's probably Talyn with clothing, I call out, "Enter!"

The door opens and Varys's sister, Nyrala, steps in. Her eyes widen as they take in my form, and I can only imagine what a state I must be in from her expression.

"Oh. I-I was not expecting you."

"I am here to help prepare you for the ceremony."

"I remember," I reply quickly. "Forgive me. I only just woke up and did not realize I had slept so long." I glance behind her. "Do you know where Varys went?"

"He is meeting with the priestess to make sure everything is arranged properly."

"Is he worried about the ceremony?"

She gives me a hesitant look. "We have had word that some of the nobles will not be attending. Then, there is the matter of the people who have already lined up outside the palace gates."

"The nobles who are not coming... it's because I'm human, isn't it?"

She nods, affirming my suspicion.

"The people outside the gates... Is he worried they will protest as well?"

"I am sure there are probably protesters among them, but the majority are not here for that reason."

"Then, why?"

"They are here because of the prophecy."

Worry churns in my stomach. "Varys says it is a myth."

"It does not matter what my brother believes," she says soberly. "The people already hope that you are one of the Great Uniters, here to usher in an era of peace for a kingdom that has seen one war after another for several hundred years."

"And what do you believe?" I ask, curious to hear her answer.

"I believe in the strength of family." Her ice-blue eyes meet mine evenly. "There are many with ambitions for the throne who would see my brother removed from rule. Varys cannot afford to appear weak in any way."

"I understand the importance of a united front," I tell her, recalling Edmynd's transition to power after our father's death. "It is the same in my brother's kingdom. I grew up in the royal court and I—"

"It is *not* the same," she cuts me off. "You are human, and yet, the gods have made you his Khio'ri." She shakes her head softly. "Do you understand the importance of this bond? Do you feel anything of it?"

At first, I'm angry and offended, but when I notice the tears in her eyes, I pause, choosing my response carefully, because I know she is simply worried for her brother. "I *do* feel something of it. But... I do not believe it is the same for me as it is for Varys. Maybe because I'm human, I do not sense it the way he does."

Her eyebrows draw together. "Varys watched our father die on the battlefield. The mantle of rule was placed on his shoulders far sooner than we ever expected, and he has borne this weight with dignity and honor. And now... he bears *this*." Her eyes lock on to mine. "This bond between you will rob him of any chance at true happiness."

Shocked at her statement, I open my mouth to respond, but she continues.

"I do not doubt you will be kind to him, for I have already seen it in the way you interact. But you are human, and if he takes you as his true mate, it is almost certain that the two of you could not have a family. He would not have an heir to secure his throne.

"It is not just his happiness, but his security that is at stake. People will view a king without an heir as weak, and someday, when he is gone, the transition of power to one not of direct descent will be... difficult at best. Our grandfather knew this. That is why he took a mistress as his true mate."

"Varys told me of this," I reply. "His queen was Fae and—"

"Grandfather could not risk making her his true mate when there was no guarantee that she could provide him with heirs." She draws in a shuddering breath. "So, I am asking you to give Varys a chance at happiness. A family... a normal life."

"Why are you asking *me*?" I shake my head in disbelief. "It is not my decision to force him to do anything."

"Because he is an honorable man, and I can already see that he cares for you. He would take you as his true mate, even knowing what it might mean for him, and what he would give up." A tear slips down her cheek. "He held our family together after our parents died, and I wish more than anything to see him happy."

I frown. "What exactly are you asking of me?"

"I am pleading with you to keep him at a distance. To let him find love with someone else."

Now I understand *what* she is asking and *why* she is asking it. She loves her brother as I love mine. "It is easy to see that you love your brother and would do anything for him," I say. "Just as I did for mine, by agreeing to this marriage in the first place." I clear my throat, forming my response very carefully. "I promise to do all I can to make your brother happy. You have my word on this."

Her gaze holds mine briefly before she gives me a solemn nod. "Thank you."

From her now much lighter expression, part of me wonders if she thinks I am agreeing to push him away. In truth, I would not have considered it before, but now... I do not know. Nothing has happened between us that cannot be taken back. Sighing heavily, I decide that we will simply take things slowly.

Last night was wonderful, but perhaps it is all happening too fast. I know my grandparents fell in love quickly, but I cannot help but think that I am leading with my heart when I should be listening to my head.

After I return from bathing, Nyrala stands behind me, combing out my long hair and arranging it in a series of spiraled braids atop my head for the ceremony. A soft knock at the door precedes Talyn's entry with my Elvish bonding robes. I'm surprised to see the embroidered flower that my mother sewed along the collar. I lift my gaze to hers. "You salvaged this from my torn dress?"

"Yes. The king asked me to save it and incorporate it into your robes. He said it was important to you." She points to elegant Elven script sewn into the hemline, the silver thread practically glowing against the green silk. "He also specified this."

I study it closely. Some of the symbols are familiar, but some I do not recognize. My ability to read Elvish is rudimentary at best. It seems the bond doesn't help with the written word. "What does it say?"

"It is a sacred vow among mates." A warm smile curves her mouth. "It means: You and no other."

Tears sting my eyes at his thoughtfulness. "Thank you so much." My voice quavers as I take the robes from her. "This is lovely."

When she offers me two small scraps of white silk, I frown. "What are these?"

Nyrala is the one who answers. "It is the clothing you wear beneath your robes."

"Undergarments?" I ask, studying the scandalous items. The bra is little more than a pattern of lace, and the other consists of a few straps framing a triangular piece of material to cover my pelvis and backside.

She nods.

I go behind the divider to change and my cheeks flare bright red when I change into the undergarments. I feel almost completely naked beneath the silken Elvish gown. The material is soft against my skin but leaves little to the imagination as it hugs me, accentuating every line and curve of my body beneath.

When I am finished dressing, Nyrala goes over the words and rituals of the ceremony to prepare me for what is involved. It sounds similar to the blessing ceremony in Caelrynd, so I am not as nervous as I would be if I had no idea what to expect.

But when she tells me about what happens after the ceremony, I take a step back. "What?" I ask, not sure I heard her correctly.

"You are to remain bound together until dawn," she repeats the last part.

"What do you mean, *bound*?"

CHAPTER 35

VARYS

I t is only an hour until my bonding ceremony, and I've never been so nervous. I was not even this anxious when we had our human wedding, but perhaps that is because I was far more worried about being attacked then. I was concerned that the marriage was a trap meant to lull me into a false sense of security and then assassinate me.

Fortunately, it was not.

Now that I am in my own kingdom, I find myself with an entirely different worry as I stare down at the long, silken green ribbon in my hands.

"What if the ritual actually works?" Aryl says, snapping me back from my thoughts. "What if—"

"It will not," I interrupt. "Inara has no magic, and the prophecy states the Great Uniters will possess great power."

"Why did the Wraiths go after her?" He poses the question that has plagued me since our attack. "You and your men should have been their target because of your magic. Not her. She is just human."

I shrug. "I do not know."

His gaze drifts to the silk ribbon. "Will you take her as a true mate?"

"If she will have me," I reply honestly.

He sighs. "Nyrala thinks you should—"

"I *know* what she thinks." Anger bubbles up. "She wants me to take a Dark Elf mistress, like our grandfather, but I will not do that to Inara. She is my Khio'ri, and even if she were not, I could not do this to another. Besides… I am already in love with her."

He blinks several times. "So soon?"

A smile tugs at my mouth. "Yes. I feel it here." I place my palm over my heart. "What I have with her feels right in a way that nothing else ever has."

"Then, by all means, ignore our sister." He grins. "If Inara makes you happy, do not worry about anything else."

"Thank you." I clap a hand on his shoulder.

"For what?"

"For being the only voice of reason in our family right now."

He laughs softly before his expression sobers. "Nyrala's intentions are good. She just wants you to be happy, you know. And… she's only trying to protect you."

"I know."

"Lord Dralyn will be upset that you will not take Melina as your mate. He might even make a play for the throne."

I sigh heavily. "I have considered this."

"What about Melina? Do you trust her to be loyal to you over her own father?"

"I do," I answer without hesitation. "She swore to protect Inara."

"And your new bride?" Aryl gestures at the ribbon. "You are certain she will not try to kill you this night while you are bound to her?"

Instantly offended, I open my mouth to defend her, but stop when I note the teasing smirk on his lips. "You had better pray she does not." I arch a brow. "Or else the crown falls to you."

His expression falls.

The door opens and Devyn walks in. "What did I miss?"

Aryl points a stern finger at him. "I am counting on you to keep your eyes on the king all night, Devyn, in case his mate tries to kill him. His life is in your hands, my friend."

"I will protect your brother, but I refuse to be present during their bonding night." He chuckles. "Besides, I doubt very much that she wants to kill him. Not from what I came upon last night, anyway."

"Is that so?" Aryl's ears perk up. "*Do* tell me more."

"Enough," I growl, even as my face flares with heat.

I know Inara said she wished for us to know each other better before we consummate our marriage, but after our kiss last night, I am not sure how she feels now.

She is comfortable in my presence, and I know she trusts me to not hurt her. Beyond that, I am uncertain where we stand. I only know she is as attracted to me as I am to her, and in a short amount of time, I have already lost my heart to my human bride.

CHAPTER 36

INARA

Once I'm ready, Nyrala guides me down a long corridor to a spiraling staircase. It's quiet in here. Only the sound of my slippers scraping across the stone steps as we climb fills the air. My heart pounds so hard in my chest I wonder if my new sister-in-law can hear it with her sharp Elvish ears.

She pushes a door open at the top and we step out into the cool night air. The full moon shines brightly overhead amidst a sea of stars. Golden and white lights flit back and forth among the trees and their softly glowing, purple, heart-shaped leaves.

I inhale deeply, enjoying the crisp breeze and the smell of earth and forest all around us. It's so different from the earth and stone dampness permeating the city beneath the mountain.

I turn to Nyrala. "I didn't know there was a passageway like this to the surface."

"This is the royal family's private passage. Magic

conceals it from the outside."

Relief floods my veins at the thought that I will not have to remain underground all the time. The thought of hardly ever seeing the open sky was discomforting. Now that I know I will be able to come to the surface regularly, a heavy weight has been lifted from my chest.

Bright orbs of golden light line a pathway through the woods. Ahead in the distance, several sets of glowing eyes blink in the darkness, but it is the ice-blue ones that draw my attention as I recognize Varys standing at the end of the path.

He is dressed in long, flowing green robes that match mine. He is so handsome, he's almost too perfect to be real.

Behind him is an identical statue to the one present at the ruined castle—the first Dark Elf king and his queen.

Nyrala falls into step behind me, and she is soon joined by Aryl. I glance back and flash a warm smile at them both, realizing they are standing in the place of my family since I am alone here.

It is a kind gesture; one I want them to know I appreciate. Even if Nyrala wants Varys to choose someone else besides me as his true mate. She loves him. I can understand this because I feel the same for my brothers. I would do anything to see them both happy.

I force my gaze to remain locked on to my husband, breathing in and out to steady my nerves. I take slow, measured steps toward him. In this moment, he is my anchor amid a wave of strangers in a strange land. And when I look in his eyes, I do not feel lost... I feel found.

My palms are damp and my mouth is dry by the time I reach his side. His lips quirk up when I turn to face him, and I answer with a faint smile of my own. Through our connection, I sense the same nervousness that flows through my veins, not just mine but his as well.

His gaze holds my own, and I frown when I notice the prominent scar on his face is somehow gone. Sensing my confusion through the bond, he whispers in a voice so low I almost miss it. "It is a glamour. I wanted to be perfect for you this night."

My heart clenches. "You are the most handsome man I've ever seen, Varys. You do not have to hide your scars from me. Not now. Not ever."

Warmth floods across our connection, and a glowing blue light shimmers across his face and falls away, revealing his true appearance beneath. I smile up at him. "Much better."

A priestess in long, flowing silver robes stands before us. Having overheard our exchange, her expression softens. Her lavender eyes are full of a warmth I had hoped for, but had prepared myself not to see, given that I am human.

She produces a small blade that glints beneath the moonlight. Dark Elves seal their bonds in blood. Nyrala told me about this part of the ceremony, but assured me that the cut across my palm would not be deep.

I remain very still as the priestess carefully slices a fine line across my left palm and then across Varys's right.

When she is finished, he lifts his right hand, staring at me expectantly. Drawing in a steadying breath, I tip up my chin and place my left palm to his. Despite my nerves, I resolve to project confidence and bravery. After all, I will have to possess both if I am to survive in a royal court with many who consider me their enemy.

Many of the Elves have gathered here because they've never seen a human up close before, and others are here because they believe in a prophecy that may or may not be true.

Although I am nervous, I push down my fears. If I am the first human they see, I will make sure they know my people are strong as I stand proud and unafraid beside my Dark Elf husband.

Varys's glowing, ice-blue eyes stare deep into mine. His words are soft and lilting, in complete contrast to his impassive expression. Behind his stoic mask, I sense a feeling of approval at the way I stand tall and hold his gaze evenly.

The priestess produces the long, green ribbon Varys gave me before. Her luminous eyes turn to me. "Repeat these words as I bind you."

Together, Varys and I speak the words as she wraps the ribbon around our joined hands, tying them together with a firm knot.

Varys's gaze holds mine, full of devotion, as he speaks the words of bonding, threading his fingers through my own. "Blood of my blood. Bone of my bone. I give you my life and my heart, that our souls may be one. You and no other."

Gently, I squeeze his hand as I repeat the solemn vow. "Blood of my blood. Bone of my bone. I give you my life and my heart, that our souls may be one. You and no other."

A faint, green light draws my attention and my head snaps to our joined hands. Varys's eyes widen as it swirls around us.

Warmth floods my veins, spreading throughout my entire body. "What's happening?" I barely manage.

Several audible gasps sound from the crowd, and the priestess stares in wonder as it begins to glow even brighter.

"The soul bond," he speaks softly. *"It is all right, my Khio'ri,"* his voice whispers in my mind as warmth wraps tight around my heart. Slowly, the light fades from the green ribbon binding our hands.

Everyone observes in stunned silence a moment before the priestess holds out a silver circlet crown. She raises it for the entire crowd to see.

The twining metal appears like vines, and in the center is a heart-shaped leaf similar to Varys's crown, but with a lovely moonstone set in the pattern.

Carefully, she places it on my head, and we slowly lower our joined hands. With my fingers still entwined with his, we turn and face the crowd.

"May the reign of King Varys and the sanishon Queen Inara be one of peace and prosperity," she says solemnly. "As foretold in the ancient Tomes of the Lythyrian."

Several in the crowd gasp, while others stare at me in awe-filled reverence before bowing low.

Varys guides me through the guests and into the woods, away from the people and the mountain that is my new home. Softly glowing orbs illuminate our path as we walk farther into the forest. The canopy above is lit with gold and silver lights that appear like stars as Pixies flit back and forth, whirling on the cool wind.

White and red petals cover the forest floor. Looking more closely, I realize they are not scattered randomly, but woven together to form a carpet. I wonder how something so fragile can be bound in this way, but then I remember this is the work of Dark Elves, and they possess all manner of magic.

Varys stops as we round a tree and heads into the forest, away from the path. "Where are we going?"

The sounds of voices carry on the breeze along with the lovely sound of stringed instruments, in the opposite direction.

Varys turns to me, a smile tilting his lips. "The reception is for our guests, not us."

I frown. "Why not?"

He lifts our joined hands. "We are expected to be alone and doing... other things."

"So where are we going, then?"

"I have a gift for you." His eyes dance with barely restrained excitement. "It is customary for a newly bonded pair to give each other something on the night of their bonding."

"I was unaware." I grimace. "I did not get you anything."

"It is all right," he assures me. "You are still learning our ways."

I lift our joined hands. "How long does this remain on?"

Although he remains without expression, his cheeks and ears flush a darker shade before he answers. "It is meant to be removed only after the consummation. But since we will not be doing that, I will remove it. Very carefully."

He reaches for the knot of the ribbon tying our hands. His brow furrows in concentration as he works to loosen it.

I start to help him, but he stops me. "I must be the one to undo this."

Immediately, I drop my hand, allowing him to continue. "Why?"

"There is a tradition. The male removes the ribbon, leaving the knot intact to ensure the bond between mates remains strong and unbroken."

I observe as he carefully loosens the knot just enough that we can extract our hands, but he does not fully untie it. He rolls it up very carefully, tucks it into a square of fabric, and places it in his tunic pocket.

He extends his hand and I take it once more, allowing him to guide me through the forest. When we reach another clearing, he points to a wooden building in the distance. "The above-ground stables are this way."

I am about to ask why we're going to the stables, but I stop when I see Devyn up ahead. He leads two dire wolves out of the entrance. I grin when I recognize Rhygar—Varys's mount—right away.

"Congratulations, my King and Queen," Devyn says, bowing low. He turns to Varys. "They are saddled and ready for you both."

I rest a hand on Rhygar's thick, black and gray fur. "I'm glad to see you again," I tell him. Shutting my eyes, I try to send an image to him to express this.

He sends me one in return of me riding upon his back, and I smile. "Yes," I tell him. "I'd love to go riding."

Varys gently strokes Rhygar's fur. "Serve her well, my friend." He offers me the reins. "He is yours now."

I take a step back and blink several times. "But I thought you said dire wolves were paired with their riders... that they chose them and—"

"I asked, and he agreed to choose you, Inara."

I shake my head in disbelief. "Varys, this is too much. I—"

"You are my mate. There is nothing I would not give you." He reaches out and gently tucks a stray tendril of hair behind my ear. "When you mentioned how much you loved riding, I thought this would be an appropriate gift."

I'm stunned into silence, touched by not only his present but his thoughtful words.

His shoulders droop slightly. "Does this... please you, my mate?"

I hate the uncertainty that flits across his expression, because it is the most perfect gift he could have ever given me. I twine my arms around his neck, meaning to hug him, but he drops his forehead gently against my own.

I beam a smile at him. "More than words can say, my Dark Elf husband."

He slips his arms around my waist. "I am glad you are happy."

As his luminous gaze holds mine, I am completely lost in the depths of his eyes. This moment is perfect... as if I were meant to be here. As if I was supposed to find my way to him all along.

His masculine scent surrounds me and my heart flutters as he leans in, his lips hovering so close to mine I'm tempted to kiss him again.

But his sister's words replay in my mind. If Varys takes me as his true mate, he might never have a family or heirs. I do not want to be the one who takes this future from him. I want him to be sure that it's me that he wants. If I let things go too far, he might regret it later, and I do not want that. Things would be so much simpler if he were human or if I were Dark Elf.

I force myself to pull back. "What about you? What will you do now that I have Rhygar?"

He turns to the other wolf. With thick, gray and white fur, its reflective, green eyes meet mine briefly before it lowers its head marginally in what I recognize as a greeting. "This is Shynar. He was my father's, and now he has chosen me as his rider." He gestures to the fields around us. "Shall we?"

"It's still dark. Should we not wait until daylight so they might see better?"

"You are thinking of them as horses." Varys grins. "But dire wolves see best in the darkness."

He's right. I had not considered this. Giddiness rises within me at the thought of riding beneath the moonlight.

"You said dire wolves bond with their riders. How do I form the bond with Rhygar?"

Varys studies me. "For horses, they allow you to tame them, and then they are yours." He rests a hand on Rhygar's coat. "But for wolves, it is different. If you want him to give you his bond, you must run with him."

At first, we simply walk past the stables and out to the nearby field, letting me get a feel for riding alone on Rhygar.

Through my connection with him, he shows me how much he wishes to run. The thrill of this anticipation is contagious, and my heart is already pounding with excitement.

I rest a hand on his fur. "All right," I whisper. "I trust you. I'm ready."

Without warning, he breaks into a gallop. The wind whips through my hair and the world blurs around us as he races through the woods faster than lightning.

I hang on to his reins as we charge through the forest, and Rhygar releases a piercing howl of pure happiness and freedom.

Varys and Shynar catch up to us as we weave through the trees.

The thrill of excitement rushes through my limbs and expands my lungs. I cry out with joy as we gallop beneath the stars, faster than a racehorse.

I've never felt so alive as I do in this moment, with the crisp night air whistling past my ears. I lean forward in the saddle as the ground blurs beneath us and the moonlight bathes the world in a silver, ethereal glow.

Varys glances over, flashing a handsome smile that melts my heart. But as fast as Shynar is, Rhygar is faster, and we quickly pull away, charging through the enchanted woods.

Before we reach the edge of a ravine, Rhygar turns and races back toward the stables at breakneck speed. Varys and Shynar are almost even with us, but not quite, and I release another joyous whoop when we reach the stables before them.

Varys dismounts and walks over to me. He pats Rhygar's neck. "Thank you, my friend," he murmurs before reaching up to help me dismount.

His strong hands wrap around my waist, gently pulling me from my seat. I wrap my arms around his neck as he delicately lowers me from the saddle until my face is level with his. My feet are not quite on the ground when he pauses, holding me close. His vivid eyes peer deep into mine, and I lean in and brush my lips to his.

I trace my tongue along the seam of his lips, asking for entrance. When he opens his mouth, my tongue finds his, gentle and exploring. Pulling me close, he deepens our kiss, stealing the breath from my lungs.

A noise off to the side startles us both. Varys moves in a blur of motion, pulling me behind him, and a low growl rumbles in his chest. "Who is here? Reveal yourself," he commands. "Now."

A Dark Elf man steps out from the shadows. His gleaming, green eyes snap briefly to me before returning to Varys. He bows low. "My King."

"What are you doing here, Lord Dralyn?" Varys asks, not bothering to hide the irritation in his tone. "Is there something wrong that could not wait?"

He flashes a cold smile. "I merely sought you out to personally congratulate you on your new bonding."

Varys says nothing. His shoulders are tense as he regards this man a moment before speaking. "Inara, this is Lord Dralyn of the High Council, and Melina's father."

He bows even lower to me. "My Queen."

Although he offers me a polite smile, his words sound forced when he addresses me by my title and congratulates me, welcoming me to Ithylian.

CHAPTER 37

VARYS

Through the Khio'rinar, I can read my bondmate's unease at Dralyn's presence, but she hides it well, standing proudly while speaking to him in return.

When he leaves, she turns to me and whispers, "Friend or enemy?" as she gestures in the direction he left.

"Both," I reply grimly.

"My King. My Queen," Devyn says, approaching. "I have woven a barrier spell around this area that stretches back to the mountain."

I know he has done this to give us as much privacy as possible. Little does he know it is unnecessary. Inara and I will not be consummating our bond this night, but I thank him anyway for his thoughtfulness.

She loops her arm through mine, and we start back toward the area where the royal tent has been set up.

We are almost there when she stops abruptly, tugging lightly on my arm, and I stop.

"Is something wrong?" I ask in confusion.

"It's such a beautiful night." She gestures to the sky. "The moon is full, and the stars are bright. I was wondering if we could just stay out here a while longer before we go back under the mountain."

My heart clenches, for I realize how difficult it must be for her to live in such a place when she has always lived on the surface, in the open.

"Of course." I pause. "But we will not be returning to the mountain this night."

"Why not?"

"There is a tent waiting for us."

"A... tent?"

"Yes. It is customary for the newly bonded couple to spend their first night in the forest and earn the blessing of the Goddess."

I do not mention it is the Goddess of Fertility, because I know from the pink bloom of her cheeks that she already knows this. After all, it is a custom I have heard many humans recognize as well.

She guides me to a small clearing in the woods and releases my arm. I observe as she sits on the grass and then lies back. Her long, silken hair fans around her head like a beautiful halo as she smiles up at me.

Tilting my head down to regard her, hazel eyes meet mine, and my gaze drops to her full, perfect lips. "Lie down," she says softly.

As I lie beside her, the thick blanket of grass is soft and spongy beneath me from the almost-constant rains of the past few weeks.

"When I was younger, we used to gaze at the stars with our mother," she says, staring up at the night sky. "We would search for patterns in the sky and make up stories about what we saw." A wistful smile touches her lips.

"Right there." She gestures to a cluster of stars in the northern sky. "That pattern was my favorite."

"Where?"

She moves closer to me, so close I can smell the soft floral scent of her hair and feel the warmth radiating from her body to mine.

"Just there." She points, turning her head slightly toward me.

The smell of the surrounding forest is earthy and damp, and the soft mint of her breath fans across my face with the cool night breeze. My skin begins to heat.

"Do you see it?" she asks.

I force myself to focus, blinking several times, unsure if what I see in the pattern is the same as her. "They are in the shape of a man—an Elf judging by the stars that make up the pointed tips of the ears."

"Yes," she replies with a smile that stops my heart momentarily.

I swallow nervously.

My people rarely smile fully, as humans do. At first, I thought it strange how outwardly expressive they are. Every emotion is clearly written across their features when they speak or interact with another. However, as I spend more time with Inara, I find myself completely enthralled every time she smiles. I am captivated by my bondmate.

"Did you ever do this with your parents?"

"Yes." I close my eyes against the beautiful, but painful, memories. "We would often gaze at the stars when we visited the summer home near the ruins of Elysarin."

The smile fades from her lips and she takes my hand, squeezing it gently. "I'm sorry, Varys. I know how hard it is to lose your parents."

I think of how fortunate I was to have had my parents

for so long, whereas Inara's mother was killed when she was a child, and her father died only a few years after that.

"Thank you," I whisper. "My soul grieves with yours."

Inara squeezes my hand. "And my soul grieves with yours."

She turns to me, and I notice the tears she struggles to blink back. "What a beautiful saying. I've always hated hearing the words 'I'm sorry' when it comes to grief," she says quietly. "It sounds so... inadequate for such a great loss."

I nod.

Silence settles in the space between us, and I am struck by how it is neither uncomfortable nor awkward.

"I did not thank you for tonight." Her eyes twinkle with pleasure. "Racing across the fields... it was wonderful. It reminded me of home."

"I am glad." I smirk and arch a teasing brow. "But next time, I will not allow you to win."

Her jaw drops. "You did not *allow* me to do anything. Rhygar and I were much faster than you and Shynar, and you know it."

I try, but fail, to suppress the smile tugging wider at my lips. "Of course you won. You are a much smaller rider. Rhygar can run like the wind when he carries very little on his back."

She laughs, playfully hitting at my shoulder. "You are just jealous that I beat you."

"Have you not heard? Dark Elves consider it poor form for a male to beat his bondmate at a race, game, or contest." I turn my nose up arrogantly. "He is taught to always allow her to win."

Her eyes widen. "Wait. What? Is that true?"

A chuckle escapes me, and she lightly hits at my

shoulder again, laughing loudly. "You almost had me for a moment. I thought you were serious."

Warmth fills me at the sound of her beautiful laughter. I love this sound, and I resolve to do all I can to coax it from her more often.

Her dazzling, hazel eyes meet mine. "You're very hand-some when you smile, you know." She gently nudges me. "You should do it more often."

"We are taught to hide our emotions," I explain. "Dark Elves rarely smile like humans do."

"Then reserve yours for me," she whispers. "Whenever we're alone, you can smile fully, and you can express all the emotion you would normally hide."

Her words touch me. Deeply. I cannot remember the last time I allowed anyone to see me fully unguarded, as she is suggesting. It means so much that I can trust her so completely. Even my own siblings have not seen this side of me. Since I became king, I have had to be strong for my family.

Trust has never been easy for me. As crown prince and then king I have always had to be careful. Everyone wants to be in the good graces of their king, but not all of them have pure intentions.

I squeeze her hand, still in mine. "I desire honesty and openness between us, and I am glad you feel the same."

CHAPTER 38

INARA

As the night wears on, the air grows colder. I move closer to my new husband, and he wraps an arm around my waist, pulling me close to his side. "We should go in," he murmurs. "It is too cold for you out here."

I want to enjoy the open sky a bit longer. "Not yet."

My thoughts turn back to the prophecy and how the priestess made a point of calling me the sanishon queen, during our ceremony. I tip my head up to look at Varys. "If the prophecy is true, it is a bad thing for us?"

I've asked him before, but it still worries me.

His lips form a tight, thin line before he responds. "It may be dangerous."

"Why?"

"To herald in the era of peace, the Great Uniters are called upon to make a great sacrifice."

A shiver runs down my spine. "What kind of sacrifice?"

"I do not know. As with all the writings of the Lythyrians, they are vague and open to many different interpretations. They simply say that it will be a great sacrifice that will stop those who seek to control the darkness."

He gently nuzzles the top of my head, and my heart flutters at this romantic gesture.

"You do not need to worry about this," he murmurs. "It is said the Great Uniters possess magic and great powers. So, it cannot be you. You are human; you do not have magic."

I still as guilt wars with fear deep inside me. Varys does not know my secret, and now that I have kept it from him, I am not sure how to tell him I've lied from the moment we met.

He caresses my chin and tilts my face up to his. "You are not alone here, Inara. I am yours, and I will keep you safe."

His gaze holds mine, and I am reminded once more of how easily I could lose my heart to this man—my Dark Elf King. But I know I must not. He is not truly meant to be mine... not if he wants a family and heirs.

"Your eyes." He studies me intensely. "They were brown a moment ago, but now they are green with a change in the angle of the light."

"Human eyes are so dull compared to those of your people. And mine are strange. They—"

"No," he murmurs. "I meant it when I said that I think they are lovely. As are you, my human wife."

I lift my gaze to his. He is so close, and I want so much to kiss him. He cups my cheek as his eyes search mine, and I realize he is waiting... allowing me to choose. He is my first. I have not kissed anyone else. An eternity stretches between each beat of my heart as it wins the war against my mind. I lean in and gently brush my lips to his.

His powerful arms encircle me, pulling me so close that

I can feel his heart beating against mine as my body molds to his. A low growl rumbles deep in his throat. In one swift motion, he rolls me beneath him. Desire burns in my veins, and I run my fingers through his hair until I reach his ears, tracing my fingers lightly over their slender, pointed tips.

He inhales sharply and pulls back.

"What is it?" I ask, worried I've done something wrong.

"My ears," he says. "They are... sensitive."

"Did I hurt you?"

One side of his mouth lifts. "Quite the opposite, actually."

"Oh." My face heats. "I did not realize—"

"It is all right," he utters breathlessly.

I shiver as the cold wind picks up. Varys lifts his gaze to the sky. "It will rain soon. We should go to our tent."

He stands, pulling me up with him. I reach up and touch my lips, finding them slightly swollen from our kisses.

Varys extends his arm, and I take it, allowing him to guide me to our tent. My pulse quickens as we enter. I'm surprised by how lavishly furnished it is. A bed sits in one corner, piled high with white fur blankets. A divider hides a tub in another corner.

I cannot deny that I am falling for him. But another part of me knows I must protect my heart. He may decide he does not want me, since I am human. He may decide to choose a Dark Elf mistress like his grandfather. I know he said his people mate for life, but... if I were to give myself to him, and then he took a mistress, I'm sure my heart would not recover.

It is good that we stopped when we did earlier... before we did something either of us might have regretted later.

When I finish bathing, I step from the tub and find a pale green sleep gown hanging where my dress had been. I pull it off the divider and slip into it. The material is smooth and finer than silk. As I move around the divider, Varys is standing by the bed. His gaze travels over me before his eyes settle on mine, desire easily read in his features.

CHAPTER 39

VARYS

When Inara steps from behind the divider, I long to pull her into my arms. Her long, golden hair tumbles down her back in glossy waves. Her silken sleep gown only reaches mid-thigh and is held up by two small straps over her shoulders. It leaves nothing to the imagination, and I struggle to suppress a rumble of arousal as my gaze travels over her.

She tucks a stray tendril of damp hair behind her ear, and through the Khio'rinar, I can sense she is just as nervous as I am. But beneath that, I sense something else.

Closing my eyes briefly, I focus on it. There is a warmth to her emotions regarding me, suggesting I am not alone in the growing feelings between us. She is falling for me just as I am falling for her. But I also sense a hesitance that gives me pause. She desires me but holds back because she is unsure about something.

I desire her, but I will not push her to give me more

than she is willing to give. We have time. There is no reason to rush what we have between us. And I will do whatever it takes to prove myself worthy of her affections, so that she will choose me as her true mate, just as I long to choose her.

CHAPTER 40

INARA

Varys lies down beside me, settling under the fur blankets. Despite them, I'm still freezing, and a small shiver runs through me.

"You are cold." He turns to me. "Come here."

"I—" I start to deny it but stop.

Nervous and flustered, I slowly scoot toward him. He loops his muscular arm around my waist, and I make a small squeak of surprise as he pulls me the rest of the way, tucking me into his chest.

I forget my embarrassment as the heat of his body radiates to mine. "You're so warm."

He tucks my feet between his calves and does a full body shiver. "And you are completely frozen, my mate," he gently teases. He pulls back just enough to arch a brow at me. "Would you really have stayed on your side of the bed, even in the cold, just because you are embarrassed to be near me?"

"Of course not," I huff in mock frustration. "And I am not embarrassed."

In truth I was, but I do not tell him this. Instead, I snuggle closer because he's right—my entire body feels like a block of ice. He shivers again, and I laugh softly against his chest.

"You find my discomfort amusing?"

I flash a warm smile. "Everyone knows a good husband *always* sacrifices his own comfort for his wife."

He arches a teasing brow. "That must be a human saying."

I laugh even harder.

We joke back and forth a bit before I begin to drift off. I curl closer to his chest, enjoying the feel of his arms around me. As I slowly fall asleep, sadness creeps over me. I'm going to miss this closeness between us if he takes another as his true mate. But at least I'll have this for a little while.

CHAPTER 41

VARYS

I lie awake as Inara sleeps. My protective instincts flare brightly, and I tighten my arms around her delicate form. Perhaps it is because she is smaller than a Dark Elf woman that this instinct is so strong.

I doubt I'll get any sleep this night as my every muscle is tense, wanting to remain alert to watch over her. I sigh heavily, trying to force myself to relax. We are in no danger here. I know Devyn and a few of my other guards are patrolling nearby. Occasionally, I catch their scent on the wind as it moves through our tent.

I curse as Inara shivers again. I should have forgone the tradition of sleeping outside, especially this time of year. Humans are more sensitive to temperature changes than my kind, and I should have considered this when the priestess insisted we uphold this ritual.

Part of me agreed because I wish to have the favor of the Goddess. I want to please her in the hope she might someday bless us with a family. I have not spoken to Inara of this, but our relationship is still so new. Even so... as I gaze down at my human mate, I realize just how far gone I am.

I did not expect to bond to, much less to fall in love with a human, but it is already done, and I cannot change what is. Nor would I wish to. Inara is intelligent, brave, kind, and beautiful—all the qualities I would have looked for in a Dark Elf mate. That she is human only worries me because of how fragile they seem compared to my people.

I am proud of the surprise I have ready for her tomorrow and believe it will be something she enjoys. She is happy with Rhygar, and I am glad that he agreed to choose her. I trust him completely to take care of my bride.

Even when they raced, I noticed how he was very careful when he made the turn around the tree at the edge of the forest. He was mindful of her and kept his movements smooth to reduce the risk of a fall. She may be experienced in horse riding, but dire wolves are an entirely different thing.

It usually takes a rider several days before they become comfortable with a dire wolf, and for the dire wolf to become accustomed to their chosen rider. But she and Rhygar seem to have already developed a deep, mutual trust, and I am grateful.

Trust. I consider this word as I recall the hesitation I sensed through our bond earlier. It is as if Inara is keeping something from me... holding something back, but I do not know what.

Perhaps it is nothing, and I am simply on edge. Although we are in Ithylian, I cannot still the worry inside me that something is wrong. I think back on the Wraith attack. If it were an isolated incident, I would not be so concerned. But there are reports of them along our borders and that of the Fae.

Because of our magic, my men and I should have drawn their attention, not Inara. I gaze down at her sleeping form. The sanishon spoken of in the ancient tomes of the Lythyrian is said to possess great power. If she had this sort of magic, her brother would never have agreed to our marriage. Of this, I am certain.

The Wraith wanted Inara, and I do not understand why. All I know is that I will do whatever it takes to make sure she is safe.

CHAPTER 42

INARA

When I wake in the morning, I'm wrapped up in Varys's arms. I lift my head to find his eyes still closed in sleep. Contentment rolls through me as I study him. His normally perfect hair is mussed. With his face completely relaxed as he slumbers, the harsh lines of his features are softened, and I imagine this must be how he appeared before he took the throne.

I remember how much my own brother, Edmynd, seemed to age after my father's death. The burden of rule weighs heavy and is definitely not for the faint-hearted.

My gaze drifts to his ears, and I'm struck again with an irrational desire to touch their elegantly pointed tips, but I refrain when I remember that he said they are sensitive.

"Why are you staring at me?" he asks. His voice is rough with sleep and his eyes still closed.

"I was looking at your ears." I laugh softly. "How do you always know?"

His eyelids peel open, and he looks amused. "It is a

secret." He cocks his head to the side. "What is your fascination with my ears?"

"I don't know," I admit. "I just… like them."

He frowns. "Mine in particular, or… any Dark Elf's?"

"Just yours, my Dark Elf husband." I grin as I reassure him.

His cheeks turn a darker shade of gray blue. "Good. It would not do to have the queen of Ithylian staring at every Dark Elf's ears that she comes across." A teasing smirk plays on his lips. "People might begin to talk, you know."

I laugh, appreciating his teasing nature.

We take turns getting dressed behind the divider, then leave the tent, stepping out onto soft green grass. The heart-shaped leaves on the beautiful purple trees rustle gently in the cool breeze. I step into a patch of sunlight filtering through the thick canopy and tilt my face up to the sun. Closing my eyes, I spread my arms wide, reveling in the warmth upon my skin. When I open them again, I find Varys studying me curiously.

"After being underground, I feel like I've taken the sun for granted all my life," I explain. "I've decided to appreciate it when I can."

He takes my hand. "I am sorry our home is in the mountain. I—"

"You do not have to apologize, Varys. I will get used to it. It is not a terrible hardship, my dear husband."

"Now that you know how to leave the mountain, you can visit the surface as often as you wish."

His words fill my heart with warmth because I know he means them. This may not be the marriage either of us was expecting, but he makes every effort for my happiness. That is as good a start as any two people can hope for.

"But you must make certain I am with you before you do, my Queen," Devyn adds, emerging from the shadows.

His sudden appearance startles me, but I quickly recover. "I will, Devyn." Smirking, I continue. "I hope you enjoy the sun, because you will be seeing much of it."

He grins. "Fortunately, I do, my Queen."

Varys guides me back in the direction of the surface stables, and I notice another building in the distance that I couldn't see in the dark. "Are we going riding again today?" I ask, excitement already building inside me.

"Perhaps later, but first, I have another surprise I hope you enjoy."

"What is it?"

"Do you truly wish to know?" His lips twitch in amusement. "Or would you prefer to be surprised?"

I laugh softly. "Surprised."

He loves to surprise me, and I love how he goes out of his way to make me feel cherished and important.

As we draw closer to the stables, I notice more details about the surrounding fields that I had missed last night in the dark. Several Dark Elf warriors spar, swords clanging in the distance. On the far side are a dozen targets set up for archery. Anticipation fills me. I love archery and am desperate to get hold of a bow and quiver.

His guards pause momentarily, staring curiously at me when we pass. They do not bow though, suggesting Varys must come here often to train among his people like my brothers do back home. It's confirmed a moment later when another Elf approaches. "Would you like to spar today, my King?"

"Another time." He gestures to the man. "This is Tamlyn. He is in charge of the armory."

Tamlyn bows low to me. "My Queen."

"Today the queen and I will practice archery. Could you fetch her a bow and quiver?"

His lavender eyes snap to me, surprise flashing behind

JESSICA GRAYSON

them. "I thought humans did not train their women in self-defense."

"Inara is a Dark Elf Queen, Tamlyn," Varys says, his expression hard. "She will train as one of our people."

All the color drains from Tamlyn's face. "Forgive me." He bows low again. "I meant no offense. I will fetch your weapons immediately."

He scurries off toward a smaller building in the distance as Varys leads me to the archery field. Tamlyn returns quickly with a quiver full of arrows and three bows, each a different size. "I was not sure which you might prefer," he says, holding them out to me.

I take each one, pulling back on the string to test the feel and weight of it. I pick the smallest one and hand back the other two.

Nocking an arrow into the string, I breathe in through my nose and out through my mouth, counting the space between each heartbeat. The world falls away as I focus on my target. This is what I love most about archery. Everything else fades into the background except for the slow inhale and exhale of each breath and the steady beat of my heart.

I exhale and let my arrow fly, watching in satisfaction as it hits the mark directly in the center of the target. I draw another one and quickly aim at the target beside it with the same effect, hitting the next four in quick succession before turning back to Varys.

My cheeks flush when I notice everyone gathered behind us, observing with gaping mouths. Normally, I would feel self-conscious with so much attention, but instead, pride suffuses me when I look at Varys and find respect and admiration shining in his eyes. I gesture to the bow. "It is a good design."

"You are a warrior," Devyn murmurs in awe.

"Indeed," Varys replies as a devastatingly handsome smile curves his mouth.

Warmth fills me as his gaze holds mine, and I sigh heavily. Gods help me, my Dark Elf King husband has already stolen my heart.

CHAPTER 43

INARA

In the two weeks since our bonding ceremony, we have not kissed again, but I know it is because he is honoring his vow. He swore he would not touch me until I asked. And I want so much to ask, but I know I should not. Especially when I think of my conversation with his sister.

Each night we share a bed. He holds me as we sleep, and I love drifting off with his arms securely wrapped around me. My new husband and I exist in this strange space I refer to as "the in-between." We are friends, but our relationship is so much more.

It would be so easy to give myself to him... to love him and let him love me. I have no experience with love, but I recognize it in the way he smiles at me, the thoughtful things he does to make me comfortable, how he includes me in every decision, and his rapt attention when I speak.

But I cannot surrender my heart to this man—not completely, anyway. Not if I expect to survive if he starts a family with someone else. Many times I have tried to broach the subject with him, but each time I cannot do it. Just as I cannot bring myself to tell him my secret.

Every day, Varys takes me to the surface to train. I love archery, but he insists I learn the sword as well. Raiden always refused, no matter how often I asked. He worried he would hurt me. I must admit, however, that I am concerned about accidentally injuring my husband. Swords are sharp, and it is all too easy to inflict damage upon someone without meaning to.

As we walk toward the armory, a small patch of nylweed catches my eye. I hold back a large sigh of relief that I've managed to locate some nearby. I found three small plants last week, but they seem to be few and far between in Ithylian. I lean down to pluck some, but Varys calls out, halting me. "Be careful with that."

I whip my head toward him. "Why? It is just nylweed, is it not?"

"Nylweed? Is that what your people call it?"

I nod.

"Here, we call it Elfbane. It is a deadly poison." He scowls. "I'm surprised to see it growing here. Usually, the groundskeeper kills any that he finds."

I want so much to tell him the truth, but the words will not come. Determination fills me. I have to tell him. I cannot keep this secret any longer. "Varys, I—"

"Tamlyn!" Varys calls out.

Tamlyn rushes over and Varys points to the nylweed. "Please make sure the groundskeeper does a thorough sweep of these fields and the surrounding forest. This should not be here."

He inclines his head. "Of course, my King."

Varys snaps his fingers and the nylweed bursts into

flame, burning the plant to ash before green grass covers the spot once more, as if it were never there.

I bite my lip in consternation. I understand now why it is so hard to find. Apparently, it's dangerous for Dark Elves.

I have to tell him.

But as I glance at all the warriors nearby, I do not wish to do it here. I'll wait until we are alone before I reveal my dark secret. For now, I'll push down my worry and enjoy the day.

As we stroll through the armory, I admire the craftsmanship of the Elves. Each weapon is a thing of fierce and terrible beauty. The bows are crafted of rich, dark wood and the swords and shields of silver metal, polished to perfection and etched with gorgeous and intricate designs.

I'm admiring one of the bows when a sudden rush of wind buffets me. I lift my head, startled at first before realizing it's Varys. I puff out a breath. "Thank goodness it's just you."

"Just me?" He arches a brow.

I huff in mock frustration. "You Elves and your inhuman speed."

A handsome smile lights his face before his expression becomes serious again. "I have something for you."

"What is it?"

Only now do I notice he has one hand behind his back. I try to peer around him, but he turns so I cannot. "Do I have to guess? Or are you going to show me?"

"Close your eyes and hold out your hands."

Tipping up my chin, I squeeze my eyelids shut, trying, but failing, to suppress a grin of anticipation. So far, every surprise he has given me has been wonderful, and I cannot wait to know what this new one is.

He places a large package in my hands. I open my eyes

and eagerly tear into the wrapping to find a beautiful bow made of rich, polished wood, carved with an intricate pattern of vines with heart-shaped leaves and tiny flowers. I pull back on the string, testing the weight and balance, and study the lovely weapon in complete awe.

"Does it please you?" he asks, with a touch of anxiety in his eyes.

"It's perfect, Varys." I'm practically beaming with joy. "I love it."

A gorgeous smile breaks across his face. "I am glad. Now, let us begin our lessons." He hands me a wooden staff. "We will train with this until you are comfortable, then we will move on to swords."

"What about my new bow?" I ask, unable to hide my disappointment. I was already looking forward to practicing with it.

"Your skill with a bow and arrow is not in doubt, my Khio'ri. We will practice archery after this."

I did tell him I wanted to learn everything I could about defending myself, so I suppose this is reasonable. I glance down at the staff in my hand, relieved we're not going to be using anything sharp just yet.

Raiden never finished training me. He refused to keep up with my sparring lessons after I got injured once, worried that I would get hurt more severely if we continued.

Varys demonstrates the best way to position my grip on the staff, and I mimic his movements through the various stances.

When he spars with Tamlyn, I'm in complete awe as he moves with a fluid and lethal grace. His motions are as mesmerizing as they are deadly. He is shirtless, and as the muscles flex beneath his skin with each movement, I admire the sheer masculine strength of his form.

He successfully disarms Tamlyn, sweeping his staff out to catch the back of his ankle and dropping him to the ground in one fell swoop. Afterward, he extends his hand to help Tamlyn back up, and they bow respectfully to each other, not as king and guard, but as fellow warriors.

It is obvious, from the way they watch and treat him, that Varys has the respect of his warriors.

"He's showing off for you, you know." I recognize Aryl's voice. He walks over, and sits beside me in the grass. "He has always been a show-off when it comes to sparring."

"Is that so?" I ask, curious to hear what else he has to say. Aryl is always making me laugh. He reminds me so much of Raiden.

"Yes, it's so." He leans in and whispers conspiratorially. "I could best him, you know, but I do not wish to wound his pride in front of his bondmate."

I laugh out loud at the sly quirk of his lips.

Varys whips his head toward us. "You know I can best you any day," he challenges, having obviously overheard his brother.

Aryl tips his head toward me. "You see? He's obviously delusional, but"—he shrugs—"he is my brother, and I suppose it is best to simply humor him."

I laugh even louder as Varys growls in response.

"Come over here and prove it, then," Varys challenges him.

Aryl grins and stalks toward him, taking an offered staff from Devyn.

Without hesitation, they begin. Their movements are so quick I can barely register them. I watch in awe as they circle each other in a deadly dance of sheer power and preternatural grace.

At first, I believe they are evenly matched until I notice Aryl breathing heavily with exertion. His movements slow somewhat as he begins to tire. Varys sweeps the staff out in an arc, hooking it behind Aryl's knee. Before he even hits the ground, Varys is over him, staff to his throat. "Do you yield?"

"Yes," Aryl shouts dramatically. "Gods, yes!"

A grin tugs at Varys's mouth as he offers Aryl his hand, pulling his brother up beside him.

Aryl makes a great show of dusting off his pants and rolling his eyes. "You did not have to be so vicious, you know. I was only teasing."

"Yes," Varys grumbles. "But you were making me sound weak in front of my Khio'ri."

Khio'ri. The word fills me with warmth, and I bite my lower lip as I watch him bantering with his brother. When he turns to me, his intense, blue eyes meet mine, and I cannot help the smile that lights my face in response.

I find myself blushing more often around my new husband. And when his cheeks and the tips of his ears turn a shade darker, my smile deepens because he is blushing, as well.

"Come." He motions to me. "We will practice some more."

I push myself up and walk toward him. Aryl hands me his staff, rolling his eyes once more at Varys before he leaves to watch from the sidelines. I'm nervous when I realize everyone is observing us, especially since I have not really done this before. This isn't like archery. I'm a novice at this, at best, not an expert.

Varys's expression softens, and I feel a strange warmth seep through my chest like a soothing balm to calm my nerves. I put a hand over my heart. Ever since our bonding ceremony, the connection between us has grown much stronger. "Is that you?"

"Yes." He flashes a handsome smile. "Is that better?"

"Much."

I glance back at the others watching us. "Maybe we should do this in private."

"You must never hide from your warriors, for they are the ones you will depend upon in the heat of battle. It is important you know each other's strengths and weaknesses."

That makes sense.

"All right"—I give him a playful grin—"but I'm pretty sure this is going to be a whole lot of weakness on my part... for a while, at least."

He laughs heartily, and I realize it is one of the few times I've heard him do this without restraint. "I love your laugh." The words escape my lips before I realize I've said them aloud.

His cheeks and tips of his ears turn dark blue. "Then I shall endeavor to do it more often."

"Good." I grin. My expression sobers when I look down at my staff. "Where shall we begin?"

He guides me through several more motions before we try a sparring match. I have witnessed how quickly he moves, and I know he is holding back so he can teach me, but I like a challenge. "Don't hold back," I tell him. "I need to know what this would be like if I were actually being attacked."

He appears ready to protest, but I interrupt. "Please, Varys. An enemy would not go easy on me."

After a moment, he agrees, his expression grim. "As you wish."

I am glad that no one seems to be watching us now. Most of the guards are too busy sparring with each other to notice what we are doing.

Breathless and panting, we circle each other. When I notice an opening, I charge toward him. At the last second,

JESSICA GRAYSON

I drop to one knee and sweep out my staff, catching the back of Varys's knee, making him stumble forward. Horrified that I nearly made him fall, I stare at my staff in shock. The last thing I want to do is hurt him.

He takes advantage of my hesitation. Lightning fast, he grabs me from behind, disarms me, and captures me in a defensive hold. His arm is banded around my waist and his other hand is holding my neck and chin, my back pressed firmly to his front.

"Never underestimate your opponent," he says. "Do not give them any opening to disarm you." So close to him like this, I take in his masculine scent as his lips graze the shell of my ear. "The secret is to never surrender. Remember that."

Oh, but I want to surrender right now in his arms as the sound of his rich, warm voice sends a pulse of desire straight through me. The muscles tighten in the pit of my stomach as I lean my head back against the solid wall of his heavily muscled chest.

He lowers his head to the curve of my neck and shoulder. A warm puff of air hits my skin as he scents me. "You can do this," he whispers. "Remember what I taught you."

I manage to break free of his hold, and we continue our sparring.

He moves in a blur of motion so fast, I barely even register his staff catching the back of my ankle. My own staff pops free of my hands, and I watch it tumbling toward the ground as the world falls out from under me. I land hard with an audible thud and the air explodes from my lungs.

He's over me immediately, his glowing eyes staring down at me in concern as I struggle to catch my breath. "Inara? Are you all right?"

Still fighting to breathe, I cannot answer.

252

He pulls me into his arms, cradling me to his chest, and brushes the hair back from my face. "Please, say something."

"Something," I wheeze.

He stills and blinks down at me in confusion.

A smile curves my mouth, and he huffs out a laugh as he hugs me even tighter. "Thank the gods. I swear... your teasing is just as bad as my brother's."

Aryl laughs in the distance.

"Again?" I arch a brow in challenge.

"Not today, my Khio'ri. My heart can only take so much. We can try again tomorrow."

Happiness blooms in my chest as he hugs me close once more. He smooths a hand down my hair and drops a warm kiss to my forehead. "I was so afraid I hurt you, my brave human wife."

"I'm fine," I reassure him when I am anything but. If I thought I was falling for him before, this entire moment just sealed it for me. It hasn't been very long, but already I'm in love with my Dark Elf husband... despite my attempts to take things slowly.

Sadness fills me as I think about his sister's words. How long will it be before he decides he wants a family?

One he cannot have with me.

If I'm eventually going to have to let him go, we cannot stay as we are. I have to protect my heart. Starting tonight...

CHAPTER 44

VARYS

As I dress in the cleansing room, my thoughts turn to our lessons. At first, I was worried that Inara's smaller size made her weak. But she uses it to her advantage, forcing my center of gravity to shift in a way that challenges everything I know. I am pleased. My wife has the heart and mind of a warrior.

When I step into the bedroom, I find Inara sitting on the edge of the bed, a pensive look on her face. It stops me short as a maelstrom of emotions flood the bond. "What is wrong?"

"I... think it might be best if I sleep in a different room."

My heart stops. "I—" I am uncertain how to respond. "Have I offended you in some way? Made you... uncomfortable?"

"No, Varys. Not at all," she denies. "I just thought you might like... space."

Something—an emotion I cannot quite discern—flares across the Khio'rinar. "Why would you think this?"

"Because I… am not a proper wife to you."

Is that what worries her? Does she think I am growing impatient waiting for her to decide to go further with our relationship? If that's what this is, I need her to understand it isn't true. "It does not matter." I take her hand in mine and place a tender kiss to the back of her knuckles. "I love simply sleeping beside you each night."

Her hazel eyes search mine as if gauging whether I am speaking truth.

I continue. "I sleep better with you than I ever did without."

"Truly?"

"Truly, my Khio'ri."

She lies down and I slip beneath the covers beside her. I hook my arm around her, tugging her back against me. When she molds herself to my body, I gently nuzzle her hair, breathing deeply of her delicate scent. Inara is mine. It matters not that we haven't consummated our bond. She is my bondmate and wife; nothing could ever change that for me. And as we drift off to sleep, I vow that I will do everything I can to reassure her of this.

When morning comes, I am called away to a meeting. I wish I could go with Inara to the surface, but the Fae king is visiting and has requested to speak with me directly.

Inara leaves with Devyn to go practice her archery while I follow Melina to the throne room.

"How long ago did he arrive?"

"Less than half an hour ago, but he is most anxious to speak with you." She pauses. "He has the look of a man with many troubles on his mind."

This is worrisome news. "Did he give any indication what his visit is about?"

"No, he did not."

When we reach the throne room, I find King Kyven pacing back and forth before the throne, his lavender wings fluttering in agitation as he rakes a hand through his short, silver-white hair. I turn to Melina. "Leave us."

As soon as the door closes behind her, I approach Kyven. "What is wrong, my friend?"

He is a new king—a young king. His father and older brother died recently, leaving him to take the throne.

I understand what it is to have such a burden thrust upon one earlier than expected. It is not an easy thing to bear. Kyven and I have always been close, but this shared experience brought us even closer.

"More Wraiths have been seen along the borders," he says grimly. "They test our defenses, trying to weaken the Veil so they may cross."

Worry gnaws deep in my gut. "How many?"

"More than one is enough, is it not?" he asks. "How are they escaping over the Great Wall unnoticed?"

I frown as I face an uncomfortable truth that has been spinning in my mind ever since the Wraith attack with Inara. "They could not. It is impossible."

"My thoughts exactly." His violet eyes flash to mine. "Someone is behind this."

"Yes, but who?"

"Humans," he grumbles. "It must be. They are the only ones who would be less of a target for them because of their lack of magic."

"I... am not so sure about that," I add, recalling how they targeted Inara, ignoring me and my own men to get to her.

"What do you mean?"

I straighten. "I am unsure if word has reached you yet, but I have taken a human bride—the princess of Florin."

He inhales sharply and something akin to worry flits across his expression before he regains his composure. "Which one?"

"Princess Inara."

I observe curiously as his posture relaxes. "Have you... met her before?"

"Not Inara."

Then he has met her sister, Grayce.

He studies me a moment, as if trying to decide something before he finally speaks. "I had planned on asking Princess Grayce for her hand to create a permanent alliance between our people. But with the increased Wraith attacks along our borders, and my growing suspicion about the humans, I am not sure it is wise."

"Wraiths attacked my bondmate and me when I first brought her back to Ithylian. We were at the Veil when they came for us. But a strange thing happened." I hesitate, not sure I should tell him, but then decide if I cannot be honest with him, our friendship is not as strong as I believe. "They attacked Inara, practically ignoring me and my men."

He blinks several times. "They went after a *human* over beings with inherent magic?"

I nod, as puzzled by this fact as Kyven.

"But that is contrary to their nature. Why would they do this?"

"I do not know, but it worries me," I admit. "Humans are fragile, compared to our kind, and the thought of anything happening to her is terrifying."

A faint smile crests his lips. "Then it is love for you, isn't it, my friend?"

"Yes," I answer immediately. "It is. And despite what you

may believe, I do not think the humans are behind the Wraith attacks. If they were, they certainly would not have allowed them to target one of their own."

"This is true," he agrees. "But, if not the humans, then who?"

"The Orcs and the Wolf Shifters hate the Wraiths as much as we do. And the Dragons... they would never ally with those creatures."

"Will you ask him?"

By "him," I understand he means King Aurdyn—the great Dragon King in the north.

"Are you still not on speaking terms with him?"

"He *threatened* to burn down my castle." Kyven gives me an incredulous look. "Am I supposed to simply forget about that?"

"You know he did not mean it." I refrain from smiling. "He was merely upset. You know he has a terrible temper."

"Yes, but threatening to burn one's home is rather serious, don't you agree?"

I try, but fail, to suppress a laugh.

"Oh," he says exaggeratedly. "You find this funny, do you? Well, I am sure *you* would have been upset if he'd threatened to burn down *your* home."

I cross my arms over my chest and give Kyven a pointed look. "You know you will have to reconcile with him some day, right?"

He drags a hand roughly through his short, white hair. "Yes, I do, but that day is not today." He pauses, visibly stewing. "Will you request a meeting with him to speak about the Wraith attacks? See if he knows anything?"

With difficulty, I manage to not roll my eyes. "Fine. I will. On one condition."

"What is that?"

JESSICA GRAYSON

"If you decide to marry my mate's sister, you must invite us to the ceremony."

Something akin to sadness flits briefly across his expression, but it is gone too quickly for me to be sure. "If she will even have me." He cocks his head. "Tell me: how did you end up bound to a human, my friend?"

I clear my throat, then relay the story of my human wedding and how important it was to Inara that her sister be present to see us wed. When I tell him how protective Inara's siblings were, and how Grayce even offered herself to me in Inara's stead, his jaw drops.

"She did?"

"Yes. She loves her sister," I stress. "Apparently, it is some sort of human tradition to offer the eldest for marriage first. But Grayce is not my Khio'ri. Inara is."

"You are blessed," he says, and something in his defeated tone gives me pause. "Inara could have just as easily refused you."

"I know."

He clenches his jaw. "I fear her sister will refuse my offer of marriage."

"Why would she when it would be advantageous for them to ally with your kingdom?"

"I did something foolish."

My head jerks back. "What did you do?"

"You must never tell anyone what I am about to reveal."

"What is it?"

"Swear you will keep what I am about to tell you a secret." He holds out his hand. "Promise me."

Reluctantly, I offer my hand. Magic swirls around our joined hands as the promising spell is woven. I wave him on when it is done. "Continue."

He sighs heavily. "I lied to her about who I was."

"*What?*"

"Before my father and brother died, my father was thinking of negotiating a marriage between me and Princess Inara."

Fierce possessiveness floods my veins. I bristle slightly at his words, then force myself to relax. This was before I even met her.

"Inara was the youngest, so my father thought the humans would be more likely to give her to me—a second son," he explains. "Things had been so tense between our kingdoms, my father doubted they'd let Princess Grayce marry my brother."

He begins pacing back and forth again, as he often does when he is anxious. I wait patiently for him to continue.

"So, I snuck across the border, disguising myself with a glamour so I appeared human."

"How did you manage *that*?" I'm shocked he was able to do this. "Magic does not work in the human kingdoms."

"Glamours do," he replies. "At least… this one did." He sighs. "I wanted only to get a glimpse of Inara. To glean whatever information I could about my potential human mate before agreeing to my father's idea. Instead… I saw Grayce."

"And what happened?"

"The fated bond," he says, and my mouth drops. "She is my fated one, Varys, but she does not know this." He swallows thickly. "I got close to her. We—" He stops short, and huffs out a frustrated breath. "I had to leave her when I received word my father had died in battle. My older brother was wounded, and I had to return immediately."

He drops his head into his hands. "I left her without so much as a goodbye, Varys. If she ever finds out that it was me in disguise, she will hate me."

"What will you do?"

"The only thing I can." He gives me a defeated look. "I

cannot live without her. I will ask for her hand and pray she does not recognize me from before."

"And if she does?"

"I don't know." His wings flutter agitatedly. "Tell me, my friend. I have always valued your counsel. What should I do?"

"I wish I could say. But I do not know what even *I* would do in such a situation."

The sound of the doors opening draws my attention, and I turn to find Inara walking toward us. I smile as she moves to my side. "I'm sorry to interrupt," she says, looking between us both. "But as soon as I found out the Fae king was here, I wanted to meet you."

Kyven bows low. "It is an honor to meet you, Queen Inara."

She smiles warmly at him, and it takes everything inside me to suppress a growl.

Kyven, like all Fae, is very handsome, and although my jealousy is irrational, I cannot help it. It is instinct for my kind to be possessive of our mates, even more since our bond has not been consummated and she does not yet carry my mark.

"It is lovely to meet you as well," she replies.

When he takes her hand and kisses the back of her knuckles, my lips curl up in a snarl and I bare my fangs.

Kyven's eyes widen as they meet mine before darting to her neck, searching for my mark. I know the moment he realizes it is not there, because he all but drops her hand and quickly steps back.

He understands I do not do this because I actually consider him a threat. It is merely instinct. His people experience the same thing. Inara, however, appears to not notice the slight tension between us, and I am relieved.

After Kyven explains the reason for his visit, he smiles

at her. "If you can convince your mate to meet with the Dragon King, Aurdyn, then I will agree to meet with the Wolf Shifter, Prince Lukas and his father, even though I worry they are more likely to try to tear off my wings than grant me an audience."

"Lukas would not do that, I can assure you." She laughs, dismissing his concern. "I grew up with him. He is a good man." I note the hint of sadness in her tone as a wistful expression flits across her face. "I will give you a message for him, from me, and he will know you are a friend and will grant you an audience."

Kyven's pointed ears perk up. "What is it?"

"Tell him the stars I saw were right."

I wonder at her cryptic message, but say nothing. I will ask her about this later.

Kyven frowns, but dips his chin. "I will do this. Thank you."

Pain stabs at my chest as her sadness seeps across the bond. She must still have love for the Wolf Shifter prince. Perhaps that is the source of her hesitance that I sense through our connection.

"Would you like me to take a message to your family, as well?" he asks. "I will travel to meet them after."

Her smile brightens. "Yes." She takes my hand, threading her fingers through mine. "Tell them I am happy."

Her words touch me. Deeply. And I smile.

"I will do this, Queen Inara."

I note he does not tell her he goes to ask for her sister's hand, but then again, I suppose he wishes to tell Grayce before anyone else. I remain quiet. I wish I had not agreed to the promising spell. I have no desire to keep this information from Inara indefinitely.

Kyven smiles at her again, and I wrap a possessive arm

around her waist, tugging her close to my side while leveling a warning glare at him.

He purses his lips and shakes his head.

Inara leans into me, satisfying my primal instinct for now.

"I will leave you two to visit some more while I go to the surface. It was wonderful to meet you, King Kyven."

"You may call me Kyven," he says, and my lips curl back in a snarl. "It was wonderful to meet you as well, Queen Inara."

"You may call me Inara." She flashes a lovely smile. "After all, I understand you two are good friends, and I hope we will see you again."

"I hope that as well," he says, nodding politely.

After she leaves, he rolls his eyes at me. "Really, Varys? You think I would steal your bondmate when I already told you I desire her sister's hand?"

"It is instinct." I narrow my eyes. "You know I cannot help it. Just wait until you have a bondmate, Kyven. The same will happen to you before you fully seal your bond."

He frowns. "And... why have you not sealed it?"

"Because I told her we would wait until she is ready." I clench my jaw. "She was betrothed to Prince Lukas before she agreed to bind herself to me."

"You stole her away from a Wolf Shifter? Are you mad, Varys?"

"I had no choice. She is my Khio'ri."

He blinks several times. "He did not challenge you?"

"No. He accepted it was her choice to wed me."

"This is not typical of their kind." His forehead creases deeply. "They are extremely possessive of their mates. More so than even our own people." He pauses. "She must not have loved him if she agreed to marry you."

"Or... she simply loved her family, and him, so much

she chose to marry me to avoid a war that could take their lives."

"There is that, I suppose," he says, feeding into my worry. "But she seems happy here with you."

"I hope so," I allow my thoughts to escape unfiltered. I wonder, again, if she still loves Lukas. I have never asked, because I do not think I could bear it if she said 'yes.' But I suspect that may be part of the reason she has not wished to consummate our bond.

Kyven rests a hand on my shoulder, pulling me back from my dark thoughts. "You are a good man, Varys. If I am reading her correctly, I believe she may already be in love with you."

"What makes you think this?" I ask, praying he is right.

"The way she looks at you... smiles at you." Sadness darkens his features. "Her sister used to look at me like that."

When Kyven leaves, I cannot help but feel sorry for my friend. I would have gone mad if Inara had refused me. The pull of the fated bond was so strong, I could not have ignored it and simply moved on with my life. It would have ruined me for all others.

As I leave the throne room, I decide to seek her out on the surface. The mere thought of my mate makes me smile. I truly am far gone, indeed.

CHAPTER 45

VARYS

When I reach the surface, Devyn informs me Inara has already left to go riding. He saddles Shynar for me. I rest a gentle hand on his thick, gray and white fur, and he leans into my touch.

His nostrils flare as he smells the food I've brought, and he eyes me with interest. "Do not worry, my friend. I did not forget you. I packed a few treats for our outing."

His ears perk up immediately. I'd meant to save these for later, but how can I resist when he nuzzles my side, and gives me a pitiful look?

I dig into my satchel and pull out two strips of dried meat. He snatches them from my hand so fast, you'd think he was starving.

"He literally just ate before you arrived." Devyn purses his lips. "You'll spoil him if you keep giving him treats, you know."

Shynar narrows his eyes and flattens his ears, obviously disagreeing with this statement.

I smooth a hand through his fur, and he bumps at my arm with his massive snout. "My father always said that a well-fed wolf is a happy one." I pull out another strip of meat, and his tail begins wagging excitedly. A smile tugs at my lips as I gently scratch behind his ear. "Isn't that right, Shynar?"

He makes a happy whine in the back of his throat and takes the treat from my hand.

"Forget what I said earlier." Devyn rolls his eyes in mock irritation. "It's too late. He's already spoiled."

Perhaps Devyn is right, but I cannot help it. Shynar is special to me. He was my father's mount. He took two arrows to shield us, on the battleground, as I held my father while he lay dying.

After Father's death, I feared Shynar would die too. He refused to eat in the early days of his grief. Nyrala, Aryl, and I took turns sitting with him every day until he finally started to eat again.

I've heard that humans think dire wolves are nothing more than aggressive beasts. They have no idea of their intelligence nor their fierce loyalty to their riders. I am honored that Shynar gave me his bond, and that Rhygar offered his to my Khio'ri.

I communicate to him that I wish to find Inara, and he projects an image of her leaving with Rhygar. When I settle on his back, he lifts his head, sniffing the wind before he heads for the forest, having caught their scent.

I close my eyes briefly, searching for Inara through the Khio'rinar. Every day, our bond grows stronger. Contentment rushes through me when I can sense that she is nearby.

It doesn't take long to find her, and when we do, she is nothing short of magnificent.

The wind whips through her long, blond hair as she

races with Rhygar through the woods. She aims at one of the many hanging targets along this path, and letting her arrow fly, hits the board dead center. She does the same with each one she passes.

My bride is as lethal as any Dark Elf warrior, and my heart swells with pride.

When she reaches the end of the path, I call out her name. She turns in the saddle. "Varys!" She greets me with a smile, rivaling the brightness of the very sun itself. "How long have you been following me?"

I move up beside her and grin. "Long enough to know I never wish to be your enemy."

She laughs heartily, and I marvel again at how lovely it sounds. "Then I suppose it's fortunate for you I'm your wife," she teases in return.

"Indeed."

She throws her head back, relishing the natural light, and the sun highlights the various shades of gold coloring her hair. Her cheeks are flushed from exertion, and I stare at her, completely enthralled. "Come. I would like to show you something."

She follows me farther into the woods. Off to the left are several fields with row upon row of vegetables. She studies them curiously as we pass. "Is this all still part of Ithylian?"

"Yes. This is where the farmers grow the food and grain to feed our people." I gesture down the dirt road we follow. "Up that way is Valdoran, our second-largest city."

She cocks her head to the side. "I thought it was destroyed in the last war."

"It was, but we rebuilt. We had to if we wanted to live. Powerful magic shields it to conceal it from our enemies."

"Is that where you're taking me?"

"No."

"Then… where are we going?"

I smirk. "It is a surprise."

"A good one?" She grins.

"Do you trust me?"

Her expression turns serious. "Yes."

Trust. Something I never expected to have from her when we first met. It means everything to me to know that I can trust her, and I have her trust in return. My heart fills with warmth as I study my lovely mate. I can hardly wait to show her my surprise.

CHAPTER 46

INARA

I follow him down a narrow path into the forest. "Are we close?"

He glances over his shoulder and nods.

The sound of rushing water echoes through the woods, and my eyes widen when we come upon a river. Glittering, blue water cascades down several small waterfalls along its length before collecting in a larger pool. Farther down, the river spills over another waterfall and into a forested area below.

Varys guides me to a large, flat, obsidian stone hanging over the edge of the collecting pool. He pulls out a satchel of food and drink. Sitting, he motions for me to do the same.

"We used to come to this place often, when I was younger," he says. "We would have picnics here."

"It's beautiful."

I observe as he arranges a platter of meat, cheese, and bread, as well as a pitcher of a dark-colored liquid. He pours me a cup and I bring it to my nose, inhaling deeply of the scent of fresh berries. "This smells wonderful. What is it?"

"Alderberry juice," he replies. "It is in season this time of year."

After we eat, I sip at my drink. I remove my shoes and allow my feet to hang over the edge of the rock and into the water. Only the tips of my toes skim the surface. I'm surprised when Varys removes his boots and does the same, except his feet are completely submerged.

He studies my feet a moment, his eyes sparkling with amusement. "Are all human women so short?"

I scoff. "Are all Dark Elf men so tall?"

He laughs, and I admire how handsome he is when laughing. Not that he isn't always handsome, but he is even more stunning when he openly smiles.

It is a perfect day. The sun is bright, and the sky is blue, filled with white, puffy clouds. A cool breeze blows through the forest, carrying the fresh scent of the trees and the earth.

Varys pulls out two small blueberry tarts. They are warm, as if fresh from the oven, and I realize it is magic that keeps them this way. I take a small bite and a soft moan escapes me as the delicious berry flavor bursts across my tongue. "This is incredible."

I turn to find Varys watching me in rapt fascination. A slow smile spreads across his face. "I am pleased you like it."

We sit side by side, staring out at the water. This place reminds me of home, and I sigh wistfully. "There's a lake near the edge of the city walls of Florin," I begin. "Raiden, Edmynd, Grayce, and I used to have a contest. We'd race our horses to the lake and back again, to see who was the fastest rider. But during the summers, when it got so hot you thought you'd melt, we would sometimes go for a quick swim." I arch a brow at him. "It's not proper for a highborn lady to do such things, so I always kept a spare set of clothing in the stables so Mother wouldn't know what I'd been doing."

Varys frowns. "You mentioned something like this before… about your clothing and how you were not supposed to even have a set of your own armor."

"Back home, women are supposed to wear only dresses and soft slippers instead of sturdy boots. We are taught to ride sidesaddle because it is unbecoming of a lady to ride astride. And it is most certainly improper for a lady to wield a weapon of any sort."

"Why are there rules like this among your people?" He frowns. "Do they not want women to be as strong as the men?"

I draw my legs up and hug my knees as I stare out at the water. "Perhaps that's part of it. It seems like they want to make human women as dependent upon their husbands as possible. Even Lukas was upset when he learned Raiden was teaching me how to use a bow and arrow. He insisted that if I had a strong mate, I would have no need of such knowledge and skill."

A low growl rumbles in Varys's chest.

"That's how I felt about it, as well." I laugh softly. "I had to ride sidesaddle most of the time, but I would ride my horse astride when no one was watching. What bothered me most, though, is Edmynd did not even want to hear my opinion when I told him we should try talking to you after you'd captured Raiden. I told him meeting your army with his would only escalate things."

Varys stills.

"All the stories I had heard of your people were utterly terrifying, and I was so afraid both of them would die. And then Lukas showed up as well." I throw up my hands as the memory returns. "Edmynd would rather have gone off and gotten himself killed, like our father, than listen to me. He could have gotten them all killed."

Heavy silence lingers between us before Varys speaks. "I am sorry about the way things happened. I am sorry you were afraid." His brow furrows deeply. "And I am sorry I stole your future when I insisted upon our marriage."

"You did *not* steal my future, Varys." I rest my hand gently atop his. "I don't regret marrying you."

"You are happy here?" he asks, and I detect the slight hesitance in his voice, as if he cannot believe what I've just said.

"More than I ever thought possible. I am free here in a way I never have been before." A faint smile crests my lips. "It also helps that the Dark Elf King is good company." He looks smug, and I continue. "He even gave up his dire wolf for me. He does not even care if I wear pants or ride like a man into battle, wielding a bow and arrow as I race through the forest."

"This Dark Elf King sounds like a good and honorable male," Varys says, a hint of a smile playing on his lips.

"He is," I agree. I gently touch his face as his gorgeous eyes search mine. "He is also very handsome," I murmur. "For a Dark Elf," I tease.

Varys cups my cheek and leans closer, studying me like I am a rare and precious treasure. "And his wife is very lovely." A gorgeous smile curves his mouth. "Or so I have heard."

"Even though she is human?" I ask softly.

"She is the most exquisite woman I have ever seen." His gaze holds mine and he whispers. "She is my heart."

Happiness blooms in my chest as I lean in and brush my lips softly to his. His fingers slide into my hair, cupping the back of my head as his tongue finds mine, deepening our kiss.

He wraps his strong hands around my waist and pulls me into his lap as if I weigh nothing. My thighs straddle him and when he pulls me close and rolls his hips against mine, I inhale sharply as the evidence of his desire presses firmly against my core.

Varys tightens his arms around me, so there is no space between our bodies. Desire burns through my veins, and each movement of his tongue against mine stokes fire in my flesh. Only a thin barrier of clothing separates us, and I gasp as the low growl of his arousal sends vibrations straight through me.

He pulls back just enough to study me, his breathing as ragged as mine. His eyes swirl with black and his fangs are fully extended.

"Why did you stop?" I barely manage.

"I want you to see me, Inara... to see what I am, my human wife, before we go any further."

I touch his face and then trace my fingers across his lips, lightly grazing the tip of one fang. "I see you, Varys," I whisper, cupping his cheek. "And I am not afraid of you, my Dark Elf husband."

I lean in and press another kiss to his lips. He pulls me closer, and my every nerve hums with pleasure as he strokes his tongue against mine. He tastes of cinnamon and earth. Slow at first, we find a sensuous rhythm.

Fire ignites deep within as he tightens his arms around me, holding me so close his heart beats against mine beneath his chest. He groans as I dip my fingers beneath the hemline of his tunic, exploring the hard planes of muscle that line his abdomen and chest.

Varys slides his hand up under my clothing, and his

touch is like fire. I arch into his palm as he cups my left breast, brushing his thumb across the already stiff peak.

Heat thrums through my entire body, and our kisses become more urgent as I unfasten his tunic and slide it off his shoulders, leaving his torso bare. His body is all lean, corded muscle, and I cannot stop touching him. He removes my dress and kisses a heated trail along my jaw and down my neck to the valley of my breasts.

I inhale sharply as the tips of his fangs graze over my already sensitive flesh. "Varys," I breathe out his name as heat pools deep in my core.

He closes his mouth over my breast, growling low in his throat as he laves his tongue across the peak. I run my fingers through his hair, holding him close, relishing the feel of him against me.

My heart beats wildly in my chest as he twists, and I'm suddenly on my back. He captures my mouth in a claiming kiss, stealing the breath from my lungs as his hips roll against mine, creating the most delicious friction.

Desire pulses through my veins as his mouth skims down the length of my body in a series of ardent kisses. Slipping his hands beneath the waistband of my pants, he slides them down and off my hips, leaving me bare except for the small triangular scrap of silk between my thighs.

He lifts his head, his eyes full of desire. "May I touch you here?"

I love that he asks instead of just taking. I've never done this before. My entire body flushes with warmth beneath the heat of his gaze. Somehow, I manage to reply in a breathless whisper. "Yes."

Carefully, he slides the silken material down my body, leaving me completely bare. My pulse pounds in my ears as he traces his hands along my inner thighs, parting me to his gaze. "You are beautiful," he whispers as he slowly guides first one leg and then the other over his shoulders.

He dips his head between my thighs, and I gasp as he drags his tongue through my already slick folds, inhaling sharply when he reaches the small bundle of nerves at the top. As he teases his tongue over my sensitive flesh, a soft moan escapes my parted lips as my entire body lights up with pleasure.

I've touched myself before, but it's never felt anything like this.

"Varys," I barely manage. "Please."

Need burns through me like fire, and I'm not even sure what I'm asking for as my body writhes beneath him. I only know that I want more.

Carefully, he slips one finger just inside my core, and I arch up into him as he continues to trace his tongue over the softly hooded flesh between my thighs.

Remembering how sensitive his ears are, I reach down and run my fingers over their pointed tips. He growls and moves back up my body, capturing my mouth in a searing kiss as he concentrates on the touches that make me arch into his hand.

My heart pounds as his gaze holds mine, full of fire and possession.

CHAPTER 47

VARYS

Dark and primal instincts rise from deep within as Inara writhes beneath me. I long more than anything to claim her completely. My *stav* is hard and painfully erect with desire to join my body to hers and seal her to me, giving her my mark.

She clings to me as she arches into my touch, and I grasp her chin, forcing her gaze to mine. I want to watch her as she finds her release.

"Varys," she pants. "Please."

Her hazel eyes remain locked on my own, and a low moan escapes her as I brush my thumb over the small pearl of flesh at the top of her folds. Her entire body goes taut as her head falls back, her lips part, and she cries out my name as she shatters beneath me. I capture her mouth in a branding kiss, and then drop my forehead gently to hers.

"Varys." She reaches up to touch my face. "That was... there are no words."

My eyes fall to the pulsing artery along her neck, and

my fangs extend with the need to mark her as mine. My nostrils flare as I inhale her intoxicating scent deep into my lungs. I long to claim her and bind her to me in all ways.

Mine.

The word burns through me like fire.

But she is my mate and my queen. I cannot take her here—not like this. I pull her close to my chest, wrapping my arms tightly around her. My fully erect stav strains against my clothing, and she inhales sharply as it presses against her abdomen.

"Varys, you did not—"

"You are my heart." I stroke her cheek as I stare deep into her hazel eyes. "I long to claim you completely. But not here, my Khio'ri."

"Why?" she whispers.

"Because you are my bondmate and my queen, Inara. Because I want you in our bed and in our chambers. I want to take you many times, and to mark you as my mate so everyone will know without doubt that you are mine."

"I am already yours, Varys. I married you twice, my Dark Elf husband." She brushes her lips to mine and whispers against them. "I chose you twice, my love."

My love.

Those two words fill my heart with joy, brighter than the sun.

As I hold her close, her eyelids flutter open and closed as exhaustion steals through her. She snuggles against me with a soft sigh, and I place a finger under her chin, tipping her face up to mine.

I can hardly believe the gods have blessed me with someone so perfect. "Tell me again," I whisper. "Tell me you are mine."

"I am yours," she breathes.

Pressing a tender kiss to her lips, I send a silent prayer

of thanks to the gods. I hold my bondmate close and listen to the sounds of her breathing becoming soft and even as she drifts away in my arms.

I'm not sure how long we slept, but it is dark when I finally awaken. Gently, I wake her, and we both dress. I would love to remain here with her beneath the stars, but it is late and she is tired. If we are gone much longer, Devyn or Melina will come searching for us, so we must head back.

Gently, I lift her into my arms, then call out to Shynar and Rhygar. They immediately come from the woods. I carefully pull Inara up into the saddle with me on Shynar's back. She leans back against me, asleep, as Rhygar follows us to the stables.

As we dismount, I carefully balance her in my arms, not wanting to wake her. When I reach the mountain, I quickly, but quietly, make my way down the stone staircase and to our room.

As soon as I reach the hallway of the family wing, I feel a presence behind me. I spin to find Devyn with his arms crossed over his chest, glaring at me angrily. "I was worried, you know. You were gone for hours."

I purse my lips. "I wanted time alone with my mate." I glance down at her. "Wait here. I will return in a moment to speak with you."

I step into our chambers and gently tuck Inara beneath the fur blankets. When I press a fond kiss to her lips, her eyelids flutter open and she gives me a sleepy smile. "Are you coming to bed?"

"Not yet. I must speak with Devyn. But I will return to you soon."

She nods, then closes her eyes again.

When I step back out into the hallway, Devyn gives me a curious look. "You love her."

"Yes, I do."

"And... she feels the same?"

Although she has not said those exact words, she called me *her love*. I believe she does. "Yes."

"Good," he states firmly. "Then you will need to convince the Wolf Shifter prince of this."

I frown. "Why?"

"Prince Lukas is threatening war if you do not return her to him."

Anger blisters through me. "He gave her up. He witnessed our human wedding. Why does he seek to reclaim her now?"

"He has heard rumors of her mistreatment."

"Mistreatment?"

He nods. "Obviously, these rumors came from someone opposed to your union, but I know not if they originated with our people or hers. We should send a response immediately if we are to avoid conflict. Otherwise, it will only be a matter of time before her brother declares war as well."

"Send a raven to Prince Lukas," I order. "Now."

"What did you wish the message to say?"

While I understand that my words will have to be carefully crafted to avoid antagonizing my enemy, I cannot stop the fury that floods my veins. I clench my jaw as I meet his gaze evenly. "That she is mine, and I will *never* let her go."

He purses his lips. "I will... draft the message more delicately than that. We do not want an actual war, Varys."

I nod. "That would be wise."

"There is another issue," Melina's voice draws my attention from off to the side. I had not even realized she was here.

"What is it?"

"My father and the High Council... many of them still believe your bond to Inara is a trap. One meant to make you let down your guard so the humans can infiltrate our kingdom from within." She pauses. "They are suspicious because you mean to bring her to the next meeting of the Council."

"She is queen. Of course, she should be there," I protest. "If she were Dark Elf, they would not even question this."

"But she is *not* Dark Elf," Melina says pointedly. "She is human, Varys. Our enemy, not very long ago."

Melina meets my gaze directly. "I love my father, but I know he loves this kingdom more than anything. If he believes it is threatened, he—" She cuts short.

"What?" I insist. "Tell me what you are trying to say, Melina."

"I spoke to him only an hour ago, Varys. He is... I cannot reason with him. He will do whatever it takes to keep the kingdom safe."

Tears brighten her eyes, but she holds them in. I understand what she tells me took great courage. "Thank you," I murmur. "For trusting me enough to tell me this."

"You are a fair king, not prone to anger or rash decisions... except when it comes to taking a human as your bondmate." A grin tugs at her mouth. "That was something quite unexpected."

"Imagine *my* surprise," Devyn adds with a smirk. "We were staring down the possibility of battle when we caught Princess Inara trying to free her brother. Varys asked her within two minutes of their meeting to bind herself to him."

I narrow my eyes in mock anger, but I cannot help the smile that threatens at their joking.

Aryl walks up to us, his face full of worry. He runs a

hand roughly through his shoulder-length, dark hair before waving a small scroll of parchment at me. "Have you seen this?"

"From Prince Lukas?"

"He is threatening war, Varys." His voice rises. "I thought your marriage was meant to prevent this. I do not understand. What gave him the idea that Inara is in danger from us?"

"It is a lie," Nyrala's voice rings out. I turn to find my sister moving toward us, her expression full of concern. "Someone… either from within our kingdom or hers has fed the Wolf prince this lie in an attempt to draw us into a war."

"Why?" Aryl asks. "I thought they wanted peace as much as we do."

I turn to my brother. "There are always some who would benefit from two kingdoms going to war. Now, we must find out exactly who."

I need to speak with Inara. Explain to her what has happened and ask for her thoughts on the matter. She knows the Wolf prince well. They were betrothed.

Even now, my stomach twists in knots at the thought of mentioning him to her. Although she said she was mine, I cannot help but wonder if she still harbors feelings for him.

Jealousy feeds the anger deep inside me. He could not have loved her. Not truly. If he had, he never would have let her go. He would have fought to keep her, not simply stepped aside and watched her become mine. He did not deserve her, and I will *never* give her up to him.

It is only a few hours until dawn, but I have much to address and I'm unable to sleep. I need to send a response to Prince Lukas before he and his warriors show up at our doorstep. As much as I wish to return to Inara, I also do not wish to wake her. Not yet, anyway.

I make my way to my private work chambers. It is rare that I use this space. I much prefer the desk in my bedroom. When I step inside, my eyes are immediately drawn to my father's old desk, near the hearth. The rich, dark wood is smooth and worn from years of use. Tapestries depicting Elves in various battles throughout our history cover the walls.

My father placed them here to remind him of the terrible costs of war. He spent much of his time in this room. Being king is a heavy burden, but he always seemed to bear it well.

I take a seat at the desk and draft a response to Prince Lukas and to Inara's brothers. I cannot have them believing that she is in trouble. The last thing we need is another war.

When I am finished, Devyn brings in several scrolls for my review. I sigh heavily as I study them for a few moments. Once I have reviewed and signed all of these scrolls, I am certain at least a dozen more will be waiting for me tomorrow.

Being king can be exhausting simply because of the amount of paperwork that is involved. After what feels like forever, I sign the last scroll and place it at the edge of my desk. It is morning now, and my thoughts turn again to Inara.

I wonder if she is awake or still sleeping. My mind drifts to what happened between us yesterday. She responded to my touch so beautifully, and I cannot wait to see her again. To hold her in my arms and cover her lips with mine.

"A raven just arrived from the north," Devyn says,

ripping me from my thoughts. "There was another Wraith attack along the border."

He hands me a scroll, and I quickly read the report. I'm relieved to see there were no casualties on our side. Even so, it is still troubling that these attacks are even happening at all. The magic along the Great Wall is supposed to prevent them from crossing.

"Send more of our warriors to reinforce the Veil," I order. "We must strengthen the magic of the barrier to—"

My heart stutters and stops as terror claws at my mind, and I stumble back a step, catching myself on the desk to regain my balance.

"My King!" Devyn grips my shoulder. "What's wrong?"

I scan the room for any threat, but see none.

A wave of terror washes through me, filling my veins with ice. It takes me a moment to realize this feeling is not my own. It is coming from Inara. *Something is wrong.* "It's the queen. I can feel it through the bond." The words leave my mouth in a panicked rush. "We must find her. Now!"

CHAPTER 48

INARA

I dream of Prince Aegryn standing at the head of his army. *His short, brown hair is red with the blood of a recently fought battle. His face twists in a vicious snarl as his gray eyes scan the horizon. In the distance stands the castle of Florin.*

He raises his arm and ushers his men forward. They march toward the palace. Wraiths hover along the edges of their formations. Their glowing red eyes are full of hunger as they bare their sharp fangs.

The image shifts and I see Varys and Aryl standing on a battlefield beside my brothers.

An arc of light slams into Varys, and a scream rips from my throat as I watch him fall.

I wake with a start as the images from my nightmare slowly recede. Tears sting my eyes as I rub them. This did not feel like a regular nightmare. It felt like a vision. I have to tell Varys. I cannot keep this secret to myself any longer.

I glance around the room, not sure if Varys even came

to sleep after he tucked me beneath the covers. I roll over and hug his pillow beside me. I inhale deeply of his distinct scent, and my cheeks heat as I think about what we did by the river.

He called me 'his heart' and said I was his. Surely that is the equivalent of "I love you" in his culture. At least… I hope it is because I'm already madly in love with my Dark Elf husband.

I had been worried he would cast me aside for a mistress that could give him the family I cannot. But it seems my concerns were unfounded, and my heart feels so light. He desires me, and only me. I can hardly contain my joy.

More importantly, I trust him to tell him about my visions.

Though it is still rather early, I ready myself for the day. When I come out of the cleansing room, a servant is leaving a tray of food for my breakfast. He bows low and turns toward the door to leave, but I address him. "Do you know where King Varys is this morning?"

"He usually meets with his guards, my Queen, but I am uncertain."

"Thank you," I reply, dismissing him.

As I stand before the mirror to check my appearance one last time, a flash of light catches my eye. I inhale sharply as sparks of energy crackle between the tips of my fingers like lightning.

My entire body begins trembling with the same strange power I felt in the ruins of Elysarin's courtyard. It has been far too long since I had any nylweed to suppress my visions and this strange, new magic.

I draw in a deep breath, trying to calm my racing heart. I need to find some nylweed and take another dose. Once I have my curse under control, then I will find Varys and tell him everything. I cannot keep this secret from him forever, and I don't want to hide this from him anymore.

It is always difficult to locate enough nylweed, especially since the Dark Elves actively burn any that they find. I'll have to search deep within the forest and pray to the old gods to guide me. I was fortunate to find the small amount I gathered the last time I went out alone, near the edge of the woods.

Light forks between my fingers again, and my unease deepens. I'm so afraid of losing control of this strange magic that is now flowing through my veins. I'm terrified that I might hurt someone if I cannot suppress it.

Quickly, I make my way to the surface. I'm surprised no one has followed me. Varys usually leaves Devyn as my guard, but I have seen no sign of him. He must be with my husband. Melina is nowhere to be seen, either, which is odd.

The sun shines brilliantly against the clear, blue sky as I stride to the training fields. Several of the guards are sparring with each other, suggesting Varys is probably not here. Rather than disappointment, however, I feel a wave of relief wash over me that I can search for the plant without fear of being caught.

Movement off to the side draws my attention, but when I search the tree line, nothing is there. Perhaps it's my own guilty conscious making me paranoid. I've hated keeping this secret from Varys. Even though I'm still worried about how he'll feel when he learns I've withheld this from him, I'll be relieved to finally be able to tell him the truth.

I walk to the armory and retrieve my bow and quiver. Looping them over my shoulder, I then make my way to the stables. I rest a hand on Rhygar's fur as soon as I find him, and he leans into my touch, projecting an image of us riding.

"Today is for riding *and* for exploring," I whisper. "There is something I need. Can you help me find it?"

When his reflective, yellow eyes meet mine, I do my best to convey an image of the nylweed.

Through our connection, I can sense him questioning this, uncertain why I would wish to search for something everyone considers bad. But he projects a vision of several patches of nylweed in a heavily wooded area.

Relief fills me that he knows where I may find some. I place the saddle on his back, adjust the straps, and rapidly mount up. "Let us go, my friend."

Rhygar leaves the stables at a gallop, heading straight for the woods. As we weave through the forest, a strange sensation prickles my skin—as if I'm being observed—but I can see no one nearby.

I'm about to dismiss it again, but Rhygar stops abruptly and stares out into the woods, scanning the trees. He senses it too. After a moment, he huffs out a breath and shakes his head before returning to our path.

The dense canopy overhead blocks out most of the sun, except for occasional spears of light breaking through the branches. A few Pixies—Day Pixies, I hope—flit back and forth among the leaves. A few stray too close and Rhygar snaps his massive jaws at them, scaring them off.

Discreetly, I pat his thick fur, glad of his protective nature. It seems he does not trust them to be too close either. After what Varys told me, I'm not too keen on meeting any Pixies up close—Day *or* Night ones.

Rhygar heads toward a clearing, and I expel a sigh of relief when I discover an entire field of nylweed. It seems the Dark Elves have not discovered this area, because if so, it would surely not be this overgrown.

I slide off Rhygar's back and pick several bunches, enough to fill both saddlebags and the pocket of my tunic dress. This should be enough to last me for a while. After I tell Varys my secret, I'll show him this place, and perhaps next time, he can come with me when I need to retrieve more.

I am eager to speak with my husband. As soon as I find him, I'm going to tell him the truth. All of it. I should have told him sooner. I want him to know everything because I trust him. Completely.

Climbing onto Rhygar's back, we head toward the mountain. With each step, I dread the conversation I know I'll need to have with Varys, but it has to be done. I want a future with him, and it cannot be built on lies.

I leave Rhygar in the stable and place the nylweed in a pack to take back with me to our rooms. Several of the guards are sparring, so most pay me no notice as I pass. When I'm almost back to the hidden door of the mountain, someone steps into my path.

"Your Majesty," a dark voice says.

I lift my head to find Dralyn—Melina's father. Like all Dark Elves, he is taller than I am, but not more so than my own husband. But the way he stares down at me makes me uncomfortable.

"Lord Dralyn," I address him, unsure what else to say as I wait for him to move from my path.

Having grown up in my brother's court, I understand how important it is to not appear weak. I tip up my chin and train my face into a calm mask, refusing to be intimidated by this man.

His gaze drops to my pack. "What do you have there, Your Majesty?"

"That is none of your concern, Lord Dralyn. Step aside, so I may pass."

He narrows his eyes and snaps his fingers. Two men appear from out of nowhere. "Search the queen," he commands.

One of the men stares at him in shock. "For what?"

"Weapons, or anything meant to harm our king."

"What are you *talking* about?" I ask incredulously. "Why would I want to hurt Varys?"

Dralyn lunges forward and rips my satchel from my shoulders, pulling out the nylweed. Using his claws, he slices a line down my tunic pocket, revealing even more.

"This is Elfbane." He narrows his eyes. "I witnessed you gathering this in the woods. It is deadly poison. You would use it to murder King Varys."

"*What*? No!"

"Take her to the dungeon," he commands the two men.

They hesitate. "My Lord, I do not believe the king would want—"

He pushes them aside and grabs my arm in a bruising grip. "You are coming with me."

Remembering my training, I twist out of his grasp and sweep my leg out, catching him behind the ankle. He stumbles back, and I bolt for the mountain door.

Something slams into my back, sending me sprawling forward. I push to my feet, but another blast hits me, knocking me to the ground. Searing pain burns through my body as I twist onto my back.

Dralyn raises his hands to use his magic again. Fear wars with anger as energy sparks across my fingers. Panic grips me as I struggle to hold back my power.

He sends another bolt of light toward me, and my magic bursts from my hands, rippling through the air in a surge of raw power.

Dralyn and the others throw up a shield at the last

second, and blue light explodes across the protective barrier.

The two men stare at me in shock as Dralyn strikes out again. Pain rips through my body, and my vision goes dark.

CHAPTER 49

INARA

When I wake, it's to a cold and dark room, and I'm lying on a pile of straw. My head pounds as I look around, barely able to see anything beyond a door with bars. I'm in some sort of cell. The air is damp, and the sound of water dripping onto stone echoes in the stillness.

My wrists are bound and chained to the dark stone wall. I jerk back, then instantly regret it as a spasm flashes through my body like fire. Tears sting my eyes and I grit my teeth against the agony.

I glance at my left forearm, where a large bruise in the shape of Dralyn's handprint stands out darkly against my skin. It is already swelling and, given a Dark Elf's strength, I wonder if he may have fractured it when he grabbed me.

Fear throbs inside me as I recall using my magic against him, and I curl into a ball as more tears gather in the corners of my eyes. They saw me use magic. Even now, I can feel it building inside me like water gathering behind a dam, threatening to overflow and break loose.

Drawing in a lungful of air, I try to calm the storm within me. I cannot lose control. If I do, I could make everything worse.

A shadow falls over me and I lift my head to find Dralyn's glowing eyes studying me like a predator closing in on its prey. "Admit what you were going to use this for." He holds up the nylweed. "Tell me all of your plans to assassinate King Varys and bring down our kingdom."

"You are wrong," I choke out. "I would never hurt my husband or betray our kingdom."

"It is not *your* kingdom." He sneers at me. "Ithylian belongs to the Dark Elves, and you are human, you traitorous witch."

Witch. I gasp as the word conjures my worst nightmares. The sounds of the woman screaming as she was burned at the stake, echoes in my mind.

As fast as a snake, Dralyn rushes toward me. Wrapping one hand around my throat, he lifts me into the air as if I weigh nothing.

The sound of a metal door swinging on rusted hinges echoes along the stone, followed by booted steps ringing out from down the hallway. I recognize the cadence of Varys's steps.

"Inara?" he calls out.

"Admit your crimes," Dralyn commands, tightening his grip on my throat.

Magic sparks between my fingers. "Let me go before I hurt someone," I wheeze. "Please, I can't control it."

His gaze drops to my hands, and worry flickers across his expression as energy crackles along the skin of my palms.

I grit my teeth, and a tear slides down my cheek as I

struggle to contain the raw power that burns deep within. Without warning, it lashes out, striking Dralyn in the chest and sending him flying backward. He hits the wall with a sickening crunch and slumps to the ground, unconscious.

I drop to my knees. Terror spikes through me as my power continues to build deep within. The stone walls begin to rumble, raining down bits of dust and debris as raw energy courses through my veins, threatening to break free of my control.

"Inara?" Varys's eyes are full of panic as he rushes into my cell. "What happened? Are you—"

"Stop!" I cry out, and he halts abruptly.

Sweat beads across my brow as I try to calm the firestorm that churns inside me, but it will not obey. It is a living thing—a destructive force that demands to be freed, ready to devour everything in its wake.

"Varys, you have to go," I gasp. "I cannot control it, and I don't want to hurt you."

His ice-blue eyes glow brightly in the darkness, highlighting the sharp line of worry creasing his brow. "Inara, what is wrong?"

"Varys, please." My voice quavers. "You must go."

The ground rumbles and quakes with terrible force, and his eyes widen in terror. "Are you doing this?"

"Yes." Tears stream down my cheeks. "But I cannot stop it. Please, Varys. Go!"

He falls to his knees before me. His eyes drop to my hands and the magic crackling like lightning between my fingers, growing stronger. The walls shake and wind swirls all around, whipping through my hair and spiraling debris throughout the cell.

I'm vaguely aware of his siblings and several guards watching from the doorway, their expressions masks of disbelief and terror.

Varys covers my hands with his own, forcing my gaze to his. "Concentrate on me, Inara," he says soothingly. "Listen to the sound of my voice."

"Varys," I whimper, terrified that I'll hurt him. "I can't control it."

"Yes, you can," he whispers. "It is part of you. Draw in a deep breath and slowly exhale. Concentrate on calling your magic back to you, Inara."

"I cannot." I choke on a sob.

"Yes, you can. It is part of you. Do not fight it, my Khio'ri. Feel it deep within. It is yours, and *you* have control—*not it*."

I force myself to focus on the fire raging in my veins. I close my eyes, concentrating on the feel of it as it moves through me and out into the world. Carefully, I draw it back, pulling it deep within. The wind dies down and the grounds and walls around us fall still again as I tamp down the maelstrom of power inside me.

"Imagine sealing it away," Varys's voice cuts through my thoughts. "You can control it, Inara. You have the strength to do this."

I imagine closing the lid on a box and locking it shut. My entire body trembles with exhaustion as the power dissipates, taking the last of my energy with it.

My eyes roll up in the back of my head and the world falls away beneath me.

CHAPTER 50

INARA

Bright light floods my vision as I open my eyes. I squint against the harsh glare coming in through a row of windows across the way. I'm lying in a large, fluffy bed with at least two layers of furs wrapping me like a cocoon.

My gaze travels over the unfamiliar room. I'm surrounded by light gray, stone walls with several tapestries and paintings of nature scenes.

My heart hammers as my memories return. I raise my hand, afraid I'll find the raw energy crackling between my fingers again, but there is nothing.

With a sigh of relief, I turn onto my side and notice Varys asleep on the chair next to the bed. Carefully, I push myself up, wincing slightly. My entire body feels like one large bruise.

Varys's eyes snap open and he quickly moves to my side. "Are you all right?"

"I'm fine."

"Your expression suggests otherwise." He frowns. "And I can sense your discomfort through our bond."

"Then why did you ask?"

He lowers his gaze. "To see if you trusted me enough to speak the truth."

A sharp pain stabs me like a knife, and I know this pain is his through our connection. He is upset that I hid my magic from him, and I suppose if our situations were reversed, I would feel the same.

"You are awake," Nyrala's voice draws my attention as she enters the room. She moves to my bedside and offers me a cup. It's filled with light green liquid I assume to be tea from the fresh herb scent. "Drink this," she says. "It will help with the pain."

Her eyes are cold as I take it from her.

She knows about my curse. They all do.

The thought fills me with terror when Aryl walks in, and I remember they all witnessed my terrible secret. Dark memories of High Mage Ylari telling me that I could be burned at the stake flood through me. My hands begin trembling so violently my cup rattles on the saucer.

Varys's hand covers mine, and he carefully takes the saucer and cup from me with the other. "What is wrong, Inara?"

Tears burn the back of my eyes, but I hold them in. "If you give me the nylweed—the Elfbane—I can suppress it." I barely manage. "I promise you. If I take it, I will not be a danger. You won't have to get rid of me. I—"

"Get rid of you?" Aryl frowns. "What are you talking about?"

"Please, do not kill me."

"Kill you?" Nyrala asks incredulously. "Why would you think we would—"

"Because I am dangerous." I choke back a sob. "That

power inside me, I don't know where it came from. I cannot control it."

"It is mine," Varys says gently. "You gained it through our bond."

"What?"

"It can be an effect of the fated bond. Magic from one mate can be shared with the other, but it is rare. Why did you not tell me?"

"Because I was afraid."

"How did you know to take Elfbane?" Nyrala asks.

"I have visions. I dream things and they happen," I explain. "High Mage Ylari taught me to hide them. That's why I take the nylweed. It suppresses my visions, and he said others use it to suppress their magic. That's why I went to find it in the forest. But Lord Dralyn thought I meant to use it to poison you, Varys." A tear slips down my cheek. "Please, believe me. I would never do that to you."

I lift my gaze to him. "I had a vision—a nightmare—right before Dralyn caught me with the nylweed. I was going to tell you that day as soon as we were alone. I just needed the nylweed to suppress my magic until I could speak with you."

"What did you dream?"

"I dreamed that Prince Aegryn was marching on Florin with his army. He had Wraiths with him as well."

"You believe it was a vision and not a simple nightmare?"

I nod.

"Then we will send word to your brother to warn him." He takes both my hands in his, squeezing them gently. "I vowed when we first met I would never harm you, Inara." His shoulders slump. "Did you really believe that I would, my Khio'ri?"

"I know now that you wouldn't hurt me, Varys. But I

did not know when we first met. I was going to tell you. You have to believe me."

"Please, leave us." Varys looks to Nyrala and Aryl. "I must speak with my bondmate alone."

"Drink that first." Nyrala gestures to the cup. "It will help you."

Varys passes it back to me, and I carefully drink down the bittersweet liquid. The ache begins to lift from my body almost immediately. "Thank you," I whisper in relief.

Her lips tip up in a faint smile and she and Aryl leave the room.

Varys's ice-blue eyes meet mine, hurt easily read in his normally stoic features. "After all that has happened between us, why did you keep this from me?"

"Ever since I was a child, I have kept my powers a secret. Women who possess magical abilities are put to death in my kingdom." A tear slips down my cheek, but I quickly brush it away. "The Mages burn them at the stake."

He inhales sharply.

"My mother had visions. So does my sister. And when I discovered these new powers... this magic... I was so afraid. Is Lord Dralyn alive? Please, tell me he still lives."

Varys growls low in his throat at the mention of his name. "Yes. He managed to escape from the dungeons during all the commotion. I've sent out word that he is banished from the kingdom. If he ever steps foot in Ithylian again, I will end him."

Relief fills me that I did not take a life when I lost control of my magic.

I continue. "High Mage Ylari has been with our family for four generations. He took pity on us and taught me how to suppress my visions with nylweed. He told me if anyone ever found out, they would either kill me or use me."

"Is that why you did not tell me?" Varys's eyes search mine. "Because you thought I would—"

"At first, I did," I admit the truth.

He lowers his gaze, but says nothing. Through our connection, I can sense both his sadness and his despair at my betrayal. I hurt him. Deeply. "I should have told you sooner, Varys."

"Yes." He clenches his jaw. "You should have."

CHAPTER 51

VARYS

She does not trust me. Not as I do her.

And it is clear to me now that she never truly did.

"Varys, I did not mean to—"

"The past cannot be changed." I force my voice to remain even to hide the pain of her betrayal. "You are safe here, Inara. That's all that matters."

She stills. "You will leave me here."

She says this as a statement, but I understand it is a question.

"We will remain here for now. I brought you to this place to protect you. The magic you have inherited from me is very powerful. Here, you can safely learn to harness and wield your power without risking harm to anyone else, or damage to our mountain—our home."

Home. My thoughts turn to the time we have spent together. I had hoped she felt safe among our people, and I believed she felt safe with me, but I was wrong.

"What about the kingdom?" she asks. "Who will take care of things while you are here?"

"This is my family's summer home—trianon—near the ruins of Elysarin castle," I explain. "It will not be difficult to attend to my duties from here. The city of Elysarin itself is within walking distance."

She gives me a hesitant look. "Do you really believe I can learn to control my magic?"

"Yes, I do."

I rub the back of my neck as I think about what could have happened if her own people had discovered she had powers. I wonder if everyone knew. Including her former betrothed. "Did Lukas know about your visions?"

"Yes."

Jealousy raises its ugly head. I hate that he knew of this but I did not. All my concerns about her possibly harboring feelings for him bubble up to the surface. "Do you still love him?"

The question escapes my lips before I even realize I've spoken it aloud. But now that I have, I will not take it back. I have to know. If she could hide something as important as her magic and her visions from me despite the Khio'ri-nar, I wonder if she concealed her true feelings as well.

"Of course, I do." I flinch slightly as her words cut deep. "But not like that. Not in the way you are thinking," she adds. "We grew up together. He is like family to me."

I study her intently, feeling for her truth through the bond. I desperately want to believe her, but after everything that has happened, I don't know if I can. I want to ask if her feelings for me were real, but I cannot for fear I will not like the answer.

"You should rest." I stand from the chair. "If you need anything, I will be in the next room."

I turn to leave, but she calls out. "Varys?"

I stop, but do not turn around. It is taking every last bit of my control to push down the emotional turmoil whirling deep within. "Yes?"

"You do not have to sleep in a separate room. You can stay here if you—"

"I do not think that would be wise," I struggle to reply evenly. I am in love with her. I gave her my heart and my soul, and I thought she loved me. But now I am not sure. And until I know, I will keep my distance and give her space.

Even if there cannot be love between us, the trust we had has been broken. I know such things can be repaired, but it takes time.

"I am sorry I did not trust you with my secret, Varys," she says softly. "I never wanted to hurt you. I truly do lo—"

"I will be next door, if you need me," I cut her off, unable to bear hearing anything further. "We will start your training in the morning."

Without waiting for her reply, I open the door and step out into the hallway. I turn left and enter my room, only to find my siblings inside. I sink into the chair across from them and drop my head into my hands. "She said she loved me. But how could she when she never trusted me to begin with?"

Nyrala places a hand on my shoulder. "She was scared, Varys. She grew up her entire life being told to hide this part of herself for fear of death."

Aryl leans forward. "In truth, if I were her, I probably would have done the same."

I lift my eyes to them. "But she should have known she could trust me. She should have felt through the bond how much I—" My voice catches and I swallow against the lump in my throat. "How much I love her, and that I would sooner end my own life than ever harm her."

"She is human," Nyrala says pointedly. "And you have not yet fully sealed the bond with a first mating. She may not be able to sense you through the Khio'rinar as strongly as you do her."

"Even if she could not feel it here"—I place my palm over my heart—"I *told* her, and *showed* her what she meant to me, but she did not trust my actions *or* my words." Doubt twists deep inside me. "How do I know what we had was not a lie?"

"Do you love her?" my sister asks gently.

"More than anything," I reply without hesitation.

"Then, you have a choice. You either choose to continue loving her or you pull away. You have not yet sealed your bond. If you find she does not love you, then it is not too late to end what was blossoming between you."

I lower my gaze to the floor but say nothing. What can I say? It is already too late; I am in love with Inara. And it is a devastation unlike any I have ever known to think she may not truly love me in return.

But I am king of Ithylian, and I have a duty to my people. I must push down my sadness and hide my despair. It should not be hard. I have done it before, when I first took the throne after losing my parents so suddenly.

Aryl and Nyrala fell apart after their deaths. I was the one who had to be strong, hiding my devastation from everyone. I am no stranger to loneliness and unhappiness.

When I fell in love with Inara, I believed I had finally found someone to share my truth with. Someone who could see beyond the mask I wear for the kingdom, and even for my own family. But I was wrong.

I trusted her, but she never truly trusted me.

Still, perhaps we can come to an understanding. If she cares for her family and her people as much as I do mine, then our marriage is the best way to maintain the alliance between our two kingdoms.

I run my hands through my hair as the memory of the nights I have held her, slept beside her, kissed her, loved her... All of them play through my mind. I want more than friendship; I want her heart. She already has mine. And despite how much it hurts, I cannot simply stop loving her. It is too late.

Now, I must wait to see if she will ever truly give me her heart in return.

CHAPTER 52

INARA

When I wake, I find fresh clothes ready for me in the cleansing room. It is smaller than our chamber in the castle. Elven magic keeps the tub full of hot water, but everything else here is rather simple, almost rustic in a way.

I make a quick meal of the bread, cheese, and fruit left for me before I step out into the hallway.

Everything here is so different from the Cyridil castle in the mountain. The rooms here are all brightly lit as sunlight spills in from several windows along the wall. The baseboards and moldings are made of rich, dark wood, intricately carved with vines and leaves, adding warmth to the space.

I make my way down the wooden stairs and into what appears to be an open living area. A large sofa and a few chairs covered in plush gray fabric sit before a stone hearth.

Across the way is a kitchen with a long counter and various dried herbs hanging from the ceiling, filling the air with the scent of lavender and spices. A few shelves hang on either side of the sink, lined with stacked cups and plates.

It is all neat and tidy, but definitely nothing like the lavish place I first imagined when Varys mentioned his family's summer home.

The front door opens, and he walks in, stopping abruptly as soon as he notices me.

Awkward silence fills the air around us.

I glance at the kitchen. "It is... quite nice here," I offer. "Quaint."

He looks down at his hands. "I am sure this must seem rather small compared to what you are used to."

"I-I didn't mean it like that," I reply quickly. "I think it's lovely here."

"This belonged to my mother's family. She grew up in this house."

"Oh," I reply, unsure what to say.

"After their bonding, my father had it expanded a bit, of course," he adds. "But it is still rather... simple." His gaze holds mine a beat before he turns away. "Let us begin your lessons."

He motions for me to follow him outside. Things are uncomfortable between us, and it is all my fault. Sadness wraps tight around my chest, and because of the bond, I am unsure which is stronger: his despair or my own.

When his blue eyes turn to me, I realize I have my answer as I see the betrayal reflected behind them. He gave me the truth from the start, and although I never directly lied to him, a lie of omission is just as hurtful. I understand that now, but it is too late.

As we step outside, I glance back to the house. The

summer home is actually more of a cottage. It has a simple thatched roof and is surrounded by fields. The main path from the front door leads to a dirt road that is a short walk to the city of Elysarin.

The ruined castle of Elysarin looms in the distance. From here, you would never know it is in such a state of disrepair as its proud towers spiral up toward the sky, their silver rooftops gleaming beneath the sunlight.

Varys is silent as we walk to the back of the house and into the gardens. The high wall surrounding the yard is made of the same light gray stone as the house and affords us privacy from prying eyes.

Just like the gardens of Elysarin castle, various flowering plants and trees, many of them glowing with a soft bioluminescence, have overrun the grounds. I can only imagine how much lovelier it must be to walk through here at night.

Trailing vines hang over the garden walls and sway in the breeze like living curtains. It is nothing like the straight rows and sharp angles defining the palace courtyards of Florin's castle. This appears wild and untamed, and is all the more beautiful because of it.

It would be easy to become lost in this place, if not for the well-worn gravel pathway that winds throughout. We follow it toward the back and find a rather large open area. Devyn and Aryl spar in the distance while Nyrala looks on from one of the wooden benches nearby. Panic spikes through me. I thought we'd be practicing alone. There are too many people here, and I'm afraid to lose control of my powers and hurt them.

I touch Varys's forearm, and he turns toward me, arching a questioning brow.

"Varys, my magic... I do not want to risk hurting them."

His expression softens. "You will not harm them. I will place a shield around us so your magic cannot escape."

"What about you? You will still be at risk."

"Aryl and Nyrala are both skilled healers. If I am injured, they will tend me."

Despite his attempts to reassure me, a slight tremor begins in my hands. I curl them into fists at my side to still their shaking and follow as he leads me to the center of the clearing.

Devyn and Aryl stop sparring, granting us the entire space for our lessons.

Varys turns to me, his gaze dropping to my trembling hands. "It is all right, Inara. Everything will be fine."

"Is it… wise for them to watch?" I swallow hard. "So many things could go wrong, and I would never be able to live with myself if I—"

Varys takes both my hands in his and gives them a light squeeze. "Trust me," he says, and I wince inwardly at his choice of words.

Through our bond, I feel the sting they give him as well. "I do," I whisper, wishing so much that he believed me. "I *do* trust you, Varys."

He averts his eyes, pinching his lips into a thin line.

It was the wrong thing to say, and much too soon.

He releases my hands and takes a few steps back before tipping up his chin and studying me with an impassive expression. One I have not seen on him since the day we met.

"Raise your hands."

I do as he says, acutely aware of everyone watching us, but I force myself to focus only on him.

He lifts his hands and sends a pulsing wave of magic all around us. Shimmering blue light encircles us within a protective bubble.

I know he says I cannot hurt him, but I'm still afraid.

"Close your eyes and focus," he says. "Allow the energy to build in your palms and hold it there."

Raw power flows through my veins like molten lava, gathering at the tips of my fingers. Heat builds in my palms. My hands shake and I grit my teeth, struggling to contain it as it begins to surge. It is as if, now that I have called it forth, it is desperate to break free.

"Do not fight it," he instructs. "Let it flow over and through you like water."

"It is *not* water," I rasp, sweat beading my brow. "It is *fire and flame*."

Intense heat boils like an inferno, threatening to consume everything in its path—me included. "Varys." My voice quavers. "It's too much."

"Do not be afraid of it," he states firmly. "Fear only takes away your control."

I open my eyes. Energy crackles and dances across my skin, threatening to overwhelm me. "Varys, please," I barely manage. "You must go. I don't want to hurt you."

"I will not leave you." His eyes flash with determination. "You can control it, Inara. This power is yours and you can—"

Primal energy explodes from my hands in an incandescent arc of blue magic, and races toward Varys. "No!"

His eyes widen, and the space between each beat of my heart stretches into an eternity as it flies toward him. Fear tightens my chest as he frantically gathers his magic and conjures a barrier spell, barely managing to raise it before my power hits him full force. It explodes against his magic shield in a brilliant display of light and power, and he stumbles back against the assault.

The raw, untamed energy curls around his shield, trying to reach him as he struggles to force it away.

"Varys!"

I try to call it back to me, but I cannot. I don't know how to make it stop!

Warmth builds in my chest, wrapping around my body like a soothing balm that flows over and through me. The power wanes, curling back on itself and returning to my hands.

As it slowly ebbs away, I sink to my knees on the ground. My entire body is trembling and tears sting my eyes as I blink them back.

"Inara!" Varys's panicked voice sounds overhead.

He drops to his knees, catching me before I fall forward. Fear spikes through me, and I grip his muscular arms. "I could have killed you."

"But you did not." He runs a soothing hand through my hair, brushing it back from my face. "It is my power as well. It came from me. And because I know it and understand it, it would be very difficult for it to hurt me." He cups my chin. "You took control of it, Inara."

I want to point out that it was only possible because of his help through our bond, but the words will not come. I draw in a shaking breath. "Please, Varys. I need to suppress it, not try to control it. It's too dangerous."

"Your magic is potent, and I will not force you to learn control. If you want to suppress it, I will grow entire fields of Elfbane solely for you, Inara." He pauses. "But until you learn to control and wield this, there will always be a danger of it breaking free, or overwhelming you, despite your attempts to push it down." His brow furrows deeply. "Magic and visions are not meant to be suppressed."

A tear slips down my cheek as dark memories return, but I quickly brush it away. "I am cursed."

Out of the corner of my eye, I notice everyone has left, probably deciding it's safer to be farther away from us.

"I am sorry for how your people regard magic," he murmurs. "We would have celebrated your powers, not shunned or considered them evil."

My voice catches as raw pain and guilt consume me. "I dreamed of my mother's death, but I could not save her. I dreamed of Father's too, but it was too late."

"Why do you blame yourself?"

"Mother died protecting me and Grayce." I bite my lip to keep it from trembling. "And then father went to avenge her death and died in battle with the Fae."

He slips his arms around me and pulls me to his chest. "It is not your fault, Inara. No one taught you how to navigate this gift, but I will find someone to teach you now, just as I will teach you to wield the magic you received from me through our bond."

"What if I cannot control my fear?" I ask, remembering how he said fear only makes it more difficult to wield.

"You will." His voice is full of conviction. "I know you can."

"How can you be so sure?"

A faint smile quirks his lips. "Because you are one of the bravest people I know."

I huff out a frustrated breath. "I am not brave."

"Yes, you are."

Before I can protest, he arches a brow. "You married the Dark Elf King—your enemy. You thought I and my kind were ruthless monsters, and yet you agreed to our marriage to keep those you love safe." His ice-blue eyes meet mine evenly. "Now, you will harness that same bravery to control your magic and make sure the power flowing through your veins can never hurt those you love."

As his gaze holds mine, I want so desperately to tell him again that I love him and I'm more sorry than he'll ever know. But an ocean of silence stretches between us that we cannot cross. I hurt him. Deeply. I hope I can prove myself... to regain his trust and, somehow, find a way back into his arms again, because I cannot imagine a life without him by my side. I've already lost my heart to this man—this enemy of mine.

CHAPTER 53

VARYS

I t has only been two weeks since Inara began her training, but she is making great progress in learning to wield her magic.

Inara raises her hands, and a glowing blue orb hovers between her palms. She grits her teeth as she allows it to build before suddenly sending it arcing toward me. I conjure an energy shield, and her magic explodes across the barrier in a brilliant display. Her magic is powerful, but such power comes at a price.

She pants heavily at the struggle to conjure another orb, but I call out. "Enough for now."

I half expect her to protest, but instead, she nods, exhausted. I know I pushed her hard, but we both agreed to try more powerful magic today.

"Let us go inside to eat," I tell her, sensing her need for nourishment.

As we walk along the garden path back to the house, a

feeling of unease travels across the bond. I turn to her, concerned. "Are you all right?"

She lifts her eyes to me, and I notice the dark circles beneath them. She takes another step and then stumbles forward.

Swiftly, I catch her around the waist and hoist her into my arms. "What happened?"

"I-I don't know. I'm just... so tired," she mumbles. "Exhausted."

"Nyrala!" I call out toward the house.

My sister rushes to the door, eyes widening when she sees my mate. "What happened?"

"I don't know. She cannot walk. She—"

"I can walk, Varys," she says weakly. "I'm just tired."

"I want Nyrala to assess you. All right?"

It is telling that she does not argue. Normally, she is very stubborn about accepting help. She must feel far weaker than she admits.

"Bring her into this room," Nyrala says, guiding me to the main living space.

Carefully, I place my mate on the sofa and Nyrala leans forward, allowing her hands to hover over her body as she moves them up and down, her eyes closed as she reads Inara's energy.

Panic tightens my chest when I observe the deep crease of her brow. "What is it? What did you find?"

"I am... uncertain."

"What do you mean?"

She looks at Inara. "You used more magic in today's session than you ever have before."

"Yes," Inara replies. "Varys and I agreed to test my control a little more each time we practice."

Nyrala's gaze snaps to mine. "You must stop."

"Why?" Inara asks. "I just need to rest, and then—"

"No," Nyrala states firmly. "You do not understand." She looks back at me, and dread settles deep in my gut. I know that look. Something is terribly wrong.

"Your magic is not like ours," she says. "We draw our power from the life force of nature around us. But you... even though you gained it from your bond with Varys... your magic draws power from your own life force. That is why you are so exhausted after each lesson." She pauses. "If you use too much magic, it could kill you, Inara."

"That explains why your magic is so powerful," I murmur, more to myself than to her. "Because it takes from you... feeds directly from your life force and emotions. We cannot practice anymore. It is too dangerous. You cannot use your magic, Inara."

"No." Her eyes flash with determination. "We *have* to continue. You said so yourself, Varys. You said if I didn't learn to control it, I could accidentally hurt someone, remember?"

I purse my lips. "That was *before* I knew it could kill you."

"Now that we know there are limits to how much I can use, we will just have to be careful."

If it were anyone else, I would probably agree, but this is Inara, and I hate the idea of her being in danger. She may have hurt me, but that does not mean I stopped loving her.

"Varys, you know I am right. It's safer for others if I learn to wield my magic, rather than risk losing control of it."

"She is right," Nyrala agrees. "If she loses control, who is to say she would not use up too much of her life force instead?"

"Fine," I reluctantly agree. "Rest, and we will start again tomorrow."

I lean down and scoop her back up into my arms.

Before she can protest, I start up the stairs to her room—my room, technically, before I gave it to her.

As we walk down the hallway, we pass Aryl. "Oh, wonderful!" A smile splits his lips. "You two have finally made up."

I level an icy glare at him, and his head jerks back in surprise. "Inara is not feeling well. She exhausted herself during our training."

"Oh," he says, awkwardly. "I thought—"

"Would you please step aside so we may pass? Or are you just going to continue blocking the way?"

He scoffs and raises both hands out in mock surrender. "Well *excuse me* for being happy for you, because I *thought* that—"

A deep growl rumbles in my chest and he falls silent.

"Have you not had your morning tea yet?" Aryl rolls his eyes. "Is that why you are so grumpy?"

Inara stifles a laugh as I growl at him again.

Aryl's lips twitch in a teasing smirk. "Fine, I will speak with you later when you are in a better mood."

When I reach Inara's room, I carefully lay her on the bed. She must be even more tired than she lets on because she makes no effort to sit up. Instead, she sinks back into the mattress with a small sigh of exhaustion.

Now that I know her magic draws from her own life force, I realize I could have killed her by pushing her too hard during our lessons. Guilt rises from the pit of my stomach. Although we may never be true mates, she is still mine to care for, protect, and watch over. I nearly failed her.

I study the dark circles under her eyes once more. "Forgive me," I whisper. "I could have caused you to—"

"There is nothing to forgive," she cuts me off. "You did not know."

"I should have." I sigh heavily, then start for the door. "If you need anything, I will be nearby."

"Thank you, Varys." Her voice follows me out into the hallway, and it takes everything inside me not to turn around. The hurt and the pain are still too raw. I must either find a way to move past it or else push her away. At this moment, I am not strong enough to do either.

I walk down the stairs to find Aryl and Nyrala sitting on the sofa near the hearth. Aryl holds out a cup of tea to me.

I half expect him to say something witty or cutting, but he does not. Instead, his expression turns sober. "I did not mean to make you uncomfortable in the hallway. Nyrala just told me about Inara's... condition. Forgive me."

"You did not know."

"Yes, but... why can things not return to how they were before?" he asks. "You seemed so happy. Why allow this one thing to come between you?"

"She *kept* this from me, Aryl." I run a hand roughly through my hair. "I *trusted* her and—"

"*Did you?*"

My eyes snap to his. "What do you mean?"

"Did you truly trust her?" he asks. "Because it did not seem that way to me."

I clench my jaw. "You know nothing."

"Is that so? Then, I suppose I was mistaken, and Inara was present in all the High Council meetings after she was crowned queen."

I wave a hand dismissively. "She is human. It is not part of their culture. I have witnessed how the human kings do not rule equally with their queens. So, I did not expect her to—"

"Inara is the Dark Elf queen now, though, is she not?"

he challenges. "Last I checked, she is bound to the Dark Elf King and resides in Ithylian. Not Florin."

I open my mouth to speak, but Nyrala beats me to it. "He is right, Varys. You are upset that she didn't trust you. But... you did not trust her completely either."

I stand, staring at them both with a thunderous expression. "You know nothing. I would have sealed her to me and it would have been a lie, because she never trusted me enough to tell me who she was."

"Magic does not make us who we are, Varys," my sister counters. "It is only a part of us. One she held back because you were a stranger."

"I was *not* a stranger. I was her husband. Her mate. Her bonded. Her fated one."

"And her enemy," Aryl adds. "You were her enemy before you were any of those other things."

A heavy silence settles as I contemplate his words.

He is right. We were bound to each other, but still...

"I do not know how to fix this between us." I sigh heavily. "Truthfully, I'm not sure it can even *be* fixed."

"The only person who can answer that is her," Nyrala says. "If you truly want an answer, you must talk to her, Varys."

"And what if her answer is—" I stop abruptly, unable to voice my worries aloud. Because she was able to keep this from me, I fear everything between us was false.

"You will not have peace until you know for sure," Nyrala says. "To move forward, you must know your path. You cannot determine that without asking the one you wish to share it with."

She leans forward. "I would see you with a family... children." She gives me a pained smile. "Because she is human, you may not be able to have that with her. So before you make a decision... you must know her heart and understand yours, as well."

She is right. I value her counsel, but it does not make this any easier. My heart is torn, and my soul is hurting. But I appreciate that she and Aryl are here, trying to help me... to help us both.

"Sound advice, as always." I place a hand on her shoulder. "Thank you."

I turn to head back up the stairs.

"What about me?" Aryl asks incredulously. "Was *I* not here offering advice to you as well?"

I glance over my shoulder, arching a brow. "Thank you, Aryl. I'm not sure what I would do without you," I add, unable to hide the teasing sarcasm in my tone.

"You are welcome, Brother." He tips up his chin with a slight smirk. "Seek me out whenever you next need council. For we all know I am the wisest in our family."

It is all I can do not to roll my eyes. A smile quirks my lips when I observe Nyrala struggling to suppress a laugh.

I make my way back up the stairs and stand outside Inara's door as indecision plays through my mind. Doubt wins out, and I decide to head to my room next to hers. I want to speak with her, but I cannot bring myself to ask the question I desperately want to ask.

My true fear is that I've already lost my heart to my human bride, and she may never have truly given me hers in return. I lie back in the bed and stare at the ceiling as I think about my predicament.

Alarm spikes through the bond, and I jerk up in bed. My head snaps toward the adjoining door to her room, and a terrified cry fills the air. "No!"

Without hesitation, I rush through the door and find her thrashing on the bed beneath the blankets. Her eyes are closed as I approach.

Gently, I rest a hand on her shoulder and reach for her through the bond, sending a wave of calm across our connection. "Inara," I speak softly. "You are having a nightmare. It is not real."

I inhale sharply as I'm pulled into her mind.

The banner of Kolstrad blows on the wind. Prince Aegryn's men march in droves toward Florin. Wraiths surround them, their burning red eyes gleaming with the desire to feed. They will feast when they reach Florin. They will bathe in the blood of their enemies as they drink of their life force.

Aryl and I stand before our army of Dark Elves, side by side, with Inara's brothers and the soldiers of Florin.

High Mage Ylari stands on the walls of Florin's castle, fighting to defend it.

A bolt of magic arcs through the air, and I watch myself fall back.

"Varys!" Inara cries out. "No!"

Closing my eyes, I concentrate and pull her from the nightmare.

Her eyes snap open, full of fear. When they meet mine, tears form at the corners and she jerks up, wrapping her arms tightly around me as she sobs into my ear. "I thought you had died. I was so afraid."

Her fear was real, as was her pain and sadness. I felt this through our connection. Even if she does not love me, she cares for me. Deeply.

I slip my arms around her waist and smooth a hand soothingly across her shoulders and back.

"It was a vision. Similar to the one I had before." Her voice quavers. "The Wraiths were there with Aegryn. They are the darkness, Varys. And Prince Aegryn is the one who seeks to control them in the prophecy. He must be."

"You are sure this was not a nightmare?"

"It felt real, but I cannot always be sure."

"You've dreamed of Aegryn attacking Florin before. It would not hurt to send another message to your brothers about this."

"What if I'm wrong, Varys?" Worry mars her beautiful face. "I could not save my parents. What if something happens to you?"

My heart clenches at her concern. "I will be careful. I have seen your vision. If it comes to pass, I will know what to do."

She lifts her gaze to mine, her eyes brimming with tears. The first one escapes her lashes, but I cup her cheek and brush it away with my thumb.

"I understand what it is to carry the burden of guilt," I murmur. "I have carried it since the day of my father's death on the battlefield." Dark memories fill my mind, and I close my eyes briefly. "He took an arrow meant for me. As he lay dying, I knew my mother would follow soon after. They were fated, and I knew my mother would not survive his death. She loved him too much."

I clench my jaw, trying to push down the pain. "If not for me, my parents would still be alive."

"You told me that the death of my parents was not my fault, and yet, you cannot even see that this applies to you, too."

"It *was* my fault," I insist. "I—"

"You are wrong. Your father knew what he was doing when he gave his life for yours. Just as my mother did when she died protecting me and my sister." She takes my hand, squeezing it gently. "When you truly love someone, the choice is already made. You'd do anything to save them, no matter the cost to yourself."

My mind replays the last moments with my father. With his dying words, he told me he loved me. Inara is right. I understand my father's decision because it is the same one I would make regarding my Khio'ri.

She hugs me and I drop my forehead gently to hers. I had not meant to make such an intimate gesture, but I will not take it back. I love her, and I do not want to lose her.

Even if things cannot be as they were, I would not see her harmed. "I am afraid to continue pushing you to learn your magic," I admit the fear deep in my heart. "Now that I know it can be dangerous for you, I cannot bear the thought."

"I will be fine," she murmurs. "I may be human, but I am stronger than you think."

"I know you are strong," I reply. "I knew it the moment we met, my brave human wife."

Her hazel eyes search mine, and I am lost in their depths. In this moment, I understand an irrevocable truth. The khio'rinar is an absolute. It will not fade or falter with the passage of time, and it will admit no other. But love is different. It is a choice. And there is no question in my mind that I love her. I am hers, and I have been from the very start.

And now, I must know if she truly is mine.

She leans in and brushes her lips to my own. My heart pounds in my chest at the first gentle touch of her mouth upon mine. I have missed the feel of her in my arms and the taste of her lips. Pulling her closer, I curl my tongue around hers, relishing the soft moan that escapes her as I deepen our kiss.

Everything inside me longs to claim her in all ways. To seal her to me, and to give her my mark. But first, I must know if she truly loves me or if her heart belongs to Lukas.

I force myself to pull away. "Inara, we must stop. I—"

"Varys!" Aryl's voice calls through the door, interrupting. "A guard is here to speak with you. He says it is urgent."

Cursing his timing, I turn back to Inara. Her eyes are full of hurt. "I understand," she whispers. "Truly."

She does not. She believes I was rejecting her, and I do not have time to explain. Whatever this message is, I must hear it. It must be important for my brother to interrupt us like this.

"I will return to check on you." I dip my chin in polite parting and leave. When I open the door, Aryl's eyes are wide. "What is it?"

"There are reports of Wolf Shifters near the capital," he says in a low voice. "One was sighted in the forest near the ruins of Elysarin."

"When?"

"Less than an hour ago." He pauses. "What if they are scouts?"

"Why would they come here? We sent a message to Lukas and Inara's brothers."

"Then it either did not reach them, and they do not know what they heard were rumors... or it did reach them, and they do not care."

His words land like a blow to my gut. Inara and I married to prevent a war, and now I may have unintentionally brought it to my doorstep.

CHAPTER 54

INARA

Varys leaves and I cannot stop thinking of our kiss. I love him and, for a moment, I thought…

Heaving a sigh, I push down my emotions.

He has changed his mind. He does not want me. Not after what happened between us.

I stand and walk to the window, pushing it open. I stare out at the forest just beyond the garden wall and toward the ruins of Elysarin, admiring the beautiful spires in the distance. Movement in the garden catches my eye and I turn toward it, studying it intently. Reflective golden eyes blink back at me from the darkness.

"Inara!" a hushed voice calls out from the shadows, and my jaw drops as I recognize its pitch.

"Lukas?" I glance around the grounds, but notice no one else nearby. "What are you doing here?"

Carefully, he makes his way through the garden until he is beneath the window. "Stand back."

I step away from the opening and my eyes widen in

surprise when he leaps through and into the bedroom. His nostrils flare and his head immediately whips toward the bed, his expression darkening.

I cross my arms. "You could have just come in the front door like a normal person."

A low growl rises in his throat. "The Dark Elf King was here."

"Of course he was. He is my husband, Lukas. What are you doing here? Is everything all right?"

The door opens and Varys steps in, freezing in place when he sees Lukas standing beside me.

Lukas bares his fangs in a feral snarl.

"Lukas, what are you—"

Before I can finish, he hoists me into his arms. A terrified scream erupts from my throat as he leaps back out the window to the ground below.

"Inara!" Varys calls out from the window. "Guards!"

Lukas barrels toward the forest, moving so fast the trees blur around us. "Lukas, what are you doing?"

"Saving you."

"From what?"

"From the Dark Elf King, Inara," he replies, not winded in the slightest as he continues to rush through the woods. "Do not worry. You are safe now. I've got you."

"Lukas, stop! I don't know what you think is happening, but—"

A thunderous roar echoes through the woods. My eyes widen as Varys charges toward us with inhuman speed. Lukas sets me on my feet, and instantly changes into his wolf form.

It's been so long since I've seen him shift. He is so much larger than the dire wolves. His russet-brown fur bristles in anger as he snarls and steps in front of me, shielding me from my husband.

"Varys!" I cry, trying to draw his attention. "It's all right. It's just Lukas."

I step out from behind my friend and my heart stops. Varys's eyes are obsidian black. His lethal, black claws are fully extended, and his fangs are bared in a feral expression full of murderous rage. "Let her go." A low growl rumbles deep in his chest. "Now."

"No." Lukas snarls. "You cannot have her."

"She. Is. Mine." Varys grinds out. "If you dare try to harm her, I will—"

I step between them. "Stop!"

They both jerk back, blinking at me in confusion.

"Get behind me, Inara." Varys starts toward me, but Lukas growls menacingly.

"Lukas won't hurt me, Varys." I turn to my friend. "And Varys is my husband, Lukas. Why are you here? What's going on?"

Lukas shoots me a brief look before turning back to Varys and leveling an icy glare at him. "We received word you were being held against your will. That your new *husband*"—he spits out the word—"was hurting you."

"That's ridiculous," I counter. "Varys is my bondmate. I love him, Lukas."

Lukas cocks his head to the side. "You do?"

I look back at my husband and find him staring at me with an expression I cannot quite discern—somewhere between hope and disbelief.

He walks up beside me and wraps a possessive arm around my waist, tugging me to his side. "I replied to your accusation days ago, Prince Lukas," Varys says. "I assured you Inara was not being harmed."

Lukas narrows his eyes. "Forgive me for not taking the word of a Dark Elf when it comes to Inara."

"I'm fine, Lukas. I have not been hurt."

His gaze is piercing as he tries to gauge my words. "Truly?"

I offer him a faint smile. "Truly."

He shifts back into his human form, thankfully choosing to shift in such a way that it appears as if he is fully dressed instead of naked. I walk toward him, and he wraps me up in a bear hug, lifting me up and spinning me around once before setting my feet back on the ground. "Thank the gods, you are all right," he whispers in my ear. "We were so worried."

"We?"

"Your family and me. A raven came with a message. We thought it was from you."

Varys's features harden. "It was a lie."

I look between them. "Someone does not want us together. They don't want us to have an alliance. But who?" Images of my vision return. "Prince Aegryn." I turn to Lukas. "I had a dream about him. Maybe he's the one behind it."

Lukas looks at me in alarm.

"Varys knows about my visions," I explain.

Lukas turns to him, studying him sharply. "Do your people have seers?"

"Yes. It is not forbidden to have visions among my kind. It is simply a type of magic. We do not consider it evil or heresy, and we certainly do not punish it by death."

"That's one thing you Dark Elves have right then," Lukas says, and Varys nods.

They finally find something to agree on.

I turn to Lukas and explain my visions to him, along with my newly inherited magic. When I'm finished, he nods. "Your visions may be right," he says. "Prince Aegryn has been hounding your brother for Grayce's hand, but she has refused him. He is threatening to withdraw his alliance with Florin, and with the constant Wraith attacks, we—"

"Wraith attacks?" I ask in alarm. "Where?"

"Throughout the kingdom. But more from the borders between Prince Aegryn's kingdom—Kolstrad—and Florin. If he was in your vision with the Wraiths, he is behind the attacks somehow. He has to be."

"Now, we must figure out how," Varys says. "I doubt he could control the Wraiths on his own."

"Now that we've determined we are all on the same side, perhaps we could sit down somewhere to talk." I look between the two of them. "Instead of standing out here in the forest."

Lukas nods, and then steps forward and extends his hand to Varys. Varys raises his hand and they grasp each other's forearms. "You are not what I thought you were," Lukas says. "It seems I was wrong about you, Dark Elf King."

Aryl and Devyn approach, eyeing the exchange warily.

"Everything is all right," I tell them, and they stand down. "It was a misunderstanding."

Despite my words, things are still tense as Lukas follows us back to the house.

CHAPTER 55

VARYS

I t does not escape my attention how closely Inara sits beside her former betrothed on the sofa as we speak. I do not like how overly familiar this Wolf Shifter prince is with my mate. Inara told him she loves me, and he seemed rather surprised by this information.

I was too, for that matter. Elation sparked in my chest when these words left her mouth, and I am exceedingly pleased that she made this declaration to her former fiancé.

"I was supposed to bring you back to Florin," he tells her. "I promised your brothers and Grayce that I would find you and return you to them."

"Thank you for coming for me," she says. "You did not need to, but I am glad to know you would have saved me if I had actually needed it."

She turns to me and takes my hand. "But now, you can report back that I am well."

"Perhaps we should visit," I offer. "I would like to speak with your brothers about these Wraith attacks." I lean forward and look at Lukas. "If Aegryn is behind this, we must find out how he is helping the Wraiths breach the Great Wall without anyone knowing."

"Only someone extremely powerful could do this unseen," Lukas adds. "But who?"

"What if Prince Aegryn possesses magic?" Inara asks. "If my visions are right, he could be the one behind the fake letters, as well. He would have the most to gain if we were at war with each other. And he would use the Wraiths to weaken us further, taking down our kingdoms, one by one."

I rub my chin. "I have fought Aegryn. If he had magic, he would have used it then. Besides, the Wraiths are too powerful for just one man to control. They would simply turn on him, too, once they were done with us. Without magic I doubt he would be able to repel them, should they attack."

"You do not need magic to defeat the Wraiths," Lukas counters. "They are not immune to the effects of an ax or a blade."

"You *do* need magic if they attack in great enough numbers," I say grimly. "That is why the Wall was reinforced with magic to repel them. Which means only someone with great power could help them cross it."

"What about the Fae?" Lukas asks.

I shake my head. "The Wraiths have been attacking along their borders as well as ours. The Fae king came to speak with me about this not long ago. It is as if the Wraiths are testing the magical barriers that surround our kingdoms, searching for vulnerabilities."

"The Fae king said he was going to speak with you about this." Inara tells Lukas. "Did you meet with him?"

"Yes, I did." A sly smirk twists Lukas's lips. "He asked

me several questions about Grayce... wanted to make certain I had no plans to court her."

Inara frowns. "Why would he ask that?"

"I believe he wishes to make an alliance through marriage as you have." Lukas arches a brow. "And you know how quickly gossip travels." His gaze darts to me. "I lost my beloved princess to the Dark Elf King and am now supposedly madly in love with her sister, who helped me through my loss."

Inara laughs, but I narrow my eyes. "You did not raise any objections to our marriage on the day of our wedding."

"You were Inara's choice." Lukas shrugs before turning to her. "We had an arrangement, and it... served its purpose."

She nods and I wonder at this cryptic statement, making a mental note to ask her about it later.

Lukas continues. "When you return, you may find your sister already engaged to the Fae king."

"I doubt it," Inara says. "Grayce was brokenhearted the last time we spoke."

Lukas's head jerks back before he narrows his eyes and growls low. "Who hurt her?"

Inara places a hand on his shoulder. "She did not give me a name, but I doubt she will be eager to court anyone else anytime soon."

He frowns. "What happened exactly?"

"She swore me to secrecy, Lukas."

I'm surprised when he does not press further, especially considering how protective he was upon hearing she was heartbroken.

As we continue to talk and make plans to visit Florin, I observe how at ease they are in each other's company. I envy him in a way. He has been involved with her family since they were children, and it is plain to see how much she cares for him.

Despite her earlier declaration, fire burns in my veins. Fierce possessiveness fills me, and I ache to seal her to me. To complete our bond by claiming my mate, so that none will question she is mine.

CHAPTER 56

VARYS

As the sun sets low on the horizon, Inara asks Lukas to stay with us, but he insists upon leaving. He says it is important for him to report back to her brothers before they send the army here, as the Order of Mages has suggested.

The last thing we need is a battle born of misunderstandings that would undermine everything we have tried to do with this marriage alliance.

Inara walks with Lukas out in the garden to bid him farewell. I observe discreetly from the shadows as he hugs her again, then leaves. She sits down on one of the nearby benches, a contemplative look on her face.

I long to go to her, but I do not know what to say.

A hand on my shoulder draws my attention and I turn to find my sister standing behind me. "What will you do?"

"We will travel to Florin."

"No," she gently admonishes. "I mean… what will you do about your mate?"

I understand what she is asking, but I don't have an answer. "I do not know."

"Do you love her?"

"Yes."

"Then what is the problem?"

I gesture in the direction Lukas left. "You saw how they were with each other."

Nyrala arches a brow. "I saw two friends. That is all."

"Did you not see the way he embraced her?"

She rolls her eyes. "I know what true love looks like, and that was not it, Brother. He is her friend, nothing more. I am certain of it."

"What if you are wrong?"

"Then what?" she asks. "Will you be like our grandfather? Take a Dark Elf as your true mate and relegate Inara to another side of the castle so you can have a family with someone else?"

Bitterness fills me as I think again of Inara's interactions with Lukas. Jealousy rises within and I clench my jaw. "Perhaps, that would be the wiser decision."

Even as the words leave my mouth, they feel wrong. I know deep inside I will never want anyone else this much. "If I took a Dark Elf as my true mate, I could have a family, but—"

Pain stabs at my chest like a sharpened blade and I still. I press my hand to the spot as I struggle to catch my breath.

"Varys, what is wrong?" Nyrala asks in concern.

"Inara," I wheeze through the deep ache.

I turn to see Inara off to the side, and her eyes meet mine, shining with hurt. I was so focused on my conversation with Nyrala, I had not even noticed her approach.

Searching the khio'rinar, I realize this pain is sadness—

deep and intense. She heard what I told my sister and believes I do not want her.

"Inara," I call out, but too late, as she disappears around a tall hedge.

Without hesitation, I chase after her.

She is hurt because she did not hear the rest of what I would have said to my sister. I have already decided that if I cannot have children with Inara, I would rather not have them at all. I will never do to her what my grandfather did to his Fae bride.

I will find Inara, and I will learn the truth this night. I cannot continue in this current state of unknowing. If what she heard upset her, maybe she desires me as much as I do her.

Or, maybe, it is merely the fear of being kept in a tower somewhere and ignored.

If Inara does not want me, I will be devastated. But if she does, I will claim her as mine and I will never let her go.

CHAPTER 57

INARA

Varys does not want me. He will take a Dark Elf as his true mate. Despair fills me. I know I have no right to feel so hurt, especially after I betrayed him, but I cannot help it. If Varys wants someone else, I will not beg him to stay with me. I have more pride than that.

I just need a moment to gather myself so I can face him and lie—tell him I'm fine no matter what he chooses. Only our political alliance matters. At least, that's what I must convince myself of before we speak again.

Quickly, I make my way to the stables just beyond the garden. Rhygar is not saddled, but surely riding without one will not be difficult. I've done this many times before with my horse. He raises his head and I run a hand through his soft fur, trying to communicate that I want to leave.

His reflective yellow eyes meet mine and he lowers his head, projecting an image of running to let me know he understands. He lowers himself and I climb onto his back, heading for the ruins of Elysarin castle.

As we take off, I hear Varys call out behind us, but I don't stop. I cannot make myself turn back. Not now, when I am so hurt.

CHAPTER 58

VARYS

Quickly, I find Shynar and follow Inara. Closing my eyes, I concentrate on our bond as Shynar follows her trail. Pain wraps tight around my chest, and I know it is not just mine; it is hers. I must speak with my Khio'ri and tell her the truth. I do not want anyone but her.

As we travel deeper into the woods, the tall towers of the Elysarin castle ruins rise up in the distance. Their silver rooftops gleam with the last light of the sun, and the vines covering the crumbling stone walls begin to glow as their tiny purple and white flowers open to the moon rising above.

When we reach the courtyard, a cool breeze blows across my skin. My nostrils flare at detecting her delicate scent, and I know she is near. A slight huff of sound off to one side is Rhygar, pacing along the far wall.

I slide off Shynar's back and walk over to him, resting a hand on his jaw. Through our connection, I can sense his desire to hunt, but he does not wish to stray far from Inara. The need to protect her overriding his own wants. "Thank you, my friend," I whisper. "Go. I will stay with her."

He and Shynar take off into the woods, searching for prey. The sound of their retreat draws Inara's attention toward me, her eyes widening slightly as they meet mine. "Varys," she breathes, placing a hand to her chest. "You scared me."

Standing beneath the silver moonlight, she is ethereal. I stare, transfixed. It has felt like forever since I allowed myself to gaze upon her fully like this. She is so lovely I cannot form a coherent thought, much less speak, as my eyes travel over the soft arch of her brows, her gently curved ears, and her full, pink lips.

Her long hair spills over her shoulders and down her back in silken waves of gold. Slowly, I walk toward her. "Forgive me," I breathe. "I did not mean to frighten you."

She says nothing. Her gaze holds mine, and I tentatively reach out and touch her cheek. Tracing my fingers over her soft skin, I observe as a pink flush rises.

She takes a small step back, lowering her eyes. "Don't," she whispers.

I drop my hand to my side. "Inara, please let me explain."

"There is nothing to explain," she murmurs, turning her back to me. "You will take a Dark Elf woman as your true mate so you can have heirs. And because I—" Her voice catches.

The wind carries the saline scent of her tears, but she quickly brushes them away, tipping up her chin. "It cannot work between us. I betrayed your trust, and you cannot forgive me. Nor do I expect you to. I simply think"—she wraps her arms around her waist—"that we should work on maintaining our friendship, if it is still there."

"Inara, I—"

She holds up her hand in a bid for silence. "Let me finish," she says, and I go quiet. "Our marriage is the foundation of the alliance between our people, and it must remain. But I refuse to be left in a tower somewhere, like your grandfather's Fae wife. I will not be kept," she states firmly. "I—"

"Please, let me speak," I interrupt.

Cautiously, I approach her, but she does not turn around. She is so close, I can feel the warmth of her body when I stand behind her. My fingers ache to touch her, but I dare not. Not before I know her thoughts and her feelings.

"Can you forgive me?" I ask softly.

She straightens and slowly turns to face me. "For what? I am the one who—"

"I pushed you away when all I have wanted to do from the moment we met was to pull you close. I was angry that you did not trust me when I had already given you my heart. I—"

"You only want me because of the bond." Her voice quavers softly. "It is the reason you asked for my hand in the first place."

"Yes, it is," I admit the truth. "When I realized what you are to me, I had a choice. I could either ignore it and hope that I could live with that decision, or I could embrace it and take you as my wife. You were human, we were enemies, and I did not see how it could work, but I knew I wanted to try."

I reach out and gently cup her chin, lifting her face up to mine. "I will never regret the bond between us. Without it, I might never have found you, Inara. You are intelligent, caring, brave, and the most beautiful woman I have ever beheld. The day we met, my heart knew what my mind refused to accept. You are so much more than my fated one. You accept me as I am… scars and all. You are my light in the darkness. You are the other half of my soul."

I take her hand and pull it to my chest, resting her palm over my beating heart. "You are my Khio'ri—my cherished one. I will never love another as I love you. My heart is no longer my own; it is yours, Inara." Gently, I drop my forehead to hers. "I love you more than life."

"You love me?" A tear slips down her cheek, but I brush it away with the pad of my thumb.

"You are my heart, my Khio'ri."

"But I am human." Her hazel eyes search mine. "You would be giving up your future. The chance to have a family."

"I do not want a future without you by my side, but I will not force you to—"

She crushes her lips to mine in a passionate kiss, and I lift her into my arms, holding her close as one kiss blurs into the next until I do not know where one ends and the other begins.

Desire pulses through our bond, stoking a fire deep within. She wraps her legs around my waist as I brace her back against the garden wall.

"I love you," she whispers. "More than anything."

"Tell me you are mine," I breathe between kisses. "For I am already yours, my Inara."

She smiles against my lips. "I'm yours, Varys."

I run my hand through her hair, gripping the silken strands between my fingers as I deepen our kiss. A soft moan escapes her as I roll my hips against hers, my *stav* hard and erect with want to join our bodies as one.

Long have I desired to claim her as mine, and now I will wait no more.

She unfastens my tunic, pushing it off my shoulders as I

remove hers. I pull down the sleek material covering her breasts. Inara inhales sharply as I cup one soft globe in my palm and brush my thumb across the sensitive tip.

I love the soft moan that escapes her as I move down her body and close my mouth over her breast, laving my tongue over the stiffened peak.

She runs her fingers through my hair, holding me close as I turn my attention to her other breast before moving even lower.

"Varys," she breathes out my name as I remove the rest of her clothing. She shivers slightly as she stands before me, completely bare.

At first, I hesitate until I realize her shiver is not from fear or the cold, but from something else entirely. My nostrils flare as the scent of her arousal fills the air.

Everything about her is beautiful.

I lower myself to my knees. Something dark and primal stirs within me as I press soft kisses down the length of her body, and the thought suddenly strikes me that she is completely mine.

Mine to cherish. Mine to love. Mine to touch. Mine forever.

Fierce possessiveness rushes through me as I press my thumb lightly against the sensitive pearl of flesh between her thighs, and she arches into my touch.

Carefully, I guide her leg over my shoulder, parting her thighs and opening her to me.

"May I taste you?" I whisper.

She looks down at me with a heavy-lidded gaze, and nods. Her mouth drifts open as I gently drag my tongue through her already slick folds. Her taste is exquisite and when I reach the small bundle of nerves at the top, her lips part on a low moan as her entire body lights up with pleasure.

I tease my tongue over the softly hooded flesh as she writhes beneath my attentions. Although I long to join my body to hers, I must wait. I want to give her pleasure first before I fully claim her.

Her delicate fingers thread through my hair as I continue to lap at her folds, concentrating my attention on the areas that make her grip me even tighter. I want only to please her. My beautiful, perfect mate.

Her entire body goes taut like a bowstring a moment before she cries out my name as she finds her release, flooding my tongue with the taste of her sweet nectar.

I kiss a line back up her body and seal my mouth over hers. Her hands move to the fasteners along my pants, but I grip her wrists, preventing her. Her eyes snap open and meet mine in a questioning gaze.

"Are you certain?" I ask, not wanting to pressure her.

"Yes," she replies without hesitation. "I want you, Varys. I love you."

I remove the last of my clothing and pull back just enough to study her. Tracing my fingers across the petal-soft skin of her cheek, I can hardly believe she is mine. She is lovely beyond all measure. "You are perfect," I whisper.

Lifting her into my arms, she wraps her legs around my waist. I trace my hands over her form; her entire body is so soft and giving. The need to claim her is overwhelming. To sink deep into her warm, wet heat and fill her with my seed, claiming her entirely—body, mind, heart, and soul.

My eyes drop to the throbbing vein in her neck and my fangs extend with the urge to mark her so every male will know she is taken. Fierce possessiveness fills me as I notch myself at her entrance. Her gaze holds mine as I begin to push deep inside her.

CHAPTER 59

INARA

The breath stutters from my lungs as he slowly enters me. At first, everything is uncomfortable, and tight heat blooms in my core as he pushes through my barrier.

"So tight," he rasps.

I wince at the slight pinch of pain, but it's quickly replaced by pleasure as he changes the angle of his hips and sinks impossibly deeper inside me. We stare at each other in mutual wonder at our connection before he leans in and captures my mouth with his own.

"I have been yours since the moment your eyes met mine," he whispers against my lips. He begins a slow and steady rhythm, creating a delicious friction between us. "Tell me you are mine, my Inara."

"I'm yours, my love."

He claims my mouth in a searing kiss and I run my hands down his back, feeling the flex of his powerful muscles as he thrusts up into me. Varys presses a series of

urgent, suctioning kisses along my jaw and down the curve
of my neck. Grazing his teeth across my already sensitive
skin, he flicks his tongue along the artery that pulses
beneath.

He pulls back and his eyes are completely black with
desire. "We mark our mates, but I do not want to hurt you,"
he whispers. "I—"

"I want you." Tracing my fingers across his lips, I touch
the tip of one fang to show him that I am not afraid. I
know he will not hurt me. "I want all of you, Varys."

His gaze holds mine, fiery and demanding, while each
stroke becomes longer, deeper, and more forceful as he
claims me. I'm so close to the edge. "Varys, please."

He growls and increases his pace. I grip him tightly as
he drives into me. As he moves deep inside my core, it is
the most exquisite pleasure I have ever known.

"You are mine," he growls as he traces his tongue along
the pulsing artery of my neck.

I tilt my head to one side, offering him better access.
"Yours," I reply, breathless.

He sinks his fangs deep into my flesh. A hot thrill
immediately replaces the initial sharp sting. When he pulls
back, he licks the two puncture wounds, sealing them.

My breath hitches as his length expands deep inside me,
almost to the point of pain, but not quite. "Varys, what
is—?"

"My knot," he grits through his teeth, and I can tell it is
taking everything within him to maintain his control.

A low groan escapes him as I tighten my legs around his
waist. I love the feel of his body joined to mine as he knots
deep in my channel, locking us together and sending me
over the edge. I cry out his name as intense pleasure
consumes me, stealing the breath from my lungs.

My release triggers his own, and he roars out my name

as he erupts deep inside me, filling me with the delicious warmth of his seed. The pulsing goes on forever, flooding me with his essence.

Our bodies are still locked together, and I'm not even fully recovered from my orgasm when he begins to move inside me once more. "You want me again?" I whisper against his lips.

"Always, my Inara," he breathes into my mouth. "Always."

CHAPTER 60

VARYS

We make love several more times before she drifts off to sleep. I study her as she lies in my arms. Her golden hair spreads out beneath her like a beautiful halo. Gently, I brush a stray tendril back from her face, staring down at her in awe.

If children were possible between us, I wonder if they would look more like me or like her.

Sighing heavily, I push this errant thought aside. Inara is human, so it cannot be.

I drop an adoring kiss on her lips, struggling to hide the depth of my need for her. Her eyelids flutter and open, and a contented smile creeps across her lips.

I kiss her long and languorously. When I roll her beneath me, she opens for me, and I settle between her thighs. "I want you again," I murmur against her lips.

She runs her fingers through my hair and cups the back of my neck, pulling my mouth back down to hers. She places the tip of my stav at her entrance, and a low growl rumbles in my chest as I sink deep into her warm, wet heat once more.

CHAPTER 61

INARA

When I wake in the morning, the dull ache between my thighs reminds me my Dark Elf husband has thoroughly claimed me. We're upstairs inside the castle ruins, in the room where we slept when we were first wed. His cloak is draped over us both to keep us warm. He must have placed it over us sometime during the night while I slept.

With his strong arms wrapped tightly around my form, I breathe deep of his warm cinnamon scent before lifting my head from his chest to gaze up at him. "You carried me all the way up here?"

His ice-blue eyes meet mine, full of warmth, as his lips curve into a handsome smile. "Your weight is slight compared to my people."

Jealousy stabs through me. "You have carried Dark Elf women to bed before me?"

Fondly, he brushes the hair back from my face. "There

has been no one before you, my Khio'ri. You are my first and my only. My people mate for life."

I remember this now. Exhilaration sweeps over me as he leans in and kisses me thoroughly. When he pulls back, he touches my face, staring at me in wonder.

"What is it?" I smile.

His glimmering eyes stare deep into mine, full of love and devotion. "I never knew it was possible to feel this way... to love someone so strongly. You are everything to me, Inara. I am yours, and I have been yours from the moment we met, my brave human wife."

Happiness blooms in my chest. "And I am yours, my love, my Dark Elf husband."

Sunlight spills in through the windows, casting the room in a soft, orange glow. I relish the feel of the sun upon my skin as we lie wrapped in each other. "I wish we could stay here forever," I whisper.

"I feel the same," he murmurs. His mouth takes bold possession of mine as he rolls me beneath him.

"Varys?" Someone calls out from below. "Inara?"

With a heavy sigh of frustration, Varys drops his chin to his chest.

I tense, already pulling the cloak around us. "Who is it?"

He purses his lips. "Aryl."

A warning growl at the door sends a shiver up my spine. "It's Rhygar," Varys explains, a hint of a smile on his lips. "He is guarding the door for us."

"Rhygar, it's me," Aryl says incredulously. "Varys? Inara? Are you in there? Tell your dire wolf that I—"

"We will be out in a moment," Varys calls back, and Rhygar quiets.

Varys and I quickly dress, then step out into the hallway.

Rhygar turns to me, gently nuzzling my side as I pet his muzzle.

Aryl stares fixedly at the ground, his entire face and the tips of his ears darkened slightly as he refuses to meet our eyes. "Forgive my intrusion. If I had known—" He stops and clears his throat. "I was worried for you both, so I came looking for you."

"It's all right, Aryl," I tell him.

He lifts his head and his eyes immediately lock onto Varys's mark on my neck. His mouth drifts open a moment before he quickly snaps it shut.

"Is everything all right?" Varys asks him.

He clears his throat again. "There have been more reports of Wraith sightings. This time, within our borders."

Varys's expression hardens. "How did they cross through the Veil?"

"Our scouts do not know. They dealt with the ones that they found, but there could be more." He pauses. "We received a message from the Dragon King Aurdyn. He has agreed to meet with you. He will arrive tomorrow."

I still. I have heard many stories about the Great Dragons and their king. He once burned an entire city to ash after their human king tried to invade their mountains. My father had no dealings with them, as far as I know, and neither has my brother. We purposely do not interact with the Dragons, not after all the rumors we've heard.

I turn to Varys. "Have you met King Aurdyn before?"

"Yes," Varys replies and I note that Aryl's expression pales at the mention of the Dragon king's name. "The last time we spoke, he threatened to set fire to our kingdom." He turns to Aryl. "Have one of the guards raise the banner over the castle to direct him here for our meeting." He takes my hand. "If you wish to remain at the summer home while I speak with him, I—"

"No," I state firmly. "I will come with you to meet him."

A smile tilts his lips, and he presses a loving kiss to the back of my knuckles. "As you wish, my Queen."

CHAPTER 62

VARYS

While I do not believe the Dragon king would actually harm us, I cannot suppress the worry in my heart as I look at my bondmate. Inara stands proudly beside me in the courtyard of Elysarin castle as we wait for King Aurdyn to arrive.

Despite her calm outer appearance, her concern seeps across our bond, echoing my own. Aryl and the rest of our guards are here as well, but my sister stayed behind at the summer home. If this were to go wrong, at least one of us must live to carry the mantle of rule, and I can think of no one more capable than Nyrala.

I close my eyes and force the dark thoughts from my mind. I have met Aurdyn before, as did my father, and despite his wrath, he and his kind have never attacked our kingdom.

For over a thousand years, a tenuous truce has existed between my people and the Dragons. King Aurdyn's subjects may have fire, but mine have powerful magic, thus making us evenly matched in battle.

"How long do you think it will be before he arrives?" Inara asks.

I am about to reply when a large shadow passes overhead, blocking the sun. I lift my gaze and see Aurdyn flying above us in his Dragon form. His silver scales shimmer beneath the sunlight as his powerful wings beat through the air. He opens his mouth and releases a thunderous roar that echoes through the forest, stopping my heart momentarily.

Inara instinctively moves closer to me, and I wrap a protective arm around her waist.

Aurdyn dips his left wing and begins a slow circle above us before he lands. The ground shakes beneath us when he touches down. He is enormous in full Dragon form, towering over us menacingly. He flicks his long tail as if in agitation. His large, dark silver wings fold tightly to his back as he lowers his massive horned head.

The scent of Inara's fear thickens the air. I dart a glance at her, admiring her strength as she stands proudly beside me, hiding her worry behind a brave mask.

Aurdyn's large, green, vertically slit pupils study us both before locking on to hers. His nostrils flare. "A human?" he asks in a booming voice. His gaze shifts to me. "Since when does your kind mate with them?"

"Queen Inara is my bondmate." A low growl rumbles through my words. "You will show your respect."

In a whirl of wind, he transforms before us into his two-legged form.

CHAPTER 63

INARA

I am stunned when the Dragon shifts into a two-legged form. He is as tall as Varys with long, silver-white hair that spills down to his shoulders, matching his silver scales. Two small, pointed black horns jut from either side of his forehead, and his dark silver wings are tucked close against his back.

Like Lukas, he is able to conjure the appearance of clothing, and he appears to be wearing dark pants. Lethal, black claws tip his hands and feet. A long, tapered tail curves behind him as his emerald-green eyes study me. His vertically slit pupils contract and expand as he steps closer.

My gaze remains locked onto his. I refuse to show any fear, despite the frantic pounding of my heart.

"I called you here to speak of the Wraiths," Varys addresses him. "They have found a way to cross the Great Wall."

His expression darkens and a thin curl of smoke puffs

out from his nostrils as he clenches his jaw. "The Mages have finally made their move."

"What do you mean?" Varys asks.

"They have always hungered for power," Aurdyn replies. "Now, they have found a way to acquire it."

"How?" I ask, stunned by his words.

"You should know, *human*. It is your kind who have helped them." He turns to Varys. "Prince Aegryn is marching even now across the land with an army of Wraiths toward the kingdom of Florin."

My knees feel weak. "How do you know this?"

"I have seen it."

"How are the Wraiths being controlled?" Varys asks. "I thought it was impossible for anyone to do this."

Aurdyn narrows his eyes. "The Mages have found a way to enslave them with magic. There are reports that a few have escaped. Those are the ones now wandering across the lands unchecked."

"But why would the Mages do this?" I ask. "They *know* how dangerous the Wraiths are."

"Why does anyone want power?" Aurdyn replies darkly. "All I know is that they are controlling the Wraiths, and they have allied themselves with Prince Aegryn of Kolstrad to march upon Florin."

"If this is true, we must stand against them," Varys says.

"I will not drag my kind into a war they need not fight," Aurdyn states firmly. "Kolstrad and Florin are both human kingdoms. Long ago, they aligned themselves with the Order of Mages to protect them from otherworldly beings, such as ourselves. If the Mages have now decided to turn their human pets against each other, that is their problem, not ours."

My anger makes me brave, and I take a step closer, meeting his eyes evenly. "Do you truly believe that Prince

Aegryn and the Mages will not come for your people too? What will stop them from attacking you after they finish with the rest of us, Dragon King?"

"That time may not even come," he replies dryly.

"It will, if they are successful," I challenge.

He studies me a moment before turning his attention back to Varys. "I have no quarrel with the Dark Elves. I came to this meeting to share what I know. That is all."

CHAPTER 64

VARYS

"If my brother's kingdom falls, yours could be next." Inara's eyes flash with anger. "How can you not see this?"

"I doubt that would happen," Aurdyn replies smugly. "My people are strong. Humans are weak."

"And I heard Dragons were brave," Inara counters. "But it seems I was wrong. You are a coward who would hide in his mountain while the rest of the world burns around him."

One of my men gasps behind us, shocked by their queen's bold words.

Aurdyn narrows his eyes and his nostrils flare. "You *dare* to insult me?"

"If I am wrong, then I will gladly apologize," she replies, as he levels an icy glare at her. "But I suspect that I am not."

A menacing growl rises in the Dragon's throat. Aryl and the rest of my guards observe with stunned expressions.

Aurdyn steps closer to her, but she stands her ground, unafraid.

Fierce protectiveness floods my veins, and I grip her forearm, pulling her behind me as I bare my fangs at him and snarl. "Do not threaten my queen, for it will be the last thing you do."

He bristles in anger and the muscles ripple beneath his scales as if readying to shift into his massive Dragon form. He steps closer, but suddenly stops, his eyes wide as he gapes over my shoulder.

I look back at Inara. Magic arcs between her fingers, crackling like lightning across her skin as she draws upon her power.

Aurdyn stares at her, stunned. "You have magic," he murmurs, more to himself than to us. "How is this possible? I thought there was only one."

"Only one what?" she asks.

"One human who possessed magic. Princess Freyja," he explains. "I saved her from the Mages. Her uncle—the king —would have let them burn her for witchcraft because of her power. Before her, I did not know humans possessed such a thing."

Inara stills, then draws her magic back inside her.

Aurdyn cocks his head to the side. "You know her."

"Our mothers were cousins. We used to play together when we were children. Tell me," she demands. "Where is she now?"

"In my kingdom, where she is safe."

Her brow creases into a small frown. "You speak of humans as if we were nothing, Dragon King, but you saved my cousin. Why?"

He clenches his jaw. "My reasons are my own."

"And I should simply take your word that she is safe with you?" Inara challenges.

"Yes," he replies firmly. "She is under my protection. I will allow no one to harm her ever again."

I stare at him in astonishment. He is in love with this human; I am certain of it. I step closer to him. "You protect *her*, but you would let her kind fall to the Wraiths while you hide in your mountains?"

"Her kind would have killed her if not for me," he growls. "They do not deserve our protection."

"You cannot judge an entire race by the actions of only a few," Inara states. "If you do not help us, Florin may well fall. If it does, then Ithylian could be next. Eventually, the Wraiths will come for your people, King Aurdyn, and I believe you know this."

"I have considered it, yes," he replies grudgingly. "But my great-grandfather trusted the words of a human king long ago, and it led to his doom, nearly costing my people everything. My kind were hunted mercilessly, and it almost caused our end.

"We survived only because we made our homes in the Ice Mountains, where most others would perish. So, you will understand why I hesitate to repeat the same mistakes as my ancestor."

I understand his reluctance to help the humans, but the Dark Elves offered the Dragons aid when no one else did. "And what of Ithylian?" I ask. "If you refuse to help the humans: to fight for Florin if they stand against the Wraiths... My people have helped you before. If I call upon you, will you honor the history between us?"

He studies me shrewdly. "*You*, I will help. The humans, I will not."

"Fine," I tell him. "Then, you'd best hope the humans do not fall to the Wraiths, because if they do, only *we* will be left to face them, when there could have been more."

"I will take that chance," he grumbles. "If this is the only reason you wished to meet, I have said what I came to say." His gaze darts to Inara, then back to me. "But I would speak with you alone a moment before I go."

I nod slightly and then turn to Inara. "I will return shortly."

She surprises me by stretching up on her toes and pressing a tender kiss to my lips in front of everyone. My kind are not usually open when it comes to displays of affection. Even Aurdyn appears surprised by this affectionate gesture.

I lead him farther into the garden, close to the castle. He lifts his gaze to the crumbling structure, studying it with something akin to awe. "Your ancestors created things of not only beauty but strength." He rests a hand on the gray stone wall. "Even the magic of these stones still lingers. If I remember correctly, this was the last building left standing, sheltering your citizens during the last Great War."

"That is true," I reply, thinking of all the lives that were lost.

"If anything had been left of my great-grandfather's kingdom, we never would have left," he says soberly. "We would have rebuilt to honor the memory of those lost and to preserve the culture of our people."

I study him keenly. Aurdyn is blunt when we are in front of others, but alone he always speaks in riddles. "What is it you are so cryptically trying to tell me?"

"You should not hide inside the mountain. Your people are not Orcs. If you stay too long in that place, you could end up buried in it, like they were."

I flinch as the story of the Orc stronghold of Grundyn replays in my mind. They were overrun by their enemies and their only means of escaping the mountain were cut off. Nearly half of their people died, and the survivors are now scattered throughout the seven kingdoms, struggling to rebuild.

I think back to Inara's words yesterday. It is difficult for her to live underground, and she wished we could stay here in Elysarin forever. Maybe it's time to rebuild. "Perhaps you are right."

His brows shoot up toward his forehead. I rarely admit such a thing to him.

"But that is not what you wanted to speak to me about, is it?" I cross my arms over my chest. "So, tell me what it is you wish to discuss."

"Your human mate," he says. "How do I win a human's heart?"

"Win?" I arch a brow. "I thought Dragons were conquerors."

He huffs out a laugh. "My female is strong of will and exceedingly stubborn. She will not be conquered."

"*Your* female?"

"She is my T'kara—my fated one. I saved her, yet she will not yield to me." He sighs heavily. "And I do not understand why."

I swallow my laughter. "That is where you are going wrong, Aurdyn. You cannot treat her as you would another Dragon. You must woo a human to win her heart, not fight her until she yields it to you… because I guarantee you, she never will. They are stronger than they appear."

"I know this," he grumbles. "But how do I… *woo* her?"

"Spend time with her," I offer. "Talk to her. Make sure she knows how important she is to you."

"How could she not already know what she means to me?" He frowns. "I saved her. I protect her. I have provided her a nest any Dragon female would envy. I made her stay behind when she insisted upon coming with me because I wanted her to remain in our home where she is safe."

I place a hand on his shoulder and meet his gaze evenly. "That was a mistake you will pay for dearly when you return. Humans are stubborn creatures, used to having their way. I have not told you the circumstances of how I met my bondmate. Even her own brother—the king—could not convince her to obey him when it came to her safety."

As I explain how I met Inara, Aurdyn listens in rapt attention. When I am done, I shake my head. "So, now you understand. You cannot force a human to do anything she does not wish, including remaining out of danger. The best thing you can do is teach her to defend herself and keep her close by your side."

"You do this with your mate?"

"Why do you think she is here?"

"There is no danger here." He replies, seeming offended. "I would *never* harm a female."

"Yes, but she is human, and I know how much anger you have toward their kind." I sigh heavily. "And do not think I have forgotten how you set fire to my last messenger."

"He was *fine*, Varys." He rolls his eyes. "I only flamed his hair. I knew it would grow back."

"You terrified him," I counter. "Now, you have a reputation among my kind for your temper."

"Dragons are not Sprites," he grinds out. "We are not supposed to be known for our friendliness, but for our fierce strength."

"Trust me. No one will *ever* confuse your kind with Sprites."

He purses his lips, but then his expression turns serious. "I must return home. If I stay away for much longer, I will incur more wrath from my human."

"She is not quite *your* human yet, though. Remember

that," I point out. "You are to court, not try to conquer."

He runs a hand roughly through his hair in frustration. "I shall remember your counsel."

Realizing that is as close to a 'thank you' as I will get from a Dragon, I sigh. "A bit of humility would probably go a long way, as well, with your… human."

He scoffs.

"Never mind." I huff out a laugh. "*That* would be an impossible feat for a Dragon."

Aurdyn narrows his eyes in mock irritation, then steps back. He shifts in a whirl of dust and wind back into his Dragon form. "Goodbye, Varys." He arches a brow. "Perhaps, when this is over, you can bring your queen to see mine. After all, they are distantly related."

Dragons are known for their over-confident natures. It's hard to suppress a grin at the fact that he is already referring to her as his queen. "Be sure to invite us to your bonding ceremony."

He tips up his chin to stare down at me imperiously. "I will do that," he replies as he flexes his wings and lifts off into the sky.

When I return to Inara and Aryl, he gives me a curious look. "What did he want?"

"Advice."

His head jerks back. "A *Dragon* asked for advice from a Dark Elf?"

I nod, but offer nothing else.

"These are strange times, indeed," Aryl murmurs under his breath.

Inara looks at me. "We must ride to Florin, Varys. If what the Dragon King says is true, we cannot trust a raven to get to my brother in time."

"I agree. And even if it did, he will need our support in a

battle against the Wraiths." I take her hand. "We will leave at dawn."

I relay my orders to Devyn to assemble the army. We will be a day ahead of them, but we will have to travel fast so that King Edmynd can ready his forces.

The rest of the day is spent sending messages back to Cyridil, informing the Council and my generals of our plan.

Once the last raven is sent, Aryl walks over to me. "Here." He offers me a cup of strong tea. "I thought you might need this."

I look up at him, expecting to see a teasing smirk on his face, but instead find a very sober expression. "Are you sure this is wise?"

I don't have to ask what he means, for I understand all too well. Despite our alliance with Florin, many of my people will be against the idea of aiding the humans.

"Florin is still under the protection of the Mages, Varys. If they are the ones behind this, then Inara's brother does not yet know he has been betrayed. We will be fighting the Order of Mages, the Wraiths, and Aegryn's army. Not to mention that we will be unable to use our powers because of the binding spell on their lands."

"We do not have a choice," I reply. "We cannot stand by and watch Florin fall."

"Would they do the same for us?" Aryl asks. "If the situation were reversed, would Florin come to our aid?"

"My brother is an honorable man," Inara's voice sounds from the doorway as she steps into the room. I had not even known she was nearby. "And I know, without doubt, that Edmynd would come to your aid if Ithylian were under attack."

"And if the Mages are behind this, which side will he choose?" Aryl asks. "There is the possibility that Aegryn marches, not to conquer Florin, but to persuade them to join his cause."

"He is right." Devyn steps out of the shadows. "The humans have been allied with the Order of Mages far longer than they have been with us." He looks at Inara. "And then there is the fact that King Edmynd was led to believe that the queen was being mistreated. We may have an alliance, but trust takes time to build."

"That is what our marriage is for." Inara takes my hand. "That's why I will go with you to Florin, to speak with my brother."

"No." My protective instincts flare. "You will stay here, where it is safe."

"I refuse to remain behind, Varys."

"Inara, please," I beg, hoping she will see reason. "You cannot ask me to take you with me when it could be dangerous."

"I'm not asking." Determination burns in her eyes. "Florin is just as much my home as Ithylian is. You cannot expect me to stay behind. Besides, you will need me to speak to Edmynd. If the Mages are behind this, they will try to turn you both against each other." She takes my hand. "You know I am right."

With a slight clench of my jaw, I sigh heavily. She *is* right. I hate the thought of her in danger, but I also remember how I first met my brave and beautiful mate. And I know that nothing I say can convince her not to come.

I pull her into my arms. "All right," I whisper as I hug

her close. It seems my wife fears nothing—not even Dragons or Wraiths.

When it is time for bed, Inara and I retire to our room. She turns to me as soon as the door closes behind us. "What kind of advice did the Dragon King ask you for?"

I take her hand and drop a soft kiss to the top of her knuckles. "He wanted to know how to win a human's heart."

A smile crests her lips. "And what did you tell him?"

I slide my arms around her waist and lift her to my chest. A low growl rises in my throat as she wraps her legs around me. Claiming her mouth in a fierce kiss, I lay her down on the bed.

I trace my fingers over her cheek and a pink flush blooms in their wake as I stare deep into her luminous eyes. "Dragons conquer their mates. I told him that human women cannot be conquered; they must be wooed... they must be worshipped."

She is perfect, and I issue a silent prayer to the gods, thanking them for bringing her to me. "I love you, my Khio'ri," I whisper. "My brave human wife."

She cups the back of my neck and pulls my lips down to hers, smiling against them. "And I love you, my Dark Elf King."

CHAPTER 65

INARA

Devyn, Aryl, and Melina ride beside us as we head toward the Veil and the kingdom of Florin's border. I am worried what will happen once we cross into my brother's lands. The Mages have spelled it so that the Dark Elves cannot use their magic there. But if we run into Wraiths, they will need it. Especially when the army arrives, if there is a battle.

I've been contemplating a solution for this, and I hope that I'm right.

"What is wrong?" Varys asks, having sensed my concern through the bond. "Are you nervous about visiting your family?"

"No, I am worried that you will be unable to use your magic once we cross the Veil."

"It will be fine, my Khio'ri. Just because we cannot access our magic does not mean we are defenseless."

"I know, but maybe there is a way to remove the binding spell."

"Perhaps," he replies, but he does not sound convinced. "I will admit that we have tried."

"Many times, I might add," Aryl says beside me.

"How does the spell work?"

"We draw our magic from the life force of the earth around us," Aryl explains. "Everything is connected. The earth beneath us does not recognize a border simply because someone drew one on a map and labeled it a different land." He pauses. "Yet, somehow, the spell placed by the Mages does this. It creates a barrier that binds our magic, rendering us unable to draw upon anything in your kingdom to use for our magic."

"The binding spell must be specific for Dark Elves, Fae, and such," I murmur, thinking out loud. "If it were not, then the Mages would be unable to use their powers as well."

"This makes sense," Varys replies.

"Any humans caught practicing magic are burned at the stake by the Mages," I say grimly. "But that also means that humans are not bound by the spell either."

Varys's brow furrows deeply. "The Mages could just as easily have included humans in their binding spell, but they did not. This suggests that they want to be able to identify those among your kind who have powers. But why?"

"I do not know."

His question plagues me the rest of our journey. Varys is right. The Mages would rather catch humans practicing magic, and execute them, instead of preventing it from happening entirely.

When we reach the soft glow of the barrier, I motion for Rhygar to stop, and Varys and the others do the same.

"I want to try something," I tell him. "You said after we were bound to each other I could cross the Veil."

He nods.

I slide off Rhygar's back and drop to my knees before the barrier. Cautiously, I touch one hand to the glowing wall. A slight tingling sensation travels from my palm up my arm. It is strange but not painful or even uncomfortable. I place my other palm on the ground just inside Florin. Digging my fingers into the damp earth, I feel the pulse of raw energy that resides just beneath the surface. Something pushes against me, an odd and heavy feeling of darkness trying to repel me, as I allow my magic to flow through me and into the ground.

Closing my eyes, I force myself to focus, trying to push through it. Sweat beads across my brow and I grit my teeth in concentration.

"Inara, stop," Varys says. "We have tried this before, but it did not work. You will hurt yourself if you use any more of your energy."

I refuse to give up. "It should not repel me, Varys. I'm human. They did not design it to keep me out. It should not resist my—"

A sharp crack fills the air, and the ground splits beneath me in a hairline fissure, spreading out like a delicate web across the earth. As I peer at it, I realize it is not the rock that is breaking, but the binding spell embedded deep within the soil.

Encouraged, I bow my head and force all my energy toward the earth, feeling the spell cracking under the power of my magic. My limbs tremble and my pulse pounds in my ears as I struggle to hold on, determined not to stop until the spell is completely shattered.

"Inara!" Varys's voice echoes in my mind, but I refuse to relent. I love him, and if I can break the spell that binds his powerful magic, giving him the ability to use it for defense, I will.

The ground gives a final quake when it's done, and I

release my hold on my power, drawing it back into myself. Exhaustion steals through my limbs, and my entire body feels weak. I struggle to lift my head to Varys and the world falls out beneath me as I collapse into the arms of peaceful oblivion.

CHAPTER 66

INARA

As my mind slowly comes back into awareness, I recognize the sound of Varys's voice beside me. "She is mine," he growls. "You will not touch her."

He stands by my bed, strategically positioned between me and the door as he faces off with my brother and High Mage Ylari. My gaze sweeps over the stone walls and the familiar unicorn tapestry above the headboard. Sunlight spills in from the balcony window and a fire burns in the hearth. These are my old chambers.

"She's my sister, and I *demand* that you let High Mage Ylari assess her," Edmynd grinds out.

"She is being tended by an Elf healer," Varys snarls. "I do not trust a Mage to touch her."

"But she is *not* an Elf," Edmynd insists. "Now, stand aside and—"

"Varys," I barely manage, and he turns to face me. He takes my hand between his, rubbing it gently.

"Inara." He breathes my name out like a sigh of relief and brushes his lips to mine. "I was so afraid. You used too much power, my Khio'ri. How are you feeling?"

"Move aside." High Mage Ylari puts a hand on Varys's shoulder.

In a blur of movement, Varys spins. He grips Ylari's wrist and pins it behind his back as he pushes him forward, slamming him on the edge of the bed and instantly immobilizing him.

My brother's hand goes to his sword and Varys sends an arc of light toward the hilt. Edmynd cries out as it burns his hand.

"Stop!" I command. My eyes snap to Varys and find his swirling black with rage. "You *will not* use magic against my own brother. And High Mage Ylari kept my secret when he could have turned me in to the Order of Mages. He will not hurt me, Varys."

The darkness in his eyes dissipates, replaced with his normal glowing blue color, as he releases Ylari and retakes my hand.

Edmynd gives him a venomous look. "How can you access your magic here, anyway?"

"I destroyed the spell that bound the Dark Elves' magic," I explain.

"Are you mad?" His eyes widen. "And how did you even do such a thing in the first place?"

"I already told you," Varys grinds out. "She inherited some of my powers through our bond. Besides, what does it matter? We are allies now, are we not, *Brother*?" Varys emphasizes the last word and arches a disdainful brow.

Raiden and Grayce walk in. Grayce runs to my bedside. "Inara, thank the gods. How are you feeling?"

Carefully, I push myself up to sitting, wincing slightly as my head begins to pound. "I'm all right."

"No, you are not," Varys chastises. "The Elf healer said you must rest to regain your strength."

"She is *not* an Elf," Edmynd insists. "Now, let Ylari assess her."

"I already told you," Varys says through gritted teeth. "The Mages are behind the Wraith attacks."

"And we're supposed to trust you, based on the word you received from the Dragon King?" Raiden scoffs.

"Yes," I tell them. "I was there. King Aurdyn had no reason to lie." I sit up straighter and a sharp hiss of pain slips out. "I dreamed of the Wraiths marching with Prince Aegryn. He would not be able to control them by himself."

"I *am not* in league with the Wraiths," Ylari growls. "I assure you, Dark Elf King, I am loyal to this family. If I were not, I would have turned the princess in the moment I discovered her powers."

Varys squeezes my hand, and through our bond, I can sense his trepidation. He doesn't want the High Mage anywhere near me, but he does not know Ylari like I do. "He is a good man, Varys. He has protected us since we were children." My gaze sweeps to Grayce.

Varys gives me a subtle nod. "All right." He turns to Ylari and issues one final threat. "You have no idea the strength of my powers, Mage." Sparks of lightning dance across his skin as he scowls at Ylari. "But if you dare harm my bondmate, I vow you *will* learn today."

Ylari blinks several times before nodding while my family stands behind him, their eyes wide and mouths gaping. The High Mage cautiously approaches, one eye on me and the other on Varys. He reaches a trembling hand and gently rests it on my forehead, bowing his head low as he concentrates.

His brow furrows deeply, and he closes his eyes. He inhales sharply and pulls away, waving his hand as if burned. "Such power," he murmurs. "I've never felt anything like it before." His gaze turns to Varys. "What she gained from you, through the bond, it is strong."

"Yes."

"What do you mean?" Raiden asks, worry easily read in his features.

Instead of answering my brother, he addresses my husband. "You were wise to begin training her, King Varys. The nylweed would not have suppressed these powers for long."

"Will she be all right?" Edmynd asks, alarmed.

I squeeze Varys's hand. "Yes, Varys has taught me to control it."

"The Order of Mages will want you dead," Ylari adds. "You are more powerful than them, and they do *not* share power outside of the Order."

Varys bares his fangs in a feral snarl. "I will end them all if they dare touch her."

"You might have to," Ylari says. "I believe she is one of the Great Uniters from the ancient tomes of the Lythyrian."

I suck in a quick breath. "What do you know of the prophecy?"

"The Order have long believed that humans may be the Great Uniters spoken of in the tomes. It is the reason the Mages have ordered the death of any human found to possess magic," Ylari says grimly. "If they are the ones seeking to control the darkness, then they would need to kill any who might become the Great Uniters."

"Which is why they would rather find and execute them, instead of weaving the barrier spell to prevent humans from accessing magic entirely," I offer as it all falls into place.

He nods.

"What do you know of the Wraiths?" Varys narrows his eyes. "Speak truth, old man."

Ylari gives Edmynd a mournful look. "Forgive me, my King. I have kept secrets because I thought to do otherwise would cause the kingdom to descend into chaos. This land has relied upon the binding magic of the Mages to keep us safe from our enemies." His eyes dart to Varys. "But now, I must speak truth."

"What is it? Tell us," Edmynd demands.

"There are two sides to magic: light and dark," he explains. "Thousands of years ago, we sought to harness both, and in that pursuit, we became divided."

"What do you mean?" I ask.

"Dark magic is powerful... more so than light, one might argue. Those who choose that path... it changes them. It shapes them into a ruined form of life. To fully embrace dark magic, there is a trade. You give away pieces of your soul as you learn to master it. Those who delve too deeply into the darkness become Wraiths—soulless beings who feed off of others."

"That's how they are controlling them," I murmur.

"The Mages can control them because their magic is born from the same place," Varys adds.

"Why is Prince Aegryn working with them?" Edmynd frowns. "It does not make sense."

Ylari turns to him. "I suspect they have promised him a long life, perhaps even to share their powers." He narrows his eyes. "But he does not understand. The Mages do not share something as potent as their knowledge *or* their power."

"Why are you offering all of this?" Varys asks.

"As I said, Dark Elf King, my loyalty is to this family above all else. I have been with them for many generations." His wizened gaze shifts to me. "I will do whatever I must to protect them. Even from my own brethren." He looks to Varys. "I could use your help, and that of your kin, to reinforce a protection spell upon the castle."

Varys turns to me. "It's all right. Go help him and then come back to me, my love."

"Are you certain?" he asks, hesitation obvious in his eyes.

"Yes." I give him a faint smile. "I promise not to go anywhere."

He places another loving kiss to my lips. "I will return as soon as I can. In the meantime, Devyn will remain with you."

Devyn gives him an affirmatory nod.

"You do realize she used to live here, right?" Raiden arches a brow. "She *is safe* in her own home."

Varys narrows his eyes. "I will take no chances with my Queen."

With that, he leaves with High Mage Ylari. Devyn bows low and retreats into the hallway to guard the door.

Raiden sits down in the chair beside me. A smirk twists his mouth. "That new husband of yours sure seems taken with you, Inara."

"He's wonderful." I cannot help the smile that curves my lips just thinking about him. "He accepts me for who I am. He had a bow made especially for me once he learned I loved archery. We practice almost every day, and now he's teaching me to wield a sword, as well as how to control my magic."

Raiden grins. "Well, then, I suppose we're going to have to be nice to him, aren't we?" He glances back at Edmynd and Grayce.

Edmynd crosses his arms over his chest. "I *am* being nice to him. It's you who threatened to lop off his head when they first arrived."

I blink at my brother. "You did?"

"He was carrying your unconscious body, Inara." He shrugs. "I was afraid he had—"

"Varys would never hurt me."

Raiden rolls his eyes. "Well, I know that *now*, but at the time, it looked rather suspect."

Grayce playfully hits the back of his head, and he winces. "I told him not to jump to the worst conclusion, but he did not want to listen." She points to Edmynd. "Neither did *he*, for that matter."

"I would have felt the same way had the Fae king showed up with you like that, Grayce," Edmynd counters.

"The Fae King?" I frown. "What are you talking about?"

With a heavy sigh, Grayce drops into the chair next to Raiden. "The Fae King is coming to negotiate a treaty between us. Edmynd thinks he is going to ask for my hand."

"Why?"

"He asked specifically if I could be present when he arrives."

"But that could mean anything," I counter. "Maybe he simply wants to meet the whole family as a gesture of goodwill."

Edmynd arches a brow, but says nothing.

I turn back to my sister. "I met him, you know."

"You did?" She blinks several times. "What was he like?"

"He seemed very nice. Like the kind of person who loves to joke but who also understands when it is important to be serious. He and Varys are friends."

"What did he look like?" Raiden asks. "I saw his father once, but I've never seen him."

"Silver hair, lavender eyes, and wings. He appeared rather young, but they all look that way, do they not? He was handsome, too, but not anywhere near as handsome as Varys."

Raiden makes a mock gagging noise. "Enough, I do not need to hear about how handsome and loving your new husband is."

"Why not?" I frown.

He wraps an arm around my shoulder and ruffles my hair. "Because you're still my little sister," he teases. "That's why."

"You are truly happy with him?" Edmynd asks.

"Yes," I reply without hesitation.

He hugs me close. "Watching you leave with him that day was the hardest thing I've ever had to do."

"It was my decision, Edmynd."

"I know. But I felt responsible anyway."

A guard steps inside and bows low. "My King, the men are assembled, as you requested."

Edmynd exchanges a glance with Raiden, then looks at me. "We'll be back shortly. I have to speak to our guards—make sure they understand the Dark Elves are our allies and friends. I do not want any misplaced hostilities when their army arrives here tomorrow."

They both leave, and Grayce sits on the edge of my bed. "You truly look happy, Inara. I am so glad for you."

"What about you? Are you still—" I stop, unsure how to broach the subject of her mystery beau. "Is your heart healed?" I finally ask.

She lowers her gaze. "I should not have told you about him."

"Why not?" I take her hand. "I am your sister. You can tell me anything."

"Because it does not matter, now, does it?" Her voice is a flat monotone, and her shoulders droop. "I was naïve. He did not want me."

"I am so sorry, Grayce, truly."

She leans in and hugs me close. "I'm just so glad you are well and happy. You've no idea how much I missed you, my dear sister."

"And I you."

"Varys refused to leave your side, even for a moment, while you were unconscious. He must be exhausted. He refused to rest or even eat anything." She nudges me. "You should have seen how pale the guards went when faced with your snarling husband and his terrifying dire wolf." She chuckles. "I overheard Edmynd asking for volunteers among the guards to stable your dire wolves, since they can hardly be kept in the regular stables with the horses."

Varys returns, greeting Grayce with a polite nod.

She stands and walks toward him. "Thank you for taking care of my sister."

"She is mine," he replies. "I would lay down my life for her."

"I can see that." She smiles and turns back to me. "I'll leave you both to rest."

Varys sits beside me and takes my hand. "Where is everyone else?" I ask, wondering where his brother and Melina have gone. I know Devyn is outside the door, but I do not know where the others are.

"Aryl is sparring with Raiden, and Melina is already in her own guest chambers for the evening." He arches a brow. "I do think our brothers get along rather well, from what I've seen. They appear to have similar temperaments."

"You mean Aryl is as much of a jokester as Raiden is?"

He barks out a laugh. "Yes. That is exactly it."

He stands. "Are you hungry? I will go find—"

"Are you?" I ask. "Grayce said you didn't eat anything, or even rest, while I was unconscious."

His expression softens. "Your brother forced some cheese and bread on me when he found me earlier."

"I'm not hungry. Not yet, anyway."

"You must eat something, my Khio'ri."

"I will." I tug at his hand. "But first, I would like a moment with my husband."

"What do you mean?"

I scoot over in the bed, and he lies down beside me. He opens his arms, and I nestle into his chest. "Like this," I sigh. "This is perfect."

He cups my chin, lifting my face to his, studying me devotedly. "I love you more than life," he whispers. "You are everything to me, my Inara."

"And you are everything to me, my love."

A soft knock at the door startles us. In a blur of movement, Varys stands from the bed, positioning himself between me and the door. "Enter," he calls out.

It's one of the servants. She blinks several times, her mouth opening and closing, before she finally manages. "Uh... dinner is ready, my Lord and... Princess, I-I mean, my Lady," she corrects herself. "Your brother sent me to retrieve you."

"We'll be down shortly," I tell her.

She bows deeply, nearly tumbling over in her nervousness, before quickly slipping back out the door.

Varys turns to me. "Do you wish to go downstairs?"

"Yes." I smile. "It will be nice to have a meal with my family again."

CHAPTER 67

VARYS

Walking down the hallway, we pass row upon row of portraits of men and women in elegant dress. I suppose they must be my bondmate's ancestors. Several tapestries of various battles and wars hang throughout. When we reach the top of the stairs, I'm surprised by how wide this staircase is. Definitely not something that would be easily defendable in a breach.

I wish Inara were anywhere but here. If I had been wise, I would have sent her with King Aurdyn, with the excuse that I wanted her to visit her distant cousin. But as I glance at my wife, I know she would not have gone. She would have seen through my excuse and refused to leave my side.

Even back in Ithylian, she would be safer than she is here. I know her brother has an army, but I do not know what sort of numbers Prince Aegryn has between his army and the Wraiths. I only hope that with Ithylian's reinforcements, we have enough to repel them should they attack.

When we reach the dining hall, I am surprised by how big it is. Tall, vaulted ceilings make it feel even larger. A long, rectangular table sits near a huge hearth with a roaring fire. Edmynd sits at the end of the table; Raiden sits on his left side and Grayce on his right. Aryl sits across from Raiden, and I note they are already sharing a bottle of wine, laughing and teasing one another.

I take a seat next to my brother and Inara sits across from me, next to Raiden. He turns to her and wraps an arm around her shoulders, leveling a mock glare at me. "You best keep her happy or else."

I frown. "Why would you think I would do otherwise?"

He gestures to Aryl as he leans in and whispers to Inara. "This one, I like much better."

Aryl raises a triumphant glass to him. "Why, thank you, kind sir."

Raiden arches a brow at my bondmate. "Are you sure you didn't marry the wrong brother?"

Aryl begins coughing into his glass.

A low growl reverberates through my chest as I narrow my eyes, but I stop immediately when Inara reaches across and places her hand over mine. "I chose well."

He laughs. "Good."

Aryl leans in and whispers to me in Elvish. "It is strange, is it not? Each of her brothers has threatened you at least three times since we arrived—vowing to beat you or end your life if you make her unhappy. Is this a human custom, I wonder?"

"I believe it is," I murmur.

I contemplate Grayce, remembering my conversation with the Fae King. The Fae are even more judgmental than my kind when it comes to humans, and I wonder if they would have difficulty accepting her as their queen.

I glance at my bondmate and think of my conversation

with Aryl. He was right. I have not included Inara in matters of rule. I assumed that since she was human, she would be like most human queens and not play a part in matters of state. I was wrong. She is my queen, and I have not honored her as such. I will be sure to do so now.

When she comes out of the cleansing room, my breath catches. She is wearing my tunic. My blood hums in my veins as I inhale deeply of our combined scent. Despite how large it is on her, it does not hide the beauty of her form beneath. We lie down in bed, and she molds her body to mine as I slip my arms around her.

I run my fingers through her long, burnished hair. She is a priceless treasure and I love her more than anything. I saw how happy she was with her family this night, and it makes me wonder if she regrets marrying me.

She strokes my cheek, drawing my gaze to hers. "What's on your mind?"

I hesitate before asking, unsure if I want to know the answer. "Do you miss your home?"

"Of course, I do. I grew up here. But Ithylian is my home as well."

My heart fills with warmth.

She reaches into the pocket of my tunic and pulls out the silken green ribbon from our bonding ceremony, studying it curiously. "Is this from our Elven wedding?"

"Yes."

"Do you always carry it?"

Gently, I tuck a stray tendril of hair behind her ear. "Yes. It reminds me of you."

"You said that couples wear it when they consummate their bond."

"It is supposed to bless their union," I murmur.

She smiles and props herself up on her elbow. "Then, perhaps we should wear it now."

Desire pulses through our connection, and I pull her to me, sealing my mouth over hers in a tender kiss. I love touching her, tasting her. I can feel the little shivers she makes as I trace my hands down the length of her form. "I want you," I breathe.

She moves over me, straddling my hips with her thighs. Intense need burns through my veins as the heat of her center pushes insistently against my stav. Only an insubstantial layer of clothing separates our bodies, and I am desperate to be inside her.

I dip my hand beneath the hemline of her tunic, tracing the tips of my fingers over her bare skin as I carefully remove her clothing. When I reach the small scrap of silk between her thighs, I extend my claws, and she gasps as I slice it away from her body.

I stare up at my bondmate. Everything about her is beautiful, and I can hardly believe she is mine.

She reaches between us and unfastens my pants, freeing me from the confines of my clothing. Her delicate fingers briefly trace over my stav before she rises and places my tip at her entrance. Her gaze holds mine, and a tortured groan leaves my lips as she lowers herself onto me.

"So tight," I rasp, savoring the feeling of her body clasping mine. Being joined to her like this is the most exquisite sensation.

She leans down and brushes her lips over the scars that mar my chest. My heart swells, for I know it is her way of reassuring me they do not matter. She loves me despite my imperfections.

Inara lifts her head and presses a tender kiss to the long

scar above my cheek. "I love you more than anything, Varys."

I sit up, wrapping my arms around her back and holding her tightly to me as I meet each movement of her hips against mine. I love the way she moans and clutches at me, breathing my name out like a fervent prayer as our bodies move as one.

"You are perfect," I whisper against her lips as I hold her to my chest.

Her channel flexes and quivers around my length with each thrust of my hips up into hers, and I know she is close.

She tightens around me, drawing me even deeper within her core. Her entire body goes tense a moment before her head falls back, and she cries out my name as she reaches her climax.

My restraint snaps, shredding the last of my control. Without breaking our connection, I flip her onto her back and sink deep inside my mate. She wraps her legs around me as each thrust becomes stronger and deeper as I lose myself in her.

Her scent is intoxicating, calling to something dark and primal within me as my knot begins to expand inside her channel.

I notice the delicate, green ribbon in her hands. Taking her left hand with my right, I speak words of enchantment, and wrap it around our wrists as it was during our ceremony. I entwine our fingers as I pin her hands to the mattress on either side of her head. A pulse of warmth extends from the contact, spreading throughout my entire body.

"Varys," she whispers my name in wonder as a softly glowing, green light surrounds us. "What is happening?"

"It is the sealing of our bond," I whisper as I continue to move deep inside her.

Her lips part on a moan as my knot locks us together and her body tightens around me.

"You are mine," I breathe. "And I am yours."

"Yours," she pants.

Primal possessiveness fills my veins as she writhes beneath me, making small sounds of ecstasy as I claim her. With my free hand, I cup her chin, forcing her gaze to mine. "I want to watch as you find your release."

Her half-lidded eyes stare up at me, full of desire, and she cries out with the force of her climax. Her channel clenches rhythmically around my length. Unable to hold back any longer, my stav begins to pulse. "Mine!" I roar, erupting inside, deep in her core, filling her with my seed.

With my stav still knotted inside her, I roll us both onto our sides and pull her close to my chest. Carefully, I remove the silken cord from our hands and the green glow around us slowly fades away.

As she drifts away in my arms, I study her lovely face. My gaze falls on the ribbon beside us. It is unusual for the magic sealing the bond to manifest as it did—glowing around us entirely. It is one of the highest blessings from the Goddess of Love and Fertility. If Inara were a Dark Elf, this would have been a sign we would create life with our joining this night.

I desperately wish that we could have a family, but I doubt it is possible. There are no Elf-human children I am aware of, and never have been, as far as our history is concerned. Even so, I will never regret my choice to take her as my true mate. Our love is enough. She is mine, and I am hers.

CHAPTER 68

INARA

When I wake in the morning, Varys is still asleep. Carefully, I turn in his arms and study him. He is so handsome. The elegant points of his ears intrigue me, and I cannot resist.

I reach out and gently trace the tips of my fingers over his left ear. With his eyes still closed, a faint smile quirks his lips. "What is your obsession with my ears, my Khio'ri?"

His eyes open, amusement dancing behind them as he looks up at me.

"I love your ears."

His brow creases. "They are just ears."

"How do you know when I'm watching you?"

He places his palm on my chest, directly over my heart. "We are bound to each other, Inara. I cannot quite explain it, but somehow… I am able to sense it."

"That isn't fair." I pout. "I can sense you, but not like that. What if you decide to observe *me* while I sleep?"

His expression turns serious, and he cups my cheek. "I

love watching you sleep." He taps my nose playfully. "And your snoring is adorable."

"Snoring?" I ask, aghast. "I *do not* snore."

A handsome smile lights his face. "Not always, but sometimes you do. It is quite charming."

"Snoring is anything but charming." I tip up my chin. "You are teasing me. I know I do not snore."

He arches a brow. "Are you sure?"

I smack at his shoulder. "Yes, I am."

He laughs.

A soft knock at the door draws our attention. "What is it?" he calls.

Before anyone answers, the sound of a horn fills the air and I whip my head toward the balcony. "Is that—"

"Our army has arrived," he says, sitting up. "We must go to meet them."

CHAPTER 69

INARA

Edmynd and Raiden's eyes are wide as the Dark Elf army approaches. Carrying the banner of Ithylian, they march in proud and perfect formation before halting in front of their king.

Varys takes my hand and steps forward. They all bow low and then straighten. The guard at the front approaches us. "My King. My Queen. We would know your orders."

"Set camp around the castle," Varys instructs. "If the Wraiths and Prince Aegryn arrive, they will know a formidable force awaits them."

The guard salutes sharply, then turns and relays the order.

Varys turns to Edmynd. "We should position more scouts along the roads to warn us of Aegryn's approach."

"Agreed," Edmynd replies. "I doubt he expects this sort of resistance."

While we wait for word from the scouts, the day grows long. I never realized war consisted of so much waiting.

Storm clouds roil overhead as the air grows damp. Booming thunder shakes the ground and lightning fingers out across the darkened sky, heralding the approach of rain. As we stare out the castle window, a few stray drops patter on the glass. I may not be an expert on battles, but I do know that rain and mud can complicate things and work against us.

A rider on a dire wolf finally gallops into the castle courtyard, and we hasten downstairs to meet him. He slides off his wolf and strides to Varys. Water drips from his armor, leaving small puddles on the stone floor as he walks toward us. "They approach by the main road on the west, my King, but so does the storm. Fortunately, I spotted fewer than a dozen Wraiths. The majority of this force comprises Prince Aegryn's human army."

High Mage Ylari strokes his chin thoughtfully. "The Mages are behind this tempest. They must be. The skies were far too clear this morning for such a storm to suddenly arrive."

It is easy to see the worry on Edmynd's face. Florin's army has superior armor, but it is heavy, and mud hinders maneuverability when it is worn.

"These are your lands," Varys addresses my brothers. "Is there anything about this terrain that we can use to our advantage?"

Raiden lowers his gaze to the floor, a contemplative look on his face. "The rains turn the ground to mud, slippery and thick. I have an idea, but you are not going to like it."

"What is it?" Varys asks.

He looks Varys up and down. "How heavy is that Elvish armor of yours?"

"Not as heavy as Florin armor, but still…" He frowns. "Why do you ask?"

"I believe we will have to fight without it."

"What?" I ask, alarmed. "You'll be defenseless."

Varys considers Raiden a moment before nodding. "I believe you are right."

"High praise from a Dark Elf," Raiden teases, but his expression quickly sobers.

Edmynd looks between them. "I will give the order."

"Wait," I say. "You cannot truly mean to go into battle without armor."

Varys takes my hand. "It is the only way. A storm is coming, and the ground will turn to mire. Our armor will only weigh us down and make it difficult to maneuver. Even though we are exposed fighting without it, we would be even more vulnerable with it on while fighting in the mud."

I understand what he is saying. While it makes sense, I cannot stop worrying about them going into battle without their armor.

CHAPTER 70

VARYS

Shynar is tense beneath me, his thick fur bristling as we stand before our army, staring out at our enemy across the battlefield. Inara and her sister are safe inside the castle walls. A handful of human and Elven guards have been assigned to protect them and the rest of the women and children who have sought shelter inside the palace.

It is strange readying for battle without armor, but I know it's the right decision.

Dark clouds spread out across the sky above us, as drops of rain begin to fall steadily, dampening the ground and turning it into mud as we feared.

In the distance, I notice less than a dozen Wraiths flanking Prince Aegryn's army. Even one Wraith would have been devastating to a human army but because my people and I are here and our magic is now unbound, the odds are tipped heavily in our favor.

The wind grows cold as the Wraiths feed off the life

force energy of the surrounding landscape. I glance to my side at Edmynd and Raiden on their horses at the head of their army, and notice them shivering. Humans alone would have been more vulnerable to the Wraiths, and I am certain Aegryn had been counting on this when he marched his army to Florin.

"Turn back now or be defeated," Edmynd calls out to Aegryn across the battlefield.

"It is not *I* who will lose this day," Aegryn replies menacingly. "I will crush your armies beneath me and—"

The words die in his throat when I unsheathe my sword and call upon my magic. Blue flame licks along the sharp blade as I hold it out beside me, showing him we are bound by the Mages no more.

Even across the field, I can see the color drain from his face. I turn to my men and give them our signal. They each raise their swords and do the same, and I watch in satisfaction as the frontline of Aegryn's army takes a small step back. Several of their horses rear up when our dire wolves snarl and snap their fangs, eager to taste the blood of our enemies.

They realize what they will face this day: an army of men and Elves who will show them no mercy.

Long have I wanted revenge against the man who scarred me with his iron-tipped blade. Today, I will finally have it.

Closing my eyes briefly, I focus on my bond with Inara. Now that our bond has been sealed, if I concentrate hard enough, we can speak to one another across the connection in our minds.

Her fear beats at me through the Khio'rinar, but it eases when she senses the wave of calm and reassurance I send to her. *We will not lose this day, my Khio'ri. I promise you this,* I whisper through the link.

Her presence grows stronger, and I turn around to find her defiantly standing atop the castle wall with the line of Edmynd's archers. Her eyes meet mine, full of fierce determination when she raises her bow and nocks an arrow.

Edmynd raises his arm and gives the signal. A volley of arrows whistles through the air, sailing over our armies. Aegryn's men raise their shields, trying to block the assault, but it's no use. Devastation rains down upon them, their shrieks and cries telling me many were hit. Blood stains the grass and bodies litter the ground throughout his lines.

Any other leader would know better than to attack, but Prince Aegryn, it seems, is not well-versed in military strategy. He calls out and leads his men forward. Releasing a battle cry, we race toward him, the ground thundering beneath us as we charge across the field. My pulse pounds in my ears as we draw closer.

Shynar leaps over the front line, and we clash with Aegryn's army in a clang of swords. Wraiths rush toward us, but I send a wall of flame to hold them back, burning Aegryn's men in the process.

An arc of powerful magic flies toward me, and I leap from Shynar's back, barely missing the blast.

Men battle all around me, and I lift my head, searching for Edmynd and Raiden, wondering how the humans are faring. I watch in horror as Edmynd falls from his horse, slamming to the ground on his back. An enemy soldier raises his sword, and I know Inara's brother will not be able to move fast enough. I send an orb of magic flying toward the man, hitting him square in the chest and knocking him away.

A loud thunk behind me is followed quickly by an agonized shriek, and I spin to find one of Aegryn's men dead at my back, an arrow through his chest.

I lift my gaze to the castle wall and Inara gives me a sober nod. If not for her, I would be dead.

The Wraiths charge us again, but we repel them with fire. It is exhausting, but with Edmynd's soldiers taking care of Aegryn's we can concentrate on combating the Wraiths. Rain is falling heavily now, making visibility difficult on the field for our human allies.

I watch as the Wraiths try to flank us, eager to reach the castle. "We must hold them here!" I yell, gesturing to the Wraiths. "We cannot let them reach the palace!"

My men concentrate their attacks on the Wraiths, but they are difficult to target. I have fought Wraiths before, but these are stronger and faster, and not easily killed. Even a direct hit with our magic does not take them down. Only repeated attacks seem to work.

Something is wrong.

I scan the field and spot three men in long robes standing along the hill line behind Aegryn's men. With their arms upraised, I observe as giant red orbs of devastating power gather between their palms. I turn back to the Wraiths, noticing the same red glow surrounding them.

Aryl is at my back, and I turn to him. "The Mages are using their magic to strengthen and shield the Wraiths from our attacks. That is why they are so hard to kill."

"We have to take them out," Aryl shouts.

"Yes, but how?"

A series of arrows flies toward Aegryn's men, but the Mages throw up their arms to conjure a shield, and the arrows bounce harmlessly off of them. But something even more important catches my eye, and I realize that to cast a shield the Mages must release their magic from the Wraiths, making them vulnerable again.

"Inara," I reach to her through the bond, trying to send what I have learned.

Another volley of arrows flies toward the men, and I know she understood.

"How can we take them down?" Aryl says. "They shield themselves."

As they raise another barrier to deflect the arrows, I notice the Mages concentrate it on their front and overhead, leaving their backs undefended.

"We have to get behind them," I tell him. "Follow me!"

Swinging my sword in a wide arc, I plow through Aegryn's men with both magic and blade. Aryl moves beside me, each watching the other's back as we clear a path to flank the Mages.

Without our armor, we can move across the muddy field without risk of falling, whereas Aegryn's men slip and flounder in the muck. Still, there are many of them, and it is difficult to wade through the bodies.

Prince Aegryn is losing. Badly. But he refuses to give up. Raiden has now engaged with him, swords clanging mightily. Aegryn is no match for Raiden's skills, and when he turns to retreat, he runs straight into King Edmynd, who slashes his sword at our enemy without mercy.

An arc of crimson light races toward the king and Raiden. Instantly, I cast an orb of magic, sending it to shield Inara's brothers.

"Aryl!" I call out, pointing back at them.

He throws another spell, shielding them further from the targeted Mage attacks.

Sweat beads across my brow as I focus all my energy on Inara's brothers, repelling the devastating power of the Mages.

I'm so focused, I do not see the danger racing toward me. A flash of red fills my vision and I turn, but too late, as the destructive power explodes against my side, sending me sprawling.

"Varys!" Aryl cries out, standing over me and creating a barrier to repel the next attack.

"To the king!" one of my warriors cries out, signaling my men to come to my defense.

My head swims and sounds echo all around me as agonizing pain fires across every nerve ending where the blast hit my side. I'm only vaguely aware of Aryl shouting orders to protect Edmynd and Raiden.

"Varys!" Inara's voice calls out across the bond. *"I'm coming to you!"*

"No!" I send back through the connection.

I twist onto my uninjured side, hissing in pain at the movement. I place my palms on the sodden ground, pushing to my feet and forcing myself to stand. If I stay down, Inara will try to reach me, and I cannot have her in danger. The world tilts and spins as I struggle to stand upright.

Horror tightens my chest as one of the Mages sends a ball of red flame toward the castle wall. I send out a blast of magic, but I know it will not be fast enough to intercept it.

"Inara!"

Green fire explodes from the wall, slamming against the red orb before it can reach them. I turn my gaze toward the castle and find High Mage Ylari standing beside my bondmate, his entire body trembling as he gathers more power between his palms to fend off another assault.

"Aryl, we have to get to the Mages."

"I know. I—"

Red flame slams against him, sending him sprawling. He lands on his side and lies there panting, but at least he's alive.

Time slows as the battle rages all around me. The Wraiths are making their way to the castle while the Mages continue their assault on the wall. Only Ylari's steadily weakening magic is keeping them from doing any real damage. Once his power fails, Inara will be in danger.

I cannot lose my Khio'ri. I will not let her die.

Slamming my palm to the ground, I dig my fingers into the muddy earth. I feel the raw and untamed energy like a beating pulse beneath my fingers. I grit my teeth against the overwhelming pain and focus the last of my energy and power.

The earth rumbles and quakes with terrible might as I draw the life force from the earth, demanding that it yield to me. With my remaining strength, I expand my magic, growing a circle of raw power beneath us.

Clenching my jaw, I bite back a cry of pain as I raise my other arm and slam my fist to the ground, releasing my magic and tearing through the earth with blistering intensity. An explosion of rock and soil ripples out like a giant wave, sparing my men and allies while knocking Prince Aegryn's army to the ground and consuming them in devastating flame.

Their agonized wails fill the air as the fire burns through them. I watch with cold satisfaction as Aegryn turns to ash before my eyes.

Raw energy pulses through our bond, and I look toward the palace. My heart stops when I see Inara rushing toward me. She drops to her knees at my side. "Varys!"

Over her shoulder, several Wraiths advance across the field toward us, drawn to our combined powers.

"You have to go, my Khio'ri." I take Inara's hand. "Please."

"No." Her eyes burn with determination. "I can save us all."

Before I can respond, Inara stands. She raises her arms and a glowing orb of power erupts from her palms. Blue energy crackles between her hands like lightning and, through our connection, I can feel the strain on her life force as she struggles to contain her powerful magic.

My sister's warnings echo in my mind. If Inara uses too much of her power, she could die.

"Inara, no!"

Waving her hands, she releases her power. I watch in awe as it slams into the Wraiths with a brilliant explosion of light. Their ear-piercing shrieks fill the air as her devastating magic consumes them, burning them from the inside out. Their cries fall silent as they crumple to the ground.

My warriors turn to her, staring in admiration at their queen.

"The sanishon of the Khio'rinar," a voice calls out from the field.

"It is the prophecy," another one says.

Inara turns her gaze to mine and then collapses beside me.

"Fetch a healer for the king and queen!" someone yells.

I gather her into my arms. Strangling tendrils of fear snake through me as her life force slowly dims through our connection. Shutting my eyes, I focus on our bond. "Stay with me, my Khio'ri," I whisper. "Please."

"Varys!" Aryl cries out, drawing my attention back to the Mages. Despair tightens my chest when they lower their shields, completely unfazed.

My energy wanes and I struggle to stay conscious. The pain in my side is merely an echo of the agony of knowing my Khio'ri is dying, and there is nothing I can do.

"Varys." A tear slips down her cheek. "I failed, my love. I'm sorry."

"You did not fail. You saved us, Inara." I touch her face, staring deep into her lovely eyes. "And now I'm going to save you."

I roll over and take Aryl's hand. His gaze meets mine and an unspoken understanding passes between us. "One last time," he murmurs, with a faint grin.

"One last time," I barely manage.

Together, we muster the last of our strength, and I pray it's enough to take down the Mages. As the raw power of the earth burns through my veins, the numbing chill of death advances upon me. "*I love you, Inara,*" I send through the connection.

I roar as the energy fills my veins like liquid fire, scorching everything in its wake, as I slam my other fist to the ground once more, sending another shock wave toward the Mages.

From the corner of my wavering vision, I notice a flash of purple wings, and I lift my gaze to find the Fae King Kyven, and a dozen of his warriors, behind the Mages. They send an arc of power straight toward their unprotected backs, incinerating them to ash in an instant.

Panting heavily, I roll onto my back. Rain falls steadily upon us. Holding Inara tightly to my chest, I stare up at the dark sky overhead and send a whispered prayer to the gods to spare my Khio'ri as I fall away into oblivion.

CHAPTER 71

VARYS

When I wake, Inara is in the bed beside me, curled against my chest. I raise a trembling hand and gently brush the hair back from her face, and she lifts her head. "Varys?"

She sits up and wraps her arms around me, peppering my face with tender kisses before finally brushing her lips to mine.

"You're alive." Relief floods my veins. "I was so afraid I would lose you."

Her face is red, and her eyes are puffy and swollen. I taste the salt of her tears as she kisses me again. "You saved me." Her voice quavers. "I feared you might die."

I press a kiss to her forehead. "We saved each other, my brave human wife."

Behind her, her brothers and King Kyven are standing off to the side. "You're awake," Edmynd says with a smile. He claps a hand on my shoulder, and I bite back a wince at the jarring motion. My entire body still hurts.

"My brother?" I ask weakly.

"Aryl is recovering in the next room," Inara says. "The Elf healer said he'll be fine."

My attention turns to the Fae king, and I force myself to sit up. "Kyven," I flash a faint smile. "You arrived just in time, my friend."

I extend my arm and we clasp forearms, his lavender eyes studying me intently. "I am glad I got here when I did."

Inara's sister Grayce walks in, and Kyven straightens, then bows low to her. "Princess Grayce. It is good to see you again."

"And you as well, King Kyven," she replies.

I arch a brow at him, and he arches one in return. I suppose this means he has not yet asked for her hand.

Edmynd looks at me and Inara. "We would have fallen, if not for the two of you." He places a hand on Kyven's shoulder. "And your help, as well."

Kyven glances at Grayce, then turns back to her brothers. "Let us consider it the beginning of a new alliance between us."

Edmynd clasps his forearm. "To a new alliance."

EPILOGUE

VARYS

It has been a week since the battle. The threat of the Wraiths is far from over. There are rumors the Mages are gathering their forces for another attack. They have not yet given up their desire to conquer the seven realms. Until they make another move, however, we have peace and the start of a new alliance.

"Are you ready?" Inara walks in from the cleansing room.

My mouth goes dry. She is absolutely stunning in her Elven gown. It is her sister's wedding day, and although we are in Florin, she insisted upon wearing an Elven gown that matches my tunic and pants, signaling to the entire world she is no longer princess of Florin but queen of the Dark Elves of Ithylian.

The long, flowing jade gown brings out the green in her hazel eyes. She is so beautiful, she is practically glowing. I slip my arm around her waist and pull her to me.

She gives me a lovely smile. "Do you think Grayce and Kyven will be as happy as we are?"

"I hope so," I reply, wondering if Kyven has told Grayce his secret.

The truth sits on the tip of my tongue, and I want so much to tell my mate, but the promise spell forbids me. I advised Kyven to tell Grayce, and I pray that he listened.

Placing a finger beneath Inara's chin, I tip her face up to mine and trace my thumb across her full, pink lips, longing to taste them. Her lovely gaze holds my own as I lean in and capture her mouth in a proprietary kiss. A low growl rumbles in my chest when she fists her hands in my tunic, pulling me closer.

I lift her into my arms and carry her to the bed, laying her down gently atop the blankets. I move over her, and she smiles up at me. "Varys, we have to go, my love. They are expecting us in an hour."

I crush my lips to hers and dip my hand beneath the collar of her dress, pulling it down to cup her breast. I brush my thumb across the soft globe, and she gasps, arching into my touch.

"Varys," she whispers against my lips.

My nostrils flare as her delicate scent thickens the air around us. It is stronger now and enticingly sweet. I kiss a line down the elegant column of her neck, to the valley of her breasts. "I can scent your need, my Khio'ri," I whisper against her skin, and then close my mouth over the sensitive peak.

She moans deliciously when I trace my hand up her thigh beneath her gown. I move her silken undergarment to one side, and she gasps as I drag my fingers through her already slick folds.

I long to sink deep into her warm, wet heat. "You are perfect," I breathe as I move lower. Pushing her skirt up to her hips, I carve a trail of kisses from her calf to her inner thigh. I place my hand on her stomach to hold her in place as she writhes beneath my attentions.

A faint pulse of energy travels across my skin and I pause. My brow furrows as I slide up her body, resting my palm over her lower abdomen.

She lifts her head. "What is it, my love? Is something wrong?"

Closing my eyes, I concentrate, searching, when I suddenly feel it again. My eyes snap open and my jaw drops as I stare down at her in wonder. "Life," I whisper. "We have created life, Inara."

"What?"

My breath catches. "You are carrying our child."

"Are you sure? I thought it was not possible."

"I am certain." I clasp her hand and place it over her womb, allowing her to feel the life spark that is our child.

Her eyes brighten with tears.

"Why are you crying?" I cup her face. "Does this upset you, my Khio'ri?"

"No," she whispers as a tear slips down her cheek. "I'm crying because I am happy, Varys."

I kiss away her tears. When I pull back, I stroke her face and gaze deeply into her gorgeous hazel eyes. "I hope she looks just like her mother."

"Her?" Inara smiles. "What if we have a son? Will you be upset?"

"Never." I touch her cheek and drop my forehead gently to hers. "This child will be the first of many."

She laughs softly and rests a hand on her belly. "And just how many do you want, my love?"

"As many as my brave and beautiful human wife will give me."

I place my hand over hers on her abdomen and entwine

our fingers, marveling at the life spark of our child. I never knew it was possible to be this happy. "You are my heart, my Khio'ri. And I am yours."

She presses her lips to my own and then smiles against them. "I am yours, and you are mine, my Dark Elf King."

ALSO BY JESSICA GRAYSON

Next book in the series - Claimed By The Dragon King

To sign up for my mailing list via my website and get a welcome gift of **2 Bonus Epilogues** (ebook) for this book go to

http://Jessicagraysonauthor.com/.

If you enjoyed this book please leave a review on Amazon and/or Goodreads.

Jessica Grayson

Of Fate and Kings Series

Bound to the Dark Elf King (This Book)

Claimed by the Dragon King

Taken by the Fae King

Stolen by the Wolf King

Captured by the Orc King

Do you like Fairy Tale Retellings?

Fairy Tale Retellings (Once Upon a Fairy Tale Romance Series)

Taken by the Dragon: A Beauty and the Beast Retelling

Captivated by the Fae: A Cinderella Retelling

Rescued By The Merman: A Little Mermaid Retelling

Bound To The Elf Prince: A Snow White Retelling

Claimed By The Bear King: A Snow Queen Retelling

Protected By The Wolf Prince: A Red Riding Hood Retelling

Charmed by the Fox Prince: A Rapunzel Retelling

Ice World Warrior Series (Scifi Romance)

Claimed: Dragon Shifter Romance

Bound: Vampire Alien Romance

Rescued: Fae Alien Romance

Stolen: Werewolf Romance

Taken: Vampire Alien Romance

Fated: Dragon Shifter Romance

Protected: Dragon Shifter Romance

Of Gods and Fate (Greek God Romance Series)

Claimed By Hades

Bound to Ares

Orc Claimed Series

Claimed by the Orc

Bound to the Orc

Night King Series

Bound to the Night King

Settlers of the Outer Rim

Rescued: Fox Shifter Romance

Protected: Lizard Man Romance

Fated to Monsters

Captured by the Kraken: A Monster Romance

Bound to the Gargoyle: A Monster Romance

Claimed by the Werewolf: A Monster Romance

Of Dragons and Elves Series (Fantasy Romance)

The Elf Knight

Scarred Dragon Prince Series

Shadow Guard: Dragon Shifter Romance

To Love a Monster Book Series (Fantasy Romance)

Taken by the Monster: A Monster Romance

Want Dragon Shifters? You can dive into their world with this completed Duology.

Mosauran Series (Dragon Shifter Alien Romance)

The Edge of it All

Shape of the Wind

V'loryn Series (Vampire Alien Romance)

Lost in the Deep End

Beneath a Different Sky

Under a Silver Moon

V'loryn Holiday Series (A Marek and Elizabeth Holiday novella takes place prior to their bonding)

The Thing We Choose

V'loryn Fated Ones (Vampire Alien Romance)

Where the Light Begins (Vanek's Story)

For information about upcoming releases Like me on

Facebook at Jessica Grayson

http://facebook.com/JessicaGraysonBooks.

OR

sign up for upcoming release alerts at my website:

Jessicagraysonauthor.com